CRISIS IN GRAND CANYON

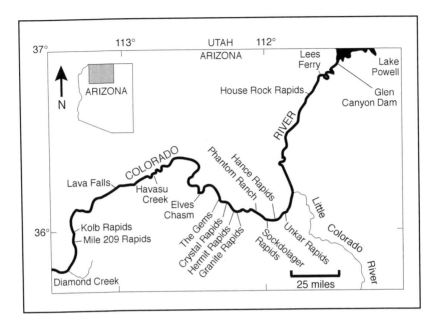

Map of the Colorado River in Grand Canyon.

Crisis in Grand Canyon

Michelle K. Rubin

CreateSpace
2017

ISBN-9781547203222

Printed in the United States of America

For David who has made everything possible

Acknowledgements

I was fortunate to have helpful, experienced, and all-around awesome Grand Canyon scientists and guides on my numerous trips down the Colorado River. They kept me safe and informed, and we shared unique experiences that I will never forget. A heartfelt thank-you goes to Ted Melis, David Rubin, David Topping, Jack Schmidt, Amy Draut East, Brian Dierker, Lars Niemi, Mike Walker, Stuart Reeder, Steve Bledsoe, Jan yBalsom, Lisa Long, Jen Dierker, Mike Yeatts, Carol "Fritz" Fritzinger, Roberto Anima, Dave Hogg, Ralph Hunter, Mary Barger, Fred Nials, and guides Annie, Jimmy, and Kirk. I know I have failed to include others who rightfully should be listed here, and I apologize.

Every person I met on the river contributed in some way to this story. However, I alone am responsible for any errors or confusions in the text.

I presented various drafts of this novel in several writing programs and received invaluable assistance and advice. Thank you to Malena Watrous and the Stanford Novel Writing Class, Robert Boswell and the Napa Valley Writer's Conference, and Jonis Agee's Master Novel Class at the Taos Summer Writers' Conference. Also, thank you to the many student writers in the classes who provided helpful critiques and comments. Thank you to Wendy Tokunaga who edited an earlier draft and whose insights and suggestions helped to create this final version of the story.

Numerous friends and fellow writers read early drafts and discussed my ideas as if they made sense. Thank you to all. My children, my mother, and my father, before he died, were always supportive. Thank you.

More recently, John Oehler provided editorial guidance and walked me down the path for publication. His generous support has been invaluable in getting this novel published.

In 1996 my husband David brought me on a Grand Canyon river trip as a volunteer with the USGS Volunteer for Science Program. I returned with him on an additional five trips and then started writing this novel. David read my drafts so many times it became almost impossible for him to keep the changing story straight. His careful reading and unflagging encouragement made this book possible. Without his support, I would still be lawyering, and this book would have remained unwritten.

A river is not its water. As Heraclitus observed long ago, the river will still be a river once these waters are out to sea and different waters fill its banks. At every moment, the river is made of different waters, and the river is the manner and process of this change. The Colorado River must change, so the Grand Canyon can evolve to what it will be.

1

Day 1. Morning

Tess wrapped her fingers around the metal flask nestled deep in the right pocket of her fleece jacket and shuffled to the edge of the river. She curled her toes into the cold, damp sand of the beach. Coarse sand grains rubbed across the skin of her feet, wedged between her toes, and coated the cuticles of her blue-painted nails. Throughout the canyon, an early morning haze settled onto the desert. At Lees Ferry the river was wide and the current slow, and the Colorado River lapped softly on shore as if it were rhythmically breathing.

The calm was deceptive. The river changed quickly as it flowed through Grand Canyon. Within days Tess' raft would enter the rapids of the Roaring Twenties, and she'd need to remember everything she'd ever learned. Then she'd drop into the inner gorge to run some of the wildest rapids in the world, and she'd need luck as well as skill.

Above the water swallows whizzed through the air, and on the road behind, a truck rumbled down the ramp. The dings and thuds of rafters rigging their boats floated across the sand. Staring into the water, Tess ignored the activity on shore and sank into the silence of Grand Canyon. She loved that silence even when her head wasn't hurting and she wasn't hung over.

She pulled her favorite pink ponytail holder from the pocket of her fleece pants and pulled her short blond hair straight back, exposing small opal studs in her ears. Brushing an index finger across each earring, she thought of her father. He had given her the earrings as a birthday present eleven years earlier, the summer before her senior year in high school. A month later he died, and the following summer, after graduation, she left home for Grand Canyon and began working as a river guide. Often it seemed a lifetime ago. That morning, it seemed like yesterday. She loved how fluid time could be—flowing like the Colorado itself—and she was excited to be back on the river, after four long days in town.

Claire stepped from the chilly, air-conditioned bus into the scorching heat of Arizona. Before her, just beyond the crowded parking lot, the Colorado River ran slow and lazy. Sunlight splayed golden on the desert river and a beaver swam circles in a shady pool. A Great Blue Heron flew overhead, and a tiny Merganser dunked in and out of the water beneath a tree. When a soft breeze blew, a wake of ripples spread across the silky water. Then the winds stopped, and the water's surface was again smooth as polished rock. Claire stood on the hot asphalt inferno and squinted in the too bright light of the desert. She inhaled the woefully deficient air, too little, too hot, and too dry for a full breath, and though she breathed through her nose, she loosened the chinstrap on her hat, hoping that would help fill her lungs. It didn't.

"I'm here," Claire said, announcing her arrival, but no one answered. The man in front of her walked straight across the parking lot and over the pebbled beach towards the river, as if in pilgrimage. Claire followed. The couple behind held hands and talked to each other, ignoring both Claire and the Grand Canyon. Camping gear, crates of food, and a bustling and busy populace crowded the flat beach. Claire's glib optimism, her conviction that all would be perfect on the two-week raft trip, started to fade.

It was only seven o'clock in the morning and already as dry and hot as a furnace. There were hot days in Santa Cruz, but nothing like this. On California's central coast it rarely heated up until the afternoon when the fog dissipated, and in the evening the fog rolled in again off the Pacific Ocean and cooled everything off, and even if the fog didn't reach Claire's mountaintop home, it set up an on-shore breeze and cooled the air. She'd often resented how that fog moderated the temperature. With just three minutes in Arizona, her resentment vanished.

She pulled off her hat to cool her head but immediately replaced it. First lesson of the desert, she told herself, was that a person needed armor for protection. Without a hat she'd be too exposed. She looked around. Almost everyone wore a hat. Only the guides, on their rafts, went hatless. A young woman with short blond hair, standing in the shallow surf of the river, went without.

Claire straightened her shorts, smoothed her shirt, and walked slowly across the blacktop to the beach. Tucking her straight brown hair under her hat, she tried to regain a feeling of wellbeing. Despite her best efforts, she was finding it hard to do. Her friend Linny was already over twelve hours late, and if Linny didn't get there soon, she would undoubtedly miss the trip. The rafts would be somewhere down the river when she showed up, and Claire would be vacationing solo.

Linny never followed the rules. She'd been that way since they met in eighth grade—always paying attention to something else— and by now Claire expected it. It was part of her charm, and Claire didn't usually mind.

Today, though, she needed Linny—nothing else was what she'd expected. Incessant noise and frenetic commotion assaulted her. Where was the paradise depicted on the river company's website? And she didn't want to travel alone, without her friend. That had never been her plan. She'd packed her cache of flasks in the large rubber bag stowed in the back of the bus. She wished she'd tucked one flask into the small backpack slung across her shoulder.

Oar rafts, paddle boats, and small motor rafts bobbed in the surf, held onshore with thick ropes tied to stakes at the edge of the sand. In between the ropes, first-aid kits and empty beer cans lay scattered. Enormous blue coolers, stacks of folded beach chairs, white buckets, and large waterproof boxes spread across the beach in a garish palette of artifice and plastic. In several pockets of sand away from the water, bright, orange lifejackets and military-surplus ammo boxes sat in a grid, and surrounding the grid, black rubber bags littered the sand, the Halloween-colored flotsam of a river expedition in the making.

An old bus made its way down the road and across the parking lot, spewing black exhaust into the clean, desert air. Soon-to-be-rafters from another rafting trip disembarked and walked to the water through labyrinths of folded tables, stacks of tarps, and crates of canned foods. Claire watched them wade through pools of bright straps coiled tight with military precision and sidestep long, colorful straps spread to dry like Mexican sashes in the hot sun.

The expedition paraphernalia of the wilderness adventures exploded across the sand. Claire tried to remember the scenes of solitude and quiet beauty she'd imagined when Linny suggested the river trip, but nothing on the beach educed such an image. In what should have been the most exquisite of natural settings, nature went missing.

For the briefest moment Claire missed her family and wished she were home, early in the day, after her children left for school and her husband left for work. Really though, she'd wanted to leave home, at least for a short while, maybe for longer, and a river trip with Linny was the excuse she needed. Once on the river, she planned to get Linny's advice on how to change her life. Perhaps Linny would convince her to leave her husband and take her kids.

When Linny proposed rafting into the heart of Grand Canyon, Claire learned everything she could about floating the Colorado. She studied photos of oar rafts skimming across the clear water and plummeting down the famous rapids. She read trip catalogues and participant blogs that described a perfect adventure. When she told Linny she'd go, she didn't mention how impeccable the timing. She didn't tell Linny that she needed time away from Paul and his drinking, that her own drinking was veering out of control. They'd have plenty of time on the trip to exchange news.

Claire and Linny had been friends for thirty years; it wouldn't surprise Linny to find out that Claire had problems. She'd had many over the years they'd been friends. Only Linny's life was idyllic. It had been perfect from the start.

"Your friend Linny called the office early this morning. Their plane was late, and they missed their connection, so they didn't get here last night with the rest of you," said the young woman who'd been standing at the edge of the river. "They should be here in an hour or so, which is time enough." She pulled a dark, metal flask from her pocket and took a drink.

Claire stared at the girl, wondering why she said "they" when only Linny was late. Was this guide-speak? Didn't anyone know proper English anymore? Linny had said Steve was staying home. That was the plan—husbands at home—and it was one of the reasons Claire had come.

"I'm Tess," the young guide said. "If you want, you can come in my raft, cause I'm gonna take your friends. I'll wait here for them to arrive."

Claire nodded assent without asking about the plural pronoun, her mind obsessing that Tess wouldn't have been her first choice for a rafting guide. Aside from the grammar issue, which Claire acknowledged was irrelevant to river running, Tess drank from a flask when most people still held onto their morning coffee mug. Claire herself had ordered five flasks on-line and filled two of them with a moderately priced whiskey, two with rum, and one with an expensive scotch. Obviously she was not a teetotaler, and even as she thought Tess shouldn't be drinking, she wished again that she had a flask in her pack. Her desire for alcohol didn't excuse Tess, in Claire's mind. Claire, after all, was a mere passenger with no responsibilities.

Claire was also a lot older than Tess who was probably in her mid twenties, which was too young to be drinking from a flask and probably too young to be guiding a raft. Tess might also be the only female guide, not that Claire had a problem with women in male roles. She herself had graduated law school, passed the bar, and now practiced law, and she knew women could be smarter and more competent than men. She was more competent than many of her male colleagues. She was certainly smarter and more competent than her husband Paul.

Realistically, though, it seemed unlikely a woman would be stronger than a man. Tess' arms were twice the size of Claire's, and Tess was stocky and solid looking, but she was still quite small compared to the men. An odd mix of feminine and rugged, the young woman was quite pretty, two small opal earrings sparkling in the early sunlight. She wore a yellow tank top, brown shorts and rainbow-colored flip-flops. She'd painted her toenails a beautiful blue that matched the Arizona sky.

"Pretty earrings," Claire said, though she really wanted to comment on the young woman's toes.

"Oh, thanks," Tess said running a finger across each. "From my dad."

With a smile at Claire, Tess jogged across the beach, climbed back into the bus, and began to unload gear. Claire hadn't time to say anything, even if she'd wanted, which she didn't. She just had thoughts, and like always, her thoughts took a while to form. She'd never been particularly spontaneous. She took a long time to form an opinion, and she needed to think before she spoke. That's why she worked on criminal appeals, rather than criminal trials. She read a trial transcript and methodically searched for errors. She examined the record with great care, taking her time. She'd known from the start that courtroom drama was not for her.

"Everyone grab an ammo box and a small dry-bag and divide your essentials between the two," Tess yelled out. "Then keep that box and bag with you, on your raft. If you switch rafts, you take that box and bag with you to your new raft. The rest of your gear, in the big dry-bags, will be tied onto a raft and will not be available to you until we camp each night."

Claire liked order. She found nothing reassuring about the disorganized pandemonium that pulsated across the sand. Even before Tess finished speaking, Claire's fellow rafters swarmed the equipment to grab the refurbished metal army-boxes and the small rubber bags. They crowded the equipment as if there wouldn't be enough to go around, and only Claire held back, waiting for the chaos to subside.

The rafters and their equipment spread across the extreme down-river section of the beach. Further up the shoreline several other commercial raft trips staked out a claim, their rafts bobbing in the river, the guides running back and forth between the rafts and the piles of equipment on shore, and the passengers grabbing necessities from grids of supplies. At the extreme up-river section of the beach, an assortment of rafts and small motorboats floated in the surf and sat on shore. Men and women climbed onto the rafts and motorboats, stacking equipment and jamming bags into tall towers, until their boats resembled out-sized Erector Sets, three-dimensional puzzles in a jumble of colors, sizes, and shapes.

"A science trip," Tess said when she saw Claire staring up the beach. "Geologists, maybe biologists. They've have been working here for years. Since before I came. Now they're collecting data for an Environmental Impact Report. It's a very big deal around here. Upriver from here is Glen Canyon Dam, and dam operations determine conditions here and further downstream on the Colorado River in the Grand Canyon, as well as water availability throughout the west. Apparently the report will determine operations at Glen Canyon Dam for the next ten years."

Tess stood for a moment and watched the scientists stash laptop computers into metal chests and strap the chests shut; they wedged cameras, compasses, and binoculars into army-surplus boxes. They wedged gear camouflaged in rubber bags beneath crates and boxes, and these disappeared into the depths of the flotilla.

The science trip was docked at the far end of the beach, blurring many details, but Tess could clearly see Brent Seeger, director of the Grand Canyon Science Program in charge of all science research on the river, and the river's number one Don Juan. She'd met Brent a year earlier when her commercial trip shared a campsite with his science trip. From the moment she saw him, she'd been astounded by how handsome he was and unable to take her eyes off him. She looked in the mirror every morning, and she knew that lopsided bangs fringed a wide face and partially hid thick, unshaped eyebrows. No one's heart skipped a beat upon seeing her. When Brent unexpectedly turned his considerable charm on her, she was flattered by his attention and savored each step of the seduction. She had no qualms about spending a night together and understood it would be a one-night stand.

That's what happened in the canyon, and the truth was, she usually preferred men a few years younger than she. Besides, she had a boyfriend. Robbie, also a river guide, was twenty-four, and they shared an apartment in Flagstaff. Brent was too old for her, and he was far outside her circle of friends. She knew he wasn't right for her. The surprise was that she couldn't forget him.

Through some trick of posture or bearing, he looked as if he might be the tallest and biggest man on the beach, though he was no more than six feet tall and inches shorter than West, the head guide of her trip. For a middle-aged man, he commanded a lot of space, and he still had the innocent air of a schoolboy. Though his short, blond hair probably had less color than it did a few years earlier, it was thick with a slight wave. His skin was clear and his cheeks ruddy. She recalled his thin top lip and full bottom lip spreading into a smile that was soft and sensuous. Now he wore bright, lime-green shorts and an orange shirt.

2

Day 1. Morning

C laire collected one of the remaining ammo boxes and day bags and carried them to the pile of large dry-bags dumped on the sand. Her gear was now on the very bottom, covered by the bags already pulled by her fellow passengers, reorganized, and tossed back. She found her bags, grabbed her flashlight, toothpaste and toothbrush, bandana, sunscreen, and other essentials from her gear and repacked. She left her cell phone in the bottom of the big bag. The introductory instructions said the canyon had no cell coverage – no phone or internet until they were back in Flagstaff.

"Is there a way to get in touch if there's an emergency?" Claire asked one of the guides.

"We've packed a satellite phone," he said, "and we can turn it on for outgoing calls, and it's usable when the canyon's wide and there's a satellite overhead. Most emergencies we handle by ourselves. Don't worry – I've never needed the sat phone."

The rafting company had sent lots of information about what to bring, and the welcome packet told what to put in the ammo box and what in the small daypack. Claire had studied the information sheets and knew what to do. There on the beach, though, the heat sapped her energy and the simple chore became unexpectedly burdensome and difficult. She pulled a flask from her bag and took a drink. Before packing the flask in the accessible ammo box, she took a second drink.

A guide stood on top of a large aluminum box and bellowed. He looked to Claire like a beefed-up version of the surfers she saw around town: about forty years old, well over six feet tall, with a long, blond ponytail down his back, and tanned, leathery skin. He introduced himself as West. A physical opposite of Tess, he looked like someone who could easily handle the Colorado.

"Form a human chain and pass the gear," he said. "Each of you is a necessary link from vehicle to raft. Use care. Take pride in your boat."

The men and women who had come in the bus formed a queue across the sand, from parking lot to water, and they unloaded the truck, grabbed the bags piled on the sand, and gathered the gear they'd scattered across the beach. They tossed everything from one hand to the next, down to the river. West said his raft, the smallest of the lot, would take the large, rubber dry-bags. His raft had a molded seat in the middle, attached atop a long metal box, and two huge oars balanced across the outer tubes. Tables and chairs had already been secured across the back of the raft, and the rafters now moved the bags over the sand to the water's edge, and the last rafter tossed them into the raft. West, Tess, and a young male guide, whom West introduced as Orion, arranged the bags in the raft, running a rope through the clip or handle of each. Like sailors on a sailboat, the guides tied everything down. The bags filled the raft, and rose up in mounds, leaving no room for passengers.

"Make sure your water bottles are filled," Tess yelled to the assembled rafters. "There's a water spigot across the parking lot."

The rafters broke formation before she'd finished speaking, sprinting across the sand in a rush to fill their bottles. Claire had filled her bottles at the lodge, but she'd had several long drinks on the beach and needed to refill. She was not, however, about to wait for her turn at the fountain. This was wilderness, she told herself, not Disneyland.

She looked down the beach. Fifteen feet from one of the largest rivers in the country, the land appeared as parched and dry as any place on earth. It was difficult to understand. It seemed the river had little impact on the landscape, though she was sure that couldn't be true. She looked up. In the cerulean sky above, the sun blazed, heating the arid air and searing the skin of the rafters. This wilderness raft trip began with a blazing heaven, parched earth, and dense crowds, not at all what Claire had expected.

Tess ran across the sand. Her short legs and muscular thighs settled into a heavy, rather graceless gait. With her backpack hanging from one shoulder, she jogged down the beach and hopped onto her raft. She pulled her tent from the top of a box and stuffed it into the bottom of a large, waterproof, vinyl bag. She crammed a raincoat, rain pants, a heavy fleece jacket, and her favorite red fleece hat into the bag and placed her sleeping bag on top. She leaned on the bag with her full weight to push the air out, rolled a tight seal, and tossed the dry-bag into the back of the raft. She tossed a smaller, second dry-bag filled with clothes and personal items.

She continued the rigging she had started earlier, preparing the raft to carry passengers and personal gear. She pulled a red strap from a large, mesh bag and passed it through one of the raft's rings and secured it to a second ring. She found another strap, tied a knot at one end, engaged the buckle, and secured the strap to her bag. She draped a long black strap across her seat, then lay two bright red straps across the black one. She hunted through the bag for small brown straps. Particular straps tied particular gear—same every trip. She always thought of her father when she assembled the gear for a raft trip. She imagined him taking inspection. He would slowly nod his head, pleased with her set-up, with how she'd remembered everything.   He'd understand how she kept the pandemonium of the expedition in check, how she balanced the yin and the yang of the river journey. She wished, as she did at the start of every trip, that he'd also been a river guide. She wished they had shared that.

She dug out the mesh cover she'd stretch across the stern, and one knot at a time she readied the raft. Immersing herself in the physical pleasure of rigging, she pulled the nylon straps through her fingers, feeling the smooth ridges of the webbing and wrapping lengths of strapping across rubber bags. When the sun found her raft, she pulled sunglasses from her bag to again darken the world. She worked for almost a half hour, her unexpectedly light, slate eyes hidden behind the gray lenses. About the time the rhythm of the chore was well established, the sun rose fully above the cliffs.

In a voice little more than a whisper, the sound dispersing in the soft breeze, she sang the words to 'Brass in Pocket' by the Pretenders. The song was her good luck talisman, and she sang it at the start of every trip. If she remembered, she sang while she rigged and then again when she started to row. One June day when she was still a small girl, her father came home with a Pretender's tape and played that one song over and over, and they both screamed out the words as they drove through the mountains.

At the start of a trip Tess relied on familiar repetitions. She started each day with the same chores. She rigged her boat the same way, finding and buckling the same straps. She always wore the same yellow shirt her first day of a trip. She planned and attended to details. Ever since the trip where her father drowned and she didn't save him, didn't even realize he was in trouble, she'd paid attention to details. She floated the Colorado, the eyes and ears of Grand Canyon, paying attention to everything. Sometimes, after several weeks, she grew bored with routine, but never with details. Thinking about it, she had a love-hate relationship with her repetitions. What she really wanted was routine interrupted by first-class excitement. Mostly, she was so grateful to be there; she loved everything about Grand Canyon. It sounded a little corny, but that was how she felt. She was pretty sure it was how all the guides felt.

Claire had spent many days as an adult camping in the wilderness and many afternoons hiking in the mountains, overcoming the limitations of her suburban childhood, learning to be comfortable in the outdoors. Yet, at the moment, she felt wretched—too hot and too dry—and she didn't know how she'd manage. Crowds of people and mountains of gear surrounded her, obliterating the calming isolation of wilderness. If Linny would arrive, things might be better. Without her, the best Claire could do was stay on the outskirts of the group and follow the rules laid down by the guides. She was good at following rules—that's what appellate attorneys did.

This trip had been planned as a get-together with Linny. They'd had several over the years. None of those times, though, did Claire have an urgent problem. Her crumbling marriage added to her stress.

She walked to the edge of the water and immersed her toes in the icy current, and for the first time she was able to block out the incessant activity on shore. In places, the water was as clear and still as a mirror, creating a perfect water reflection of the cliffs, brown and taupe hills and rock formations that looked nothing like the mountains of California. She dropped her gaze deep into the river and settled in the green and gray flattened mesas of a distorted vista.

In the trees across the river, unseen birds rustled the leaves. Overhead, the cloudless sky stretched to the limits of her sight in every direction, promising that raingear would be superfluous. If the beach hadn't been crawling with people and concealed by equipment, it might have been as seductive as the river. In its crowded, disordered state, though, it had little appeal.

"The calm's deceptive," Tess said, walking up behind her. "The river changes quickly as it flows through Grand Canyon. Calm here, wild only a few miles downstream. But there's always that silence that I love."

West assembled everyone at the edge of the water to go over the rules.

"Free-form democracy, even anarchy, flourishes on the river," he said, "but the underlying structure of a river expedition is a tight hierarchy. River rafts operate like sea vessels, and the head guide has the authority of a captain. No one tells a captain where to go or what to do. Whatever the head guide decides is the law. Just so you all understand, I'm the head guide."

He introduced the other guides – Orion, Riz, Theresa, Mark, and Tess. Claire realized she was wrong about Tess being the only woman. Theresa looked even less promising as a guide than Tess did – she looked like she could be Tess' mother.

West explained a few more rules, then yelled that it was time to go, and everyone around Claire ran to secure a place in a raft. West pushed his raft, loaded with baggage but no passengers, offshore and climbed aboard. The rafters climbed into the other rafts, grabbed paddles, settled along the tubes, and let loose with screams and hollers when their rafts moved into the current. It seemed to Claire that everyone but she knew exactly what to do. The rafts passed before the cliffs, layered and subtly shaded, and where the river channel bent and turned, they disappeared from view. She wasn't sorry to see them go. At least a small section of the beach was now emptied, and Claire sank to the sand, watched the water, and began to relax.

"Are those your friends?" Tess said.

Claire turned to see Linny and her son Dirk dragging their large bags across the sand. She hadn't seen Dirk in several years, and at sixteen he looked older and much taller, but otherwise not that different. He had Linny's fair complexion and very light hair, but where Linny's hair was board straight, his hair was a cap of tightly wound curls. Both mother and son were slim and handsome. Dirk was now a head taller than Linny, who had always been several inches taller than Claire. He had the same scowl on his face that he'd had since he was a small child. Claire realized, with a shock, that she had never seen him smile.

Linny was talking into her cell phone.

"Call you later," she said, hanging up.

"I'm so sorry," she said, turning to Claire and Tess. "Air travel is impossible. Our flight was canceled and the next one delayed, and we missed our connection. For a while, I didn't know if we'd make it."

Dirk didn't say anything. He just pulled his bag down the beach to where Tess and Claire stood. When he reached Claire he dropped his bag and gave Claire a nod. Claire hugged him. Neither said anything. For her part, Claire didn't trust herself. She was angry that Dirk was there but knew that wasn't his fault, and somewhere in her brain she knew she couldn't blame him—he was just a kid.

"I thought cell phones didn't work," Claire said to Tess when she saw Linny talking on her phone.

"There's coverage here, on the beach at Lees Ferry," Tess said. "None in the canyon."

Claire nodded at Tess and then at Linny. She didn't offer help with Linny's bag, and she didn't smile, or speak. She was intent on making Linny uncomfortable, but her friend appeared oblivious to Claire's distress.

"Are we very late? Do I have time to run to the restroom?" Linny said.

Tess gave her approval and turned to instruct Dirk in fitting his life vest, packing his ammo box, and filling their water bottles.

As soon as Linny left for the toilet, Claire went to fill her water bottles. Only two people now stood in line.

"Water's too clear," the man in front of her, tall and handsome in lime-green shorts, said to the man standing in front of him.

"Yeah, as clear as I've seen it," the first man responded. "The fucking dam."

"Maybe this report will do something. Finally change what's going on."

They talked about sediment sampling and sonar equipment, and Claire eavesdropped. She learned that they planned to measure river sediment and beach sand, and they worried that the dam was destroying the river's ecology. They wanted data to show the damaging effects of the uniform, low flow from Glen Canyon Dam. They wanted the Bureau of Reclamation to use the data in their report to alter dam operations. She listened until they left and it was her turn to pump water.

She was bent over the pump handle, trying to hold the water bottle in her left hand while keeping a steady stream of water flowing with her right hand, when Linny grabbed her from behind and clasped her shoulders, throwing off her pumping and knocking the bottle from her hand, spilling the water she'd already pumped.

"Oh, let me do that," Linny said. She grabbed the tipped bottle and the second bottle standing nearby and held an open bottle under the pump and waited for Claire to get the water going again.

"Thanks," Claire said before she could stop herself.

"Here mom, you need to fill your bottles also," Dirk said, handing Linny two bottles. He got in line behind Claire with his bottles.

3

Day 1. Morning

I 'm ready to go!" Tess yelled while they continued to pump. "Get a move on!"

While she waited for her passengers, an engine coughed, gasoline fumes spewed across the sand, and an old pick-up truck drove onto the middle of the beach. A young couple, perhaps in their early twenties, though they looked like they could still be in their teens, flung open the truck doors and stumbled out. The man, of medium height and stocky, climbed into the truck bed; the woman, who was short and sleight, stood on the running board. They pulled at ropes and buckles and untied knots. Muttering in soft and sometimes not-so-soft voices, they unloaded two worn kayaks, one yellow and one red, from a dilapidated frame bolted onto the back of the truck.

The woman and then the man pulled off the black fleece pullovers and leggings of early morning. The woman wore a tight, pink T-shirt and small, blue shorts. She was very thin, almost waif-like, with little chest and no hips. A body made for river clothes, Tess thought. Her long hair was as dark and as straight as a Navajo's, but her skin was very fair. The man stripped down to his bare chest and Speedo. He looked like he spent his afternoons in the gym, or perhaps at the beach. His short hair was as light as the woman's was dark, and his body was tanned and muscled. Together they packed their gear.

Tess continued to watch and listen to the couple. The woman looked over at her and smiled, and Tess gave a small wave. The woman looked around the beach.

"We're the only kayakers," she said to the man, her fingers pulling at her pink shirt, stretching it into odd angles.

The man stayed crouched over the yellow kayak, and he didn't look around the beach. He looked up at the woman.

"We're prepared," he said. "You're strong."

"Look at these boats, Tim, and all their supplies. We've got almost nothing," she said.

"Ellie, we're fine."

"What if we forgot something? What if something happens?"

Ellie stood with her hands on her hips. Tim continued to pack his gear. He looked up at her again and smiled. After a minute or two, she squatted near the red kayak and pawed through her gear. She cinched her sleeping bag smaller, sorted then stuffed a minimal assortment of clothes into a dry-bag—wadding shorts into a ball and jamming shirts into jacket pockets. Occasionally she folded a shirt or smoothed a pullover. Tim stuffed his clothes, using knees and elbows to push the clothes inside his bag, and he cinched the bag shut and tied it to the kayak shell. A water filter, cans of food, and a small cooking pot lay on the sand.

The man talked to himself as he packed, and the woman stopped what she was doing and stared at the river. They were quiet, and they didn't create anything resembling a commotion, but something about their behavior drew Tess' attention. She started to walk over to them. She wanted to tell them that kayaking had been her first love, that she kayaked before she rafted. The summer she turned eleven her father dragged a battered, blue kayak to the edge of a deep, swimming hole. Then he presented her with her old life vest and a new helmet. A Park Service Ranger reached the couple first, and Tess returned to wait for her passengers.

When Claire and Linny had filled their water bottles and walked back across the beach, Tess helped fit their life vests. The two remaining vests looked worn and used. Tess handed Claire a jacket with foam panels pounded thin and straps dried stiff, as if rigor mortis had set in. Claire's concern showed in her face.

"Don't worry," Tess said. "It's totally safe."

She then handed them paddles and showed them where to sit – Dirk on the left side and Claire and Linny across from him on the right side of the raft. Dirk climbed in and perched on the outer tube of the raft, with his left leg dangling in the water and the paddle at his side. Linny sat in front of Claire, and they both sat inside the raft, with their feet tucked beneath them, and they leaned to their right, across the outer tube, to paddle. Tess was certain the women felt awkward, leaning out as they did, but she knew it would take at least a few days before they considered straddling the tube as Dirk did. She believed Dirk was safe sitting on the edge of the raft. She was surprised, though, that his mother didn't say anything about how he sat, didn't even seem to notice.

Claire, on the other hand, looked across at Dirk several times, and then back at Tess and straight ahead to Linny. She too said nothing.

"Normally we'll have a couple additional rafters," Tess said. "I can take up to six paddlers." She sat in a molded seat, her hands gripped on long oars that skimmed across the water.

"Pretty nice to have our own private raft," Linny said.

With seeming reluctance, Claire agreed.

"Well, since we're so private," Tess said, "why don't you tell me where you live and something about yourselves, for a start. We'll do trip introductions later, when we do the big safety talk, but we can start early. I grew up on the Kern River in California. Came here right after graduating from high school."

"You mean you never went to college or anything?" Dirk said.

"No college. I knew I wanted to be a river guide from the time I was in elementary school. And where do you live?"

"New York City," Dirk said.

"Never been there," she said.

"Living in New York's great," Dirk said. "The best part of my life. The city's amazing."

"We've been in New York since before Dirk was born," Linny said.

"And I live in Santa Cruz, in California," Claire said. "Well, in the mountains outside town."

"Oh, a bicoastal friendship," Tess said. "That's cool." She thought how she had a boyfriend, but no real girlfriends. She'd never had girlfriends.

The raft skimmed across the water. The river, the air, and the bushes along the shoreline were all still. Once they left the beach at Lees Ferry, silence replaced the shouting. They rounded a bend in the river, and the world simplified—there was nothing but river, rocks, and blue sky. Not even a single cloud disturbed the view. The cliffs rose straight from the water and the sand beach disappeared. Mountain ranges emerged in the distant haze, mesas beyond the cliffs. Nearby, the rocks changed color, adding a new, deep purple to the desert tableau. Tess relaxed into her seat.

Claire tried to relax. She wanted to focus on the canyon, but she thought how she was friends with Linny and hardly knew Dirk.

After another bend in the river, the white sand reemerged, washed in from the surf, to disappear beneath the green and brown bushes crowding the shore. Reflecting the bushes, the water turned green at the edges. Mirroring the sky, it sank deep blue in the center of the river.

In front of her, Linny turned her head back and forth. She turned around to look at Claire.

"Not too much to look at," she said. "I don't see any animals. There are supposed to be rapids. This water's barely moving. I didn't expect Pirates of the Caribbean, but still."

"You won't be disappointed in the rapids," Tess said. "Just wait. And West can probably give you as good a time as Johnny Depp, if you're interested."

"She's married to my father," Dirk said. "At least for now."

Tess shrugged her shoulders. Claire waited for Linny to say something, but she didn't. Her friend paddled and looked forward, and Claire thought she saw Linny tense her back, but she wasn't sure. A short time later Tess called out "Four Mile Wash," and they passed under a large bridge.

"Navajo Bridge on Route 89A," Tess said. "From this point, we leave behind roads and civilization and enter into Grand Canyon's Marble Canyon and the desert wilderness. You crossed over the bridge right before you got to Marble Canyon Lodge."

"We're in a spiral," Linny said. "Or going in circles. Circling down into hell, like Dante's Inferno. C'est la vie. C'est ma vie."

Claire had crossed the bridge the previous day. They'd stopped to look down at the water below. Two rafts had passed beneath them, and someone watching from the bridge had said "private trip." Even then, Claire had been unable to imagine herself floating the river. In the high desert that stretched around her in all directions, as far as she could see, the river appeared insignificant. She had to take it on faith that it was also grand.

Tess worked her oars. She leaned on her left oar, steered the raft away from the edge of the river, where the water was calmest, and ran the small rapids on the right side. As her oars vanished into the foaming froth, all sound, except that of rushing water, disappeared. The raft moved down the main current, over the waves lined up like dishes in a dish rack.

The baggage raft rowed by West, and the four other oar and paddle rafts with their guides and twenty-seven passengers had pulled to shore about two miles beyond the bridge. When Tess' raft pulled up, several rafters sat on their rafts' outer tubes with their feet dangling in the river. Others strolled the sand or splashed in the water. A few walked up a dry creek bed. Overhead a narrow string of wispy clouds floated across a southwest mesa.

"Are we camping here?" Claire asked.

"No, just having lunch. We need a bigger camp for this group." Tess said. "It's a nice beach, though. A private trip, or the scientists, could camp here if they get a late start. Most trips like to go farther before stopping for the night."

Tess pulled up to one of the rafts, and a guide jumped up and pulled their raft close and used a metal clip to secure it to a staked raft. Claire slid across the outer tube into the water and sloshed to shore.

"Are you the person who was late?" a man about her age asked her.

"No, I'm her friend. I was here on time."

4

Day 1. Afternoon

Claire walked along the shoreline through the shallow surf. Muted and soothing colors surrounded her, with brown fading into tan, and gray into burgundy, accented by the deep blue of the sky reflected in the water. It was like nowhere she'd ever been, the scale and topography of the canyon beyond her comprehension. Instead of mountain ranges visible in the distance, the cliffs now rose vertically and towered overhead, as if pushed forward by the faded mesas previously crowded on the horizon. The silence and utter calm, a complete about-face from the noise and commotion at the launch, surprised her. Even her mountaintop, weighted down with monumental redwoods, lacked the peace that floated down the Colorado.

The ice-cold water stung and numbed her feet as she waded in and out of the river, and she lost all feeling in less than a minute. Looking down through the crystal clear effluent she watched her feet turn white, and with each step she took the coarse sand held the imprint of her sport sandal. The air was still extremely hot, but a gentle breeze coursed along the river just above the water, and all around her the massive walls of Grand Canyon rose up and dwarfed her.

For the first time since arriving she felt the magic of being outdoors, and she forgot that Linny had brought Dirk. It no longer mattered that Linny had been late. Only the river mattered as she walked along the shoreline of the Colorado. Only the mountains and trees had mattered when she first moved to the mountains.

Claire pulled off her shirt, placed it on the sand, and folded her sunglasses on top. She adjusted her bathing suit and dove into the frigid water. Goose bumps spread across her cold-red arms, and as soon as she stood back on shore, she shivered. She wiped a cool hand across her still-hot face. She dried her hands with her shirt, shook herself like a dog, then wriggled her arms through the sleeves of her shirt and fastened two middle buttons.

In shallow stretches where the current petered out, Claire could see to the riverbed, and in deep pools her gaze sank into an emerald abyss. Where the water stilled, its glassy surface mirrored the cliffs into a two-dimensional cubist canvas. In the river's riffles, sunlight ricocheted between sculpted water and smooth cliff, and silver sparkles danced across the rocks. The water's sparkling transparency was as breathtaking as its chill, the water as clear as a swimming pool.

Someone called that lunch was ready, and Claire turned to see a table set in the sand, near the river. Again rafters lined up and jockeyed for position. This time a sizable number of rafters didn't join the queue but waited on the beach. Food is less important than gear, Claire thought, or no one is worried about running out of food at the first meal, except, perhaps, Dirk, the youngest of the group, who stood at the very front of the line. He'd probably been ready to eat for hours. Claire's son Greg, four years younger than Dirk, was ready for lunch as soon as he finished breakfast. On weekends and during the summer, when the kids were home, Claire spent most of her day in the kitchen preparing food. She hadn't minded in the beginning, but for the past year she resented every minute. She always thought there was somewhere else she wanted to be, though she didn't always know where that was.

She wasn't particularly hungry, but she made her way to the buffet and made herself a sandwich. She loved having someone else plan and prepare the meal. It seemed the ultimate luxury, and she didn't care that she wasn't hungry. Accustomed to living with a strict routine, when it was time to eat, she ate. She didn't even think about taking a beer or pulling out the bottle she'd stashed in the ammo box. She drank only furtively before five o'clock. To openly drink in the morning or afternoon would require her to acknowledge her drinking problem. She could dismiss the two drinks she'd had earlier on the beach because no one had seen her. She wasn't like Paul, who started drinking mid-afternoon and didn't stop until he passed out.

"I ate a big breakfast," Linny said as she took only a can of Diet Coke and no food. "I'm not yet hungry."

Dirk came and sat on the sand near Claire and Linny. He had just made a second sandwich.

"This is really good," he said.

"Must be the scenery," Claire said, surprised at how perfect the meal also tasted to her. "I've never been a sandwich person, and I agree—this is great."

Neither Dirk nor Linny answered. Dirk concentrated on his eating, looking down at his food and studying the ingredients. Linny sat with her eyes closed and her hands around the soda can.

"We're gonna camp at 8 Mile," Tess announced. "After we get camp set up, Orion will lead a hike up Jackass Creek if anyone wants to go. And before that we've got our first semi-real rapids! Enjoy!"

Claire wondered whether she would join the hike, and she looked around to find Orion, to see who he was. Theresa, the older woman guide, ambled up to Tess to talk. Claire didn't want to be in Theresa's raft. I am both sexist and ageist, she thought to herself. It is pushing my limits for me to raft with Tess.

"We're going to do a little shuffling around to set up for the rapids, even though it's small," Tess yelled across the beach. "I need a few more people, to balance out the rafts. I want you and you and you."

She pointed at two men and one woman. They seemed not to understand what was happening, and Theresa walked over to explain the situation to them. When she finished, they untied their ammo boxes and day bags and carried them to Tess' raft.

Tess stared at the water, thinking it wasn't quite right. The river looked calmer than usual and the flow more modest than was normal. Undoubtedly something about the dam. The scientists hated the dam and it's effect on the river. The biologists wanted a river with warm, slow backwaters to protect young fish, and the dam made that impossible. The water released by the dam came from the bottom of the reservoir and was extremely cold. The geologists wanted a variable flow with higher highs and lower lows to replenish the canyon's sediment. They believed the dam and the steady flow of water stripped the canyon of its sand. The most comprehensive solution to the canyon's problems called for removal of the dam, but only the most radical people on the river wanted that. Tess thought of herself as radical, but she wasn't that radical. She wanted a natural river, but she liked rowing under controlled flow conditions. Without the dam, it would be like the old days, and could be too wild. She might not be up to the challenge.

Tess wondered if all the research done actually made any difference. For more years than she'd been there, scientists collected data and wrote reports, but nothing seemed to change. She imagined a roomful of men in Washington, D.C., men who had never visited Grand Canyon, making decisions about its future. The imagery fit with her basic skepticism of science and her total cynicism about government.

On a more personal level, Tess didn't really care for the researchers. She found them too intense and controlling for her tastes. They were also somewhat delusional. Though each studied only a tiny issue, and the research of any one of them was unlikely to change the Grand Canyon or have a major impact on the Colorado River, each thought he or she was irreplaceable. She knew no one was irreplaceable, even if Brent was unforgettable.

"It's getting crowded here," Linny said. "Where should we sit?"

Claire shrugged. How could she know which seat was best? She didn't know anything about rafting. She looked to Tess for advice.

"Do you want excitement or an easy ride?" Tess asked.

Claire didn't even know what she wanted. Linny wanted some excitement. Dirk wanted lots of excitement. Tess arranged the rafters, putting Dirk in the left front of the raft and one new man in the right front. She put Linny in the middle right and Claire behind her. She placed the other new man behind Dirk and the other new woman behind him. Claire was certain she should introduce herself to the new rafters, but everyone seemed too busy for her interruption.

Tess rowed and the passengers paddled. The river ran fairly straight, almost due south and only slightly to the west. They aimed directly into the brutal sun. Claire laid her paddle across her knees and turned to the ammo boxes strapped in the center of the raft. She pulled open her box and pulled out a bright orange and purple sarong she'd bought years ago when she visited Maui. She draped the cloth over the top of her hat to provide some shade like an umbrella, and the purple fringe fell across her arms. It might not look stylish, but she was too hot to care. She just hoped it would provide some relief. If it had been windy she would have needed to secure the cloth, but the slight breeze she'd felt earlier had disappeared.

"Try dipping the fabric in the river," Tess said. "It will become a personal air-conditioner."

Claire followed the advice, and the other rafters eyed her with envy.

"O.K. Claire, sit on your shade screen," Tess said. "Everyone stop paddling - raise your paddles out of the water - and follow my directions."

Tess stopped rowing, and the raft stood still as if the river and time itself had stalled. For a moment there seemed to be neither sound nor movement, neither past nor future. Just beyond the bow of the raft the water turned glassy and smooth, and without effort they flowed onto the polished surface that fanned out across the river. At the edge of the shiny surface, up ahead, the river dipped and disappeared.

Almost imperceptibly the river funneled the raft down the tongue of the rapids. Tess angled one oar and then the other in the water to adjust placement of the raft, keeping it centered in the strongest current in the middle of the flow. As they approached the dip where the river disappeared, Claire saw splashes of water leaping into the air, the only sign of the water and rocks that she knew must be there.

"Paddle" Tess yelled, her voice rising above the low roar that simultaneously arose from the jumble of rocks that now appeared before them.

Claire dropped her paddle into the water, gripped the handle, and paddled as she'd been taught during lunch. Straight paddle in the water ahead, pull hard, straight paddle lifted out behind. Repeat. Repeat. In an instant they were through the rapids.

"Back paddle," Tess yelled.

Claire lifted the paddle and dropped it into the water behind, then pushed the paddle forward and lifted the paddle out ahead. In a matter of seconds the water calmed and the excitement was over yet adrenaline continued to course through her body, and she strove to quiet her breathing. She remembered that Tess had described Badger Rapids as semi-real. Claire thought it real enough.

"O.K. for a warm up," Linny said.

"This is awesome," Dirk answered. "Can't wait to tell the guys at school."

Tess rowed them to river-left, and Dirk and the man across from him jumped from the raft and pulled it up the sandy beach. The guides and the rafters pulled all the rafts from the river and lined them up along the beach and tied the rafts to stakes pounded into the sand. West stood on the beach and bellowed.

"O.K." he yelled. "I need everyone's attention and everyone's help. We've got to unload the rafts before you move. We'll unload your personal gear at the end. Line up across the beach and hand off equipment from one person to the next. No one walks up the beach carrying anything. You pass it along."

"Dirk, you stand in the raft," Tess said. "John, you stand near West. The rest of you spread out across the sand, between the two."

Claire climbed to the front of the raft and jumped onto the sand. Others got into line behind her.

"Different and special rules for the port-a-potty," West said. "Known on the river as the groover."

Laughter rippled down the assembly line like a wave through water. Even in Grand Canyon, toilet humor triumphed. Claire caught each item that Dirk tossed to her and turned around and tossed it to the woman standing behind her. She looked up the line but didn't see Linny. Linny stood dipping her toes in the water at the far end of the beach where the sand disappeared. When the rafts were almost completely unloaded, Claire caught a bag, and Linny appeared behind her taking the bag before she could throw it.

West directed the action and indicated where to place the gear. He designated a section of the beach as the camp-kitchen, and the rafters carried all kitchen supplies there. Tents went in a sandy spot farther from the river and chairs in a place at the edge of the surf. As soon as the rafts were unloaded Claire found her bags and dragged them to an empty area to set up her camp. She assembled her tent on the small rise of a dune with a view of the river.

5

Day 1. Afternoon

O K. rafters. We're hiking up the creek. Anyone who's interested, follow me."

About half the group, maybe a dozen rafters, shuffled across the sand to where Orion stood. In his early 30's, Orion looked very comfortable on the river. Medium height, lanky, and a little bouncy, he'd been barefoot on the rafts and beach but slipped on flip-flops for the hike. Claire couldn't place his accent and thought perhaps he'd grown up in southern California, the land of sun, surf, and perfect diction.

Dirk was at the mouth of the creek before Orion finished speaking. Linny walked the other way while he spoke, distancing herself from the organized activity. Claire joined the hikers. She waited back a little, wanting to get at the end of the line that she knew would form. She was a strong hiker and didn't worry about keeping up, but she hated having someone walking right behind her. Instead of looking ahead, she'd turn around to see what that person was up to. When she was last in line, she need only worry about a wild animal running up and pouncing on her, and that unlikely possibility caused her almost no anxiety.

"This canyon makes it all the way up to the road," Orion said. "We could walk up and back, and I've done it, but there's no reason to unless you're leaving the river. We'll just do the lower section."

Claire followed the hikers across the loose sand of the wash. Within moments they left behind the frigid, green river and entered the blistering, rust-colored, desert canyon. The canyon walls slumped to the ground, as if they'd melted in the sun, and large boulders littered the canyon floor, preventing a direct march up the slot canyon. Orion picked out paths between the massive rocks, and where he couldn't find any, he blazed a trail by climbing onto the walls and scampering across the rubble. He stuck to the shady side of the canyon where possible, but even in the shade the air was feverishly hot and still.

Though the landscape was bone-dry, and the layered cliff looked nothing like her coastal mountains, Claire felt comfortably at-home. Hiking, whether in the desert or in the forest, had a rhythm that she recognized, and her body moved in familiar ways. She bent her knees and lifted her legs to climb; she wedged her sandal into the sand to balance. She trailed her hands across the rocks and felt a coolness she didn't find in the air.

"We're rafting through a whole series of rock formations," Orion announced. "At the rim near the launch at Lee's Ferry is the Kaibab, a marine limestone. A little later, the river cuts down through the Coconino Sandstone. You can now see that sulfur-colored sandstone at the top of the canyon. We're moving into older and older rocks as we move deeper into the canyon. Eventually we'll reach Vishnu Schist – 1700 million years old. The rocks here are only around 250 million years old."

Leaning against the rough, jagged cliff, Claire felt the grittiness of the rock: shale and, above it, sandstone—nothing like the hard granite of the rocks in the Sierra's—and she wondered how old the Sierra rocks were. It was something she'd never thought about.

"What's the name of that kid hiking ahead?" Orion asked.

Claire looked up and saw Dirk climbing the cliff wall.

"Dirk," she said, her stomach muscles clenching.

"Hey Dirk, we're not going that far. Come back," Orion yelled, and Dirk stopped and turned around.

A big difference between twelve and sixteen, Claire thought. Greg wouldn't turn around if she called. Maybe it was that Orion called, rather than she or Linny.

"If you like to climb," Orion said to Dirk when he rejoined the group, "I'll take you up to Deer Creek Falls and Elves Chasm. There's really cool stuff down here."

"Like this rattlesnake?" a man about Claire's age said.

Orion shot over next to the man, and everyone else crowded behind them.

"No, that's a California King," Orion said. "Not poisonous but rare to see here. Its usual habitat is farther down river."

"Are there rattlesnakes?" someone asked.

"Sure are."

"Are we gonna kill the snake?" the man who discovered it asked.

"We don't kill anything."

"You'll kill a rattler if we find one."

"No."

Claire didn't even kill spiders she found in the house. She had a spider catcher, and she'd use it to scoop up the spider and take it outside. Her kids would be furious if she killed a spider. They didn't believe you should kill anything. She drew the line at mosquitoes, though. She killed mosquitoes. She also killed rats and mice. For her, that was a necessity of country living.

"How can you not kill rattlesnakes?" Dirk said. "We kill rats if we find them. And cockroaches."

"It's different in a city," Orion said. "Out here we try to keep nature's balance. We leave the snakes unmolested so they can eat the rats."

6

Day 1. Evening

Dirk didn't say much, but that was O.K. with Claire; she almost liked him. He had a rather sullen attitude, much like he'd had since he was a little boy, but he wasn't challenging in the way that Greg was. He was competent and independent and seemed able to think for himself. Maybe when her kids were older she'd enjoy them more. Right now, if she were honest, she experienced Greg and Sarah as obligations. Greg talked all the time and was, above all, annoying. Sarah didn't talk much, but she was passive, unformed, and uninteresting. They weren't the adorable youngsters they'd been, and they were not yet companions. Paul used to be Claire's companion, but he'd become increasingly angry, and now she tried to keep her distance. Though his verbal abuse never became physical, she kept the kids out of his way.

So far, Claire had spent more time with Dirk than she'd spent with Linny. She didn't know what to make of that. It felt like she'd come on the trip alone.

The hot afternoon turned into a warm evening. Claire searched the sand for a small, flat rock, and when she found the perfect one, she turned ninety degrees to the water, pulled her wrist back, and released the stone to skip across the river. It sunk below the surface after only one bounce. Sometimes nothing went her way.

She checked her watch. It was 5:20, and she was free to drink openly according to the rules she'd set for herself. On her way to get her flask she found a bucket of cold beer sitting on the sand. Apparently she wasn't the only one waiting for a drink. She looked around the beach. Every guide except West and Theresa had a beer, and Linny sat in a chair at the edge of the water, holding a beer in her right hand. Claire pulled a Heineken from the tub and dropped onto the sand.

A Great Blue Heron flew overhead, soared on an updraft, and perched on the end of a top branch in a tree across the river. Claire pulled binoculars from her bag. The heron resettled on a neighboring tree. She looked around to offer the binoculars for viewing, but no one stood near her, and no one seemed interested. No one else watched the bird.

When she finished a second beer she walked up to her tent, found a towel at the bottom of her dry-bag and took the towel and her small bottle of Dr. Bonner's Liquid Soap down to the river. Upriver the shoreline curved out of view of the camp, and she walked along the water looking for privacy. Around a bend, in the area West had previously designated for women only, several women bathed by squatting in the surf. She walked a little farther along the river and found a large, flat rock on which to balance her towel and soap, and she waded into the water.

The water was icy, almost too cold to tolerate, but she forced herself to ignore the pain in her feet and lower legs, and soon the pain turned to numbness. After washing she felt clean in a way she hadn't thought possible when she'd learned the only option for bathing was to sit in the flowing river. She smelled like peppermint, and considering the alternatives, she thought that exceptionally good. Her skin dried as soon as she stood up, before she'd fully emerged from the river. She hadn't done a full hair washing, but she'd splashed her hair with her hands and wet it down. That felt good enough for the first day, and her hair dried as soon as she finished toweling it, and she worked her fingers through the strands releasing any tangles. By the time she finished with her hair and checked on her bathing suit, it too was completely dry. She could hardly believe how good she felt. A half-hour warm water shower wouldn't have left her feeling any more refreshed.

As she walked back to camp, soft, warm air brushed across her skin. Though conditions in the canyon were rough and harsh, and that had been one of her greatest concerns in coming, for the moment she felt pampered and indulged beyond the limitations of the desert. She tossed her things on top of her bag, pulled out her flask, grabbed another cold beer, and settled into a chair at the edge of the river.

"There's no shower," Linny said. "I thought they'd set up a shower stall. That's what they did on my friend's trip."

"I washed in the river, up there, around the bend," Claire said. "It was great."

"Doesn't sound great," Linny said, and she rose from her chair and walked to her bags.

Dirk, apparently destined to be Claire's companion, pulled up a chair and sat down on the other side of Claire.

"Everyone on this trip's so old," he said.

"Not the guides—Tess, Orion, and Riz aren't that old," Claire said.

"Yeah, but mom said I couldn't hang out with them."

Really? Claire thought. Linny's worried that a kid educated in New York City's best private schools is going to blow off college to run rivers? Or did she worry about alcohol and drugs? Probably more of that in New York than here. At least here the supply was limited by what could be stuffed in a bag and brought down the river. He wasn't her kid, though, not her responsibility. She just shrugged.

If he had been her kid, and if her husband Paul had made such a rule, she would have objected and overruled him. She could see Paul saying that. He liked to set limits; he wanted to control everything.

He hadn't wanted her to take this trip. He couldn't stop her from going, though, since they didn't have that kind of relationship, and she wasn't that kind of wife. He asked her to call him every night, and she promised she would. When she learned Grand Canyon had no cell coverage, Claire offered to keep a diary so Paul would know what she'd done, in case she couldn't remember when she got home. She was ecstatic to avoid having a daily conversation. He accepted defeat.

Dirk left to skip stones across the water. Linny returned from her bath, dumped her things in a pile, and took Dirk's chair.

"Dinner!"

"Thank God; I'm starving!" Linny said. She jumped up and headed straight for the makeshift kitchen.

Claire waited for most of the rafters to fill their plates and the line to disappear. Even from her chair at the shoreline she could smell the food, and she was soon hungrier than she thought possible. The bar-b-que chicken was plump and perfectly browned with just the right amount of black charcoal. The mashed potatoes were white and smooth, and the salad included her favorite vegetables, crisp and fresh. She filled her plate thinking again how perfect that someone else did the planning, shopping, and cooking. She had no doubt the food would be delicious.

It wasn't that she didn't like to cook. She liked cooking, and she loved baking, and she enjoyed spending time in the kitchen. But doing the same thing every day, day after day, sapped her energy. She hated how Paul and the kids expected her to take care of their meals, and then she berated herself for feeling like that. Of course they would expect food – they, like everyone else, needed to eat, and in the family's division of labor, cooking was her job.

Linny sat surrounded by other rafters, and Claire found an empty chair at the edge of the water next to West and Tess.

"Can I sit here?" she asked.

They looked up and nodded enthusiastically. Both had their mouths full. Claire sat down, heard the water rushing across the rocks at the edge of the beach. The shade from the cliffs across the river extended part-way up the cliffs behind her. She took her first taste of the food. It was as good or better than anything she'd ever eaten. Everyone was eating, and no one was talking, and Claire couldn't remember the last time she'd eaten in such complete silence. She didn't miss her family's dinnertime conversation. She didn't miss her family.

After dinner when the dishes were washed and the pots and pans put away, Linny stood up and stepped away from the large group of rafters and walked towards Claire. Claire saw her out of the corner of her eye. After the quiet dinner and the companionable solitude, Claire had no interest in a serious conversation with Linny, and Linny looked serious. Claire had drunk too much to think about Linny, talk about Dirk, or figure out her own life. Gripping the sides of her chair to steady herself, she stood up, walked up the small hill to her tent, and climbed in.

7

Diary Day 1

A very busy day that started early at the lodge at Lees Ferry. We met at 5:30 for breakfast, then assembled for the bus ride to the launch site. Linny didn't arrive on time (per her usual), and when she did arrive, she had Dirk with her! So, that was a big surprise.

Rafting the Colorado River through Grand Canyon is amazing. The water is freezing cold and clear, the air is blistering hot, and the sky is a deep blue. Much of the day we float the river. Our guide rows with huge oars, and we passengers sit along the edge of the raft with paddles, sometimes paddling and sometimes not, and the current pushes us down the river. Today we ran small rapids, and that was super fun.

When we reached our campsite, we set up our tents on the sand, away from the river, and the guides prepared dinner. Tonight we had absolutely delicious chicken. Too spicy for Sarah though – she wouldn't have liked it.

After dinner, before clean-up, the guides held a meeting to lay out the rules of the river. Pee in the river and poop in the can. Throughout the day—wash hands with soap and water or use anti-bacterial gel. Cleanliness and safety first, they said – just like I tell you kids! Always wear a lifejacket when on a raft, or when climbing around near the river. If you end up in the water, turn to face downstream in a sitting position with feet out in front and look for a way to get back in the raft.

Tonight's as quiet as it is at home. Except for the rush of the river. I miss you all.

8

Day 2. Morning

Tess walked through the dark camp announcing the arrival of morning. Claire forced herself to wake and dress, and she quickly assembled her gear, stumbling down to the water from her over-night perch in the sand. As the campers arrived, the sun shot a few narrow rays of light above the cliffs across the river while the rest of the canyon remained shrouded in deep shadows. Downstream, gray water flowed into gray cliffs, fading into the somber gloom of early morning.

Claire poured herself a full mug of coffee from a large pot. Back at the tents rafters chatted, a woman sang, and someone whistled, but they all grew quiet when they reached the river. No one risked disturbing the palpable calm rising from the water. The coolness of the river spread onto the beach and surrounded Claire. It reminded her of stepping into the fog at home and being transported to another world. When they first moved to the mountains she'd walk into the fog- filled forest just to feel cut off from everyone else. She hadn't done that in several years—she'd forgotten.

As dawn lit the sky, the stillness of the river and the desert settled onto the sandy shore. Claire stood mesmerized by the river canyon until the smell of frying eggs and sizzling bacon overpowered her. Rafters lined up for breakfast, and the beach burst into activity. In addition to the plates of bacon and fried eggs, English muffins and sectioned grapefruit filled the large steel bowls that had held last night's salad. At the end of the table a carton of orange juice sat alongside a large tub of tea bags.

Ignoring her five-year-old self, with eyes bigger than her stomach, Claire forced the responsible, adult part of her brain to limit the food she piled onto her plate. She thought of how much food there'd been the night before and would likely be again that evening. She reminded herself that lunch would be served between breakfast and dinner.

She'd never had an eating problem; she was neither overweight nor underweight. What was it about providing food every day for her family that had become such a chore that being served a buffet felt the ultimate luxury?

"Ugh," Linny said. "Who wants to see this much food in the morning?"

"I guess I do, if I don't have to cook," Claire said.

"I never make breakfast," Linny said. "Everyone's on his own in the morning. I have no idea what Steve eats, and Dirk's not hungry in the morning. Usually he goes to Starbucks for a coffee and a scone."

Dirk was at the front of the line, just as he'd been at dinner. As Claire watched, he took more food than she thought possible for one person to eat.

"Lucky for us we've got at least one teenager on the trip," Orion said. "We won't have to worry about too many leftovers."

Claire laughed along with several other rafters. She noticed that Linny, still standing next to her, didn't laugh. Dirk took his plate of food and searched for a chair without looking at his mother or Claire.

The sun peeked through a notch in the cliff, letting sunlight pour through the rocky cut to stream beneath the canyon's suspended mist, as if it came direct from heaven. For a few golden minutes a marigold light washed across the river as the canyon emerged, caught in the beam of a spotlight. With sun shining directly on her face, Tess closed her eyelids to let the pure, unadulterated brilliance soak into her. The sun moved, rising higher in the sky, again behind the cliffs, and the moment passed. Tess resumed serving.

When she finished, she climbed back onto her raft to rig a large beach umbrella in the back of her boat. She tucked herself in the tiny refuge of shade as the sun rose, drinking from a half-empty bottle of Southern Comfort. It was barely morning. The day was off to a good start.

Claire hadn't thought about having a drink until she noticed Tess drinking, but then she couldn't shake the idea that she too needed something. She pulled her flask from her bag and took a long drink. She was so focused on tasting the liquid as it slid down her throat, she didn't see Linny and Dirk approach. Dirk looked at her without saying anything. Linny was watching one of the guides on his raft, and Claire didn't think Linny had seen her. Shrugging, she put away the bottle, trying hard to appear less guilty and embarrassed than she felt.

The rising sun now lit the far wall of the canyon and some of the beach, leaving the river itself in shadows. Claire turned to look back upstream as splashes of sunlight and shade spread across the water and the mesas. The mixture of glimmering light and opaque darkness was magical. The beach was still in shadows when they launched, and cool air rose from the river and fell onto the raft.

Claire sat in the middle seat on the right with Linny in front of her. The man who'd been in the front seat moved behind Claire. The man who'd sat in the middle of the left claimed the front seat, forcing Dirk into the middle, across from Claire. Claire had the feeling these were the seats they would keep for the rest of the trip. The guides stood in the water to push the rafts off the shore; then they jumped onto the boats and bounced along the outer tubes in a graceful dance on the way to their seats. No one missed a step.

The man in front of Tess said that he was from Colorado Springs and they'd had a huge snowpack and everyone in the state knew the Colorado River was going to flood as soon as the snow melted. Tess told him that mattered in the mountains – down here the river was dammed. She didn't say anything more, but she wondered why the water level seemed so low. The dam operators should be releasing water if the river was going to flood upstream, filling the reservoir.

Claire leaned out over the water. It was clear enough for her to see straight through to the bottom. She would have thought it the most natural river in the world, if she hadn't heard the scientists complaining that the river's clarity was an unnatural result of dam operations. Apparently the river should have been dirty brown, filled with sediment. Instead, the current flowed exquisitely clear. Downstream, the gray-silver river disappeared behind a gentle fold in the rocks.

"I heard the scientists at Lees Ferry say that the water was too clear," Claire said to Tess. "Why would they want the water dirty?"

"The beaches are disappearing," Tess said. "Glen Canyon Dam blocks the sediment from flowing down the river, catching it in the reservoir above the dam. Because of the dam, there's no sediment coming down the river to replenish the beaches when a storm whips the sand off the shore. Also, wind blows sand off the ancient archeology sites, exposing them, leaving too little sand in the canyon to cover them back up. If you see Grand Canyon as an eco system, it's unbalanced and in trouble. It's changed enormously since the building of the dam."

"So many things are in trouble," Claire said, and Linny turned around to face her.

Claire nodded, affirming what she'd just said. It was true. Her life was falling apart. She'd come to Grand Canyon to decide whether to leave Paul. At some point she'd tell Linny, hoping

Linny would know what to do. But maybe she wouldn't. What problem had Linny ever had?

9

Day 2. Morning

This is Hot Na Na Wash," Tess yelled, "next we're coming up to House Rock Rapids. Follow my instructions."

They drifted into the tongue of the rapids, the smooth glassy water that drew the raft down the river to the hidden waves. At the back of the raft, Tess stood on the top of her seat, staring downriver. She didn't expect to find anyone waiting at House Rock Rapids. Although it was the first significant rapids in the Grand Canyon, it couldn't compete with the later rapids, and the truth was, if House Rock Rapids posed a problem, you were on the wrong river—you shouldn't be rafting the Colorado. Every commercial guide knew to avoid the large hole on the left channel by making a right run. Many of the private rafters didn't know this, but few of them stopped to scout. Instead, they let the current carry them down into the unknown, as a preliminary test of their rafting skills which none of them expected to fail.

Riz's and Orion's rigs each commanded a channel of the river below the rapids, and the yellow kayak floated between them. Tess didn't see the red kayak. The two guides stood and pointed into mid-stream, their signal for where they wanted her to go.

"Something's wrong," she told her passengers. "Pay attention. Paddles up."

The raft seemed to stall at the top of the satin tongue, as it always did, where the water backed up before narrowing into the smaller channel. While they hovered, Tess heard nothing beyond the roar of the water and felt nothing except the soft canyon breeze against her face. She pulled her oars from the water and let the raft fall slowly, sliding down water as smooth and polished as reflective glass. Only when it slid from the tongue and tumbled into the churning froth, did she drop her oars back into the river, ready to fight the current.

"Paddle!" she yelled.

Keeping her eyes on the water where the guides had pointed, she entered the rapids as she always did, and when she slammed into a first wave, she aimed for the right channel. Rocks, honed razor sharp, threatened the raft. An immense, out-sized boulder, a mythical Charybdis, commanded the left channel of the river, and a fierce current pushed the raft toward the rock and the hole behind it. Her muscles tensed and her heart beat faster. This was the danger of the rapids, the hole she needed to avoid.

The rush of water drove her left, and Tess strained against her oars to force the raft toward the narrow channel on the right, where she needed to be. Her body relaxed and her breathing steadied. She'd trained a lifetime for such a moment. She looked into the river but saw nothing, only waves grown monstrous. She steadied the bow of her raft into a succession of waves, and Orion, downriver, motioned her farther right. With little room to maneuver, she let up slightly on her right oar, pulled harder on the left, and powered into the next wave, pitching down into frothy water and bouncing blindly across breakers. For what seemed like an eternity, the raft was submerged, drenched, and cut off from directions, and for a moment, she could find no air to breathe. They skirted the edge of a whirlpool, and a gigantic back wave threatened to fold the raft on itself and slam it into a rock.

As a menacing dance of waves surrounded the raft, a tint of red refracted in the river and a flash of yellow emerged in the whirl of water to Tess's left. Luminous froth rose from opaque depths, and Tess's raft hovered in the mist suspended above the waves. Without thinking, Tess jammed her raft against the current, pulled backwards to where the kayaker might be, and pressed her oars against the flow of water to steady the raft. Not knowing if her eyes tricked her or if she saw another flash of yellow next to her raft, she acted purely on instinct and pulled the oars onto the tubes, wedged her feet against crates, leaned from the raft, and grabbed the edge of a life vest. The body resisted, but she yanked it into the air and onto the baggage piled behind her.

"Paddle harder," Tess yelled.

The raft hit against the kayak and pushed it free, and without pause, she grabbed her oars, twirled the raft in pirouettes, and pivoted the boat around. She pulled hard to veer right into the calmer water. By the time she had dropped the oars and turned around, the yellow kayak and other rafts had pulled next to her.

Claire clutched her paddle as if it could save her. She felt her heart drumming against her chest. She didn't turn around, deliberately ignoring the urgent words yelled back and forth by rafters and guides, and instead shutting her eyes and folding onto her knees. Her heart continued to race. She paid no attention to what was happening in the back of the raft, and only tried to quiet herself.

Linny climbed over her to join Tess. In the hushed quiet that fell over the raft, Claire heard Linny talking to the rescued person, who was vomiting. She also heard Linny talking with Tess. If she didn't know Linny was an investment advisor, she'd think she was an EMT. When she finally opened her eyes and turned around, Claire saw everyone crouched around a young woman in a yellow life jacket. Claire couldn't help noticing how much more buoyant that new, paneled life-vest looked than her faded orange one.

The young woman held Tess' right hand between her two hands. She seemed to be saying the same thing over and over. Perhaps she was thanking Tess, but she spoke so softly that Claire couldn't hear.

Tess, focused on the young woman, and pumped up on the adrenaline rush of the rescue, didn't hear what anyone else was saying. Eventually she realized Linny was talking to her.

"You lifted her over your head," Linny said. "I heard stories about women like you. I guess they're true."

For a moment, Tess saw herself as a mythic woman, a sprite with supernatural strength. She could row the river looking for boaters in distress, for mortals swept into rapids, and she'd pluck them from turbulence, from monstrous waves, and flip them onboard. She'd be the Wonder Woman of the Colorado. She'd rescued swimmers before, but nothing quite so dramatic. This was good—good enough to make her a river legend. Too bad there were so few people as witnesses. She'd have to rely on Orion and Riz to spread the word. She'd have to somehow make sure that Linny told them.

Linny started to tell the woman what she needed to do, and West told the young man in the yellow kayak what he needed to do. The couple refused the suggestion to stop kayaking and camp at the next site, and they insisted they would continue down river. They didn't waiver – they seemed to know what they wanted. Linny started to argue with them, then stopped. Claire realized the couple were probably in their early twenties, only a few years older than Dirk. Those were important years, she thought. Dirk was still a child, while these people were adults. Linny couldn't tell them what to do.

"I kayaked with my father when I was a kid," Tess said when they were again floating the river. "I stopped when my father drowned."

"You didn't tell the kayakers that?" Claire said.

"No, I didn't want to jinx them."

"I hope their kayaking doesn't end with a drowning," Linny said.

"The woman Ellie seemed a lot less sure of what they were doing back at put-in. Now there's no stopping her," Tess said.

10

Day 2. Morning

The heat was brutal. Beads of sweat ran down the edge of Claire's face, while her sunglasses slid down her nose on the sweat that dripped from her forehead. She retrieved her cloth shade, dipped it in the water, and draped it across her hat.

Linny sat in the back of the raft, on a cooler next to Tess. She had stayed in the back, even after Ellie left, to talk to Tess. She had an opinion about everything that had happened. In fact, as Claire knew, Linny had opinions about everything that had happened since they were fifteen; she was the most assured, opinionated person that Claire knew, and Claire knew many lawyers, all with strong opinions. Linny's tough judgments might have been the main reason Claire hadn't yet mentioned her marital problems. Everything she knew about Linny's and Steve's marriage made it sound perfect. What would Linny know about a troubled marriage? She'd believe it could be easily fixed.

The river moved slowly, and Claire stared into the water. It was still clear, but had taken on a greenish tinge, as if from algae. She wished she knew more chemistry to understand why that would be. At the edge of the river, on the sand, uniform ripples spread across the beach. When the raft swerved closer to the shore, she saw air bubbles popping in the sand.

"Did the kayaker make a mistake, or does that stuff just happen?" Dirk turned and asked Tess.

"Nothing just happens," Linny said. "We're all responsible for the things that befall us."

"Well, that's certainly overstating the case," Claire said before she could stop herself.

"No it's not," Linny said. "You can refuse to take responsibility, if you want, but that doesn't mean you're not responsible. You need a certain amount of experience to kayak a river like this. Maybe she doesn't have it. You also need a certain amount of confidence. And maybe she doesn't have that."

"I didn't see the kayaker get into trouble," Tess said, "so I don't know what happened. Lots of unexpected things happen in the water, though. You expect the river to act a certain way, but it doesn't always do that."

"Then you need to be prepared for that," Linny said. "And it's a choice to prepare or not prepare for the unexpected."

Dirk turned in his seat and faced forward. He didn't argue with anyone, nor did he restate his question. Claire realized, for the first time, how difficult Linny could be as a mother. She always had an answer, and there was nothing she didn't know. Claire's own mother had been like that, and Claire learned at a young age not to argue with her.

Linny was her friend and not her mother, but Claire didn't want to get into a disagreement with Linny. Though Claire often spent her days making arguments for indefensible positions, and she sometimes won, she had never won an argument with her friend. Linny was always the self-proclaimed victor. Still, Claire thought Dirk had raised an interesting question.

"What do you think Tess?" she said. "Was the kayaker competent or unprepared? She looks very young to be doing this."

"My dad died kayaking on the Kern River," she said. "He was very experienced and knew what he was doing, but he died. Sometimes there's no clear answer."

11

Day 2. Morning

The river swept over boulders, surged past time-weathered walls, and filled the canyon with a low rumble; the rafters entered the series of rapids known as the Roaring Twenties. With no assist from the passengers and only minimal guidance from Tess, the raft raced left and right and down the middle as the river threaded its way through the mesas. The rapids and waves came in quick succession, the river gradient steep and the current strong. Tess told them they would pull to shore for lunch after a stop in Paradise.

A beautiful, sandy beach and a narrow canyon appeared on river right. Claire was turned sideways, trying to see up the wash, when the water hit, and she took the full force of the wave as a violent slap to her cheek. Water smacked her left eye and knocked her head back and around. She straightened herself out, tucked her feet underneath the tube on which she sat, and held tight to her paddle. Frigid water gushed down her life jacket, soaked her shirt, and trickled across her skin. In an instant the rapids disappeared and the river calmed. She brushed the water from her face and shook out her cap. The moment of intense excitement had passed.

They continued floating. Water moved swiftest in the middle of the river. Near the left bank the current curved back on itself and flowed upstream, gurgling as it spread onto the sand. Tess pointed to the upriver flow and called it an eddy. Across the river bighorn sheep clambered up a rocky slope. Linny was the first to point them out.

The raft hit the next big rapids with a series of waves, and the very first wave doused Claire in an icy deluge and plunged her underwater. Small rapids appeared one after another in an uninterrupted onslaught, and water sprayed across the raft from bow to stern leaving no one dry. After running several rapids in quick succession Claire learned to recognize the roar announcing the rapid's approach, and she could identify the rapids' telltale swell. The extraordinary number of small rapids numbed her to their potential for excitement. Instead, she took them in stride as preparation for surviving the large waves. When a large wave hit she squeezed her eyes and gripped her paddle until the water drained away and the raft reemerged. If a particularly large wave quickly followed before she had time to recompose herself, she pinched her nose, clamped her mouth shut, and gasped for air.

In a break between rapids she pulled on a long-sleeved polypropylene shirt for warmth, working quickly to re-buckle her life jacket before the next wave hit. Though the temperature of the air now soared into the nineties, the cold water left her shivering. She tucked her hair under her hat and cinched it tighter.

She looked up and saw a sparkling oasis springing from the red rocks. A moment earlier, she'd seen no trace of the hidden garden, only solid rock walls. Now several silvery waterfalls reflected the glistening sunlight and gushed down the cliffs, disappearing into the lush greenery on the riverbank. From her seat on the raft where she baked in the sun, it all looked cool and irresistibly inviting.

"Careful if you explore Vasey's Paradise," Tess said. "There's poison ivy."

Claire jumped ashore and instantly warmed up. The sunny beach was scorching, and the sun quickly dried every inch of Claire's clothing. She removed the layers she'd added for warmth, not quite understanding how she'd been chilled just moments earlier and now was overcome by heat.

Claire, Dirk, and a few others assembled in the surf to follow Orion through the vegetation to the waterfalls. Tess stayed on the raft and pulled out a bottle of gin before they left. Linny climbed from the raft and sat on a rock at the edge of the river.

The slight breeze at the water disappeared as soon as they entered the brush. The greenery was beautiful, but as hot and humid as a steam room, nothing like a desert. Claire felt too overwhelmed to continue, but she followed the person in front of her, and before she made a decision to turn around, she stood before a spectacular cascade of water, exquisitely beautiful.

Dirk strode into the mist, but he didn't get far – the water as impenetrable as a steel door. He tried a second time. Claire had been psyching herself up to march in, but after watching him, she just splashed herself with water, turned around and headed back to the raft.

Everyone was hungry and ready to eat, and once they started talking about lunch, it was all Claire could think about. She paddled imagining the sandwich she would make herself.

"We'll have lunch there," Tess said as they neared Redwall Cavern.

From the middle of the river, the cavern looked rather insignificant, a smallish opening in a huge, immense and towering rock face. Once Claire stepped onshore, the cavern became a gaping expanse like nothing she had ever seen – a huge, natural amphitheater, carved from a massive cliff of red-colored limestone by a flooding Colorado River. Several raft groups had already stopped, and people threw frisbees and cart-wheeled and tossed a football. Lunch tables lined up across the sand. Still, the cavern was so large and the beach so wide, the many people running across the sand appeared like a scattered few. Claire forgot about food as soon as she stepped ashore.

Dirk took off running across the sand and disappeared into the cavern. Claire and Linny walked, and their sandals sank deep into the soft, surprisingly cold sand.

"This is amazing," Claire said. "Did you know that John Wesley Powell estimated 50,000 people could fit in here? I read that in the guidebook this morning."

"Ready to go back?" Linny asked.

"I just want to see how far back I can walk," Claire said. "I want to see if there's an echo. Then lunch."

Claire walked and walked. The cavern seemed to go on forever, and eventually, without reaching the end, she turned back. She saw Linny walking at the other side of the cavern. As Claire watched, Linny turned around and walked over to sit at the water's edge next to the woman they'd rescued from the swamped kayak. Claire joined them.

"This is my friend Claire," Linny said. "This is Ellie."

Claire smiled, said hello, and wandered off. She'd come on the trip to talk with Linny, and that hadn't happened yet, and maybe she no longer cared. She was comfortable, as usual, with her own thoughts. She hadn't bothered to chat with the other rafters; she had no reason to talk to the kayak woman.

Food, though, was of interest. She couldn't believe her appetite, especially considering that she occasionally skipped lunch at home. She made the sandwich she'd day-dreamed about: two slices of whole wheat bread, double the amount of roast beef she'd eaten all of last year, tomatoes, and sprouts. It was almost too wide to fit in her mouth.

She found a chilled can of sparkling water and sat on the sand with her feet in the surf. The frigid water washed across her toes, in sharp contrast to the broiling sun that baked her ankles and calves. Dirk sat down next to her.

It'll be nice when Greg is old enough to sit quietly and doesn't need to give a running commentary on everything he sees, thinks, and feels, Claire thought. She tried to remember Dirk at twelve. Had he too talked incessantly at that age? She had no recollection of him.

"So, what do you think of Grand Canyon?" Linny asked as she sat down.

"Cool," Dirk answered.

"Articulate," she said.

Claire gave him a smile and what she hoped was an agreeable nod.

"What do you think, Linny?" Claire said.

"I think there are insufficient regulations about who can do this," she said. "That girl Ellie doesn't have enough experience."

"You sound like a lawyer," Claire said, "while I, the lawyer, don't have any thoughts about regulations but love seeing cliffs beyond cliffs in the distance. The mammoth rock walls sometimes spring up straight from the river, and sometimes there's a sandy beach before the cliff. I pictured the desert looking boring and empty, like the Sahara. This is spectacular."

"I can't wait for the big rapids," Dirk said.

12

Day 2. Afternoon

The air was as still as a held breath, the sun straight overhead, and the day almost too hot to endure. Claire again draped her cloth across her hat to provide shade. Her eyelids drooped; she had trouble keeping herself awake and slipped into a stupor.

When she opened her eyes, the river rolled out in both directions, as far as she could see, smooth and polished. The water placid and nonthreatening, she enjoyed the small undulations and riffles. On the left side of the immense silver sluice, the canyon wall rose overhead, massive and stately, blocking much of the eastern sky. A palpable sense of tranquility floated down the river. Claire should have felt calm, but instead she felt small and alone. She pulled at the brim of her hat, pulling it down onto her forehead.

She swept her eyes across the horizon that opened up downriver. Mountains rose in the far distance, the gauzy image of a mirage in the vast sweep of an open continent. Nearer to the raft, high above the water, canyon wrens swooped down the cliffs, emitting a friendly twitter of descending tones. She was happy to have the silence of this inner canyon replace the chatter and chaos of Lees Ferry. The river wrapped Claire in the stillness of a silken shawl.

Three weeks ago she'd borrowed a book of Grand Canyon photos from the library. One showed a man standing tall, clutching the oars of his raft piled high with provisions. He stared down the river, and behind him a craggy cliff blocked sun and sky and shadows spread across the water. Studying the photo before the trip she anticipated serenity. Imagining herself at the photographer's viewfinder she created a composition of grand solitude.

At that moment on the river, though, she couldn't quite capture those feelings. Solitude implied a welcomed seclusion, but Claire instead felt isolation and loneliness, as if the magnitude of the canyon diminished her. She'd arrived at Lees Ferry expecting to feel empowered by her journey, certain that having an adventure without her family was just what she needed. Yet, at the moment, nothing felt right. Perhaps it was the estrangement she felt from Linny. She hadn't planned on a trip by herself. She'd planned a get-away with her friend—her friend who'd shown up late, with her teen-aged son in tow. Claire still didn't know why Dirk was there, and she hadn't really talked to Linny. She felt in limbo.

"This is the site where another dam was to be built, the proposed Marble Canyon Dam," Tess yelled out to them. "It's our good fortune that the Sierra Club stopped it years ago."

Turning around and looking upstream, Claire saw the river winding up the canyon. Facing downstream, the river disappeared into folds of sensuous cliffs. She couldn't imagine a large dam in that place. She wasn't even sure what it would have meant to have a dam there, though she understood that much of what she now saw upriver would be under water, beneath a large reservoir. It would no longer be a flowing river. It wouldn't be the mighty Colorado. It was impossible to envision. She applied more sunscreen and pulled her hat lower on her forehead.

The distant plateau faded to obscurity, and above the canyon rim clouds blew across the sky and gathered at the limits of her vision. Black shadows spread down the parched cliffs, and dark streaks of rain spilled from the clouds. In all ways, except the most essential fact of rain drenching the ground, a storm had arrived. All around her, the desert sand remained dry as powdered milk, a miracle of evaporation.

"What's the word for when rainfall evaporates before hitting the ground?" Dirk said.

"Virga," Linny answered, before Claire could say anything.

Tess pulled the raft onshore, next to Orion's raft.

"We're going to take you all on a short hike to see Indian ruins," she said. "No chance of rain."

13

Day 2. Afternoon

Orion again led the small group. Dirk took the place right behind him, and Linny joined Claire in the rear. Before they started, Orion told them that several years earlier the Park Service had tried to protect the ruin by moving the trail that led to it. The service crew blocked the old path and disguised it. Hikers stopped visiting the site, and commercial guides were told to stay away. The big-horned sheep, though, refused to change their patterns. They ignored all efforts to close the path and trod over pebbles and stones, pushed aside branches and logs, and scraped over barriers, to hobble down the old route. After a short time, the barricaded path again appeared well used, and eventually the Park Service re-opened the trail.

"So the animals are even more unruly than the tourists," Linny said. "I like that."

"You'll like this site," Orion said. "Last time I was here potsherds lay strewn across the sand. They were everywhere. It was hard to walk. Apparently, successive floods from a sediment-laden river provided enough sand to bury successive settlements. Over the years the wind blew sand onto the beach and buried the village. A new settlement would be built. That one would be flooded and buried, and then another settlement built. The surface site contains a pueblo with four or five rooms and, possibly, a kiva. Maybe 950 to 1150 AD. And there's much more below that, still unexcavated."

"I heard the scientists at Less Ferry say the river has no more sediment," Claire said.

"Yup," Orion said. "It has no more sediment because Glen Canyon Dam was built. And because of the dam the river doesn't flood anymore. So, things are changing. Ruins are exposed now rather than buried. We now see that pueblo and kiva that were hidden for hundreds, close to a thousand years."

Dirk was turned around, not looking where he was walking, and he slipped on a slope of loose rocks. Claire saw it happen. The narrow trail sloped downhill, and Dirk was unable to stop his fall. His arms scraped across spiny bushes, and his legs slid over polished boulders. As the slope steepened, his body picked up speed, and he rolled through a jumble of brush and rocks, snapping the branches of the dry desert plants and pushing the loose stones into a freefall, until he plummeted into a jagged ravine. Claire grabbed Linny's hand, but Linny pulled free and scrambled down the hill.

Dirk fell almost twenty feet before breaking his fall with his hands. When the loosened stones stopped tumbling down the cliff his loud gasp echoed across the rocks. He lay there without moving. Orion reached him, followed by Linny. From the trail Claire couldn't see what was happening, and she slowly made her way down the slope.

"Just wait," Orion said to Dirk. "No rush."

Dirk pushed against Linny and pulled himself up. His face, the color of faded straw, contorted in pain.

"Catch him," Claire said. "He's going to faint."

He leaned against Linny and held his right hand out for her, Orion, and Claire to see.

"You've dislocated your finger," Orion said. "I'll get it back in the socket.

He looked up at Linny and told her not to worry, that he'd done it before. He looked at Claire and told her it would be O.K.

"Maybe there's a doctor on the trip," Linny said. "Or someone with more experience."

"I've had wilderness first aid; it's O.K.," he said.

"No, I want a doctor."

A spasm shot through Dirk, and he leaned to the left and vomited.

Orion moved closer to Dirk. He rested Dirk's fingers in his palm. Without saying anything more, he took hold of the top joint of Dirk's index finger, gripped the misshapen appendage, and pulled until Claire saw the bone under the skin pop back into the lower joint and slide into the socket.

The air rushed from Dirk's lungs and he fell forward, onto his raised knees. Linny bent over him, her face rigid with concern. She glared at Orion.

"He's O.K.," Orion said. "That's a dislocation. The pain depletes you."

"I'm O.K.," Dirk said.

Claire walked back to the trail and told the hikers waiting there that Dirk had dislocated his finger in his fall and Orion had fixed it. She didn't elaborate. When Dirk, Linny, and Orion rejoined the group Dirk's fall and recovery became the topic of conversation. Linny was effusive in her praise of Orion's skill. Listening to her talk, Claire thought, you'd never know that she wanted someone else to help Dirk. She wondered if Linny herself remembered. She expected that Orion did, but maybe not. Maybe he was used to it.

They sat down and waited for Dirk to regain his strength. As Orion said, Dirk was young and wouldn't be indisposed too long. They were back on the trail in fifteen minutes and reached the archeology site about a half hour later. Orion kept them all on the edge of the site while he stated the rules. Look, but no touching, no moving, no removing.

Claire and her family had vacationed in National Parks throughout the west. She knew the motto – "Leave only footprints and take only photographs." It was one of the first rules her kids learned. They understood it long before they seemed to understand her admonishment to clear the table or place laundry in the laundry basket. That rule alone made sense to them.

Since even her kids accepted the rule, Claire was surprised by the group's reaction to Orion. Everyone had an opinion on the appropriateness of the rule; several suggesting it was unnatural. Someone said, "You can't control human nature." Someone else said it made no sense to have an unenforceable rule. Among her friends in California, no one ever questioned the need to leave artifacts, even natural formations, undisturbed. It was something they accepted and believed, a basic tenet of living in the west. Her kids, with their penchant for moral indignation, followed the law to the letter.

As they headed into the area of crumbled walls, Linny walked slowly and soon fell behind. Claire turned to wait for her and saw her crouched on the sand. She walked back and saw she was examining an exquisite specimen of pottery with an intricate, black-line design. Linny grabbed Claire's shirt to pull her down. Claire stooped and before she could say anything, Linny cupped her hand over Claire's mouth.

"Shh," Linny whispered. "Don't say a word."

As soon as Linny removed her hand, and Claire got a look at the pottery shard, she shook her head at Linny.

"No," she said, "You can't take it."

"I can," Linny said. "I'll preserve it. It'll look great on my sideboard, and here it'll be lost, or crushed, or something. If I don't take it, it will be destroyed."

"No," Claire said. "You can't."

Linny seemed genuinely startled. Perhaps, Claire thought, no one had ever told Linny no.

"I'm rescuing it," Linny said.

"Linny, you can't take it."

She watched until Linny dropped the piece and then Claire used the heel of her sandal to scrape up dirt and cover the artifact. Orion called everyone to the center of the ruin. Claire pushed Linny ahead and followed.

Orion had found a large section of coiled clay, part of what he called a Tsegi Orange Ware bowl. He pointed out the features of the pottery specimen, noting the shape, the color and design. He then commented on the exposed, crumbled walls of the ruin, showing where the archeology was newly uncovered and where it had been long-exposed. He identified rings of fire-cracked rock and told them how the ancients roasted agave plants in shallow fire pits covered with rocks. When the meal was cooked, the ancients threw off the fire-cracked rocks, creating a large ring of fired rocks. Finally, he walked them to the edge of the site where he pointed to a prickly–pear cactus with exceptionally large pads and huge yellow flowers.

"Ancient peoples cultivated indigenous plants," he said. "They kept gardens, just like we do. Someone planted this right here.

"Come on, we've got a river trip to do!"

14

Day 2. Evening

They camped on a large, sandy beach at the mouth of a canyon. Claire set her tent up and sat in the doorway looking across the sand. She pulled a flask from her bag and drank. After a few minutes of straight drinking she dropped her bottle into her small pack and walked back to the water. She sat and watched the river. Linny had hiked down from the ruin with Dirk, and she hadn't talked to Claire since the potsherd incident.

"Are you interested in the Colorado River?" Orion asked Claire. "You knew about the sediment."

"I just overheard some scientists talking," she said. "Of course I noticed the clear water. It's as clear as a mountain stream in the Sierra's."

"The Colorado's no longer a natural river," he said. "Hasn't been for many years, since Glen Canyon Dam was built. The dam controls the river, and it prevents sediment from flowing downstream. The dam and the steady flow of water strips the canyon of its sand. It also prevents the river from flooding. The scientists want to have controlled floods to benefit the river, and they've talked the authorities into having small floods. From what I know, any significant flooding, that will really help, is a long way off."

"Before coming, I thought the Colorado would be the most natural river in the world," Claire said.

"Yeah," he said, "you'd think that. Glad your friend is O.K. It can be scary when things happen down here."

Orion skipped across the sand to where West's raft was tied. With barely a muscle rippling West pushed several crates of food and supplies and a large box of emergency gear in the rear of his raft. He stood with his feet slightly apart, as if he were Atlas preparing to lift the world onto his shoulders, and hoisted supplies and pulled straps. The muscles in his lower arms lengthened and stretched as he pulled on the ropes tying down the gear, and the lower bicep muscles bulged out from the short sleeves of his shirt. As he worked Orion hopped into the raft and danced to the rear to sit near West.

Claire drank much of her flask. It bothered her less that Linny was angry.

"I might just see what West has to offer," Linny said as she sat down next to Claire. "Steve and I are getting a divorce, and we're sending Dirk to boarding school in Massachusetts. He doesn't know yet. That's why I brought him here – to tell him. I thought you could help me. Since you're my friend."

"I didn't think you'd ever been anything but happy," Claire said. "I'm the one with problems, not you."

"Are you and Paul separating?" Linny asked.

"No. I didn't say that. It's just that you and Steve always seemed so good together. You never said anything was wrong."

"Well, nothing was. Now it is. Things change."

"What changed?" Claire asked as she slipped her bottle back into her pack.

"It isn't working. It's not what I want, and it isn't what Steve wants, though he doesn't realize that yet."

"You mean this is your idea? Your decision?" Claire said.

Linny nodded. Claire tried to imagine taking that initiative, if that's what it was. She was sure her situation was worse than Linny's, yet she couldn't even decide what to do. Linny said she was no longer happy, so she was breaking up her family. Was that the right thing to do? What did that mean Claire should do?

"Can't you just take separate vacations, like we're doing? Just take a break?"

"I could. But I want to be happy all the time, not just a few weeks a year. I don't want to accept the status quo just because I'm afraid to make a change," Linny said. "You wouldn't do that. You always do what's right."

Claire sat in silence. She didn't think she'd done anything right in a long time. Was it simply that she'd become afraid of change? Should she leave Paul like Linny was leaving Steve?

"When did this happen?" Claire asked.

"It hasn't been right for a while," Linny said. "But it also hasn't been bad, so it's been hard to do anything. Steve's a good man. I want to stay close. I thought we would, but he's angry now, and I don't know how that will be."

Well of course he's angry, Claire thought. You're ruining his life. And think what you're doing to Dirk.

"You don't think there's a way to work things out?" Claire asked.

"Of course there is," Linny said. "I could stay married, Dirk could live with us, we could continue on. But that's not fair to me. I want to make the most of my life. I want to be as happy as I can be."

They sat without saying anything for a minute.

"It's hard for me to explain this," Linny said. "I've tried. I tried when I told Steve. And when I told my mom and sister. I haven't told anyone else. I hoped you would understand, or at least try to understand."

Claire put her arm around Linny's shoulder and hugged her. That was the best she could do. She didn't understand at all, and she wasn't sure she wanted to. Linny sounded so selfish and cold that Claire couldn't even remember why they were friends. At the moment, they seemed to have nothing in common.

On the other hand, why shouldn't Linny be happy? Why shouldn't she live as she wanted? People got divorced all the time, and spouses and children survived. Why should Linny sacrifice but not Steve and Dirk? Claire might be too afraid to improve her life, but that didn't mean Linny should be.

"We're so different," Claire said. "I've always admired your adventurous spirit and how you go for what you want. I would never have arranged this trip, or anything else we've done, but I'm with you wherever you go."

Tess called everyone dinner, and the conversation ended. Claire had noticed Tess drinking steadily since they set up camp, and she hoped the guide could cook even when intoxicated. She followed Linny to the food line and filled her plate.

"We need a little safety talk," West said when everyone was seated and eating. "The surprising thing about rafting is that most accidents happen off the river. Being on the water turns out to be quite safe. It's when you're in camp or hiking up a wash or hanging your laundry on a cliff that someone gets hurt."

Next to her Linny stiffened. Claire looked at Dirk, and he ate his food with his head down.

"You're not upset with Dirk, are you?" she asked Linny.

"Of course I am," Linny said. "Things need to go according to plan."

15

Diary Day 2

The food's amazing. I hope it will give me some ideas and inspiration for when I get home. French toast and a fruit compote for breakfast. Lunch a fabulous buffet of meats and vegis and bread and condiments. There are always cookies for dessert. Dinner tonight was Mexican – chicken enchiladas with a spicy, flavored rice and a green salad. And our young, female guide made a pineapple upside-down cake for dessert! It was baked in the biggest dutch oven that I ever saw, with red-hot charcoals placed in a ring below the pot and in a circle of coals on the lid. Tess said she cooked it like that for fifty minutes.

The river was beautiful and surprisingly tame today. Or maybe I'm just getting used to it! The river's controlled by a dam, so nothing unexpected happens. It might have been a little slow for all of you today – hours floating in the hot sun, drifting off to sleep and jolting awake when my head fell too far to one side.

We stopped at a huge waterfall, and then at a cavern as large, maybe larger, than a baseball field. I thought I'd go under the waterfall, but it was too strong for me. And I thought I'd walk to the back of the cavern, but it was too far. I'm wimping out all around.

We climbed to an Indian ruin and saw an ancient village. Pieces of pottery were still scattered on the ground—black on black mesa pottery and Tsegi Orange Ware. Circles of rocks (called fire-cracked rock because the stones were discolored and cracked by fire) showed where the Indians had hearths and underground ovens.

Perhaps if you were all here to see this with me I'd be more adventurous.

16

Day 3. Morning

C laire dressed as the gray light of morning spread across camp. Over her bathing suit she pulled on thin pants, a shirt, a sweater, and a jacket, piling layers of polyester, polypropylene, and fleece to protect her from the chilly morning air. She'd peel off the layers as the day heated up, stuffing the excess clothes into her day bag. Life seemed so simple when she only needed to think of herself. Most days at home, she had no time to dress until everyone else left the house.

She crawled from her tent and looked around. As she watched, a diffuse yellow light spilled down the western cliffs, like icing dripping on a cake. On the eastern cliffs, black shadows still hid all detail. Between the sunlight and the shadows, the river flowed down the spectrum of color from black to dark green. Only the tinkling call of a canyon wren and the distant rumble of the downstream rapids disturbed the quiet of the morning, and neither was much of a disruption.

The wind emitted a slight whisper as it swept up the canyon, and the waves released a soft murmur as they brushed to shore. Claire heard them only when she stood still listening. The canyon was so quiet, she felt as if she'd been placed in a large bottle with a stopper, with the specific purpose of keeping the world of noise at bay.

The sun rose a little higher and the world brightened, and upstream the river flowed calm, amid splashes of sunlight and shade. Downstream, water tumbled over the rocks of the small rapids. The canyon had not yet begun to heat up; waves of cool air rolled steadily off the chilly water. Claire remembered when she first moved to the mountains. She attended to each minute change in weather – where the fog was, what direction the wind blew, whether the temperature was rising or falling. It had been important to her sense of knowing her place in the world. She wasn't sure when she'd stop noticing the details, but she had. Lately her days blended one into the other, undifferentiated.

She stuffed an already emptied flask into her bag and zipped a full one into the right pocket of her fleece jacket, then took it out and packed it with her gear. Just because Tess drank all day didn't mean she would. She would at least try to stick to her five o'clock rule. She shuffled to the edge of the river. An early morning haze still clung to the desert.

Claire had been on the river only a couple days, and everything in Grand Canyon still seemed new. She found no comfort yet in any of the trip routines, but she could barely remember the daily habits of her life at home. Two days had somehow become a lifetime. Staring into the water she let herself sink into the reality of Grand Canyon. She hadn't thought anything could be more nurturing than a morning in the redwoods with the night-time fog still settled in, when she could see only a few feet in any direction. But here in the canyon, the chill of the water numbed her toes while the rush of the river got lost in the large expanse of the desert. The shadowed mesas loomed large in all directions and spread to the horizon, and finite space grew infinite. The fog isolated her in the mountains; the river canyon connected her to the universe.

It seemed to Claire that the nature of time also changed in the canyon. It felt as if time itself flowed with the river. Time sped up and slowed down in ways she'd never before experienced. Grand Canyon days simultaneously rushed by and inched along; time flew and stood still. At home the days marched by, one after the other, at the same, constant pace with little seeming progress. If something didn't happen one day she could take care of it the next day. If she missed an opportunity on the Colorado there was no second chance. And yet she was also certain she could wait all day for a moment that never came. The canyon itself changed only in geologic time, a measurement off her temporal scale.

Claire watched Tess pull her silver flask from a bag and take a drink. It was not yet eight o'clock, and it was not her first drink of the morning. Earlier, Claire had seen Tess quickly down a beer.

She turned from the guide and looked across the river. The sky was cloudless, the jeweled tones of early morning already dissolved to an anemic hue, and the mesas themselves, so sharp and clear just a short while ago, had grown indistinct. In the distance vast deserts extended across the plateaus and disappeared in the diorama of Arizona's mesas, mountaintops and valleys. The horizon faded into obscurity at the edge of the seemingly boundless landscape.

Where Claire sat, the top layer of the beige beach sand had already dried pale in the early heat. All around her, rafters ambled through camp. She rose and started to walk along the river headed upstream. She needed to do something other than watch Tess drink or wait for Linny to appear.

The path was narrow, only two feet across, flat, and sandy, and completely different from the mountain trails she was used to, which were studded with rocks and criss-crossed with tree roots. No longer worrying about tripping, and freed from the need to watch each footstep like she did at home, Claire looked up at the cliffs and over at the river as she walked. The world felt large. She'd gone only a short distance when three feet in front of her a large rattlesnake coiled, ready to strike. She stopped when she heard the rattle.

She'd seen many snakes near home and in the Sierra's, but she'd never been within striking range. Now, she was too close to notice anything except the tongue flitting in and out of the tiny mouth. Its speed and regularity mesmerized her. Only the danger compelled her to move. Telling herself to breathe, aware that her life depended on it, she forced herself to stay calm and to move slowly backward. As she took each step and moved further and further away, the snake relaxed, and eventually it sank back to the ground, stretched out, and slithered across the sand into the brush. It was almost three feet long, a light tan color similar to the soil, and with dark blotches that became bands near the tail.

Claire waited. There were no sounds in the still, quiet desert except her heartbeat, loud enough for anyone to hear. Eventually her breathing returned. When the snake had fully disappeared into the bushes and she had lost track of it, she turned around and returned to camp.

Every few steps she paused to lift her head for a broader view and to look more closely where she was going. Forewarned was forearmed. She'd pay as close attention on these trails as she did on the trails at home. Overhead the sun pushed higher into the sky. On the cliff beyond the river, a band of apache plume cut a wide swath. The beauty of the canyon, of which she'd still seen only a small section, took her breath away.

As soon as she returned to camp she found Tess and told her about the rattler. Tess listened and nodded and told Claire she'd done the right thing.

"Will you warn the others?" Claire said.

"No need," Tess said. "Doing that doesn't protect anyone; instead, it sends people off to look for the snake, and we end up with a problem where we didn't have one."

Linny had walked up behind Tess as she finished speaking.

"You saw a snake?" Linny said.

"It's long gone," Tess said. "And it wasn't near camp."

"Was it poisonous?" she asked.

"A rattler," Claire said.

"You saw it also?"

Claire nodded. It didn't seem necessary to tell Linny that Tess hadn't seen it.

"I think I'd die just seeing one," Linny said.

"Of course not," Claire said. "You're good at taking care of yourself."

"What do you mean?" Linny sounded defensive, or aggressive, Claire wasn't sure which.

"That you take care of yourself," Claire said. "You wouldn't die on seeing a rattler. Nothing overwhelms you."

"And you?" Linny asked.

"I cope."

Linny frowned and shrugged. It wasn't exactly what Claire wanted to say, wasn't exactly what she meant, but it was close enough.

Tess looked at the two women. She'd witnessed several romantic relationships (two marriages and one new coupling) disintegrate on the river. The danger and uncertainty of the trip, plus the unrelieved togetherness, added stress and things fell apart. She could imagine this friendship failing. Claire and Linny would need to be a lot more skilled at intimacy than they appeared to be.

17

Day 3. Morning

It looks like the river is smaller than it was last night," Claire said to Tess. "The rafts were all floating in the water when we docked, and now they're beached on the sand."

"It's the dam," Tess said. "The dam produces electricity, and dam operators drop the river level overnight when demand for electricity is low, and the shoreline rises highest in late afternoon when electricity demands peak and Glen Canyon Dam increases its release of water. Not quite natural, but that's the Grand Canyon tide table. We've gotten used to it. We know when the river will get its lowest, and how low, and where we should stake the rafts.

Problem is—there's a high snowpack at the headwaters in Colorado, and the dam should be releasing more water, to make room for the increased supply when the snow starts to melt. Doesn't seem quite right."

"O.K. listen up," Riz called out. "We need everyone to join us, push the rafts out into the river, and load the gear."

Claire found a spot in the line of passengers that stretched across the beach. She saw Dirk farther down the line. Linny had disappeared. Under West's command, they pushed the rafts off the sand and into the water. They quickly loaded the gear.

Linny had mentioned to Claire that she was interested in West, and, sure enough, by the time they'd finished packing the rafts, she was standing off to the side, having a tête-à-tête with the rugged guide. As Claire watched, he put his arm around Linny and hugged her. Claire knew that Linny would have grabbed her gear and hopped onto his raft, leaving Dirk and Claire behind, if only West were rowing passengers instead of baggage.

"Hey Tessy!" West called. "Time to get the fuck outa here."

Tess grabbed her small backpack and ran across the sand. She readied her raft, watching Linny from the corner of her eye. She noticed that Dirk also watched his mother.

Back on the water she settled into a comfortable rhythm and slowly moved the raft down the undulating river. The early rays of sunlight flashed above the eastern cliffs and cast luminous daggers across the canyon. Everything about the moment was perfect. With eyes wide she imprinted the beauty in her mind. When she was off the river attending to errands in Flagstaff, she'd picture the water and the sunlight and remember exactly why she spent most of her time in the canyon.

She gazed at the river's reflections in the water, mesmerized by the changing flow. When the current was slow, the raft dawdled, and when it was swift, they moved quickly down the river, its rhythm constantly changing.

In places the canyon narrowed to less than eighty feet across, and canyon walls rose an incredible mile high, and in these places the sun shot like a lightning bolt across a thread-width sliver of sky. In those places, the day grew warmer and warmer, but the sun itself remained hidden. Where the canyon widened, the egg-drop sun dragged across the idle expanse of sky, fully exposed, and the day lengthened. In those places, the day became almost unbearably hot and stifling, and the sun burned exposed skin.

Tess had turned around to look back upstream when the two kayakers floated into view, headed right down the middle of the river. The woman led in her red kayak, and the man followed in his yellow one. They bounced down a small riffle without a problem. As she watched, they passed her raft and the other rafts, then rounded the bend in the river and disappeared from sight.

Claire thought she'd like to kayak the next time she came, and she wondered if Paul would want to do that. Maybe, she thought, his folks would watch the kids.

Linny called to the kayakers as they neared Tess' raft, and she tried to catch their attention. She waved her arms and motioned for them to pull over near the raft, but they either didn't see her or ignored her.

18

Day 3. Afternoon

There's the science trip," Tess called out to her passengers. "Looks like we're stopping to see what they're doing."

She followed the other guides and pushed her raft onto the sand on river right. She saw Brent across the beach, easy to spot in his bright shorts. The science rafts that she'd seen at Lees Ferry were staked at the shoreline, and the guides for those rafts ran over and helped secure the visiting commercial rafts. West knew each of them. Tess knew several, but not all.

"Find a scientist to explain what they're doing," Tess urged. She knew that would free her to have a drink with the science crew.

The scientists stood in the middle of the beach around an enormous, open trench. A woman in her thirties walked over and asked if they'd like a tour. West answered that they would.

"Follow her," Tess said. "You'll learn a lot."

The woman introduced herself as a sedimentologist and started lecturing.

"We're working on a study that measures sand loss in the canyon. This river was historically muddy, but now it's clear. There's insufficient sediment in the water, and the beaches are disappearing."

"The sand on the beaches comes from the river, not from erosion of the rocks?" Linny asked.

"Well, it's more complicated. In the near term, some comes from river water, and some is deposited by the wind. The big question is what effect the dam is having on the movement of sediment down the river. Come look."

A man in bright lime shorts strode across the sand to Claire. Claire recognized him from the water line at Lees Ferry. She was surprised he remembered her. He introduced himself, telling her his name was Brent, and she followed him across a nondescript, flat beach, across plain, beige sand to the open trench. With the geometric imprint from the sole of a sport sandal, someone had paced a perimeter contour for a trench, fifteen feet long by three feet wide. Half a dozen men and several women, all wearing work shirts and big hats, stood around the trench shoveling sand out.

"O.K." one of them said, "Time to take turns."

All but one of them stepped back. A young man stepped inside, dug for a while, then stepped out. Everyone took a turn until the hole was too deep to offer an exit and the person inside cut stairs into the wall at a narrow end, and the trench became a tiny basement, like an empty wine cellar on the beach. Claire stared into the pit and watched grains of sand flow down the cut surfaces of the drying walls.

"Now it's my turn," Brent said.

He descended the steps, crouched in the trench, and scraped a trowel across the middle section of the upper wall. As gently as if he were unearthing an ancient relic, he smoothed away ridges and gouges and rubbed the wall flat. He pulled a Chinese calligraphy brush from his pocket, dusted the surface, and whisked away loose grains of sand to reveal tableaus of deposition. The undifferentiated chaos of subtly shaded stripes became an elaborate pattern of rippled layers in an array of desert colors that spread across the chiseled wall.

Like an artisan restoring the Sistine Chapel, or an artist stripping whitewash from an ancient panorama, he painstakingly scraped and planed surfaces, smoothing the sand and transforming the trench. Wrap-around murals splashed across the sand with top-to-bottom scallops of gold and amber and intricate, multi-colored patterns. The sand below the surface was strikingly beautiful and bore no resemblance to the plain, unembellished sand of the beach.

"See the climbing ripples? Thin bands of lightly pigmented sand in shades of beige and brown?" he said. "Evidence of a flood on the Colorado River. And see the coarser sand grains in the upper layers? Proof that sand was scarce, even back then. It's all here, everything we need to know to evaluate the changes made by Glen Canyon Dam. And I still know the science, even though I'm now immersed in the politics."

The woman who had escorted them across the sand carved an oblique furrow along a lower edge of the trench and exposed a pattern of multi-colored scallops in the sand. She told them they were geologic structures from a time before the silvery water ate into the golden bank.

"Further evidence," she said, "that the sand bar was more extensive before the dam. The dam is producing electricity, and it has made it safer to raft the river, but we don't really know how it is changing the river."

19

Day 3. Afternoon

A ll of a sudden the perfect day disappeared, and the canyon grew unbearably dry and hot. Wind blew upstream with the ferocity of a small tornado, and the guides found it almost impossible to row down the river. Tess strained at the oars, but the raft moved backwards, its loss of progress evident from landmarks on shore. The rock that they passed moments ago they passed again, the Colorado's variation on the Sisyphus story, and Tess, not remembering why King Sisyphus had been punished, wondered at the wrong the rafters had committed. She imagined it was Claire, somehow deceiving Brent and diverting his attention from Tess. Before her Claire hunched over and buried her head in her lap, her hands holding her cap down over her hair.

Tess turned the raft around and rowed facing upstream, with her back to the wind. She strained with every pull on the oars, now able to use more force than she could muster when she pushed on the oars, and they very slowly inched down the canyon. Slowly, the scenery changed.

Claire lifted her head just enough to see the cliffs. Several mountain goats climbed the cliffs on river right, seeming to jump up the vertical slope. On river left a cluster of Utah Century-plants sprang Dr. Seuss-like from the rocky desert into giant, stiff, flowering stalks. With their slow, tedious progress Claire had time to examine everything. The wind uniformly bent each bush into a ninety-degree angle, and beyond the beaches Claire observed the contact between one rock formation and another. She watched the rocks change colors.

Onshore, close to the water, the sand advanced in waves across the beach letting Claire gauge the effects of the wind on the sand. It organized the sand grains into ripples extending from the water to the cliffs, and then it lifted the sand into suspended walls, clearly visible from the raft. Tess again turned the raft around, facing downstream. Even though they stuck to the middle of the river, tiny grains of sand flew off the beach and exploded against Claire's arms and legs and stung her cheeks. It felt as if Tess rowed them through a sand tunnel, rather than down a river of water. Yet the scientists had just explained how the river was sand-deprived. Claire thought how intolerable the canyon would have been with a full supply of sediment.

The wind howled. Gusts blasted up the canyon, pushing the rafts upstream and imbedding sand grains into Claire's clothing. The green of her shorts dulled. The sky blue of her cap turned dusty. Claire tasted the sand in her mouth, abrading her teeth. She was thankful at that moment for the sand deprivation. Tess again turned the raft around.

A bald eagle glided overhead soaring gracefully, seemingly unaffected by the wind. Eventually the gusts stopped blowing and the wind died down, and Tess turned the raft back to face downstream. They bounced through a long series of waves as the river tumbled over the rocks at Nankoweap Rapids. Though rather gentle rapids, the gradient was steep enough to rush the raft down the river, and Tess rowed with just a slight push on her oars, without much assistance from the paddlers. The raft swept down the glassy tongue, then hovered, suspended, in the crescendo of the rapids' roar. The river slowed, and Tess' oars shot ripples across a satin-smooth surface. They drifted into a pool and washed into an eddy.

They found the yellow and red kayaks pulled to shore at the far end of the beach, and the guides pulled their rafts up right next to them. The kayakers sprawled at the edge of the sand, near the cliffs, far from the water and far from their kayaks. Several of the guides and Linny waved. As soon as the rafts were beached, Linny jumped out and ran across the sand to where the kayakers sat. Claire helped secure the rafts and stood at the edge of the river looking out across the water. A few minutes ago the wind overwhelmed her. Now the wind had nearly disappeared, and the heat baked her. Grand Canyon, she thought, a place of extremes. She looked back at the kayakers who lounged companionably with Linny.

"I'll talk to Ellie," Tess said to West. "Too easy rapids for such problems. Why don't you call Linny so I can talk to them alone?"

Ellie and Tim had removed their two life jackets and tossed them across the kayak hulls to dry. They had pulled off outer clothing, jackets and pants, but still wore more than the warm, late-afternoon air required. Even from a distance, Tess could see that Ellie, so thin, without any fat, shivered.

Tess strode across the dry beach as West called to Linny. She felt the tiny grains of sand wedge between her toes as she walked, and she made exaggerated motions to kick the sand into a spray behind her, just for fun. When she reached the kayakers, she stretched out next to Ellie.

"Well, you might feel warmer if you take off your wet clothes," she said. "The sun will heat you."

"Thank you for rescuing me," Ellie said. "I'm not really sure what happened. I don't remember all that much. I saw the rocks and then the current swept me into the rapids. The kayak got stuck, I guess."

"I couldn't reach Ellie," Tim said. "I tried but was overpowered and got swept downriver. I couldn't get back up. It's our honeymoon." He leaned over and took Ellie's hand.

"Who had the experience for the permit?" Tess asked.

"Me," Tim said. "I kayaked here two summers ago. It was different; I didn't have any problems."

"Different every time. You never know what the canyon will do," Tess said. "Never know what any river will do."

Everyone except West, Tess, and Theresa assembled for a hike to the Anasazi Granaries. Linny didn't want to join, but Orion insisted the excursion to the 900 year-old food and seed storage facility not be missed. He pointed out the distant cliff structures, looking inaccessible on a vertical cliff wall and said the hike was steep but short and relatively easy. He wouldn't accept Linny's 'no' as an answer.

Linny joined Claire at the rear of the hiking line. They were still walking up the sandy trail towards the cliff, stepping around rocks, when Dirk called to them from the first granary, built into the face of the cliff about 700 feet above the river. He balanced on a ledge in front of a small window built into the rock. If he were Claire's child she would have freaked out—scared for his safety and concerned he was misbehaving. Linny waved. Orion said something Claire couldn't hear.

"Hurry up," Dirk yelled. "This is totally cool."

They picked up their pace. The trail got steeper, and Claire found herself taking a breath with each step. She looked down, paying attention to each footstep. She didn't like that feeling that came with walking on a ledge or balancing on a wall. She didn't like being hyper vigilant. Ahead of her, one after another, the rafters reached the site and exclaimed their appreciation of the view.

When she reached the granaries, she stood on the ledge where Dirk had stood and looked around. The ledge was wider than it had looked from below, more secure and stable. The granaries themselves were constructed of small horizontal rocks, layered one on top of the other to create a wall with an opening onto a large cave. Being there, peeking inside, Claire imagined the lives the early Indians had lived.

Downstream, the canyon widened. Although she'd been told that the river cut through the rock, this was the first time that she could actually see it. On a raft on the water, it was hard to imagine how the flow of the river changed the landscape. From a perch on the cliff, it became obvious that the river had created the canyon. It was a startling change of perspective. There among the cliffs and mesas, the Colorado River, glimpsed through the desert haze, though a mere glint of ribbon, wielded immense power.

Claire chose not to follow the narrow trail along the base of the granary. Instead of continuing along the cliff face, she turned around. She didn't know yet what to expect from the big rapids, but she knew that balancing on a rock ledge hundreds of feet above the beach wasn't for her. She scrambled back down the trail, and found going down a lot easier than going up, though that was not her usual experience in hiking. Perhaps it was her deep focus on getting down from the cliff. Linny walked to meet up with Dirk.

Theresa and West lay stretched out on the sand near the rafts. West lay on his stomach, his head up. Theresa lay on her side, her head propped in her arm. Claire knew Linny would have jogged right over there and joined them, but she was not Linny. She walked to the farthest raft and sat on its edge with her feet dangling in the water. She appreciated how good it felt for the moment to be alone.

20

Day 3. Afternoon

After battling the winds earlier in the day, it felt like rafting through heaven to skim across the water in the still afternoon with the sun starting to dip to the west. Tess made small, easy movements on the oars, and they floated the wide meanders through the deepening haze. The canyon's stillness sank deep into Claire's bones and calmed her. She hadn't realized how tense the wind had made her until the tension dissipated. Her eyelids fluttered and drooped behind the dark lenses of her glasses. After several minutes she slipped into a light doze.

"Hey look!" Linny turned around and poked her.

The raft moved along the current on river left, and they startled deer drinking from the river. In another moment they floated past a lone beaver grappling with a jumble of logs. Claire was letting her eyes close again when Tess pulled the raft beside a small family of river otters splashing in the muddy delta of a tiny stream. The canyon's quiet deepened and expanded along with the river's peacefulness, and Claire grew calmer and less tired.

She loved being in a place so sparsely populated. Now that she was there, she understood that the canyon's scarcity of people was one of its biggest draws. It would be a different experience if a steady stream of rafts lined the river. She'd always been one of those people most comfortable alone. If it hadn't been for the solitude of the canyon, she'd never have been able to tolerate the intense closeness of the rafting group. She was pretty sure that Linny felt differently. Linny, she knew, enjoyed being part of a group. Whenever possible, Linny sought out new rafters with whom she could strike up a conversation. She looked for the kayakers and took it upon herself to know them. She participated, as she'd done since middle school.

Claire shifted in her seat and strained to see around the river's bends. When the water moved slowest and the raft was the calmest, she climbed to the back, pulled up the drag bag that cooled the beer in the water and grabbed two cans. It was before her appointed hour of five, but she was ready for a drink, and beer was more acceptable than whiskey. She climbed back to her seat, leaned forward, and offered a beer to Linny. Linny looked at the can and shook her head. Claire pushed the extra can down below the tube of the raft, where it would stay cold and she could retrieve it later. The other she immediately opened and drank.

Without any warning they passed a group of about a dozen campers, all completely nude. On a flat section of beach near the water, two young women practiced yoga, moving from warrior one to warrior two as the rafters floated by. Camping gear, scattered besides empty rafts, included brightly colored dry bags, a skillet, and a first aid box with a large red cross. Claire thought Dirk might fall from the raft trying to get a better look.

Tess asked Dirk if he wanted her to row back up river so they could float by again. Everyone, except Linny, laughed when he shouted "YES!"

They floated through the late afternoon until the day dissolved into evening. Tess pulled behind the other guides and beached their raft on river left where the Colorado curved right and a thick carpet of sand unrolled into an emerald pool. For several moments no one moved, and they sat in their rafts immersed in the beauty that surrounded them as crystalline water lapped the shore. The air had cooled, and the large sun hovered just above the western cliffs and seemed to stall. They watched as it finally slipped behind the mesas and shadows spread down the rocks.

West staked the rafts and then sat on the sand, staring into the river. Linny joined him.

Tess watched the water. It didn't seem right. If it was true that folks near the river's headlands in Colorado were preparing for floods, then the water here should be high, to make room in the reservoir. She wondered what the scientists on the river thought about it.

21

Day 3. Evening

I need to tell Dirk about the divorce this evening," Linny said.

"Why?" Claire asked, even as she realized the answer.

"Because I'm going to spend the night with West, and Dirk won't understand that unless he knows about the divorce."

"He won't understand even after you tell him."

"Well, I'll feel better about it."

"Linny, this isn't the right time or place for this discussion. You and Steve should tell Dirk when you're all together. And it should be in a safe place, not in the middle of the wilderness. And not where there's no escape or privacy for Dirk."

"That's all true, but this is how it is."

"No. Just forget about West. He's not important. Dirk is."

"Of course West isn't important and Dirk is. That goes without saying. But I want to spend the night with West. And I'm as important as anyone."

That was the thing about Linny – she was smart. She discarded the bullshit and got right down to the issue. Claire never really thought she was as important as anyone. She put her children's happiness above her own. Until recently, she put Paul's happiness above her own. Linny didn't ignore Steve and Dirk; she just valued herself equal to them. All Claire could do was shake her head. How could she possibly argue with that? Using Linny's logic, Linny wasn't wrong, not by a long shot.

"I can't help you," Claire said.

"You have to," Linny answered.

"Listen up everyone!" West called out. "I know it looks perfect right now, but the sky's real dark in the west, and our weather comes from the west. So, we can expect some serious rain tonight. Have your rain gear accessible, and do a good job putting up your tents."

Linny and Claire both looked off to the west. Down the canyon that almost sapphire blue sky had turned pitch black.

"You luck out," Claire said. "In a downpour no one will know where you are."

"Doesn't matter," Linny said. "We need to tell Dirk tonight."

Claire walked to the raft and pulled a flask from her bag. Claire needed time to think things through—Linny was going too fast for her. Shouldn't she and Linny first talk about Linny's problems before she announced to Dirk that she was getting a divorce? Didn't Linny want her to problem solve, like she wanted Linny to problem solve for her? Didn't Linny want to know Claire's opinion?

If she remembered her high school physics correctly, she corresponded to matter in a solid-state, while Linny was the more volatile gas, the least stable form. Perhaps they'd each do better if they both strove for fluidity. She slipped off her river sandals and stood barefoot. She liked feeling the sand below her feet. As she pushed down, the sand rose between her toes.

The canyon wall glowed in the setting sun. The air was warm and just slightly balmy. Perhaps the coming storm had already brought moisture. All around her campers set up their tents. Claire did the same, but she couldn't force herself to pay adequate attention. Instead, she set up the tent on auto-pilot and returned to standing barefoot, drinking, and watching long rays of sunlight turn white sand to gold on the river bank.

Linny had been her lifeline in high school. When Claire didn't know up from down, or right from left, Linny pointed the way.

She brought Claire into her group of friends and provided her a social life. She provided Claire with her first drink of rum and her first joint. Claire welcomed the kindness of Linny's family when her own felt impossibly cruel. She wouldn't have survived without Linny, and she owed her a lot. She took a long swig, capped the bottle, and grabbed the beer she had stuck into the sand.

Claire was trying to calculate her debt to Linny when Linny walked over.

"O.K." she said. "It's time. Come with me."

Claire should have tightened the lines of her tent and better prepared for the storm, but she nodded without objection. Pulling her rain gear from her bag, she threw it into her tent, piled her bags up near the door of the tent, and zipped everything closed. She always tried to be ready for whatever was going to happen, that was the foundation of her legal training, but she knew she wasn't ready for talking to Dirk or braving a storm.

Dirk was skipping rocks across the river when his mother told him she wanted to talk. Linny walked them to three chairs that she'd set up far from the others, up the beach. Away from the river, the kitchen, and the tents, no one was likely to join them.

Claire could tell that Dirk thought he'd done something wrong and was trying to figure out what it was. She tried not to look at him. She didn't have anything to say and had no business being a part of the conversation. She knew that; Dirk would know that. If things were being done right, she wouldn't be there. No doubt Dirk would resent her presence.

"Dad and I are separating, and we're getting a divorce," Linny said. "I thought you needed to know."

"Yeah," Dirk said. "Dad told me before we left."

Linny stared at him. She didn't say anything.

"Is that all?" Dirk said.

Linny nodded, and Claire knew how stunned Linny must be not to have anything to say. Linny would have prepared a long explanation for Dirk explaining her feelings. Had Linny ever said nothing?

"Yeah, well, O.K.," Dirk said. He stood up and went back to the river, back to skipping rocks.

"You didn't tell him about boarding school," Claire said. "Do you think Steve did?"

"No, I'm sure he left that for me, but I wasn't ready to jump right into that."

"I'm too tired to do anything about dinner," Tess said to West when they'd unloaded the rafts.

He nodded and didn't say anything. She walked across the beach and climbed onto her raft. She sat facing upstream, her back to the wind, her eyes closed. The wind was still gusting, but it was not yet raining, when West called dinner.

He had prepared as nice a meal as anyone could want, but Tess was too exhausted to enjoy it. She filled her plate and sank onto the sand and stared at the river. She'd camped at the same spot on a trip in the late fall. She remembered that dinner—steak, rice pilaf, and salad. She'd been able to deliberately burn her steak, just like she wanted. She remembered the beach and sitting on the sand. She hadn't been nearly as tired.

They ate dinner, and as soon as the dishes were done, as if the guides had a direct line to nature, the weather changed. Though it was not yet fully dark, gray clouds drooped into a gray river, and the sky slipped down the cliffs until the canyon disappeared. Only when lightning bolted across the otherwise veiled heavens, did earth and sky again separate. Thunder ricocheted off the canyon walls, and their vibrations rumbled through Claire's body spreading from heart to limbs, into fingers and toes. Without further warning the clouds ripped open, and torrents fell.

Waterfalls plunged down the sheer cliffs scouring the pastel walls. The water drew sediment from the rock, turned pink then red, and splashed to the canyon floor in a bloody deluge. In a very short time the gushing water triggered avalanches of rocks cascading down the sloping walls. The rain pounded, the river swelled, and rocks crashed onto the rain-soaked beach. Claire crawled into her tent and stared out the doorway and across the beach, through a gray film of rainwater.

Winds ripped along the frame of the tent and pulled at the corners; under the weight of the rain, the walls sagged until they almost touched. Water dripped down the creased folds on the inside walls of the tent and puddled on the nylon floor. Claire wrapped herself in her sleeping bag. She wanted to shut her eyes and let the explosion of rain drops lull her to sleep. It mirrored how she felt. She had no idea how Linny or Dirk felt. She was uncertain where Linny slept.

22

Diary Day 3

I learned a lot about Grand Canyon today. Geologists and biologists are doing research and experiments here. They're collecting data for an Environmental Impact Report about how to operate Glen Canyon Dam. We stopped and talked with a group of researchers for a while this afternoon.

The scientists believe the dam's current operation schedule alters the river. The biologists want the river to again be warm, with slow backwaters to protect young fish. The water now is absolutely freezing, and they said that's because the water released by the dam comes from the bottom of the reservoir where it's super cold. So, instead of native, warm-water fish, the introduced trout, a cold-water fish, are taking over. (I'm not sure what I think about that – I do love trout, and I never heard of the endangered chub.) The geologists want a variable flow, with higher highs and lower lows, and occasional big floods, to replenish the canyon's sediment. They told us the beaches aren't as nice as they used to be. It's hard for me to imagine anything better than this.

Our guide, Tess, sings 'Brass in Pocket' by the Pretenders whenever anything significant happens on the river. She says the song is her good luck talisman, and I think she really does believe in magic. Something significant happens many times during the day—rapids run well, a raft properly rigged, a cloud offering a moment of shade. Lucky for me I really like that song, even if I don't believe in talismans.

Another guide, Orion, has a travel stereo hooked up on his raft, and he blares the music of Jimmy Cliff from a playlist on his ipod. Lucky for me I love Jimmy Cliff's music!

We climbed to an old Indian granary built right into a canyon wall. We stood right there, in the place the ancient Anasazi stored seeds and grains—a stone and mortar structure, under a large overhang, in a cliff thousands of feet high. Seeing what the ancient Indians had built, I could begin to imagine the life those Pueblo people lived. It was a day's adventure for me; yet those people must have run back and forth, up and down the cliff, getting food and storing seeds. I understand how they lived, but I can't really understand being that fit or that comfortable out here. It seems like a very hard life.

The weather's been perfect – dry and warm during the day, cooler in the evenings. Until now it's been a lot like California weather, but tonight there's a thunderstorm—nothing like California. Thunder reverberates down the cliffs, and lightning flashes on and off in the dark night. It's scary and intense hearing rocks crash down the face of the cliffs onto the sand where we're camping. The guides had instructed us to set our tents in the middle of the beach, away from the cliffs, and we all followed directions, so I don't think any one will be injured. Unfortunately though, I didn't do a very good job of staking my tent and fly, and everything is sagging, and the rain drips down the inner wall and collects on the floor. I'm writing this using my headlamp, wrapped in my sleeping bag, hoping I'll be able to fall asleep when I put my notebook down.

23

Day 4. Morning

Amazing, absolutely and totally amazing," Linny said as Claire emerged from her tent.

Linny must have been waiting for her because Claire saw her friend's legs, tanned and shapely, outside the door as soon as she unzipped the tent flap. She had no doubt what Linny was talking about. It was the exact same expression Linny had used the first time she'd had sex in high school, back when Claire wasn't even dating. Linny had gone on to describe the night in great detail, and Claire had tried to imagine how she could ever get herself in that situation.

So many years later, she didn't want to hear Linny's description of her overnight activities. It was neither Linny's first time having sex, nor Claire's first time hearing about sex. Though she still might not know everything, Claire knew enough.

Linny gave her a hand and pulled her up. Claire stood still, waiting for Linny to say more, but Linny just combed her hair with her fingers and paced back and forth. Claire was both relieved and surprised by Linny's silence. Not wanting to say the wrong thing, she said nothing.

"I'm not sure how to describe this," Linny said. "We don't usually talk about sex."

"That's O.K., I'm fine not knowing the details—we're not in high school."

"No, I want to tell you. It was such an amazing, incredible, obviously indescribable experience."

Again Claire said nothing. She wondered if Linny remembered telling her about sex with Scott Robertson. Probably not. For her part, Claire no longer remembered what Linny had said. She'd forgotten the words Linny had used, the nouns, adjectives, and verbs, maybe even adverbs, and without those particular words, she herself would never try to describe sex. Not that she'd had any need to. Even to herself she'd never tried to put into words her best times with Paul.

If she were forced to say something, if someone demanded it of her, she'd probably look for a poem to express what she felt. Someone would have to be really good with words to get it right. She supposed Linny could be that good.

"Maybe it's because we're in Grand Canyon," Linny said, "sex seemed like a rafting experience. First, we drifted through the languid entry pool, and I started to anticipate what was coming. I knew it was going to get way more exciting, and I imagined I could hear the rapids growling. I tried to ignore it and stay calm, but as I rode the glassy tongue into the v-waves, trying to keep steady, I knew I would soon float over wave after wave. It felt like it could go on forever."

What?" Claire said. "You don't even know these words. This is your first time rafting."

Linny laughed. "It's how West describes sex. What do you think?"

Claire looked at Linny's flushed, eager face. Her annoyance and jealousy disappeared, and even her envy dissipated. Of course Linny should be happy. If Linny wasn't happy, there was no hope for Claire.

"It worked for you," she said and laughed.

24

Day 4. Morning

Tess pulled into the current and sped down the river. Without the wind to fight against, her body again rested loosely on her seat, her feet anchored against the frame, her hands gripped the oars, and her arms, far from slack, hung soft. She wriggled her shoulders and rolled the muscles down her back. She felt comfortable and confident. The exhaustion she'd felt the day before had vanished. It was a new day.

With the storm passed, a clear, powder-blue sky reigned, and hot air filled the canyon, snuffing out the tiniest breeze. The weather would again be a problem—just a different problem. Sweat dripped down the inside of Tess' shirt, front and back, and accumulated at the waistband of her shorts.

"It's still morning," Tess told herself.

As the stillness closed in on the rafts, Claire felt as if she were suffocating. The backs of her thighs stuck to the rubber tube of the raft, and the raft became a cage; she felt trapped, like an animal locked inside, peering into the larger world. It was, in some vague way, how she felt at home, with the sameness and the routine trapping her, the tall redwoods standing guard and staring her down. Sometimes she thought she should pay for an office and get out of the house.

Certainly nothing on the Colorado River was routine for Claire. Every foot of the canyon, each sandy beach and each bend in the river exposed an unexplored world that awaited discovery. Blossoms of prickly pear, hedgehog, and barrel cacti dotted the rocky cliffs. The river descended, and a sandstone formation surfaced below the softly eroding contours of the Bright Angel Shale. Where the river quieted, otters frolicked in still pools and mallards splashed at the shoreline. The river cut through the canyon in huge meandering folds. The canyon opened onto seemingly infinite vistas of incomparable beauty, but Claire couldn't shake the feeling of being confined.

"We're gonna stop at the Little Colorado River," Tess said, "known in the canyon as the LCR. It's a side tributary into the main Colorado. If it's running clear, we'll stay for a while."

She too felt oppressed by the unseasonably hot air and was happy to follow Orion and the other guides as they steered to river left and headed towards the mouth of the smaller river. The LCR itself was hidden, enfolded in the haze of distant mountains, the tributary marked only by the huge boulders scattered across the Colorado where the two rivers merged. The milky turquoise water of the smaller river flowed past the boulders and into the confluence where it mixed with the clearer Colorado.

The pale azure water of the LCR looked like it came from somewhere else – maybe Greenland or Iceland—though Tess had never been to either country, nor seen their waters, so she couldn't know for sure. Mostly, the water seemed unnatural, like it had to come from somewhere strange and foreign. It wasn't until the water of the LCR merged with the water of the larger river and the Colorado diluted the smaller flow, that it looked natural.

Already a half-dozen rafts parked at the edge of the swampy beach. The red and yellow kayaks were pushed into the brush, half hidden. Tess breathed a sigh of relief as soon as she saw the kayaks. She wanted another go talking to Ellie and Tim. She didn't understand why Ellie had been so fearful on the beach and so confident after almost drowning. It didn't make any sense.

A stand of sturdy reeds marked entrance to the desert canyon. Tess hopped from her raft, tied and fastened it, and once the raft was secured, she stepped from the beach into a labyrinth of dense, swamp-like grasses. Her passengers followed. Leading them through the maze, Tess turned right then left, wherever the reeds gave way, and sometimes she muscled her way through the stand of razor-sharp stalks, when that seemed the only way into the canyon. The vegetation grew surprisingly thick and sturdy in the irrigated desert-sand, and the reeds closed in and surrounded the rafters as they made their way into the side canyon. Many reeds stood more than six feet tall and soared above them. In the midst of the dense grasses the canyon disappeared and the roar of the water faded. For a brief moment, they could have been anywhere. Tess took several more steps, emerged onto the LCR, and again could have been nowhere else. No matter how many times she visited, it always thrilled her.

The LCR flowed a light, milky turquoise. Up from the confluence, the side canyon glowed surreal, looking synthetic and fabricated, like one of the vivid velvet paintings her Uncle Ray collected. Rock edges stood sharp, as if cut in relief, and water frothed iridescent. It was a sharp contrast to the main canyon where the Colorado flowed a deep, translucent green, through a subdued landscape of muted tans and browns.

Tess led the rafters up the trail on the bank of the winding river, past small cascades and satiny pools. At the top pool, the guides urged the rafters into the silky effluent. Claire followed instructions and removed her life vest and pulled it on upside down, with her legs through the armholes. It had the feel of an ill-fitting diaper.

"It'll cushion you going down the slide," Tess said.

Claire dipped her hand into the water before entering. The pool felt as warm as a South Pacific sea, nothing at all like the frigid Colorado. One after another the rafters stepped into the pool. One after another they slid across polished rocks and spilled down the cascading rapids, bouncing from the top pool into the middle pool, and then down to the lower pool. Claire sat on the edge of the river and slipped into the water. It was as warm and gentle as a soothing bath.

Dirk scooted past her, on his second run. She followed Dirk into the middle of the pool where it was a little too deep to stand. The upside-down lifejacket buoyed her, though she was a good swimmer and didn't need the assistance. She steered toward the small waterfall and floated with the current. With her feet in front, she whooshed down the rocks and emerged below the turbulence, again floating in a calm, warm pool, as carefree as a child. Nothing was dangerous, and nothing was scary. It was pure fun, and she couldn't remember the last time she'd so enjoyed herself. She paddled towards the fall and slid into the lower pool.

She took several turns slipping down the slides, and when she finished, she looked around. On the rock ledges along the river, sunbathers draped across smooth boulders, and rafters picnicked in the spray of the falls. She had seen so few rafters on the river that it was a surprise to see such a large number of people in one place. Somehow, everyone had converged there, at that spot.

Linny started to walk towards the kayakers, but Tess caught up with her and told her she needed to speak with them alone. She told Linny to stay where she was. Tess hadn't wanted to say anything to anyone about checking on the kayakers. Expressing her fears for them might, in some way, jinx them. She was superstitious like that. Many of the guides were. They knew what the problems were without having to say anything out loud, and they all tried not to say anything out loud. She didn't tell West anything. He was probably thinking the same thing. She wished she hadn't had to say anything to Linny, but she didn't want Linny there.

Tess sat down next to Ellie.

"I was thinking about yesterday," Tess said. "Maybe you're tired, and you should let us take your kayak. It's not a permanent commitment. We'll take it day-by-day – hour-by-hour. It's too risky to be on the river when things aren't exactly right."

"I don't know what happened yesterday," Ellie said. "I feel great."

"Well, it's easy to feel good on the LCR – this isn't the Colorado. This isn't Grand Canyon," Tess said. "The water's warm and milky. You're not in your kayaks. You're sunbathing on smooth, flat rocks. This doesn't really count."

"No, I've felt really good the whole time," Ellie said, "except for when I almost drowned."

"But that's it," Tess said, "You did almost drown. You should probably stop and think about that."

"No, I'm good," Ellie said. "I did have a problem, but I survived. It won't get worse than that."

Tess had nothing more to say. If Ellie was continuing down the river, Tess wouldn't jinx her confidence. She wished she'd said more the day before, when it might have mattered. Maybe she hadn't because she'd gotten caught up in the wonder woman fantasy. She felt old, talking to this couple with no sense at all of their mortality.

Dirk swam over to Linny and motioned for her to join him in the water. She slipped in and joined him and Claire.

"We've got a geology side trip for you," Tess announced. "Follow me."

She had righted her life jacket and now waded into the river at a spot where the channel grew wide and the water shallow. Everyone in the group followed suit. Dirk, Linny and Claire followed in line to cross the river. Claire was surprised at how strong the river felt as its currents swept her legs and threatened to topple her. Even in the middle of the river, though, the water stayed below her knees, permitting a safe ford of the stream. She sprinted across the shoal and onto the sandy beach.

The sand at the river's mouth lay white and soft, and each footstep sank deep. Claire avoided the footprints of the rafters before her, to feel her own feet plunge through as if into a warm, downy snow. After only a few steps, the sand became less soft and more hard-packed, and the rafters skimmed its surface, stamped with ripples and dimples, as they hurried upriver. Farther upstream, under the imprint of geologic processes, the sand turned red and extremely hard.

When they reached the hardest sand, Tess kicked off her sandals and twirled barefoot, sliding across the sand curls in a desert tango. The rafters and guides joined her in wiggling across the sand. Linny and Dirk danced something that looked like a waltz, with Linny leading. Claire felt only a little older than she had tumbling down the cascades.

The dancing over, they headed back to the rafts. As soon as she reached her raft, Tess pulled out the bourbon. She'd drunk almost half the bottle by the time West, the last in line, arrived.

"Water's a little higher than when we pulled in," West said. "It's changing."

Tess had been sitting there for a while, but she hadn't noticed. Maybe West was right—it was subtle and hard to tell.

"Dam must finally be releasing water, to keep up with the snow melt and spring floods," Tess said.

"If that's it, that's a good thing," said West.

25

Day 4. Afternoon

They stopped for lunch shortly after leaving the Little Colorado. They had been hungry before leaving, but the guides said it was more convenient to set up lunch on an accessible beach. Claire had no doubt that was true, and she didn't mind waiting, or being back in the raft – the long break had soothed her. Instead of a cage, the boat now felt like her window on the world, bringing Grand Canyon right to her.

Tess tossed her sandals aside and wiggled her feet into the sand as she prepared the meal.

"You're always doing food prep," Claire said. "You like to cook?"

"Actually, no," Tess said. "I rarely cook at home, but I love to cook on the river. Cooking in the canyon provides structure to my day. In the morning, I'll dig my toes into sand that's as cold as leftover porridge, and at noon, like now, I'll stand on sand hot as bacon grease. Preparing dinner, I feel the day winding down. I stand barefoot in sand that's cooling in the shadows of the cliff and it's as if the beach itself had been pulled from an oven and set aside."

Tess laughed as soon as she'd finished answering Claire. She'd given a long, poetic explanation to an off-hand remark. What was happening to her?

Claire didn't think about Tess' answer as much as her own feelings about cooking. She prepared breakfast, lunch, and dinner without thinking of the useful structure it provided to her day, without thinking of the poetry that was available to her as a cook.

Her only thought a constant one of responsibility. The Santa Cruz Mountains weren't the Grand Canyon, but they were exquisite in their own right. On the other hand, Tess said she cooked on the river, but not at home, and being on the river was not the same as being home.

This was the fourth day of Claire's trip—time to think about why she'd come, even if she wasn't yet ready to plan the future. She'd come for a break, yet she knew the particulars of her life were not the problem. She felt oppressed and bored by the sameness of every day. The challenges she confronted—challenges she found only burdensome—neither inspired nor exhilarated her. She'd come to Grand Canyon hoping to talk with Linny, but she no longer thought that would happen, and she didn't think Linny could help her.

Linny had arrived with her own problems and, typical of Linny, she'd found a unique solution. For the first time in her life, though, Claire felt that Linny was making a mistake. Perhaps Claire was too resistant to change. Perhaps she couldn't imagine Linny's life as less than perfect. Perhaps she was threatened by Linny's daring.

In high school, Linny had been popular, with an abundance of friends and easily obtained social standing. Claire remembered Linny's routines on the pom-pom squad. She could name all of the good-looking boys that Linny dated. Cataloguing adolescence like that might sound corny, but that was Linny's life, and Claire had always thought Linny was charmed. Nothing dragged her down, and she floated through the turmoil of high school unaffected. She wore expensive, preppy clothing, and she always looked perfect, even after gym class. As Claire well knew, that, of course, was the ultimate cliché.

Claire, on the other hand, had been so self-conscious she spent nearly an hour getting dressed in the mornings, choosing what to wear when nothing seemed right. She was one of the smartest students in her class, and she knew it, but she rarely raised her hand to answer a teacher's inquiry. Most papers she wrote came back with an A+, and she wrote additional papers for extra credit to counter-balance the low participation grades she invariably received.

If she hadn't been friends with Linny, she might not have had any friends. Claire never quite understood what Linny saw in her, but she'd accepted the friendship without hesitation, and over the years, their friendship evolved. Linny pushed her places she was reluctant to go and forced her from her comfort zone. Seeing what Linny could do, helped Claire to expand what she did. For her part, she thought she grounded Linny and helped her to accept that not all limitations were bad.

Perhaps they hadn't been in touch regularly enough over the past few years, and Linny, not seeing enough of Claire, had lost sight of how normal people lived. Still, Claire knew that if she told Linny she wasn't happy, her friend would want Claire's life to change—she'd want the best for Claire. Perhaps she'd encourage Claire to do what she, Linny, was doing. Linny took action; she had little time for thinking. Claire, on the other hand, analyzed and evaluated until the time for action had passed. She and Linny didn't see the world the same way. Sometimes Claire thought it was because Linny's mother was her biggest advocate, while Claire's mother never paid her daughter that kind of attention. Sometimes Claire thought it was just that she and Linny had different personalities.

Linny walked over to Claire.

"Why'd you take your wedding ring off?" Linny said.

"I left it at home," Claire said. "So I wouldn't lose my finger if I fell in and had to be rescued. I read something about that in a book."

Linny shook her head. Claire had wanted to be alone with Linny for days. She'd wanted her friend's attention since she'd arrived. She'd wanted her advice from before she left home. Now she wanted to be back on the water.

It was more than how differently they reacted to the world. Linny was always ready to take the bull by the horns, as the saying went, and Claire loved that about her. But she couldn't do the same. She needed to let things unfold and unravel at a slower pace. Linny would jump into the middle of the pond from a rope swing. Claire would slip in from the bank. That was the difference, and that parsing of motivation mattered to her. It wouldn't even make sense to Linny.

26

Day 4. Afternoon

O K. Dirk," Tess said, "This afternoon's for you. We're starting the big rapids, and your life's about to become awesome."

Dirk didn't say anything, but Tess could tell he was excited. She herself was excited. The adrenaline rush she got from the big rapids was probably why she spent her days on the river. What she loved the most, though, were the subtle changes in the canyon. She loved how a thin layer of clouds softened the sunlight. She loved that all around her the mesa ranges set boundaries in the far distance, and the spacious, vast expanse belied the actual, solid verticality of the canyon. She searched for the beaches that had disappeared from view. She tried to imagine the canyon before the dam.

Claire also noticed the changes in her surroundings. Many times during the day she wondered what Paul would think, and every time she knew he would love it.

Linny, on the other hand, seemed unmoved and rather unaware of the canyon itself. As far as Claire could tell, Linny hadn't come to Grand Canyon for the nature. When Tess pointed out a changing rock formation, Linny glanced at it and then turned back to chatting with the man across from her. When Tess commented on how the dam had changed the canyon's vegetation, allowing tamarisk to grow and threatening the native mesquite, Linny didn't appear to listen. Claire didn't think Linny had any interest in tales of how sand dunes used to sweep across the landscape and now lay hidden beneath the brush.

Linny's current concern, as she told Claire, was looking for the kayakers. Apparently she had wanted to talk to them, and Tess didn't let her. It was as if they were her best friends, as if she had come to the canyon with them, not Dirk and Claire. Claire might have been more upset at how Linny ignored her, if she hadn't felt sorry for Dirk and how Linny ignored him.

"Tim, and particularly Ellie, are so inexperienced," Linny said. "I'm really afraid for them."

"You don't even know them."

"You saw what happened."

Claire just shook her head. She worked hard to stay on top of her own business—her natural inclination for the past year or so was to let things slide, and she had to fight herself to stay focused enough to manage her affairs. She couldn't remember the last time she got involved in someone else's business. Once, when she was young, driving on the New York State Thruway with her mother, brother, and sister, a large truck jack-knifed and blocked all the lanes in their direction, and they ended up in a traffic jam, slowly inching down the highway. They were on their way home from her aunt's house and stuck on the road for hours. She looked out the window and studied the people in the cars around them, making up stories about their lives. With her focus on the unknown inhabitants of the other vehicles, the time sped by. Lost in her own world, she commented on how much she enjoyed observing everyone and speculating on their lives. Her mother responded with derision.

She might occasionally imagine the lives of others, especially when people-watching in a city, but she didn't often give her friends advice, and she kept her interactions with strangers to a minimum. On a rare occasion she blurted out a foolish, inappropriate suggestion without anyone asking her opinion, and sometimes she couldn't avoid an unpleasant, unnecessary exchange with a stranger. If it weren't for Linny, she wouldn't even know the kayakers' names, and she saw that as a good thing, or at least not a bad thing.

The first big rapids, different than anything else they'd run, were Unkar Rapids. Claire heard it before she saw the rocks and the whitewater. In front of them West's raft entered the rapids on the right.

"He's taking the easy route," Tess yelled over the water's roar. "We're not going that way."

They ran the smooth, satiny tongue to the end, and immediately Tess angled them to the left.

"Paddle, paddle, paddle," she screamed. "Harder!"

They broke through a large entry wave, and Claire pulled furiously on her paddle, dropping it into the current as far as she could reach and keeping the paddle perpendicular to the river and pushing the raft up to meet the paddle, trying to move away a river of water, as Tess warned them of the hole that they had to avoid. A series of large, rolling waves pushed them downstream. Exhilaration and excitement claimed every inch of Claire's being.

"Back paddle!" Tess yelled. "Now!"

Dirk, normally showing no emotion, screamed with what sounded to Claire a mixture of fear and joy. In front of her, Linny shrieked. Claire moved her paddle to angle behind her, and she pulled it forward in an attempt to slow the raft's descent, but nothing stopped the raft. They powered through the waves and just skirted the hole and somehow managed to miss the many rocks that consumed the left side of the river. The strong current below the rapids swept them downstream without a pause.

"Fun, huh?" Tess yelled out, and all around Claire heads nodded and bobbed.

More than fun, it was amazing. Claire had never experienced anything like it, and she remembered from reading the guide that

Unkar Rapids were not, by any stretch of the imagination, one of the bigger rapids. She was glad Tess hadn't cheated and avoided the waves, like West had. If they were going to run even bigger rapids, they needed practice. Besides, as Tess said, it was fun, and she loved how much Dirk and Linny enjoyed it.

"That was what I was expecting," Linny said. "I could have skipped the first three days. Don't you think?" She turned and looked at Claire.

Claire wouldn't have missed a moment since they left Lees Ferry, except perhaps for Ellie's rescue and some of Claire's conversations with Linny. Being out in nature made problems disappear, or at least made life seem more manageable. Running a river required every paddler to think and focus, and worry about serious matters. In comparison, everything else became easy.

Many women married the wrong man, and sometimes Claire felt a connection of sisterhood when she thought about her marriage. This wasn't one of those times. Now she felt nothing but an awareness of lost opportunity. She thought of Paul and the kids, and she missed them.

It wasn't often that she felt a part of a team, but she did now. In the middle of the rapids, she and everyone else needed to hold their paddles upright so the blades entered the water on the vertical. They needed to push forward or pull backwards, depending on Tess' call. She needed to squeeze the seat beneath her legs to keep herself in place, so she could paddle. She needed to feel the shock of the icy water across her face and chest without moving or flinging her paddle, ready to take action. She needed to listen for and follow instructions. She was an essential part of the raft's success, as were each of the other paddlers. Usually, she was either in charge or she was inconsequential, and she wasn't particularly comfortable in either of those roles. She liked being right in the middle, a cog in the wheel.

Out of the rapids and floating in the calm water, she no longer followed directions and could do what she wanted. Instead of letting her mind run, ruminating on what she had or hadn't said, or what Paul had or hadn't done, she relaxed. Instead of thinking thoughts unrelated to the canyon, she observed the scenery. The current lapped against the raft, and when the sun angle dipped, the green translucent water disappeared, and the river flowed like liquid mercury, its surface opaque and silver. Downstream cliffs retreated into the distant rosy haze of Arizona, and the extraordinary river and vast canyon faded. Claire's problems vanished.

Obviously only her attitude had changed. Happiness and sadness could be found anywhere, and things were good and bad, important and inconsequential. Reality was often less important than how she was feeling. She could focus her attention on what was wrong, or she could look for what was good. She believed her appellate work was important, and she was good at it, and it brought her satisfaction. Early in her career her work sustained her, and she could say the same about raising her kids.

Her work was still important, and she improved and became increasingly more effective, but for some time it hadn't brought her the satisfaction that it had earlier. It was similar with her children. Caring for them was certainly important, perhaps more important than it had ever been, but it no longer brought her satisfaction. Now she wasn't sure she was any good at it and thought she'd been better when they were younger. For quite a while, she'd spent most of her time working and raising a family, and now neither sustained her. Still, she had no plans to stop working or raising her children. She had no illusion that responsibility and satisfaction correlated or even coexisted.

"Running these rapids is great," Linny said. "Perfect to get my new life kick-started."

She turned around, leaned close and told Claire her plans. She was done living someone else's life. Her first decision, she told Claire, was not to live the life her mother planned for her. Claire listened and looked at her friend with amazement. In that moment Linny looked very much like her mother Alice. It was the first time Claire had noticed the similarity. She thought about the older woman and the life she'd foreseen for her daughter. Certainly, Alice had never imagined Linny rafting down the Colorado. Nor could she have imagined her getting a divorce.

When they were in high school, Alice used to take Claire aside every few months and tell her that Linny was destined for great things. Claire would whole-heartedly agree. It was as if Linny were their secret project. She thought it wonderful that Alice recognized Linny's potential. Her own mother, a single mom traumatized by her husband's early desertion, watched over her three children looking for fault. Claire was in high school when she understood that her mother had never gotten over her husband leaving. She felt the world owed her for her burden. Only years later, after Claire had married, did she realize that she and her siblings were the most significant part of that burden.

Second, Linny told her, she wasn't living the life Steve mapped out for her.

"What do you want to do differently?" Claire asked.

"I want to put my happiness first, where it belongs," Linny said. "I just want to live and see what happens. I don't want to live within the constraints that Steve sets. He's so controlling. He's rigid, uptight."

Linny had never said anything like this before. Claire had spent a lot of time with Steve, and she'd never thought to characterize him as extreme. Yes, sometimes he seemed a little rigid, but no more than other people, especially successful ones accustomed to having people do what they wanted. Linny herself had very strong opinions; she wasn't that different. He was as fast a thinker as she was, and as successful professionally. Maybe that was too much competition. Claire had no way of knowing. In many ways Linny and Steve existed in a world beyond her life experience.

Steve certainly had opinions, and he knew about a lot of things, but she'd always liked that about him. If he was occasionally abrasive and obnoxious, Claire always thought he meant well. He seemed to care about Linny and Dirk. He even seemed to care about Claire and her family. If you divided the world's men into those who were good and those who were jerks, she'd always put Steve in the good column. At this moment, Claire thought that was enough to ask of someone. Linny apparently did not.

Linny's mother Alice had thought Steve was the perfect husband for Linny, and if anyone had asked her, Claire would have agreed. They had the same interests and goals, as far as she could tell. They had both wanted to live in New York City. They had both wanted children, though Claire never knew why they had only one child. And look at Dirk. He was a good kid, no trouble.

"A very big change," Linny said, "is Dirk going to boarding school in Massachusetts. That will let me create a whole new life. I hadn't realized until now how important his leaving home is."

27

Day 4. Afternoon

Tess steered the raft down the main current of the river and watched the passing landscape, acutely aware of the starkness of the harsh desert. When the river held calm, the water sparkled as if a million diamond lily pads scattered across its surface. It all clicked into place, and things felt right. She liked her life simple and unambiguous, and floating down the Colorado, Grand Canyon's splendor as backdrop, was dramatic and thrilling, but also, in a way, simple and unambiguous.

They passed through the desert tableau—the cliffs awash in shades of taupe and rust, burgundy and yellow. In the dunes beyond the beach, cacti bloomed with yellow, magenta, and red flowers, a neon invasion in a khaki canyon. On the other side of the river a turkey vulture circled back and forth above the cliff, swooped down into the canyon, and then rose back up and retraced its flight. A soft breeze blew the strands of hair that had escaped Tess' elastic. She loved the tickle of her hair in the wind. She loved the smell of the canyon. She loved being on the river.

They pulled onto the shoreline, pulling in behind the motor rafts with the science gear. The scientists had passed them the previous evening while they set up camp. Tess had thought it late to still be rafting on the river, and she'd hoped, for a fleeting second, that the scientists would stop and camp with them—a fantasy of spending the night with Brent. They didn't stop, though, and apparently they'd made it all the way down here. Tents and cots were scattered across the sand, interspersed with piles of dry-bags. Several guides sat drinking on one of the rafts. A young woman sat hunched over a laptop. Tess knew the others were out working. She knew Brent was focused on what he was doing, not on her.

"Hey Sarah," West called. "Will you take these folks on a science excursion?"

"Send them over," answered the woman working on the computer.

The guides directed the passengers to scramble off the rafts. On shore, the rafters waited for the young woman, and she led them across the sand toward the large gully at the up-river end of the beach. Claire hoped the excursion would be interesting. She feared it was merely an opportunity for the guides to drink, and she had low expectations for the science. Together they marched up the canyon.

"I can't wait to see what they're doing here," Linny said, as she joined Dirk up front.

The temperature rose at least twenty degrees as soon as they left the water, and Claire walked up the dry creek physically pushing her way through the heat that packed the narrow canyon. The soles of her shoes scrunched the pitted tan pebbles lining the path, and she snaked through the citadel of vertical red stone to enter another world, completely surrounded by desert, cut off from the river. The sun beat down, the vast silence stifled every thought in her head, and she slowed her pace. By the time she made it to the work site, she was beat. The man who was not wearing the lime green shorts at the water faucet at Lees Ferry, the one talking with Brent, was already explaining the work to her group.

"The Colorado winds through a sculpted fortress of stratified rock and desert talus," he said. "It carved out this canyon over many, many years, and before the dam it was a typical desert river filled with sand. It was muddy and rather unattractive. Now the river's clear and radiant, and you all like it, I'm sure, but it's unnatural. Before the dam regular floods brought sand to replenish the beaches. Since the dam those beaches are quite diminished.

"One of the things we're doing here is measuring the sand that's here and the sand that's disappeared from the canyon, to figure out if we can change the situation by changing the flow of the river through the dam. The problem's more complicated and harder than we expected."

"After we saw you, yesterday I think, though I'm having a little trouble keeping track of the days, I considered the problem of the sand in the canyon," Linny said. "It seems relatively simple, in that sand will always be sand, somewhere, part of some ecosystem—extinction is possible only as part of some colossal blast converting matter to energy. So, there's no real risk of sand disappearing. On the other hand, my canyon guidebook says there's a risk of extinction for the humpback chub, a native fish."

"Uh oh, we've got a biologist in our midst," the man said, smiling at Linny.

"No," Linny said, "I really was just thinking about it. And I don't know anything about it, other than what you've told us and what the guidebook says."

Claire couldn't remember a time she spoke up like that without knowing as much as, if not more, than anyone else. When she went to court, she was always over prepared. Though she spoke to her friends and family without knowing much of anything, she never spoke up in a group without being well informed. She couldn't even talk with West.

"You're right. Right about the relative simplicity of sand studies and right about the vulnerability of fish. Sand gets washed down the river—it doesn't disappear. Before Glen Canyon Dam the mud brought sand from above the dam area to the beaches downstream. That same mud and fluctuating water temperatures supported native fish: Humpback Chub, Colorado pikeminnow.

Today the clear water has little sand, and the beaches don't get replenished. The cool, clear water of the river fills with non-native trout, particularly rainbow and brown, and the natives get pushed out. It gets complicated."

Claire listened. That's how it always was with Linny. She could think about anything, even things she knew nothing about, and even when Claire thought she wasn't paying attention. Claire, on the other hand, took so much longer to think—even about things with which she was familiar.

From across the sand Brent caught her eye and smiled, and while discussions continued about the status of the river, he walked over to her and stood next to her.

"Maybe we'll have a chance to spend some time together," he said, his voice so quiet Claire almost doubted what she heard.

"Look around you," he then said to the assembled group. "Sometime in the past, a powerful stream cut through these rock walls, deepened fissures, and carved channels. Gushing water smoothed cliffs and rounded pebbles and the colossal canyon walls slowed the water and altered its course. The natural forces acting now aren't quite as extreme, because of the dam, but this is still a dynamic river canyon."

"Could the Colorado flood, even with the dam?" Linny asked.

"That's not an easy question to answer," Brent said. "The dam can certainly be breached, if it's not operated correctly. That would be water flowing over the top, and it would look like a flood from the perspective of someone on the river. But it would be more limited and contained than a real flood. We don't know if the dam can fail, which would result in a catastrophic flood. Sometimes you don't know if something can break until it does."

"Well, that's certainly true," Linny said.

28

Day 4. Evening

Claire set up her tent and sat down inside the vestibule, stunned by the intensity of the past few hours and the magnitude of the rapids they'd run. She was still recovering, catching her breath from the runs through Hance Rapids and Sockdolager Rapids, every cell of her body alert. Her mind racing with why they'd run the rapids so late in the day. Camping upriver near Papago Creek and running the rapids early the next morning, when they weren't so tired, had seemed the better idea to Claire, but Tess said the guides wouldn't sleep if they faced whitewater first thing the next day. The logic seemed backwards to Claire. She was certain it was more problematic to find the energy to run rapids in the late afternoon.

Not that she complained. The guides rowed, and she found the fortitude needed to sit on the raft. Tess announced that they'd run Hance rowing left to right, and immediately out-sized boulders hovered in the mist above the river, and whirlpools and holes appeared and disappeared. Seconds later the raft tumbled into a steep granite gorge where the canyon walls dropped straight from the heavens into the water, and the sandy beaches that had previously lined the river vanished.

"On to Sockdolager!" Tess yelled as she rowed out of one series of rapids and into another.

Claire hadn't been prepared for any of it, and even now, more than an hour later, she was merely going through the motions of setting up camp, not quite fully aware of where she was or what she was doing. Linny stood before her.

"That was awesome, don't you think?" Linny said, and Claire nodded.

Claire pulled her bag closer and dug out a full flask.

"You brought a flask?" Linny asked, and again Claire nodded.

"Drinking by yourself from a flask? That isn't good Claire. You shouldn't do it. Put the flask away, and we'll go have a beer."

Claire shrugged, stuffed the bottle into her pocket, and followed Linny across the beach.

"Dirk, get us two beers," Linny yelled.

"Three?" he answered.

"Two," she said.

"I'm really sorry about you and Steve," Claire said. "If there's anything I can do, you know I will."

"I know," Linny said. "There's nothing. It just doesn't work any more, and I can't fix it. I'm willing to try something new. I'm ready to move on. Maybe I've already said that, and I'm repeating myself, but that's how it is. Anyway, I can't remember what I said to you and what I said to my mom and sister."

"We are like family," Claire said.

"Yes, so I'm telling you to cut back on the drinking."

"I should," Claire answered as she gripped the flask in her fingers. But I don't want to, she said to herself. You do what you want, and I can do what I want. She turned around and took a long swig with her back to Linny.

"Is Paul still drinking?" Linny asked when they sat down near the river.

"Yeah, quite a lot," Claire said.

"Well, that's the problem," Linny said. "If he drinks, you'll drink. If your friends are assholes, you'll probably become an asshole as well. I'm not going to hang around Steve and turn into someone like him. If you stay with Paul, you need to figure out how to do it without taking on his problems."

29

Diary Day 4

What a day! We did as much today as the 3 previous days put together. At times it was so intense I could barely think – I just held on and tried to do what I was told. And I know – you all think that's impossible.

The day started out calmly enough. We left the frigid water of the Colorado to swim in the warm waters of the Little Colorado River. Wearing our life jackets upside-down, like over-sized diapers, we slipped down natural water slides into deep pools. It was like playing in a natural amusement park. Greg would have loved it. Sarah would have enjoyed swimming in the pools, but maybe not sliding down the falls. Dirk had a great time—a change from his usual, more sullen self. It's too bad there aren't any kids on the trip for Dirk to hang with.

We started the big rapids today. It was exciting, exhilarating, and frightening, all at the same time. I don't know how the guides do it, going from one set of rapids to another, maneuvering and planning, remembering the sequence of waves and rocks. It was all I could do to just sit there. The water comes at you faster and stronger than seems physically possible. Maybe that's why there aren't more kids – it could be dangerous. If an adult got flipped into the water, O.K., but if a kid got thrown from the raft—that would be serious.

We stopped again for a science lesson. It's almost like the Grand Canyon is a big laboratory, and the river itself is an experiment. There are hydrologists and geologists here measuring the water flow and the sand movement. They're trying to determine the best way to run Glen Canyon Dam to benefit the Colorado River. Everything is controlled and managed, yet, at the same time, amazingly wild. Not sure how that works.

30

Day 5. Morning

Claire's alarm went off at seven a.m., a half-hour before the scheduled breakfast. At sunset she had calculated where the sun would rise, and she had positioned her tent so the first sunlight of the morning, rising over a low mesa, would fall on her face when she sat up. She hoped to trick her brain into equating light with warmth and thinking the air was already heated. She hoped to make it easier to crawl from her cozy sleeping bag, and it amused her to think she was following the lead of the scientists and trying her own little experiment in Grand Canyon.

That morning the canyon was exceptionally cold, and even though her calculations were accurate enough, her tricks weren't helping. The first rays of sunlight were too weak to warm her eyelids. She didn't give up. She sat with her face turned into the early light until eventually her closed eyes glowed red. In the muddle of her sleepy brain she allowed her mind to confuse light and warmth, and though the air was still frigid, she imagined herself warm, and with a flash of sunlight seared into her eyelids, she pulled herself from her cocoon. She felt around in her bag and found the small stainless flask of rum. With her eyes shut, she took a small drink, telling herself the drink didn't count until she opened her eyes. It was so cold, and she was still tired; she needed a little extra help to wake up and get dressed. Linny was wrong—this had nothing to do with Paul; he wasn't even there.

Outside her tent the canyon felt like winter. She would have liked to wrap herself in her sleeping bag, but once she was dressed and outside, there was no going back. Tess stood at the edge of the river staring across the water, and Claire walked over to her.

"Spectacular, isn't it?" she said.

"No," Tess said, after a hesitation. "That's not what I was thinking. Just ten years ago there was a beautiful beach right there, across the river. Tamarisk bushes now crowd the river's edge, and there's sand exposed only back against the cliff, hardly visible from here. The steady flow from the dam has allowed seedlings to take root and bushes to colonize. I can't stand here without envisioning the beach as it once was, and it was spectacular."

To herself Tess questioned the effectiveness of the science investigations. So many years of work, and still the river and canyon degraded. From her perspective, the scientists knew little about protecting the magic of the canyon.

Claire also kept her thoughts to herself, not wanting to contradict Tess. She knew the Santa Cruz Mountains near her home well enough to notice changes and to mourn development and distressing transformations of the natural habitat. During droughts the trees thinned and exposed previously hidden places. Most of Grand Canyon looked to her like it had existed without change since the dawn of time.

On his raft, Orion was hooking up his ipod and plugging in the small speakers he had brought on the river. The music started in the middle of a long jam by Railroad Earth, a change from the usual reggae.

Claire and Tess watched the current. Downstream were several small pools of water that looked still, almost lifeless.

"Those are eddies," Tess explained. "They look static, but they aren't. Eddies have complicated existences, different from one minute to the next and never really still, no matter what it looks like."

"O.K. Back in the proper groove," she said, and she threw up her hands, wiggled her hips, and danced into the make-shift kitchen.

"Good morning Claire," Linny said.

Claire turned and noticed that in the early morning sunlight, her friend's hair and skin had little color. Even so, her enthusiasm and exhilaration transformed her. She was perkier than anyone but Tess could be that early in the day.

"I had another great night," Linny said. "And it is a perfect morning."

"Breakfast is ready!" Tess called, sparing Claire unwanted details.

Claire walked over and eyed the stack of pancakes and bowl of cut pineapple.

"I'll start with coffee," she said.

"I'll stick with coffee," Linny said.

Dirk walked by with his plate piled high with pancakes. He glanced at his mother.

"Feed them and they're happy," Claire said.

Linny looked at her but didn't say anything. If she had to guess, Claire would say that was a new idea for Linny. Yet Claire knew her kids felt loved when they were fed. How was it possible that Linny didn't know this? Did boys in the city really take care of themselves?

"Hey Dirk," Tess called, "I want to show you something."

She sat on the sand near the river with a jumble of thin, slender sticks piled next to her. In her hands she held a tiny board, less than four inches long, with a hole drilled into the center. Dirk balanced his plate of food in one hand and sat down on the sand facing her. He stared at Tess while he ate.

Sticking a short twig into the carved-out hole, Tess held the board steady between her knees, and quickly rotated the twig by rubbing her palms together. She held her breath and rubbed as fast as she could, and friction between the twig and board created heat, then hot ash, and in a mere second, the twig burst into flame. The half-a-dozen different sticks she tried all performed on cue and caught fire quickly.

"Awesome," Dirk said. "Can I try?"

Tess helped him hold the board steady and choose the right stick, but nothing happened. Seeing his discouraged face, Tess leaned forward and whispered. She adjusted his hands and chose a different stick. The twig burst into flames as soon as he started rubbing. He was as proud as a child taking his first steps, and Tess was almost as pleased. She didn't often have such an interested pupil.

She picked up several longer, very slender twigs, holding them in one hand and slowly bending them with her other hand. One by one, as she twisted and twirled, the twigs took on the shape of primitive replicas of deer.

"Like the archaic figurines found in the canyon," she said.

Several rafters sitting nearby clapped. When Claire walked over for a closer look, she saw that Dirk had already returned to making fire. Linny had walked over to West as soon as Tess called to Dirk.

31

Day 5. Morning

Floating in formation, the rafts swept down the current. Claire settled in, adapting quickly to being on the water again. The soft breeze blew the hair off her face. The cold air rose from the river, and the warm air settled down from the upper plateau. The cliffs on the left bank still hid in shadows, but those on the right bank glowed golden in the morning sun. No one on the raft said a word.

Claire felt the alternating warmth and chill and watched the light and darkness chasing each other. As she floated down the river a feeling of peacefulness swaddled her. It was still early morning that time of day normally filled with chaotic, frantic activity meant to assure that everyone in her family arrived where they needed to be. Here on the river there was neither chaos nor frenzy. A person could breathe and dream.

Until all of the sudden, the peace was gone. The rafts turned a slight bend in the river to face a sandy beach upriver from a side canyon. Twenty men stood on the beach, though not one raft bobbed in the surf. Instead of rafting gear, the men wore cowboy hats, denim, and cowboy boots.

"Hopi Indians from the nearby reservation." Tess said.

"How'd they get there?" Linny asked.

"A trail comes down the side canyon, from the rim," Tess said.

The men assembled into a loose circle and began to chant and dance, paying no attention to the rafters who now pulled to shore. While most of the men softly chanted, an older man, whom Tess recognized as an elder of the Hopi tribe, walked into the middle of the ring and began reciting the ancient words of a prayer. He spoke with a flat intonation, evenly spaced sentences of syllabic words, much like a string of rosary beads, and Tess strained to hear what he was saying. Though she didn't know the language, the consonants fell so sharp, and the words rang out so clear and sounded so understandable, that it seemed she could make sense of it if she tried. When the elder quieted and the chanters grew louder, she relaxed her efforts—the chanting musical rather than narrative, and not offering the illusion of easy comprehension.

Tess had observed many chants over the years, and she knew Hopi chanted at the change of seasons and to bring rain. They chanted in celebration of victory, and to ease the pain of defeat. They often chanted public grievances. Hopi called this world the Fourth World and the lives they lived here the Fourth Way of Life.

"Hopi legends prophesy the Fourth World and the Fourth Way of Life to be difficult. They say that life is simple, but the path is difficult."

All of the sudden the Hopis turned their attention to the rafters. A translator stepped from the circle and explained to the assembled rafters that the Hopi predicted a period of dark annihilation, flood and destruction.

"Prepare!" he said. "The river will flood, and there will be no way to stop it."

Tess looked back at the river. The Colorado still looked calm, and the water level hadn't changed significantly while they'd been in the canyon. If anything, she thought the river should be rising more, as the dam released in preparation for the snowmelt. It appeared to be a long way from flooding. Anyway, the river could flood only if the dam failed. The men continued chanting and dancing.

Tess studied the men. Three of the older men had very long hair, braided or pulled into a ponytail; most had shorter hair, chin length. Tess recognized one of the men as Ray Tewa. They'd been on a trip together the previous October, checking out sacred sites.

"This looks like a scene from a novel—the setting of an Edward Abbey story," Linny said. "The only thing missing is Abbey himself."

"You've read Abbey?" Claire said. "He's awfully western for a New Yorker."

Linny shrugged her shoulders. Tess had read all of Abbey's books. All the guides had.

The chanting continued, occasionally staccato, mostly melodious, until a final roar, followed by silence. The circle disintegrated.

Tess waved Ray over.

"Better get off the river before it floods," he said.

"Look at it," Tess said. "Calm and low. This river isn't close to flooding."

Almost a minute passed before Ray said anything. Tess had learned that sometimes American Indians, and Hopi and Navajos in particular, needed to gather words before they spoke. Their conversations often took a long time. She waited. When Ray finally answered, it was with a hard edge to his voice.

"The mountain snow is melting, and the river will flood," he said.

"But Glen Canyon Dam and its reservoir hold back the runoff," Tess said. "The dam is built to handle the snow melt."

Ray's face clouded.

"The river will flood," he repeated. "That is the prophecy."

An over-reaction, Tess thought. When it came to Grand Canyon, it was easy to lose all sense of proportion. Hopi, Navajo, and Hualapai all warned of cultural annihilation. Whenever someone discovered the degradation of a sacred site in the canyon, the tribes complained that they were being wiped out. Yet after years of atrocities, they survived.

She turned away and pulled the small flask from her pocket. The hard, raw liquid running down her throat focused her. People worried too much about the future, she thought. Today, not tomorrow, was most important. Today the river looked perfect. Today she was back in the canyon and Brent was a possibility. Today she was headed down the Colorado into the heart of the canyon.

Claire saw Tess take a drink and she wished she had her own flask with her. She was tired of being the good girl. She was tired of self-control and self-improvement. Right now she would absolutely love a drink and it made no difference in the world whether she waited until five o'clock.

32

Day 5. Afternoon

Tess rowed past one side canyon after another, one dry wash after another. On either side of the empty creeks, and along the Colorado itself, craggy cliffs rose before distant mesas. In some sections of the river, flat, sandy beaches stretched along the water, with sand dunes behind them, and other times sand dunes rose in waves right along the shore. Then, without warning the sand vanished and polished rock plunged straight into the water.

Overhead, clouds gathered and dispersed. Out over the mesas, wisps of thin, white clouds faded into a sky almost white in some places, and a deep, dark blue in others. Soothed by the gentle roar of the river and the monotony of the distant mesas, Claire relaxed. For a while, she shut her eyes and dozed in the swelter of the searing sun. They floated the river's currents, and she woke when the raft slipped into the glassy tongue at the top of the rapids and the river's rhythm, foremost in her consciousness, gave way to a pregnant hush. With a constant prevailing wind sweeping across the dry cliff walls, the air was at times hard to breathe. The chill of the morning had long vanished, afternoon temperatures rose above one hundred degrees, and the heat quickly grew oppressive.

All of a sudden Claire felt like she'd never make it another nine days. She, who had thought her salvation was wilderness, was desperate for a break from the wild. They passed under a black, narrow suspension bridge, and Tess yelled out "Kaibab Bridge." Just beyond the bridge she pulled onto the sand at a beach crowded with rafts, kayaks, and people.

The trucks and extraneous equipment of Lees Ferry were absent, but the commotion of the put-in suddenly reappeared just past River Mile 87. People called to each other, and they climbed on and off rafts and moved and rearranged gear. Hikers pushed through the crowd. A string of mules clomped across the overhead bridge, adding to the cacophony with their loud brays. It took less than a minute on the beach for Claire to again wish for the solitude of the isolated desert.

"This must be Phantom Ranch, the confluence of the Colorado and Bright Angel Canyon," Linny said.

Tess nodded. "We'll take a break here—maybe 1, 1 ½ hours. No more. Your guides will psych themselves up for the big rapids coming, and we'll tighten straps and otherwise prepare the rafts. Though many of us like to drink, as you may have noticed, we sit this one out. We've got Horn Creek, Granite, Hermit, and Crystal rapids just downstream, and that's sufficient to keep us sober.

"You can follow the trail to the canteen. It's just a quarter mile. You'll like it. It's air-conditioned. Take money if you want to buy something, and be back in a little over an hour."

"Can I have some money?" Dirk asked before Tess had even finished talking.

Linny pulled open her ammo box and took out a wallet. She handed Dirk ten dollars.

"What if there's a tee-shirt I want to get?"

She handed him a twenty. "I'm coming up there. Find me if you need more," she said.

She turned to Claire. "Want to go?"

Claire nodded and pulled open her ammo box and dug for her wallet. She'd known Linny since they were schoolgirls, yet everything Linny did now seemed unusual, even incomprehensible. In Claire's world, no one gave money to a child without also giving a lecture about its value, and Claire couldn't remember the last time she'd given either child any money, even with a lecture. Nothing her children wanted ever seemed worth the cost. Sometimes she wondered if she refused her children money because of her values, a shortage of funds, or a stinginess of character. What would Dirk think of the way her family lived, she wondered? How would Dirk have reacted if Linny had refused him?

Claire followed Linny across the beach towards the trail. A large tree cast shadows across the sand, its shade empty, and just as they passed a man ran up the beach, dropped his pack to the ground, fell to the sand, and stretched his legs and arms across the migrating shadows, taking up as much of the shade as possible. He wore hiking shoes, not river sandals, with army-style shorts and a cotton shirt, not the quick-dry, synthetic clothes that the rafters wore. He looked hot and tired, and he lay with his head propped up and his eyes wide open, staring at the bridge. Claire turned and followed his gaze. A train of mules roped together, hobbled the path across the bridge. Ahead of them, a family struggled with their packs, looking as if they might not make it to the canteen.

Claire and Linny stepped from the sand onto the trail. The winding path of packed dirt, hot and dusty, and smelling of fresh mule dung, teemed with people. Rafters, like Claire and Linny, walked in both directions, to the canteen and back to the water, scraping their river-thonged feet in the dirt and kicking up the dust. No one, apparently, had the energy or inclination to properly pick up his or her feet. Everyone looked weather-beaten and a little tired.

The path meandered up a picturesque little valley, Bright Angel Canyon, and though she was hot and felt like zoning-out, Claire forced herself to pay attention. In contrast to the sweeping, grand views on the Colorado, the perspective in the valley was intimate and personal, demanding a different contemplation. At first she looked up and around, as she had on the river, but that was no longer the primary panorama, and she trained her gaze down, and held it steady, and she looked where she walked. Graceful trees grew along the bank of a small stream, shading the water. Grass and tiny wildflowers emerged from the sand and dirt. A cozy, peaceful landscape replaced the harsh desert tableau, and for a moment the Colorado, with its excitement and danger, disappeared. If Claire stood with her back to the river and her eyes focused on the creek, she might be in picturesque Sebastopol after an apple harvest.

They reached the canteen, fashioned from roughhewn logs and stone. Of all the magnificent sights in Grand Canyon, this place was at the bottom of the list, and Claire could think of no reason to go inside.

Linny gave Claire a soft push on her back, and they climbed the steps to the canteen door and pulled it open, entering a shabby lunchroom, its only possible charm the chilled air streaming from its cooling system. Though Claire had never been much of a fan of air conditioning, it amazed her to walk into the freezing cold room straight from the scorching canyon.

"Perfect," Linny said.

A food counter and souvenir shop stretched the length of one wall, across from rows of long tables. Groups of rafters sat at the tables. Dirk stood in line in front of a glass display case.

"Let's see what Dirk's up to," Linny said as she walked over to him.

Claire walked past Dirk to the postcard rack and spun the holder and looked at the cards. She picked one with a photo of the granaries, where they'd hiked up the steep trail to the prehistoric caves. She chose a second showing Vasey's Paradise, with a view of the waterfall from the river. For a third card she picked one of the Little Colorado River.

"If you want to write these cards now," the clerk said, "you can use this pen, and we sell postage stamps. Later, we rubber stamp the card to say that it was carried by mule out from the Grand Canyon. People like that."

"Yeah," Claire said, "I'd like that."

The clerk looked only a year or two older than Dirk. What a great job for a kid, Claire thought, and she walked to an open seat at a near-by table. She doubted the cards would make it home before she did, but they would show Paul and the kids that she was thinking of them. She'd always loved getting postcards when she was a child. Her father would send them from his business trips, from cities like Chicago and Minneapolis, addressed to her and her siblings, and even though it meant her mother would spend a couple days talking about how irresponsible her father was, it was worth it. One time he sent a card from Austin, Texas with a photo of the Alamo.

The granary card was definitely for Paul. It was the least exotic, but the most historical. She addressed the Vasey Paradise card to Greg and the LCR card to Sarah.

"Look what I got," Dirk said.

He held up a brown tee shirt with a drawing of the Grand Canyon.

"Looks large," Claire said.

"That's the style," he answered. "Who you sending cards to?"

"Paul and the kids. You going to send a card to your dad?"

Dirk stopped folding his shirt. He looked down at the table, avoiding Claire's gaze.

"No," he said, shaking his head and resuming folding.

33

Day 5. Afternoon

When it was almost time to get back on the water, right before their passengers returned, West walked over to Tess. "Water's higher than when we pulled in," he said.

Thinking about the coming rapids and planning her routes, Tess hadn't noticed. West was right—the water was much higher.

"Dam's finally releasing water, to keep up with the snow melt and spring floods," Tess said. "I guess that's a good thing, unless you're running the rapids."

"Maybe," said West.

Claire, Linny, and Dirk were the first passengers to return to the rafts. The beach was even more crowded than when they arrived, and every inch of the shoreline was taken up with rafts and kayaks. Parked at the far down-stream end of the sand, right before the beach disappeared, Claire recognized the science rafts.

"Ten more minutes," Tess yelled to them, waving them towards the large tree at the back of the beach.

"Want anything to drink?" Claire asked.

Linny and Dirk shook their heads, and Claire walked over to Tess' raft. Her small day bag was still clipped to the rope that ran along the center tube, and she grabbed the bag, pulled out her small flask and re-clipped the bag. Seeing others drinking in the canteen and on the beach, she couldn't stop herself. She needed a drink—needed some whiskey, though whiskey wasn't her favorite.

"Looks good," Tess said, "but I've got to wait. No drinking for me until I'm ABC – alive below Crystal Rapids. Then it's time to celebrate!"

"Any problem with me drinking?" Claire asked.

"Definitely not," Tess said. "It's what I would do if I were you."

The first sip burned Claire's throat, as it always did. The second sip went smoother. After the third, she replaced the flask and returned to sit under the tree with Linny and Dirk. Linny spotted the kayakers pulling onto the beach, and she jumped up and walked over to them. Claire and Dirk watched her go.

"That's how my mom is," Dirk said, "always butting into other people's business. She talks to my friends about their schoolwork and their college and career plans. No one has a problem that she can't solve. She can figure out anything. So she says."

"She is pretty good at getting things done," Claire said.

"Yeah, unless it has to do with me, or dad. Then she doesn't have time or something."

Claire wanted to defend Linny to her son; that was her role as best friend. She just didn't know what to say. It would be like defending Paul to her kids when they'd seen him drunk, yelling at her, or they'd watched him march into their rooms, kicking aside whatever lay on the floor. They were sacred of him, though she knew he'd never hurt them. She'd lose all credibility if she said anything in support of him. What could she say about Linny that Dirk didn't know?

"Is your family happy?" Dirk said.

She hadn't expected that question. Dirk was sixteen years old, caught in the middle of a divorce. Would it be too dishonest to lie to him, or too great a burden to tell him the truth? What was the truth, anyway?

Sometimes we're happy," she said, "and sometimes we're not. Maybe that's how most families are—both happy and unhappy."

"My friend Zach's family is worse than mine. Every time I go to his house his parents are yelling at each other. And there's never anything to eat. Not even in the freezer. But they're not getting divorced, so maybe they're not really worse. Alex's family is definitely better. His mom is always home when we go there, and she gives us snacks and drinks, sometimes she even orders pizza for us."

"O.K. Time to go!" West stood on his seat and waved his arms back and forth. His booming voice commanding attention.

Dirk jumped up and ran across the sand. He met up with his mom, and they unclipped their life vests from the raft. When Claire reached the raft, she unclipped her life jacket and slipped it on.

"Tess," Linny said, "that young kayak couple is pretty spooked about the large rapids coming up."

"I'll go talk to them," Tess said.

She walked over to West and spoke with him, nodding towards the kayak couple. Then she walked over to them.

"Damn," Linny said. "I should have mentioned this to West, not Tess. It might have re-sparked his interest in me."

"God, mom," Dirk said. "You can be so lame."

Claire hadn't known that West had lost interest, and she wanted to know more, but she wouldn't have that conversation in front of Dirk. She said nothing, and then, before she could give it a second thought, she noticed that the river's water level had risen while the rafts were parked. She could tell which rafts had been there the longest by how far into the river they floated. As they waited for Tess to return, a private rafting trip untied and took off.

"They want to continue in their kayaks," Tess said when she returned, "but they want to go with us."

"You mean to rescue them if they have a problem?" Dirk asked.

Tess nodded.

"So, we'll wait fifteen minutes or so for them to rest up. Then we'll go."

"Can I go back to the canteen?" Dirk asked.

Tess thought for a moment. "Sure, why not," she said. "Fifteen minutes, though, no more."

Dirk tossed his life jacket to his mom, and Linny and Claire walked back to sit under the tree.

"It feels like one of our hottest days," Claire said when they'd sat down. "Feels like ninety-five degrees. Do you think it's hotter than usual, or just feels hotter because we're not on the river?"

"It's hot," Linny said. "The kayakers were all bundled up, though. You'd think they were on a river in Alaska."

"We could do that next time," Claire said. "A river trip in Alaska, with bears, and guides with guns."

"I don't know," Linny said. "This trip didn't turn out as planned. I wanted to talk to you about Steve, to decide what I should do, but then I couldn't handle things being in limbo, and stuff happened, and now it's all decided, and I'm getting divorced. And Dirk's signed up for boarding school, only he doesn't know it yet. And I'm isolated down here when I have lots of things to do. Hard to imagine wanting to go to Alaska."

Claire looked over at her friend, who sat there with her eyes shut. It was the first time she could remember Linny looking defeated.

"Do you want a divorce?" Claire asked.

"Well, things aren't very good, and divorce seems a way to move on, but I hadn't planned that. I planned to separate. I know it's tough for Dirk, but he'll manage. It's tough for me, but I'll manage. Life isn't always easy."

That was an aggravating thing about Linny, Claire thought. Just when she felt compassion towards her friend, when she felt sympathy for her, Linny would say something completely out of touch with Claire's life.

"No, life isn't easy," Claire said. "It's not a float trip on the Colorado."

34

Day 5. Afternoon

O K.," Tess said, "We're entering the inner gorge—running some of the wildest rapids in the world. We need luck, as well as my skill, so I'm wearing my pink cap and my special earrings. If I can, I'll try to sing my song."

Swallows whizzed through the air above the sand, and nearby, hikers clomped across the bridge. The dings and thuds of rafters adjusting the rigging on their boats bounced across the water.

Claire sloshed through the river and climbed into the raft. As she took her seat, an old man with dark skin and long gray hair hobbled across the sand towards their raft. He made his way through the surf and stopped right in front of Tess, and he stood for at least a minute without saying a word, examining her face. She studied his face in return, and she too said nothing. Claire felt less anxiety than she thought the scene warranted.

"I went down the river last week," he said. "Used my medicine pouch on the narrow beach below Whitmore Wash, river Mile 188, and I left it there. Please get it for me."

The old man explained that the pouch was filled with his most powerful herbs and objects. He insisted it be picked up as soon as possible, so it wouldn't be swept down the canyon when the river flooded.

"I can't replace my pouch," he said. "If it's swept away in the flood, that medicine is lost."

"I'll look for the pouch," Tess said, "but the river won't flood anytime soon. It's only April. There's no chance of flooding until the summer monsoons, three or four months."

"The river will flood," he said. He nodded to the rafters sitting in the raft, turned around, and walked back to the beach and across the sand towards the path.

"What's that about?" Linny said.

"Hopi Medicine Man," Tess said. "I've seen him and know his reputation, but I never talked to him before. I guess we'll look for the medicine pouch. It's a very big beach."

"Like looking for a needle in a haystack?" Linny said.

"Worse," Tess said.

As the raft sped away it passed under Bright Angel Bridge, and Claire watched the hikers and mules on the Bright Angel Trail. The trail followed the river for a short while. Where it turned up a canyon, the rafts ran the easy rapids. The kayaks took the run ahead of Tess' raft, and none of it looked very difficult to Claire.

"O.K.," Tess yelled. "Now we start. Pay attention."

The river narrowed, and the canyon walls moved closer to each other. Big waves rose up from the water and blocked the view downstream. The raft rushed along the current in the middle of the river.

"Back paddle, back paddle!" Tess yelled. "We want to go left."

Claire tucked her feet under the large side tube and forced her paddle into the current. Ahead of her she saw Linny straining to see down the river, and she knew Linny was looking for the kayakers who had gone before them. She wished Linny were more concerned about their raft – sitting behind Linny she could see that Linny hardly paddled, though Tess continued to yell directions to them.

Eventually the raft turned to the left and surged over the big waves. Before them, in the middle of the river, Claire saw Ellie's red kayak sucked down into a whirlpool. Ellie floated farther downstream, at the edge of the river, holding onto Tim's kayak.

Tess swung the raft towards the middle of the river, knocked the kayak, and pushed it down the current. So much happened so quickly, Claire could hardly register it all.

"We made it down the first rapids!" Tess yelled.

"Bring on the next one!" Dirk answered.

"What about Ellie and Tim?" Linny said.

Tess turned around to see the kayakers, and Claire followed her gaze. Tim held Ellie's kayak close to his as Ellie climbed back into it. She settled in and adjusted the skirt that covered the kayak opening. Claire couldn't imagine swimming through such rapids and immediately getting back into her kayak. She couldn't imagine swimming any rapids and returning to the river under any conditions. Ellie looked almost waif-like, but she must be extraordinarily tough, Claire thought. Or maybe she was only doing what she thought Tim wanted.

"They look good to me," Tess said. "Water's high, but manageable."

As the rafters watched, Ellie and Tim nodded to each other, and each gave a thumbs-up sign to Tess.

"O.K.," Tess said, "Off to Granite Rapids."

Whatever routine they'd developed during their days on the river, whatever rhythm they'd adapted to—it all vanished when they entered the Inner Gorge. Nothing was ordinary, and all became extraordinary. The river snaked its way through the granite rock, dark and forbidding, with very little landscape revealed beyond the towering cliffs. The gorge deepened. The visible world diminished. Canyon shadows replaced the hot sun, and constant splashing from the over-sized waves dropped the temperatures. Most importantly, the river demanded constant attention. There was no time for dozing. Claire wished Linny would be more conscientious in her paddling.

They passed several dry creeks running into the Colorado, offering quick glimpses beyond the river and a mental escape from the morphology of the canyon. Trinity Creek dropped down onto a small beach from a narrow chute carved into the rock, but before Claire could appreciate the expanded view, they ran down Salt Creek Rapids and entered the glassy tongue of Granite Rapids. Huge waves bounced off the cliff on river right and hit up against waves bouncing off the cliff on river left. Claire could see neither the current nor an entry or exit. The river appeared to be completely closed off and inaccessible to the small oar raft.

"Paddle!" Tess yelled above the roar of the water.

Claire tucked her head down, looking away from the rapids and focusing in front of her on Linny's life jacket. She tapped into every reserve of strength she could find. When the waves crashed over her, she saw nothing but water in every direction. She barely breathed; there was no air. She lost track of where they were and what they were doing. Forcing her feet under the raft tube for security, she pushed on her paddle following Tess' directions. Her only thought, buried deep in the back of her mind, was a wish to get through the rapids as quickly as possible. Running these larger rapids terrified her.

They continued down the river, and she saw nothing except the orange fabric of Linny's life jacket. When the roar of the river momentarily subsided, she heard the screams of everyone around her. She'd known Linny for most of her life, but couldn't distinguish Linny's screams from the screams of the other women in the raft. Sometimes, she was not sure whether the screams she heard were her own. Dirk's screams she recognized only by the pitch of his teenage exuberance.

They progressed through the rapids, and the water poured down and flowed off her, until finally the deluge ended and the river again appeared in front of the raft, rolling flat and straight between towering cliffs. They were through the rapids and past the danger, but her heart pounded in her chest the same as it had in the midst of the maelstrom. Her back ached from the tension of holding herself rigid.

"Don't get too comfortable," Tess said, "the next rapids are coming up in a fast mile."

Linny turned around to face Claire. Her blond hair was plastered straight against her scalp. Water dripped from her chin and down her neck. She should have been miserable, in the way that Claire was, but Linny's smile took over her whole face. She appeared to have not a care in the world.

"That was perfect, Tess," she yelled, looking to the guide at the back of the raft.

Then she looked at Claire and froze.

"You're white as a sheet, Claire. You alright?"

Claire nodded and forced a smile at her friend. What had been too much for her had been perfect for Linny. Where Claire emerged terrified, Linny appeared exhilarated. Linny stared at Claire for a moment, then turned back around.

"This is awesome," Dirk said, and Linny whooped in reply.

Another short mile on the fast-moving water through the shady canyon, and they approached Hermit Rapids.

"We've got five waves in a row," Tess yelled over the roar of the water. "Each wave bigger than the preceding one. Hang in there! We have to make it to the end, through all five!"

The raft, which usually dawdled in the tongue of the rapids, rushed forward without delay.

"Where are the kayakers?" Linny yelled, turning around to look for them.

"They're there," Tess answered over the roar of the rapids.

"Turn around, Linny, you're making me nervous," Claire screamed.

Hermit Rapids rode wilder and longer than Granite. Waves rose up and crashed over the raft, one after another. After each wave crest, the raft pitched down into a deep valley of water, nothing but the rushing river visible, and the rafters had no time to prepare, respond, or even react. Tess shouted orders to the rafters to back-paddle, or paddle, or hold position, in a seeming endless sequence of instruction. Claire heard her guide's commands and tried to follow the directions. Most of the time she stared at Linny's back, and when she looked up, just for a moment's relief, she saw only water. Only the orange vest in front of her anchored her to the raft. She understood they were headed down stream, that being the only way a raft could go, but she had no sense of their orientation. If it weren't against the laws of physics, they could have been riding the waves back upstream, or going up and down the same wave, over and over.

"Paddle!" Tess screamed above the roar.

Claire squeezed both hands around the rubber handle encasement, pushed her paddle into the water and pulled on it. It barely budged. The raft itself seemed in limbo, perched at the edge of a wave. Claire had lost count of the waves. Tess had said there were five. Claire thought they'd run three or four, possibly even five. Suddenly the raft lost its balance and the front disappeared, submerged under the water.

"High-side!" Tess yelled.

The rafters in the front of the raft, the ones now waist-deep in the river, grabbed at handholds, forced their way through the rushing water, and pulled themselves toward the back of the raft. Following the directions Tess had given days earlier, everyone in the low part of the raft moved to the high part of the raft in an attempt to keep the raft from flipping. Linny held onto Claire's shoulder and dragged herself behind Claire. Claire grabbed Linny and moved back.

The front of the raft, now empty and lighter, without the weight of the passengers, rose up, and the water drained from it, and the raft slid down from the crest of the wave. That last wave had been the fifth one. They had run the entire rapids, and a calmer river flowed before them. Claire swept her hand across her face, brushing away the clinging water. She breathed deeply and tried to slow her breath. She could feel the adrenaline pumping through her veins. In the blink of an eye the river grew placid. Claire remained agitated and charged up.

She looked across the canyon, hoping to calm herself with her observations. In places the shiny canyon walls were so dark they looked purple. Where they were less reflective and more opaque, they appeared merely black. At the top of the cliffs Claire caught sight of rock layers in bands of varying colors and textures, but along the river now, where the rocks plunged into the water without benefit of beaches or brush, the layers disappeared. Solitary trees emerged from the craggy surfaces; otherwise, the massive rock walls encased the river without vegetative relief. It was a journey to the center of the earth.

"Hermit Rapids was about the waves," Tess said. "If we run Crystal Rapids on the right, which is what I hope to do, Crystal is about the holes."

As far as Claire could see downstream, there was barely a current. The water surface was flat, reflecting a detailed depiction of the overhead sky and the steep rock walls plunging into the river. Ahead of the raft, the yellow and red kayaks cut through the swirl of reflected colors as they floated on the surface of the water. The air barely stirred. The up-river breeze, which had slowed their journey most afternoons, had taken the day off, leaving behind a suffocating stillness.

In the distance a few splashes appeared to jump up from the river. Beyond that, Claire saw only the rock of the cliffs in the far distance. Nothing more was visible—from where she sat, it looked like the river just ended. She'd been on the Colorado long enough to know what that meant—the river fell on a steep gradient and dropped out of sight. All around the raft her senses registered a peaceful, calm river, but her brain, educated over the past days, told her to be alert.

Within a short time the raft picked up speed, and more splashes rose up from the water's surface, and the river plunged down until all of a sudden the rapids appeared before them. They had barely entered the rapids when Ellie's red kayak, running the rapids right before them, slid sideways on a wave and plunged into a hole on the right side of the river. The kayak rose up from the water like King Arthur's sword from Lake Elsinore. It was perfectly straight, perpendicular to the river, an extraordinary sight.

"Holy shit, back paddle, give me some time," Tess yelled.

Even as she yelled, she knew her rafters would be of no use. They weren't strong enough, nor focused enough. It was up to her. She pulled on her oars as hard as she could, but the raft sped down the river, cresting the waves, and passing by the hole that held the kayak. In a few more seconds, the raft skirted along the edge of a second wave and passed a second hole. All Tess could think about was the kayak sticking up from the river, and then the river calmed. They had run the rapids.

Neither the red nor yellow kayaks arrived downstream. Tess blew on the whistle tied to her life vest. The rafts that had preceded them down the rapids, the rafts now idling in an eddy, turned around and circled back towards her raft.

Tess quickly explained the crisis to Orion. West hadn't yet run the rapids. His was the last raft of their group, and he was still behind. Tess was certain he'd be able to do something. She'd never had a problem he couldn't solve. Orion and Tess agreed that she'd stay put and watch for the kayakers. He and the other guides would pull to shore and walk upstream, along the bank, carrying throw-ropes and rescue equipment.

"Someone's coming!" Linny yelled.

A raft barreled down the final wave, followed by two more rafts.

"A private trip," Tess said. "They won't be much help."

The private raft trip spread across the river, each raft facing upstream. The other rafts in their group followed Orion and rowed to shore. Claire watched the guides tie the rafts to the rocks and the passengers climb from the rafts onto the rocks. They spread out along the shoreline, life jackets on. The guides also wore their life vests, and they slung ropes across their arms and chests, slipped first aid kits into backpacks, and carried bright-colored bags in their hands. They walked over the rocks and headed upstream.

Tess watched them until they were out of sight, then she turned the raft around, to face up river. No one on her raft said much. Dirk had climbed onto the cooler to stand next to his mother. One of the other women bent her head down and appeared to be praying. Tess watched the woman from the corner of her eye. She wasn't accustomed to prayer.

Just then another raft rushed down the rapids. Tess saw West as soon as the raft emerged from the waves. She hadn't realized how certain she'd been that he would rescue the kayaker until it was evident that he hadn't. He looked at the rafts spread across the river and rowed to the bank. Within seconds he had tied his raft to shore, grabbed a rope and his pack, and run up the rocks; he was quickly out of sight.

Time had become increasingly distorted since they'd been on the river; sometimes Claire found it hard to know if mere minutes or an hour had passed. She'd thought the repetitiveness of the rowing or the huge expanse of rock warped her senses. Or the hot sun or the open blue sky had dulled her normal feelings of awareness. Perhaps, untethered to usual activities and a normal routine, she'd drifted into a separate canyon reality where she lost her ability to keep track of the day. Sitting in the raft, though, waiting for the kayaker to be rescued, there was nothing except the slow creep of time. She felt each minute pass, expecting to see the kayak at any moment. Everyone waited.

"What's going on?" Linny asked. "Where are they?"

"Rescues can take a long time," Tess said. "Sometimes it can take hours, many hours."

"How's that possible?" Linny said. "You throw the rope and pull the person out. Can anyone survive hours in the river, like that?"

"When you've got the force of the water, with a strong current, pushing in one direction, it can be really hard to get through."

"Then how does it happen?"

"You work at it, and everyone cooperates, and then there's a small break, and something changes, and the person, or the boat, or both, are freed. One time I hit a wave wrong, and my raft tilted onto its side and wrapped around a rock, with the current pushing us against the rock with all its force. It took about three hours of me really pushing on one oar, and passengers pushing on paddles, and a couple guides on shore pulling on ropes that we tied to the raft. Eventually it worked and freed us. Every guide has had that experience."

Tess didn't answer Linny's question about whether someone could survive being in the water for a long time. No one pressed her on it. An hour, then another passed. For a moment, she closed her eyes against the unrelenting brightness of the day.

"Look!" Dirk said.

The red kayak careened down the current. Tess couldn't be certain, but it looked empty. The yellow kayak appeared next. A figure sat upright with a paddle, and across the shell, in front of the paddler, another figure lay sprawled.

Tess blew on her whistle.

"Everyone paddle," she said. "Get us over to the kayak."

One of the passengers on the private trip yelled that she was an ER doc. Her raft pulled up to the kayak, and she leaned over, and she and another passenger lifted Ellie to their raft. They pulled off Ellie's helmet and tossed it aside. Tess could see a young man pumping Ellie's chest and then the woman doctor put her mouth to Ellie's. Tess pulled up next to the private raft.

The doctor gave directions in a monotone voice, repeating the same sentences over and over, whenever she wasn't breathing for Ellie.

"When a person is unresponsive and drowning is likely," she said, "compress the chest, using two hands, one on top of the other, pushing hard with the whole upper body. After thirty compressions, start rescue breaths—tilt the victim's head back, lift the chin, pinch the nostrils, and begin breathing."

"Was she breathing at all? Conscious?" Tess asked.

The doctor shook her head. After maybe a dozen resuscitations, the doctor jerked back, and Ellie coughed. Water spewed from her mouth. The man compressing her chest moved to the side and raised her to sitting. The doctor swept her hands across Ellie's face and into her mouth. Ellie continued to cough. She opened her eyes. Tim burst into tears.

Tess turned to shore and gave the rafters waiting on the rocks a thumbs-up signal. They cheered.

35

Day 5. Evening

The private raft trip pulled to shore on river left at the next campsite. The doctor climbed from the raft with Ellie and delivered her to the dry sand. After a round of beers gathered from all the rafts, as well as whiskey provided by Tess, the boaters said they needed to leave to make it farther down the river, to stay on their schedule. Each of the commercial guides suggested they stop for the night and make up the time the next day, but the private rafters insisted on leaving.

The remaining rafters and kayakers set up camp. The beach was too small for the number of people, but no one complained. Claire was happy to have the rafts, guides, and other campers near by, almost on top of each other. The closeness provided a sense of security, which she desperately needed. The kayakers settled themselves in the middle of everything, and they did whatever anyone told them to do. They, Dirk, West, and Theresa seemed to be the only people not drinking. For everyone else, alcohol became the sustenance of life.

Claire finished her largest flask and stopped counting the number of beers she downed at four. Even as she drank she knew she'd had more than she could handle, certainly more than was good for her. She'd drunk too much to pay attention to how much anyone else was drinking, but she had the feeling everyone drank too much.

Orion announced that dinner would be very simple, and they didn't want anyone helping. The guides would do it themselves. Guides and passengers looked at him as he spoke, and no one moved. After a while, West stood and pointed at each guide and then pointed to the kitchen that remained unassembled. One after another, the guides rose and went to work. The passengers remained seated, sprawled on the sand. Claire smiled at Linny and passed her another beer.

"Last one," Linny said. "For you too."

Claire nodded. Even in her inebriated state, she knew she'd never tell Linny to stop drinking. She wouldn't want to say it, and Linny wouldn't want to hear it. It wouldn't happen. That meant, Claire thought to herself, that they didn't have a very reciprocal friendship, and she accepted that. She was grateful that Linny cared about her, so grateful, in fact, that she wanted to cry, thinking that Linny would tell her to stop drinking.

"I have some rum," she said. "Is that O.K.?"

Linny shook her head.

"O.K.," Claire said, nodding, agreeing to do as Linny instructed.

Claire expected Linny to join the kayakers, to badger them, or whatever it was she did. But Linny stayed next to Claire, as if they were tied together. Each of the rafters found a spot and sat in that one place. Only Dirk roamed the beach, walking back and forth, as far as he could in each direction until the sand disappeared and the cliffs blocked his path. He collected stones and threw them into the river.

As the sun dipped behind the western mesas and the beach slipped into the shade, cool air sank down from the desert rim and settled into the canyon, spreading across the sand, comforting the rafters. A memory of scorching heat still lingered in the waves of warmth that radiated from the ground and bluffs, but Claire felt almost cool in the feathery breeze that wafted up the canyon and brushed across her skin. She pulled off her hat, faced the breeze, and wove her fingers through a tangle of hair matted against her scalp. She felt even cooler as the sweat from the day dried from her head. She wondered why she hadn't taken off her hat earlier. She leaned over to Linny and told her to take off her hat, and she watched as her friend shook her hair free.

There was little sound except for the guides preparing dinner. The water rushed by, but quietly. Claire removed her sandals, stood, and slowly walked barefoot across the beach. She sank into the sand. Soft powdery grains collapsed around her feet as if she walked through a deep, dry snow. It had the feeling of childhood, only sweeter.

She was concentrating on her footsteps, aware of only her own sensations and not fully placed in the world, when she felt someone grab her hand. Linny clasped her hand tight and stood next to her. Claire remembered that Linny's firm grip was surprising to many people. Her delicate features and blond hair hinted that she might just gloss over the fundamental rules of handshakes, but her personality and professional success dictated otherwise. Linny's mother had given the girls handshake lessons when they were in high school. She said a firm grip was essential to making a good first impression, as important as how they styled their hair and what they wore. Claire had taken the lesson to heart. Linny had also.

"Time to set up our tents," Linny said, dropping Claire's hand. "It's gonna get dark soon."

She headed for the pile of bags, pulled hers from under several others, and dragged it across the beach. Claire shuffled across the sand and found her bag. She followed Linny and set up her tent so the two tents almost touched. As the sun set, the sky turned a darker blue, and then black. Claire looked up to a sky splattered with stars. She had to work just to keep her eyes open, and she pulled her pad and sleeping bag from her bag and spread them on the floor of the tent. She looked for Linny but didn't see her, and she climbed into the tent and lay down, on top of her sleeping bag.

She shut her eyes, planning to rest until the call for dinner. She never heard the call and woke only once, in the night when all was still and quiet. She shut her eyes and immediately fell back to sleep.

36

Diary Day 5

It's almost impossible for me to write about this day, and actually I am writing this entry after breakfast the next morning on day 6, since I fell asleep last night before dinner and before I could write anything. One of the kayakers who's been traveling down the river at the same time as our group almost drowned. A major rescue effort pulled her from the river unconscious and not breathing, and a doctor on another trip administered CPR and revived her.

When I get home, I can explain how she got trapped in the river, and exactly how the rescue proceeded, if anyone cares. I will never forget the details.

It was incredibly scary for everyone, and a very clear reminder of how dangerous the river can be. No one talked about it afterwards. No one talked about anything. The kayakers spent the night with us, and our guides fed them and helped them make camp. Even those of us peripheral to the drama had trouble with the simplest tasks.

We'll see what today brings.

37

Day 6. Morning

The wakeup call found Claire in the same position, on top of her sleeping bag, as when she lay down before dinner the night before. Though she'd had more than a full night's sleep, she was still not quite ready to start the day, and she buried her face in her hands to block out the emerging light. Lying still with her eyes closed, she took inventory of her person.

She couldn't deny that she'd had too much to drink, but to put a positive spin on it, she told herself that she'd certainly had days when she felt worse. At least she didn't have the flu. Being that sick on the river was almost impossible to imagine, and really, her situation wasn't too bad. What she needed to do, she told herself, was change her clothes, wash her face, brush her teeth, and comb her hair. If she did all that, she'd feel much better. If she made herself look presentable, she could fake it, and then she'd make it. That was her mother's motto – fake it till you make it.

With her eyes still closed, she sat up and unzipped her tent. If only it weren't so bright outside—that damn light assaulted her, seeping through her scrunched eyelids. She wished she'd opened her eyes before she'd opened the tent. That would have been smarter, but it would have required planning ahead. For a fleeting second she considered starting over—zipping up the tent, blocking out the sunlight, and then opening her eyes, but she knew that was ridiculous. She could no more go backwards in time than a raft could travel up river.

She sighed, thinking what the morning was likely to be. She'd be unable to do anything but the most simple tasks. That's why she knew she wasn't an alcoholic—she could calculate exactly how alcohol impaired her, and she put herself in such an impaired situation only rarely. Paul, on the other hand, had no idea what happened to him when he drank. He didn't realize when she and the kids stayed in their rooms and kept out of his way. He didn't notice when they hurried about without talking. He was too wrapped up in himself to pay attention to anyone else.

That was the thing she still needed to think about. What was she going to do about Paul? At the moment, the answer seemed easy. She should go home, find an apartment to rent in Boulder Creek or maybe Felton, and move the kids and herself out. Since she hadn't thought that before, she considered that it might be an alcohol-fueled solution. There might still be some alcohol in her blood. Could it be that easy to solve her problem? Probably not. It wasn't that easy to change a life. Maybe it was for Linny, but it wasn't for her.

She pushed herself out of the tent and stood up. Linny crouched on the sand, near the river, talking to Ellie and Tim. As Claire watched, Linny put her arms around the two kayakers and touched her head to theirs. At the corner of her eye, Claire saw Dirk standing near the kitchen table watching his mother.

"Breakfast," Tess called.

Claire didn't think she could eat, but coffee was certainly in order. By the time she washed and dressed and made it to the table, her mug was one of the few remaining in the aluminum box, and the coffee was almost gone. She poured what was left and handed the empty pot to Orion.

"You're first on the next pot," he said.

She moved closer to the river to drink what she had and wait for a refill. As she stared at the water, the science rafts floated down the current, into view, and pulled onto the beach.

"Tessy, girl, are you making me breakfast?" the guide on the larger raft yelled.

"I can give you lots more than breakfast," she shot back.

The scientists whooped, and they and their guides climbed from the rafts and headed for the kitchen. Claire followed them— she wanted to be first on that next pot of coffee, as Orion had promised. She needn't have worried. The scientists weren't eating or drinking. They'd come to talk. She refilled her cup and left.

Tess was still looking around the kitchen, distracted by morning chores, when Brent started talking.

"Something's not right," he said. "First the water level was really low – too low considering the snowmelt runoff in the headwaters. I had come thinking the river would be higher. Well, now it's higher, which makes no sense considering it was so low a couple days ago."

"So what do you think?" West asked.

"What I think is too weird to say," Brent said. "If I tell you what I think, you'll think I'm crazy, a paranoid conspiracy nut."

No one said a word, and Brent continued. "I think the dam operators are altering water flow to manipulate the data we're collecting for the EIR. Extreme winter storms had increased the snow pack in the mountains, and early spring rains caused quick melting of the snow. It would have been easier to get our data a month or two ago, but we wanted to be here when the river was running at its highest, swollen with snowmelt, laden with sediment runoff from the tributaries. I think the operators tried to reduce the flow, but it was too much, and now they're releasing it. The worrisome part is that they may not be able to control it."

"What are you saying?" said Tess.

"I guess I'm saying, prepare for a breach of the dam."

38

Day 6. Morning

"The scientists are doing research here, behind this beach," Tess said, "and we're not leaving for an hour or two, so anyone who wants can join them."

Linny, Claire and Dirk joined the expedition.

"Tess said the river level fluctuates as the dam increases and decreases water output for electricity production," Linny said. "But, I think the river looked higher yesterday, and a little higher again today."

The three scientists in front of them stopped and turned to look at Linny.

"Yes," one of them said. Are you a hydrologist?"

"Are there hydrologists in New York City?" Linny said. "Not one of the usual Wall Street careers."

Everyone laughed.

"We'll let Brent answer your observation," someone said.

"We think the increased flow must be snowmelt from the headwaters in Colorado," the scientist said. "Extreme winter storms increased the snow pack in the mountains, and early spring rains caused quick melting of the snow. The dam might be releasing water to prevent an overspill. Maybe that's what we're seeing."

Claire studied Brent's left hand, to see if he wore a wedding ring. He did. She didn't know why she looked.

"We're hiking out to where we've placed several anemometers," Brent said. "We'll download the data they've been recording. We do this every month or so."

Claire adjusted and aligned the chinstrap on her hat. She drew the brim down lower on her forehead for increased shade. She smoothed the front of her light blue sun shirt, checking the alignment on the buttons, making sure the proper buttonholes met up with the appropriate buttons. She pulled at her shorts, centering the seams, though she wasn't sure why. She wasn't someone who usually fussed with her appearance, but she needed an outlet for her agitation, and fidgeting with her clothing was the best she could come up with. She felt as if she were over-caffeinated, which she probably was, but she knew the correct diagnosis was that she had a hang-over. Sweat dripped into her eyes and down her cheeks and neck. A swell of nausea rose through her chest. Just at that moment, for some unknown reason, Linny patted her on the shoulder, and Claire felt better.

Being on the river with Linny was changing Claire's friendship with her. She understood Linny a little bit more, and seeing Linny handle the wilderness in her own way deepened Claire's appreciation of her friend. She wondered if it would have helped her relationship with Paul if they'd taken the raft trip together. Perhaps she and Paul could have changed the course of their lives with a Grand Canyon adventure. Sometimes, just one little tweak, and lives, like creeks, ran a different course. At the moment, the real question was whether she cared enough to try.

They walked through scraggly brush and through a break in the rock. Suddenly the landscape opened onto a wide expanse of sand dunes, hidden behind the cliffs, away from the river. Two anemometers stood before them, lined up on a dune, and a third lay on its side, partially covered by sand, its base bent and twisted. Claire and the other rafters watched the researchers dig it free. One of them held the metal frame against a large piece of driftwood while another hammered it straight with a small rock. Someone retrieved a larger rock, partially buried in the sand, and he used it as a hammer. When they finished their repairs, one of the researchers pushed the instrument base deep into the dune and adjusted the sensors. Brent handed another scientist a computer case to hold open as he downloaded the wind data. He faced into the wind that had begun blowing soon after they arrived, and angled the computer as best he could to minimize its sand exposure. Claire was surprised at how interested she was.

"What do you do with this information?" she asked him when he'd finished.

"It helps us determine whether the sediment changes we see in the canyon result from river flow or wind, whether it's fluvial or eolian," he said. "And that helps us figure out whether or not dam operations are harming the canyon. Basically, we want to use the information to figure out how to best preserve the camping beaches and protect the ancient artifacts."

"Complicated," she said.

"Yeah," he said. "And that's just the sand and archeology story. When you add in how to protect the native fish, it's super complicated."

Before he could say anymore, Tess appeared to round up the rafters and return them to the beach.

39

Day 6. Morning

W e're through most of the biggest rapids, into the part of the canyon called the Gems," Tess said when they were back on the raft. "Gems as in Agate, Turquoise, Ruby, and Sapphire Rapids. We've entered the upper granite gorge."

Claire looked back and forth across the river. The geologists had piqued her interest in all-things geologic.

"I wonder what these rocks are," she said, thinking aloud.

"The silver rock is schist," Linny said, turning around, "and the pink veins through it are pink granite. I just found it in the guidebook. It's amazing, isn't it? Look over there, it looks more like granite than schist."

"Actually, river left is a tan schist," Tess said.

"I'm so happy we're here," Linny said.

"Me too," Claire said, thinking the same thing at the same time.

"That geologist seemed awfully interested in you," Linny said. "I was ready to make a move, planning what to say, but he's walking next to you, talking to no one else."

"You have an over-active imagination," Claire said. She turned around to straighten the strap she was holding and noticed that Tess was looking at her, her eyes in a squint and her mouth in a frown.

A mountain goat climbed the steep cliffs on river right. It wasn't very graceful, but it ascended the rocky wall without slipping, and that seemed a miracle. Claire leaned forward and tapped Linny on the shoulder to point it out. On river left in a patch of soil on a small ledge half way up the face of the mesa, a cluster of Utah Century-plants sprang up into giant, stiff, flowering stalks. Claire pointed them out to Linny.

A quarter mile downriver, a bald eagle glided effortlessly overhead.

"That's only the third one I've ever seen in the canyon," Tess said.

With little fanfare, they had entered a magic kingdom. Towering cliffs of silvery rock rose up from the river and reflected, maybe even refracted, the intense, desert light, bouncing sunlight back and forth across the water as if they were made from splintered mirrors instead of rock. The river itself sparkled in a shimmering labyrinth of reflections, and the water ran clear, with the slightest hint of a translucent green. Claire understood the reason was insufficient sand and mud in the river, and the geologists blamed the dam, believing a desert river should hold sediment. She was certain a rafting river should be clear.

Currents rushed the raft down the steep gradient, and Tess' oars shot ripples across the river's surface. They rode through a long series of manageable waves, skimming the water like dandelion fluff blown across a field. Then, without warning, the currents disappeared, and the raft drifted haphazardly across the suddenly lazy river. The sound of rushing water disappeared, and the staccato twitter of swallows and wrens filled the canyon.

Tess grabbed a beer from her stash and popped it open. Before her Claire sat straighter, and Tess knew the other woman was feeling the taste of the cold refreshment as if she herself held the can. When Claire turned to watch Tess drink, Tess offered her a beer.

Claire had turned to watch Tess enjoying the beer, not to get one herself, but she couldn't turn down the offer, and she told Tess yes and took the can offered by the guide. Once she took a drink, she couldn't stop, and she drained the can quickly and drank a second. When she took a third can, Linny turned around.

"Hey, what's going on?"

Claire looked at the unopened beer in her hand and shrugged. She wasn't sure what was happening.

"I'll take that," Linny said and took the can from Claire's hand.

Claire didn't object. She knew that Linny cared about her more than anyone else, and she trusted Linny. She had no idea if Linny trusted her. Sometimes she thought Linny didn't need to trust anyone, that Linny was totally self-sufficient. She thought she cared about Linny enough to take her friend's beer away, but she wasn't sure.

Before Claire could think anymore about her situation or Linny's, they drifted into the calm tongue of the rapids.

"You know, the river's pretty high," Tess said, "and that could make these rapids more difficult than I'd normally expect. Pay attention. Listen for my commands. We could be in for a rough time."

Claire adjusted herself and planted her feet straight forward. She tightened her grip on her paddle and watched the river in front of the raft. Small splashes and larger waves rose from the water. She was grateful she hadn't had a third beer, and she silently thanked Linny. Tess stood up on her seat and peered down the canyon.

"No problem," she said. "Piece of cake."

Claire relaxed, and her mind wandered. After five full days on the Colorado she'd learned a lot, not the least of which was to trust her guide's pronouncements and recognize her skill. Tess steered the raft down the middle of the river on the main current, and it rose and fell on the waves, as if on a giant roller coaster. All around her the paddlers whooped, and Claire realized she too was involuntarily yelling. The anxiety that often tempered her excitement had disappeared. With no cares weighing on her, all that remained was a child-like joy in everything they did and saw. She hadn't expected that a Grand Canyon trip could do that. She hadn't understood that such a feeling was even possible at this time of her life. It wasn't that she felt like a child, she just felt fully appreciative of the world.

The red and yellow kayaks passed them on the right. Both kayakers raised their paddles in a wave. They were close enough for the rafters to see the big grins lighting up their faces. The rafters waved back, and Linny gave them a thumbs-up. The kayaks, lighter and floating atop the river, sped ahead.

"They're looking good," Linny said, turning around to yell at Tess.

"Yeah," Tess said. "Good when things are going well, not so good when it gets more difficult."

"Will they be O.K.?" Linny asked.

Tess shrugged her shoulders.

40

Day 6. Afternoon

W e're gonna run some rapids," Tess said, "have a late lunch, and take an afternoon hike. Then we'll make camp."

On shore the massive blocks of schist and granite devolved into sculpted panels with flutes and crags, and the silvery colors of the rocks became increasingly more pronounced, deeper and shinier. Buttresses of Redwall Limestone still towered over it all, creating a seemingly impassable barrier. And then an even larger, distant mountain appeared beyond the Redwall. They raced down the river. The water, swift and deep, occasionally frothed. Waves rose and fell. An unexpected hole appeared in the current, but the guides swept past without incident.

It wasn't until they pulled to shore and Claire looked at her watch, that she realized how late it had become and how hungry she was. Several other rafting groups had already pulled onto the shore. Claire saw the red and yellow kayaks on the sand at the lower edge of the beach. She looked for the science rafts but didn't see them and immediately realized they couldn't be there since they'd stayed behind at the beach that morning.

"Elves Chasm," Tess announced. "We'll have lunch then hike up the canyon. This is one of the best hikes on the Colorado."

As they stood on the sand and the warm sun quickly dried their river-drenched clothes, a group of male hikers returned to their beached rafts. Linny talked with the men until they climbed into their rafts and launched from the shoreline. She stood in the surf and watched their rafts disappear around a bend in the river. Dirk walked into the water, then back across the sand, back into the water, and back across the sand. Claire figured he was used to entertaining himself, and though she felt critical of Linny when she thought that, and felt certain that Linny should pay more attention to Dirk, she also wished her children were more independent.

Tess called for volunteers to help prepare lunch, and Claire washed her hands using the large squirt bottle of disinfectant and joined the few volunteers. She helped pull loaves of bread and jars of pickles from the aluminum boxes on the rafts. Thinking how she didn't enjoy making lunch at home, she consoled herself with the thought that at least she always did what was needed, and there was satisfaction and virtue, if not pleasure, in that. The kayakers walked by, climbed into their kayaks and pushed out into the river. A group of rafters left, and others arrived. Linny talked to everyone.

The rafters assembled for the hike right after lunch. They started up a steep but easy embankment and followed a sandy trail that wound past dry rock terraces dotted with blooming barrel cactuses and scrawny bushes. As they made their way towards a distant ravine, a few red monkey flowers grew from cracks in the rocks, and the path became more difficult. Claire watched each footstep, trying to step securely, but sometimes she slipped on loose dirt, and other times she scrambled hastily over rocks that appeared to offer no stable route.

The pace slowed, and she balanced on huge boulders and stopped walking when the person in front of her paused. They stood at the mouth of a narrow canyon, and in an exquisite arrangement of geologic features, enormous boulders of travertine marble balanced atop pink bedrock, across from a massive cliff of sandstone. One after another, the hikers entered a green oasis dotted with hanging, Maidenhair ferns, and soon they stood before a stunning waterfall splashing into a crystal clear pool. For a moment no one disturbed the beauty, and then Dirk dropped his pack, pulled off his shirt, and dove in.

Linny followed, and he dragged her across the pool to stand under, and then behind, the pounding water. By the time Claire prepared herself to join the swimmers, the water was crowded, and Dirk and Linny had begun to climb the rocks in a cave behind the fall, and they disappeared from view. Claire slipped into the frigid water and submerged herself. She didn't force herself into the waterfall, but watched as Dirk and then Linny perched on the ledge above the fall and jumped into the middle of the deep pool. When Dirk grabbed Claire's hand, she followed.

They pushed their way through the water of the pool, avoided the pounding cascade of the waterfall, and climbed up the rocks behind the fall. In a few steps, they entered a cave, and in the darkness of the cave, climbing a natural staircase carved into ancient rock, Claire lost her nerve. All she could think of was turning around and climbing back down. If she made it to the top, she'd have no place to go except over the fall, and she no longer wanted to do that.

It was pitch black ahead, and she couldn't see where she was going. She felt her way in the dark dampness, crawling up stairs that were both rough and slippery at the same time. Looking over her shoulder, she felt the presence of two people, almost touching her heels. Beyond them she could hear more people, though it was too dark and twisty to see anyone.

Trapped in the tunnel with no choices, she continued, and in a moment she was back in the light on the ledge atop the lowest part of the fall. Above her the water hugged the rocks and cascaded down the cliff in a series of rivulets that diverged into trickles and fused into larger streams. Below her the waterfall, which hadn't appeared too large when she looked at it across the pool, dropped a seemingly unbridgeable distance.

Dirk seemed anxious to jump again, but he wanted Claire to go first.

"Sit down, right there against the rocks," he said. "Then swivel around, with your legs hanging down, and push off. It's easy."

She did as Dirk instructed, trying to ignore the fact that she was taking directions from a sixteen-year old boy who'd said no more than a few words to her since they'd arrived. She sat down and moved until her back fit snug against the wall of the cave. She swung around, letting her legs drop over the ledge, and she pushed herself from the rock and cannon-balled into the pool below. She quickly pulled herself away from the pounding water and watched Dirk jump down. They gave each other a thumb's up sign, and she followed him back up to the top for another jump.

Feeling more comfortable for her second jump, Claire didn't tuck herself into a tight cannon-ball as she had done on her previous jump. She wanted to jump free form as many of the other rafters did. She stood and jumped off the rock, waving her arms and legs, and she landed on her back.

When she pulled herself from the water and turned around to look for Dirk, he was gone. She saw Linny, but not Dirk. Tess came over to her.

"Don't worry," she said. "Orion has taken him up to the top of the fall. It's a hard hike, and we don't usually do it, but Orion said he promised Dirk."

Claire didn't go back for another jump. Instead, she strolled along the creek to the mouth of the open canyon. There, away from the fall, where the water was more stagnant, algae turned the water a bright, almost iridescent green. The pool reflected the clouds and the sky, and the green color became a backdrop for a panorama of the celestial dome.

"Time to go," Orion yelled about forty-five minutes later. "We've got some river miles til camp."

Dirk scampered down the trail with a huge grin. He had several gashes across his shins, but Claire didn't hear him say anything to anyone about where he'd been or what he'd done. She didn't hear Linny ask. Back on the water, the sun hovered just above the west canyon wall, and while they moved farther downriver, shadows swooped down bluffs and bolted across beaches. Rocks and boulders darkened into obscurity, and sand and water fused to a single composition.

"There's more water flowing now than there was last night, which was more than the night before," Tess said to no one. "Let's hope it means nothing."

41

Day 6. Evening

"Hold off a minute before unloading," West said when all the rafts had pulled to shore. "Let's think about the water level."

"I'm still hoping it doesn't mean anything," Tess said.

"I'm thinking it's a bad sign," Orion said.

"Safety first," West said. "Make camp higher up the beach, farther from the river. Give it room to flood, if that's what it's going to do."

"You don't really mean flood," Linny said. "since it's controlled by a dam."

"Yeah," West said, "the dam means it shouldn't flood, and there hasn't been a real flood, unplanned and all, since 1983."

"I thought Glen Canyon Dam was completed in the early 1960's." Claire said. "How did the river flood twenty years after the dam?"

"Nothing's infallible," West said. "People screwed up."

"Enough chatting," Tess said. "We need the kitchen set up. I've got dinner to cook."

While the guides and rafters assembled the kitchen, the science rafts pulled onto the beach, downriver, at the far edge of the sand.

Linny looked over at Claire and raised her eyebrows.

"Hard to understand why we're friends," Claire whispered under her breath so no one but Linny would hear. "You're impossible."

"But you're considering the possibilities, I can tell."

Claire shook her head, but she wondered if Linny knew her better than she knew herself.

Claire watched the researchers trudge across the sand, unloading equipment and dragging their dry bags up the beach. They were too far away for her to pick out Brent. She wondered if Linny really thought she'd have a one-night stand, or something like that, when she knew there were so many reasons that wouldn't happen.

Claire considered herself attractive enough for most purposes, but she was nothing like Linny, and she both looked and felt her age. She was an average, forty-four year old woman with straight, brown hair mixed with a few new strands of gray, cut several inches below her chin. She wasn't the kind of person others paid attention to, nor a person who had unusual experiences. That was always Linny. Linny made things happen.

Even more relevant, Claire was married, and she'd been faithful to Paul for fifteen years. She'd had only one small involvement with a high-profile criminal attorney when she was first married, and that hadn't progressed beyond a few hesitant kisses in a darkened parking lot after late-night meetings, before they each headed for home. He wasn't married, and she'd only been married a year and a half at the time, and she didn't fully appreciate the commitment and attention that marriage required. She'd loved Paul back then and valued her marriage; she just didn't think a few kisses could hurt when Paul didn't know about them.

It was painful to now remember the person she was back then and how cavalier she'd been. In all the years since, she'd rarely even flirted with anyone, and no one had given her a second look that she'd noticed. She supposed Linny would say that reckless, carefree person was still somewhere, tucked deep inside, but Claire didn't think so. She hoped not.

"Don't get too worried about whether the river will or won't flood," West announced to the group. "Just try to notice the river and the canyon. It takes about four or five trips through Grand Canyon until you can really see it. For most of you here, this is a first trip."

"Are you saying only guides really sees the place?" Claire asked, immediately regretting the hostile tone of her question, like an attorney on cross-examination. She hadn't meant to sound like that; she didn't know why she did.

"No," Tess answered. "Lots of people come back multiple times. They get hooked."

"It's our second time," said a man in his late fifties. "We first came eleven years ago, when we were around your age."

Orion had hooked up his travel stereo, and once again it blared the music of Jimmy Cliff across the sand. Claire loved music, particularly reggae, but she didn't want to hear anything right then, and though she usually helped prepare the food, she walked away from the kitchen. She grabbed her bags and headed towards the cliff, needing a few moments alone.

She'd been on the river less than a week, a relatively short amount of time, but long enough to realize she'd arrived in Grand Canyon unprepared. Mountain hiking and camping didn't provide much in the way of preparation for two weeks in a desert wilderness. The temperature extremes were extraordinary, almost unbelievable, and she would never get used to the intense dryness. Also, knowing she'd spend all day every day with the other rafters and guides, she'd come expecting to feel hemmed in, and yet she felt lonely, though she was never alone. Then there were the physical difficulties and the danger. She'd thought only of spending a couple weeks with Linny figuring out what to do with her life. Instead, each day brought new challenges, and nothing was turning out as she expected.

She found a half-filled flask in her bag and pulled it out. There wasn't much that just a little whisky, even the thought of whisky, couldn't make better, and even before she took a drink, she felt calmer. Her situation appeared less dire. She watched the river. The kayakers pulled onto the beach, half way between the rafters and the scientists, and Tess walked over to them.

On the water, Claire had felt a chill rising from the river, but it hadn't yet spread to shore,. The sandy beach was still hot—a full, height-of-the-day hot—and Claire sat as still as she could and imagined cool air slipping down the cliffs and settling into the canyon. She tried to force her body to cool. It was a trick she'd learned as a child, but she hadn't done it in quite a while, and never in a place with such temperature changes. When she was younger she loved late afternoons when the air had not yet cooled, and she alone could feel the approach of a cooler evening. She'd learned to turn an imminent forecast of shade to a physiological advantage, training her body to register a temperature drop before air temperature actually fell. She'd never mentioned it to anyone; no one she knew would have understood, and she could only imagine the sarcasm her mother would have expressed. It was her secret that the mercury soared, and she alone sensed an impending chill.

Claire pulled out her tent poles, clipped the poles in place, and assembled her tent. She pushed the pegs into the sand, scavenged a dozen rocks to hold the pegs, and staked the fabric. She pulled guy-lines and straightened the tent's alignment. After years of practice, she could put up a tent without thinking, and she took comfort in doing something so familiar. For a brief moment she considered offering to set up Linny's tent but dismissed the thought.

"Dinner is served," West boomed out across the sand.

The dinner menu was stir-fried chicken with broccoli, rice, salad, and cheesecake, rather boring. Linny had told her that the day before they had tacos with fish, tomatoes, and cilantro, and Tess had made a pot of Spanish rice on the stove and set up the grill for heating tortillas. Linny said it was a memorable dinner, and Claire was sorry she missed it.

The kayakers joined them, but the scientists stayed down at the far end of the beach, and Claire felt a little disappointed.

"The water's looking higher," Tim said. "It was already high in the early morning and got higher through the day."

The guides looked at Tim, and they all nodded. Then they all shrugged. Claire looked from one to the other, but no one said anything.

"Any reason I can't ask the scientists?" Linny said. "We talked about it a little this morning."

"Nope," West said, after a small hesitation, and a glance at Tess, and Linny jumped up and walked down the beach, kicking sand, as Claire rose to start cleaning the kitchen.

She was almost finished when Linny returned with her arms linked elbow to elbow with a researcher on each side of her, Brent on one arm and a young woman on the other arm.

"Here's what we know," said Brent. "In early spring, warmer temperatures melt the winter snow that's fallen in the mountains, and the resulting runoff increases the river flow down here in the canyon. That's what happens every spring. A week ago the flows seemed lower than expected, and yesterday and today the flows are higher than you might expect.

"We got confirmation this evening from our office that dam operators kept the flow artificially low over the past month, and the reservoir has filled. It's now at unprecedented levels, and the operators are trying hard to get the water out as quickly as they can. They're even sending water through the by-pass chutes, which are rarely used and which make the flow greater than normal. So the river's high. They say they are not worried about the flow or the dam – the situation's sufficiently under control."

"But the river's going to be higher than usual?" Linny asked.

"Probably," Brent said. "Probably O.K. for motor rafts."

"We're in oar rafts," Linny said.

"And kayaks," Tim said.

42

Diary Day 6

Here's a little more about yesterday, now that I'm not as exhausted. I didn't even eat dinner last night, and I love to eat. I can't remember ever missing a dinner unless I was sick. Apparently I missed one of the best meals of the trip.

Anyway, about the day's early activities: We got an early start, as usual, and floated down the river, past a sandy beach. Our guides pulled to shore. About twenty Hopi Indians formed a circle and began chanting, and we climbed from our rafts and stood nearby listening. It was quite an experience – they chanted together in their language, in a simple melody, and punctuated the chant with yells, and then explained themselves to us in English. The men believed the Colorado River was going to flood, and they warned us of the danger.

Our guides seemed unconcerned. Tess, who rows my raft, said that people get all riled up about Grand Canyon, out of proportion to the real situation. By the time you read this, you'll know I'm safe and there was no problem.

We left the Hopis, went back on the river, and pulled off at Phantom Ranch for another strange experience. It's the crossroads of the Colorado River – the intersection of the river and two hiking trails from the rim, the Kaibab Trail and the Bright Angel Trail. There are bridges across the river and mule trains going up and down the Bright Angel Trail carrying people and supplies. Backpackers head into Bright Angel Canyon and the canteen there. After days of being on our own, seeing few people, it felt like we had arrived at a busy bus station (without the buses.) I thought I was ready for something livelier than the river, the sand, and the cliffs, but I was wrong. It was overwhelming instead of stimulating.

The canteen sells souvenirs, snacks, and drinks. Dirk bought a tee shirt. I mailed you postcards that will be carried out of the canyon by mule.

After our stop, we hit the big rapids. This was more exciting and scarier than anything I can remember doing, ever. The waves were huge, and the raft sped down the water, and all I could do was try to follow the directions yelled out by our guide as water smacked me in the face and drenched me. Much of the time there was too much water for me to see beyond the raft, and I stared at Linny's orange life vest in front of me. I couldn't think or make decisions on my own. Everything happened too quickly. The guides are really experienced, though, and we all went through without a problem.

A young kayak couple traveled through the rapids alongside us, and they didn't make it through so easily. The woman's kayak got stuck in a drop in the river that they call a hole, the front of the kayak under water, and the back stuck straight up, and the woman stuck there. The water pushed us down the river before we could help, and our rafts stopped when the water calmed, and several of the guides pulled out safety ropes and other rescue equipment and climbed to shore and hiked back up along the river to the middle of the rapids where the woman was stuck. Another trip came down the rapids, and they too waited with us.

We waited a long time, but our guide didn't worry. She said rescues take a long time. Finally, the kayak came into view, racing down the river. It was empty. Then the other kayak came, with the kayaker paddling and a body sprawled across the front. A doctor in one of the waiting rafts administered mouth-to-mouth and saved the young woman. It was terrifying.

This morning several rafts with scientists stopped at our beach. They had previously set up anemometers (instruments which measure the wind) at the back of the beach where we couldn't see them. Our guides were happy for a short break, so we passengers joined the scientists and hiked to the hidden instruments. They are looking for data to help revitalize the beaches along the river and to determine whether the operations of Glen Canyon Dam are hurting Grand Canyon.

Back on the river we floated to a place called Elves Chasm. Amazing. There's a trail through some scrub brush and rocks and then, all of a sudden, there's an enchanted grotto with clear water, huge boulders, hanging ferns, and waterfalls cascading down the cliffs. It's like something out of a Disney movie, but for real. We climbed up to the top of the lower fall and jumped down, through the fall, into the pool. Dirk did it first, then Linny, and I followed.

43

Day 7. Morning

W e're changing our routine a little," Tess said. "We'll finish breakfast and load the rafts, as usual, but then we'll take a hike, right here, up Blacktail Canyon."

Claire had noticed the side canyon when they pulled to shore the day before, but she'd been too tired to explore and, besides, there hadn't been any time. They'd made camp, had dinner, and before they finished cleaning, it was getting dark. When she woke in the morning, the sun rising across the river caught her attention, and she forgot all about the canyon behind her. That early sun bleached all color from the rocks beyond the narrow sandy beach, and only the rocks still tucked into the shade at the edge of the river and across the river retained pigment. A forecast, Claire decided, for a very hot day.

By the time they started walking, the temperature had risen and the color had disappeared from much of the landscape. Though the air felt clear, a haze spread along the river and across the sand, and everything appeared pale and dull in the desert light. Only when the hikers entered the canyon did the tall cliffs cast a morning shade onto the dusty, primitive path and provide welcome relief from overexposure in the sun.

"We've been rafting through increasingly older rock layers," Orion said. "The Colorado River cuts down through the rock formations, from newest to oldest, exposing a geologic history. And it all makes sense, and works, until we get here to the Great Unconformity."

He indicated rocks at eye level, pointing out the Tapeats Sandstone, an orderly, layered, sedimentary exposure in a rich, earthy brown color, overlying the Vishnu Schist with its undifferentiated, vertical bedding pattern in a tan and gray blend. The sandstone didn't fade into the schist; the schist didn't merge into the sandstone. The two rock formations were so distinct and clear it looked as if a physical barrier separated them.

"This unmistakable boundary marks the disappearance of 255 million years of rocks," Orion said. "We know from finding some of the missing formations in other parts of the canyon that there was a period of widespread geologic upheaval between 820 and 770 million years ago. The rocks that had been deposited in this space, between the layers we see here, were uplifted after they were deposited, and then eroded. They're gone from most of the canyon, found only in down-faulted wedges in a few exposures.

"This sandstone formation has lined the Colorado River for much of our journey so far. And the schist is exposed now in the heart of the canyon. Here you can see the contact."

"Named the Great Unconformity by John Wesley Powell," Linny said.

"Let's keep going," Tess said. "We're headed toward a small, clear pool."

Claire expected something like Elves Chasm, but instead of opening up, the canyon narrowed, and in places she walked a path between two towering cliffs touching both walls with her hands. Surprisingly, she didn't feel claustrophobic. She felt centered and connected. Out of the bright light, the schist gained muted, hidden color and a luminescent beauty. The shallow pool at the end of the walk was perfectly clear, but filled with insects and bugs, and no one jumped in.

A lizard darted across the dirt, its mottled brown markings camouflaging it and leaving it almost indistinguishable from the hardened desert sand. Claire watched it disappear up the rocky cliff.

"Back to the rafts," Orion said, and he turned around, and everyone followed.

Back on the river, back in the Tapeats Sandstone, the sun shone almost directly overhead. Hemmed in by geology, but without the personal grounding she'd felt in the slot canyon, Claire stared at the rocks trying to decipher the layers and identify the strata. She knew Tess, and possibly Linny, could help, but she didn't ask. The sun was hot and the air still, and she felt too heavy to talk. She dabbled in the geology as an intellectual, abstract curiosity, without actually attempting to figure anything out. Occasionally she saw a trail leading up a side canyon or through a break in the rocks. She'd drop the geologic puzzle she'd been piecing together and imagine the people who had hiked there and the places they'd found at the ends of the paths.

After the intensity of the previous days, Claire enjoyed sitting on the raft, baking in the sun. The sun made her lazy and sapped her energy, and she welcomed the calm, hoping it would restore her equilibrium, reestablish her sense of control. The large rapids were spaced farther apart, the wind was calm, and little demanded her attention.

"We've got a treat for you," Tess said, waking Claire from her daydream. "West is pulling to shore up ahead. Those small motor rafts on the beach are used by archeologists, so we can stop and see what they're up to. Maybe it'll be Lucy Stanley, I like her."

The rafters climbed from the rafts, and followed West up a steep path through the rocks.

"Hopis have a special name for archeological sites," he said. "They call them 'places where our ancestors walked,' and they describe archeological fieldwork as 'looking for footprints'.

Archeologists from the Park Service catalogue the ruins on the river."

They reached a small clearing up on a terrace. A man stood with his back to them.

"Definitely not Lucy," Tess said.

The man turned around. He stood about five feet ten inches tall with a medium build, and he was dressed in a Park Service type uniform—regulation shorts, a short-sleeved shirt, and a hard brimmed hat. He had short, dark hair and a neatly trimmed dark beard. He adjusted his wide-brimmed hat and tucked his shirt into his shorts, squared his shoulders, and stared at the rafters ascending from the path.

"Hey Parker," West said. "What're you up to?"

The rafters spread out and walked across the dunes that rolled back towards the cliff. Some trudged up the sand and slid down. A few knelt and dug a hole and sifted the sand through their fingers.

"What you need to know," Parker said in a loud voice that carried across the sand, "is take only photographs and leave only footprints."

Even while he spoke, one of the men dug through the sand, picking up potsherds and stuffing them into his pockets.

"What the fuck are you doing?" the archeologist bellowed.

Tess quickly intervened, and the man tossed several artifacts back onto the sand. The archeologist stood with his hand out, and he collected additional pieces until the man turned his pockets inside out and scraped grains of sand clinging to the cotton fabric.

Claire stared across the landscape and tried to envision the ancient village site that must be buried under the sand. No structures or stonework were exposed. Wherever she looked she saw only sand and scattered potsherds. As she stared at the sand, she saw a worked piece of turquoise right in front of her, at her feet. The relic's deep pigment and squared edges stood in sharp relief against the colorless, rounded grains of the sand. With its bright color and squared form, it popped out from the sand, and the piece lay exposed on the ground like a shadow print of black on white. A small hole had been drilled along the top edge of the stone, and even from a distance the piece appeared magnificent; she stooped and picked it up.

The archeologist went crazy. That was the only way she could describe it. He began shaking and jumping up and down, but for a long time he didn't say anything. Claire held the piece in her hand and watched him. It took her a moment to realize he was reacting to her.

"You can't take that," he said.

"I wasn't taking it," Claire said. "I was looking at it."

"Let me see," Linny said, and she took the artifact from Claire's hand.

"No!" Parker screamed. "Put that down."

The guides jumped to action, placing themselves between Parker and Linny. Later, when she thought about it, Claire decided that the guides hadn't worried about her overreacting to Parker, but they'd worried about Linny's response. Maybe they knew Claire could be yelled at, and knew Linny couldn't. For whatever reason, West and Orion moved in front of Parker, and Theresa and Tess moved next to Linny.

For a moment no one else moved. Claire wanted to back off and move away from the crowd. The last thing she wanted was to be involved in an actual fight, out there in the middle of the wilderness. She put her hand on Linny's arm and felt Linny stiffen. Of course Linny wouldn't back off.

The archeologist slipped through the guides and lunged at Linny, grabbing for the relic clutched in her hand.

"You can't take that," he said.

"Don't you dare touch me," Linny answered. "Get your hand off me!"

Before Claire knew what was happening, Linny pushed both her hands against the archeologist's chest. He fell back and landed on his butt. Orion and West cornered him. Tess corralled Linny.

"Are you fucking crazy?" the man yelled.

To herself, Claire thought yes, maybe she is. She'd never seen Linny get so hot.

"Let's take a look," Tess said. "Quite an amazing piece of stone. What can you tell us about it, Parker?"

"It's old," he said, answering automatically, as a scientist rather than a protector, forgetting he was in the midst of an altercation. "Probably crafted in another part of the canyon—there's no known turquoise here. Possibly traded from outside the canyon, maybe southern Arizona."

Tess had taken the turquoise from Linny, and she held it out for everyone to see in the flat palm of her hand. She stroked the polished surface with her fingers. The curved edges were smooth and polished, and the chiseled grooves were rubbed soft and silky. Tess had seen many artifacts in the canyon, but none like this, with such exquisite workmanship. Holding the turquoise in her palm was quite a sensory experience. She wished someone would take the piece to a museum, but she knew enough to know that wasn't how it worked.

When everyone had seen the pendant, Tess handed it to the archeologist. Turning his back to everyone, the man stooped and pushed the turquoise into the sand, then he stomped the ground until it was well hidden. He stood on the sand above the buried treasure, his feet firmly planted, while the rafters walked from the site and made their way back towards the river.

With the immediate drama of the archeology find over, Claire remembered Dirk. She looked for him, wondering how he'd handled Linny's confrontation, but she didn't see him. Only when she stood at the edge of the terrace, with a view down to the river, did she see Dirk sitting on the edge of the raft. He sat facing the river, dangling his feet in the water. Theresa, the older guide whom Claire had paid little attention to, sat behind Dirk with her hands on his shoulders.

44

Day 7. Morning

Too bad you had to meet Parker, rather than Lucy," Tess said when they were back in the raft. "Archeology is really cool, unless Parker's explaining it."

"That turquoise pendant was something else," Linny said.

"I've found amazing artifacts down here," Tess said. "Last year I found a very plain neckband from a jug, and I took photos of it and showed Lucy, and she said it could be one of the oldest potsherds ever found in the canyon."

"What did you do with it?" Dirk asked.

"Just what Parker did with the pendant—buried it in the sand. Parker can be an asshole, but he always protects the archeology and almost always follows the rules. Lots of stuff's buried in the canyon. I've found obsidian pressure flakes scattered across the ground and fire-cracked rock poking up in rings. Those fire pits—pairs of concentric circles of rocks burned gray by fire and straight-cracked by high heat—are really fun to find. Lucy told me that using archeology to decipher human history is like figuring out a thousand-piece jigsaw puzzle with only a quarter of the pieces, and every time you're in the canyon, you can look for another piece to the puzzle."

For Tess, archeology provided a different way to organize her thoughts about the world. She liked thinking about the lives of ancient peoples, especially here, where their presence was so evident.

"I guess that's what all scientists do," Linny said. "The world's a puzzle, and they try to solve it. You've got rocks in Grand

Canyon formed a billion years ago, and the canyon itself took several million years to form. That's a geology puzzle, I would imagine."

Tess agreed, and the rafters, listening, all nodded, and Claire, who had known Linny since they were children, found that her friend still amazed her. There seemed to be nothing Linny didn't know about. As much as Claire was fascinated by archeology or geology or any other science, she was dependant on someone else framing the subject in a way that she could access. Only with the law could she set the framework. With everything else, she needed an established viewpoint. Sometimes she thought she was waiting for Paul to tell her how they were going to separate.

The rafts again lined up, one after another, and headed down the river. Tess was certain the water was higher than it had been just days before. The beaches were narrower than on her last trip, and the water moved more quickly. She knew she wasn't wrong. She'd been in this place before, just last month, and these beaches had less sand, and the river ran faster. She needed to talk to West about it, away from their passengers.

Claire sat in her usual spot on the right side of the raft, and as they moved down the river, she leaned out over the water and brushed her hand against a colossal rock slab, fifty feet tall, protruding from the water and falling back against the cliff behind it. It rose from the river as if from a world hidden deep below. More likely, Claire thought, the huge rock had cracked off a section of canyon wall hundreds of feet up, fallen down the cliff, and settled in the river. Or perhaps it had formed right where it was, there in the river, and the rock around it had eroded. In any case, Claire knew she noticed the rock only because she sat within scraping distance. On the other side of the boat, she wouldn't have noticed this monolith. On the other side, something else would have caught her eye.

45

Day 7. Afternoon

By afternoon an intense wind blew up the canyon, forcing sand off the beaches and stalling the rafts. In a section of the river with no rapids, where she didn't need to see where she was going, Tess turned the raft around to face upstream while she rowed down the river. This forced the rafters to sit with their backs to the wind, watching where they'd been and trusting where they were going as they inched down the canyon. Tess knew no one liked going backwards, and she did it only when it was absolutely necessary.

Claire folded her body over her knees, sheltering her face from the sand and water spraying through the air; she closed her eyes and tried to relax. She felt hotter and her skin felt drier than any time during the preceding week. When the wind gusted, Claire found it hard to breathe, as if she couldn't quite capture from the wind stream the small amount of air that she needed. On shore the few isolated bushes at the edge of the water bent into the river. Then, without warning, the wind subsided, and Tess pushed on the oars, and they again moved slowly down the river, and again Claire breathed.

Throughout the early afternoon, time slowed and stopped and started up again, and as they continued to face upstream, the river they'd already run disappeared around wide bends, the only sure sign of progress. In calm moments Claire turned around to see where they were headed. When the wind again picked up, as it invariably did, she turned back to stare upriver. She wondered if this weather forecast the approach of a storm.

As the wind swept up the river, it rearranged the sand on shore into ripples extending from the edge of the water to the base of the cliffs. It also spread the sand in waves across the canyon, the air lifting the sand into suspended curtains of sediment, a gossamer veil billowing out over the river.

"Change of plans," West announced as the rafts huddled together in an eddy below the large rapids. "We like to hike a side canyon when we're down here, but not today. Too much fucking wind. Not to mention we're too fucking slow and too damn tired."

Back in the current, Tess continued to push the raft down the river. With the sun overhead, the towering cliffs lost all shadows, and the shadings of red and purple that had highlighted the canyon disappeared from the washed-out rocks. The magnificent layered rock formations that revealed ancient sediment deposition vanished from the lower section of the canyon; instead, cliffs of dusty, hazy brown rock dropped into brown tinted water. The rocks and the river had changed color, creating a monotone world. The only sensory input Tess registered, other than the soreness and ache in her muscles, was the unrelenting push of the wind and the occasional roar of the rapids.

"I need everyone to paddle, using all your strength," Tess said. "It's the only way we're going to make it."

Claire hadn't noticed that she'd stopped paddling, but she had. She imagined the others had also, though she hadn't paid them any attention. Instead of pushing on her paddle, she merely dipped it into the water. Now she straightened her back and gripped the rubber handle. She braced her feet as best she could and leaned into the stroke. For the first few minutes, it was invigorating to have something other than the wind to think about. Quickly her arms ached and her back tired.

"This is a great workout," Linny said in front of her.

"I'll race you," Dirk answered.

46

Day 7. Afternoon

Most days the routine had them pulling off the river in late afternoon, giving everyone time to set up camp, explore, bathe, and relax. This day, they were still on the river as dusk approached. The wind hadn't died down for more than a couple minutes at a time, and most of the day they spent on the water, moving slowly down the canyon. Claire tried to paddle, to help Tess as much as she could, but she found it exceedingly difficult and tedious. Her arms hurt, her shoulders ached, her back stiffened, and all the time her mind wandered; again and again she lost her focus and forgot to paddle. Tess, sitting right there behind her, rowed hour after hour throughout the afternoon without stopping. Claire had no idea how she did it.

A week of adventure in Grand Canyon had slowed the tempo of everyone's life, interrupting the crazy multi-tasking demanded by the modern world. With no screens to study, Claire spent hours each day watching the river splash against the cliffs, looking away only to check the clarity of the water or the extent of the cloud cover. She imagined others did the same. Perhaps some of the rafters composed poems or symphonies in their heads. She couldn't tell by looking at them. She could only tell that one way or the other, everyone had settled into the new reality.

The slowness of this day, however, taxed each rafter's patience, and everyone seemed antsy. Tess tried to alleviate their boredom by imparting some of the social history and pointing out the natural features they passed.

The rocky, dry terrain sprouted cacti in abundance. Where not a spoonful of soil could be seen from the river, Barrel Cacti dotted a schist slope. Depending on the light, the schist looked dull and featureless or shiny and craggy. Always, the geologic formation looked like a relic from prehistoric times, an emissary from the earliest days of the earth's formation. Tess reminded everyone that the schist had looked silvery when they'd hiked up Blacktail Canyon. Here it appeared dark black, like a rock from earliest creation that had not yet absorbed any color.

"Can you see the three rock formations on river left?" she said. "Schist's at river level. The red sandstone and shale of the Supai Group is farther back and appearing above it. Above that, a little cap at the rim, is a very light-colored Kaibab Limestone."

The schist rose in straight columns, the sedimentary rocks stretched out in horizontal layers, and, from their vantage point on the river, huge blocks of limestone appeared perched on top of everything else. It was a new way for Claire to view the world. Since living in Santa Cruz, she'd grown accustomed to the verticality of the redwood forest in the mountains and the horizontal expansiveness of the Pacific Ocean at the coast. In Grand Canyon the geologic formations piled up, one on top of the other, vertical mixed with horizontal.

The kayakers pulled up beside them.

"We're gonna get a campsite. Join us," the man seemed to say. It was hard to hear over the howl of the wind, but Tess gave a thumbs-up, and the kayakers moved ahead.

"Paddle, paddle," Tess yelled to them. 'That's the only way we'll get off this river."

Claire fixed her eyes on the polished, scalloped rocks at the edge of the water and paddled. She counted strokes, and when she reached one hundred, she counted backwards. At zero, she started over. Tess turned the raft around so they were again facing into the wind. After hours on the river, nothing had changed—the wind hadn't died down, the blowing sand hadn't disappeared.

Claire tucked her head down and focused on her paddling. When she looked up, she saw the kayaks ahead, on the beach just before the river disappeared down the rapids. The guides didn't often camp above rapids; Tess said it gave them bad dreams. Claire hoped today would be an exception. She was tired and it was late, and she wanted to get off the river. West, in the first raft, angled to shore.

47

Day 7. Evening

W e wanted to get another ten miles downriver," Tess said, "but there was no way."

"So, what's that mean?" Linny asked.

"Means up early tomorrow and on the river late, especially if we want to hike."

"What about this trail heading up the side creek?" Dirk asked. "Can I walk up that now?"

"Too late," Tess said. "It'll be dark soon. We can go tomorrow morning, before breakfast, if you want."

Dirk nodded his head and went off to set up camp. Once again Claire thought how much more mature he was than her kids. They would never just accept a rational, reasonable answer when it didn't let them do what they wanted. Linny didn't seem to appreciate Dirk. Or, she seemed to assume he would be a rational and reasonable person, and she expected proper behavior. Even Claire's husband Paul, age forty-six, wasn't rational and reasonable, and his behavior was anything but proper.

The kayakers had pulled off the river at the far end of the beach, right next to the rapids. They waved when the rafters dragged their rafts from the water at the upstream edge of the sand, as far from the rapids as possible.

"I'm gonna talk to the kayakers," Tess said. "Orion, you're on for dinner."

Orion asked for everyone's help, and they prepared, ate, and cleaned up in record time. A full plate was put aside for Tess who didn't return from her visit to the kayakers until they had finished.

Tess pulled West aside before she ate, and they talked. She couldn't provide the assurance he wanted. She hadn't convinced the kayakers of anything. Neither Ellie nor Tim was willing to cut their trip short, and Ellie, particularly, seemed too inexperienced for the high water level they were experiencing. Tess thought West might try talking to them as the voice of authority. He told her he'd try.

A string of clouds moved up the canyon. Claire picked up a handful of sand and tossed it into the water. As she stood there watching the current, the sky darkened from sapphire to indigo to midnight blue, and the cliffs faded from vibrant oils to soft pastels to a faint, erased sketch. She hadn't realized it was so late. A planet appeared, then a satellite. The wind, which had died down during dinner, picked up again, and sand whipped across the beach, and though it seemed more and more likely a storm was coming, she waited to see a first star. Then she waited for a second. At that moment, she felt safe, though she knew she had no shelter and was, in fact, at nature's mercy. Eventually, white stars scattered across the blackened sky, a celestial negative of the archeologist's obsidian flakes sparkling on pale sands. Stars littered the sky, and the Milky Way lit the heavens. Maybe, she thought, she'd been wrong about the winds signaling a storm.

Tess finished dinner and pulled out a flask, and while she drank she stared into the dark canyon. At the edge of the river, out of the current, water bubbled onto the sand, released into soft pops, and seeped back to the main flow. When the wind quieted, the sounds of someone setting up camp echoed across the canyon's stillness. The darkness enveloped her. As evening drew to a close, clouds blew furiously across the sky, and one by one the stars vanished. The storm she'd known was coming finally arrived.

The folds in Tess' shirt filled with grit; sand grains wove into the fabric of her shorts and turned them brown. Her skin felt as coarse as sandpaper, and her eyes filled with dust. Invisible winds lifted sheets of sand from the beach on the opposite side of the river and hurled them across the water. Every gust blew handfuls of sand into her face.

Claire walked up the beach to check on her tent. Everything was tied down and covered, and even with a storm coming, nothing needed to be done. Though several passengers and the guides still sat at the river and she thought about heading back to shore to join them, she climbed into her tent and lay down.

Almost immediately her world shrank to the small confines of her tent. Wind blew through the camp like a speeding train. Rhythmic pulsations shook her tent and rippled through her body until she forgot where she was, aware only of the blowing, howling wind. Periodically the bellowing stalled and an unnatural quiet rushed in, followed by a loathsome roar. Streams of wind seeped into the tent through miniscule openings in the seams and zippers. A fine spray of rain blasted the fabric with a mixture of water and sand.

She lay on her sleeping pad and waited in the dark for another moment of quiet, invariably followed by the wind's roar and rumble and another spray of water and sand, and the pattern repeated over and over, again and again, through the elongated night. Eventually a heavy rain fell. She listened to the rain on her tent as the first rays of morning sun percolated into darkness, and she finally fell asleep dreaming of floods.

48

Diary Day 7

All in all, this wasn't our most exciting day, and I'm not sure any of you would have really enjoyed being here. It was windy almost every minute of the day, and you all would have hated it as much as I did. Sarah says she doesn't mind wind, but I'm pretty sure she would have minded this. The wind blew up the canyon, making it almost impossible for the rafts to make a steady progress down the river. We inched along, sometimes pushed backwards.

I never complained once. No one here even knew that I have a wind phobia. I wore a baseball cap, tucked my hair under the cap, and kept my chin down. I pulled up the collar on my shirt. The thing about wind, especially here, is that it really dries you out. I feel like a prune. My hands feel like sandpaper.

At home we worry about the wind toppling the huge fir trees. There's no such threat here—the wind won't collapse the cliffs. It won't send rocks flying. But it will lift sand from the beaches, spray it across the river, and spread it down the canyon. It embedded the sand in my skin and clothes; it coated my scalp with sand and filled my mouth with sand.

O.K. Enough. The good parts of the day: I woke up to tracks on the beach, outside the tent. They looked like bird and mice tracks. Birds are benign enough, still, I'm happy to sleep all zipped up and secure from roaming mice.

We started the day with a short hike up Blacktail Canyon, a side canyon near our camp. It was early morning and just starting to warm up—the perfect time for a walk. In the shadows, the cliffs appeared polished and full of color. Later, when the sun shone on the rocks, they lost all pigment and looked washed out and dull.

The highlight of the day was our visit to an archeology site where ancient peoples lived. Archeological features pockmark the canyon landscape, and scattered within these sites are pottery pieces called potsherds and worked stones called lithics. Some places there's jewelry, other places—human bones. It's totally exciting to walk across the sand and uncover a potsherd or a turquoise pendant right where an old Pueblo Indian left it. The archeologist told us about a sharp stone he found that he thought was used to attack a wooly mammoth around 10,000 B. C. Linny said she'd read in the guidebook that the oldest discovered artifacts near here were only several thousand years old. So the question is, did the archeologist discover something to change that date?

A bizarre rule is that no one is permitted to take anything from the canyon. You know the national park rule – take only photographs and leave only footprints. Well, even when someone finds a rare and exciting artifact, all he can do is bury it back in the sand. Even the archeologist, working for the Park Service, can't collect artifacts. If the piece is really important, like the wooly mammoth dagger, the archeologist takes a photo and records in his journal exactly where he found the artifact, but that's it. You need a collecting permit to take anything, and those permits are hard to come by.

The archeologist said the early cultures revolved around seasonal changes on the river, expecting floods from late summer monsoons and winter storms, anticipating drought in early summer and late fall. They moved up and down the canyon depending on the season. He also told us that finding artifacts sweetens the arid landscape with a sense of history. I thought that was a nice way to think about things. Greg, Sarah, want to be archeologists?

49

Day 8. Morning

Sitting on her sleeping bag inside her tent, Claire took inventory of herself. The muscles of her calves, the ones she used to climb in and out of the rafts and up and down the sandy beaches, twitched in a pattern of their own design. If she bent her legs and pressed her feet to the ground, she could quiet them, at least for a short time. When she did that, her hips ached, deep inside her pelvis where the bones connected. On the surface her scalp itched, and too much dirt caked her fingernails.

She didn't remember brushing against bushes or pushing through shrubbery, yet small cuts and scratches covered her lower arms. New scrapes added a shiny patina to her shins, and she did remember banging into the raft's metal storage boxes every time she climbed from one place to another. She squeezed antibiotic cream on the scrapes, ignoring her better judgment that she should first wash her hands and her legs. She rationalized that the river water wasn't very clean, and when she remembered the sterile wipes she'd brought, pushed to the bottom of the bag she'd left on the beach, she shrugged her shoulders and turned her attention to something else.

She rubbed salve into her severely chapped hands and rough, scaling feet, trying to regain the feel of normal skin. As soon as she finished rubbing the lotion in, the skin felt as rough as it had before, the lotion disappearing to no seeming effect. She hoped she wouldn't need to gray tape her feet as she'd seen West do when the skin of his heels split open.

She felt as if her body was failing her after a mere week in the desert. She wasn't strong enough to paddle the raft down the canyon. She was ill equipped for the sun, heat, and extreme dryness that each day brought. She was starting to break down. She hadn't slept well the previous night, and she hoped that was all it was— missing one night's sleep. She hoped a good night's sleep would restore her confidence and change her mood. Yet dry skin didn't plague a body deprived of sleep. Why was she falling apart? She couldn't remember feeling like this before.

She unzipped her tent. The sun was up, the day bright, and the wind calm. The storm had passed, and the canyon in daylight wasn't nearly as scary as the canyon at night. She found a patch of sunlight and stood with her eyes closed and her face to the sun, letting its warmth spread through her. Her mood lightened.

"Did you know that Grand Canyon is considered one of the seven natural wonders of the world?" Linny said.

Claire opened her eyes to see her friend standing before her. The sky remained cloudless and the sun bright; her mood started to darken.

"I was reading the guidebook this morning," Linny said. "The biggest rapids of the canyon are Lava Falls, another forty-five miles or so down the river. And the Vishnu Schist, exposed here in the Inner Gorge, is the oldest rock in the canyon – 1700 million years old."

Claire was certain she also knew something worth repeating, but she wasn't about to start her day reciting facts. Except, of course, if she could think of something remotely relevant, she would repeat it to Linny. Unfortunately, she couldn't remember anything, though she'd read the Grand Canyon guidebook at least twice.

"Orion's going to take me up the Tapeats Trail," Dirk said. "Want to come?"

Claire wanted to go, but not if Linny was going. She'd had enough lectures.

"Yeah, I'll get my water," Linny said and ran to her tent.

"Thanks, Dirk," Claire said. "Not this morning."

She thought of Paul. Sometimes it seemed they had been married too long, that her misery had no discernable beginning and no likely end, and during those times she thought she should leave Paul and start anew. Other times she thought the years disappeared too quickly, and if they just had a little more time, if she and Paul applied themselves and paid attention, they could work it out.

How typical, she often thought to herself. I never know if I should be stricter or more lenient with the kids. I don't know if I should do more or less work for the appeals I take. I don't know if I should quit or stay in my marriage. On the river, she now thought, rafters needed a mixture of rough and calm, not either-or. Rafting Grand Canyon wouldn't be as popular if the huge rapids disappeared, and it wouldn't be possible if the calm moments vanished.

Tess was moving gear around her raft, when Claire walked to the edge of the river to ask a question.

"Tess, did a Mormon really live here with multiple wives?" she asked.

"Yup," Tess answered. "In the 1800's a wagon road followed Vermillion Cliffs east from Utah, and the site where we launched, now known as Lees Ferry, was one of the few places to cross the Colorado. John Doyle Lee moved to the site and operated a ferry across the river during the 1870's. After he was executed in 1877 for the massacre of non-Mormon pioneers, his seventeenth wife Emma continued to operate the ferry."

"That seems impossible," Claire said. "I'm having a hard time having one husband. Just one-on-one seems too hard."

"I haven't even gotten that far," Tess said.

"I don't imagine it's easier with more people involved."

"I wouldn't think so," Tess said. "It's fun, but a challenge, to keep all the personalities on a river trip happy. And usually, only a couple people, at most, are sharing partners."

50

Day 8. Morning

The kayakers didn't join them for breakfast. Instead, the young adventurers hit the water early, before the rafters had assembled on the beach, while the canyon still slept in the shade. Tess dragged around the kitchen without enthusiasm, absorbed in her worries about Ellie and Tim. She'd counseled them to stay with the rafts, when it was clear they wouldn't abort their trip, but they'd rejected everything she advised. She knew she hadn't gotten through to them. West told her he'd talked to them, but he'd also had no luck. The couple was certain they'd been through the worst.

As she ate, Claire watched a honeyed sunlight drench the cliffs and beach. When it was time to go, she stood in the sunshine facing east with her eyes squeezed shut and her face upturned until she warmed up, and then she climbed aboard the raft. In an instant all traces of warmth vanished; she might have stepped into a walk-in cooler. As Tess rowed and the passengers paddled and the raft moved downriver on the current, they created a slight breeze that chilled them even more. No one said a word, each rafter wrapped up in his own discomfort. The stillness of the canyon floated just above the water, a perk for their cold, punctual start.

They'd only been on the river for a short time when the canyon narrowed and all traces of sand again disappeared from the banks of the river. The craggy cliffs dropped straight into the water. Claire imagined she could reach across the canyon to touch the deeply hued metamorphic and igneous rock. On the other side of the raft, Dirk held his arms out, as if he were trying.

"Granite narrows," Tess said. "Narrowest point on the river. In another mile, we're stopping."

Small pockets of sand emerged on both sides of the river, and the guides steered the rafts to river right and pulled onto a sliver of beach. The red and yellow kayaks had been dragged from the water, and they rested on a ledge of rock.

"Deer Creek," West yelled across to all the rafts. "One of the best hikes in the canyon."

The rafters gathered water bottles and slathered sunscreen. Tess walked among them urging them to tighten their sandal straps. It was a spectacular hike and not too long, she said, but somewhat technical.

Within minutes they reached the magnificent falls with a drop of almost two hundred feet. Cutting through the horizontally layered Tapeats Sandstone, the water fell with such force onto the igneous rocks below that it set up water and wind currents across the small plunge pool. Dirk waded in, aiming to crouch under the falls like he'd done at Elves Chasm, but with no luck. The power of the falls was too great, and he couldn't get close. No one else even tried.

The grotto wasn't quite as delicate as Elves Chasm, and Tess needed to assure everyone that it would get better and was worth the effort. They'd only seen the lower part of Deer Creek, she told them. As soon as they rested, they'd continue up the trail, to the top of the falls and the view up the river.

They took a trail heading up an adjacent hillside. Claire recognized the poison ivy lining the path; it wasn't very different from the poison oak that covered the mountains near home.

"Are you familiar with poison ivy?" she asked Dirk, and when he shrugged, not really understanding her question, she grabbed his shirt to make him stop, pointed out the plant, and described its unwelcome effect.

The trail wasn't too hard, until they needed to angle out over a bottomless slot canyon, with their lower bodies balanced underneath on overhanging rock. Claire didn't think she could do it. She watched Linny and Dirk and several other passengers. She saw that the physics of the angle kept each hiker's body firmly planted on the trail. She saw that it could be done, if only she could quiet her fears.

"We'll help," Tess said, before Claire had said anything. "West will be on the far side of the overhang, and he'll take your right hand. Hold the overhead rocks with your left hand. Give me your pack. I'll be here, and I'll guide you. We've done this before."

Linny and Dirk were around the bend in the trail and out of sight. All the other hikers had continued down the path. No one but Claire remained.

"I know my fear is irrational," Claire said. "I think I'm going to fall into the crack."

"That's not the way to do it," Tess said. "Just do what we tell you. Don't think at all."

Claire shook her head. A semantic trick wasn't going to help her. For an instant she wished she were older. Maybe if she were mid-fifties, just ten years older, she'd be comfortable turning around. She'd be old enough to stop. But how could a woman her age, a woman in her prime, as all the literature said, not make it to the top? Linny, of course, was oblivious to Claire's distress. She didn't know Claire wasn't right behind her. She didn't know Claire.

No one has fallen, Claire told herself. No one has disappeared into the bottomless crevasse. If that had happened, they wouldn't continue hiking this route. She handed Tess her pack, then she grabbed the cliff with her hand and inched forward. She held her other hand out, waiting for West to grab it. She needed several more steps before he could reach her. The muscles in her right thigh started to twitch.

"Keep moving," Tess said. "Press down on your right foot."

Claire shuffled her feet forward, keeping contact, and felt West grab her hand. With the security of his grip, she made it the rest of the way, tilted out from under the overhang. Tess followed. West squeezed her hand then left them, walking quickly to catch up with the others, and Tess stayed behind Claire, to bring up the rear.

The trail continued over rough, horizontal ledges, through the slot canyon of Deer Creek Gorge, and they walked along a rock shelf part way up the cliffs. Claire had never imagined anything so spectacular: a narrow channel of curving walls that glowed in reflected light, the hikers suspended mid-cliff. Far below, the slender, clear Deer Creek wound through the layered bedrock, and above, an impossibly blue sky appeared in slivers between the towering rocks.

"We're almost at the patio," Tess said, "and that's the best part."

The upper canyon widened, and the creek below disappeared from view. A wide bench of smooth, sedimentary rocks spread out alongside a rushing creek as it cascaded into a waterfall. Small groups of rafters reclined on the sandstone, the image of complete relaxation. The bright yellow flowers of blooming cacti provided spots of intense color. It might have been the most beautiful place Claire had ever been.

"Worth it, huh?" Tess said, and Claire nodded.

She'd only been resting a few minutes when Orion announced he was organizing a group to climb down into the gorge. Dirk and Linny were the only rafters who wanted to go. Tim and Ellie, the kayakers, sat nearby and asked if they could join. Linny couldn't have been happier. Dirk didn't seem as delighted.

Claire strolled across the patio, along the creek, looking for its source, and stopped where the running water emerged through a screen of small trees and flowed into a very small pool. Watercress bordered the pond on one side. She turned back, uninterested in wading the pool and pushing her way through the brush.

The explorers returned. Dirk told of climbing down into the gorge and wading in the creek until it dropped in a huge waterfall. Linny said it was scary. Claire was happy to have stayed where she was. She took deep breaths to prepare herself for the hike back.

51

Day 8. Afternoon

The rocks changed again. They were back in the Tapeats Sandstone. Tess announced the change to her rafters, and as everyone peered at the cliffs, noticing the change from the metamorphosed rocks of the morning, Bighorn sheep appeared on the talus canyon slopes. Tess pointed these out also, commenting on their huge, curved horns that curled back on themselves and their light brown fur that blended perfectly with the rocks. She explained that they frequented rocky slopes where their excellent climbing skills were an advantage, and that they were most often seen in late fall to winter, when they rutted.

"Now, in spring, the males and females live separately, which is why we see only the males with the big horns. The smaller-horned females and their new babies are somewhere else.

"The water's still getting higher," she said without thinking. "Every day it's higher."

"Isn't that what the scientists said?" Claire asked. "I think they expected high water for the next few weeks."

"Yeah, but this seems higher than you'd expect from an increase spill to accommodate snow melt. Well, maybe not."

Tess shook her head, to focus her thoughts. She shouldn't have said anything about the water. She didn't want a raft of anxious paddlers. In all her years guiding, she'd never said anything to make others nervous. Why was she starting now?

Claire looked at the river downstream, in front of the raft, and turned around to look up river. She couldn't tell if the level was significantly higher than it had been. She had no frame of reference against which to measure the river. The water did look different, though, and she realized with a start that the water had been changing. The clear, sparkling water they'd rafted for over a week had turned a dull, muddy brown.

"When did the clear water turn brown?" she asked.

"Yesterday it lost its sparkle, but it was subtle; today is the first day it's really muddy-colored," Tess said, not knowing how to lie or change the subject.

Claire thought about it and remembered noticing that the water had turned brown, blending with the rocks. She'd thought it had been the river reflecting the color of the cliffs. She thought that was the previous day, though it might have been the day before that.

"Does the water color have to do with the water level being higher?" Claire asked.

"Possibly," Tess said. "It means there's more sediment in the river. More mud. The question is how it got there."

"What are the possible options?" Dirk asked.

Tess took a deep breath. "The most usual is that a side creek flooded and brought in sediment. That happens. But it happens when there are huge storms in the area, and I don't know that we've had anything like that recently. Last night was a localized storm, not a regional one.

"What else?" Dirk asked.

"I don't really know."

Claire understood that Tess knew more than she was saying. Dirk shrugged his shoulders and turned back to paddling. Linny looked at Tess then turned away.

Claire's first thought was that she could rely on Tess or Linny. She didn't need to figure this out. Her second thought was that she always did that—waited for someone else to take the lead.

Linny had researched colleges when they were in high school, figuring out where each of them should apply. They both went to Paris, chosen by Linny, for a semester during their junior years. They celebrated their graduations with a trip to Ireland, again chosen by Linny.

Maybe, Claire thought, it was this pattern of acquiescence that caused her problems with Paul. She never fully asserted herself. She acted as if he were Linny, and he wasn't anything like Linny. His choices weren't nearly as good.

When they stopped for lunch, Linny paced across the sand. Claire watched her for a moment, then caught up with her.

"It's impossible not having internet access," Linny said. ""I need to know things."

"What?" Claire said.

"Why the river's muddy."

Claire nodded. They had become so accustomed to instantly knowing everything. No one made decisions anymore without a surfeit of information. Perhaps Linny would figure out how to get information when no one else could. Claire left Linny and made herself a sandwich. She heard Dirk tell his mom that he and Orion were going to walk up Kanab Creek.

"We're not going far," he said. "We're not going to make it anywhere near the falls."

Linny nodded absent-mindedly. Claire stood up to join them, but realized, as she was about to call to Dirk, that she hadn't been invited.

She picked up a soft drink and carried it over to a woman sitting at the edge of the river, staring at the cliffs across the canyon. Amy was probably around fifty, though Claire, afraid that she might be very wrong, would never actually make a guess.

"I think there's a condor sitting on that ledge," Amy said. "It's hard to see. This is the first I've seen, if that's what it is."

Amy pulled out a pair of binoculars and held them up to adjust the focus. The dark creature on the opposite cliff spread its wings.

"It's a condor," she said, "I can see its number. No. 87." She handed the binoculars to Claire. Tess walked over.

"Oh, I've seen 87 before," Tess said. "It hangs out in the canyon."

"They have numbers?" Claire said.

Tess explained that California Condors were one of the rarest birds in the world, and Grand Canyon was participating in a condor re-introduction and recovery program. As part of that program, all condors were captured and tagged.

"In the last few years," she said, "several condors have frequented the canyon. I think No. 87 has a nest nearby."

The condor flew off, heading up the canyon.

"Time for us to head down. We're stopping at Matkat."

52

Day 8. Afternoon

Several miles down the river the shoreline along the left bank filled with rafts—rafts tied to rafts tied to rafts.

"Matkatamiba Canyon," Tess said. "Hardest part of this canyon is parking the rafts. Everyone stops here, just like the Little Colorado and Phantom Ranch."

Orion pushed his raft between two others, and one of his passengers jumped off and pulled the raft onshore. Theresa, West, Riz, Mark, and Tess tied off behind Orion, securing their rafts to his raft and to each other's rafts.

"I guess you've done this before," Linny said, and everyone laughed.

To reach shore, the rafters on Tess' raft first climbed onto Theresa's raft, then Orion's raft, and from there they climbed onto rock.

"Is this really worth it?' someone asked.

"It is so worth it," West said.

The rafters assembled on shore and followed West and one another, single file, up the trail. Within minutes the wide river corridor and then the harsh desert sunlight vanished. The trail narrowed, the walls closed in, and the hikers entered a shaded slot-canyon, narrower and curvier than any they had seen. The exquisite striated limestone walls of the canyon reflected or emitted (it was impossible for Claire to tell which) a filtered glow, and the hard stone of creamy-gold tan and blue-slate gray seemed to soften. For the second time that day Claire stood surrounded by extraordinary beauty, beauty even greater than that of the canyon itself.

She spread her arms and put a hand on each undulating wall and felt the cool rock beneath her fingers. She splashed through a trickling stream of clear, warm water. Dirk balanced with both feet on one wall and braced his back against the opposite wall, and he maneuvered down the narrow canyon without stepping into the creek, keeping his feet dry.

A small waterfall spilled down smooth, stone steps, and the rafters climbed up the cascade to an even narrower canyon with a steady flow of sparkling water and intermittent, deep pools that forced those wearing long shorts to roll up their pants legs to keep them dry. Dirk walked with a foot on each wall. Where the canyon was too narrow for Claire to place both her feet side-by-side, she walked with one foot placed in front of the other. In the tightest spots, she kept her feet pointed straight ahead but turned her body sideways and sucked in her stomach. She didn't know if Paul, with his newly acquired beer-belly, could have made it through.

She wished her kids were there. She'd never been anywhere like this—shimmying up and down the beautiful, slick cliffs, splashing in and out of the deep or shallow, crystalline pools and the clear, narrow streams. It was a fantasyland, but so much better in being real and natural, and one of the most tactile, sensual experiences she could imagine having out of doors. She stepped into a small pool, and the tadpoles scurried away. Tender, young plants cascaded down the rocks in a flowering, hanging garden. Greg and Sarah would have loved it as much as she did; she was certain. She didn't know about Paul. She never knew about Paul anymore. But maybe she wasn't being fair. Who wouldn't love Matkatamiba?

The narrow gorge eventually expanded into an open amphitheater, and the muted, pale colors that had radiated in the confined canyon now shimmered in the golden sunlight. They'd reached a hidden place, invisible from the river, and it took Claire's breath away; she felt momentarily disoriented by the sheer magnificence of the oasis.

"Being here almost seems like a religious experience," Linny said, and Claire, who wholeheartedly agreed, thought how uncharacteristic it was for her friend to express such sentiments.

"I wish I had a video camera," Linny added. "Still photos won't really capture the majesty. But I'll try. Go stand over there, and I'll take your picture. Dirk you too. Over there, next to Claire."

Claire and Dirk stood and moved as Linny directed. Claire didn't mind. It gave her an opportunity to stand still and look around. One moment she'd observed a two-dimensional world created by the likes of Dr. Seuss, where thin, horizontal layers of different colored rocks stepped into amazing configurations, and the next moment the landscape morphed into a sensuous, three-dimensional jigsaw puzzle, the rocks undulating and curving all around her.

When Linny had finished photographing, Claire took a few snapshots of her own. The afternoon quickly disappeared, and Claire had been sitting for only a couple minutes, soaking up the calm peace that spread down the hidden canyon, when West called the rafters to assemble for the hike back to the rafts.

Back on the water, a little over a mile downriver from Matkatamiba, just after Mile 149, the rafts entered the quiet, calm tongue of Upset Rapids. The hypnotizing magic of the ethereal side-canyon vanished, and the dangers inherent in running the Colorado River reappeared.

"We've got to avoid the huge central hole," Tess yelled. "There's a super big drop on the other side."

The escalating roar of the water drowned out all other sounds. Tess offered additional instruction, but no one heard. A soft canyon breeze caressed Tess' cheeks, mocking the anticipated danger, and for the moment Tess hung suspended in the anticipation of the rapids. She pulled her oars from the water and balanced them on the side tubes of the raft. She let the raft descend slowly, gliding along water as smooth and polished as reflective glass. Only when the raft slid from the tongue and tumbled into the rapids did she drop her oars back into the river to fight the current.

They slammed into the first wave, and the water pushed the raft toward the hole that she needed to avoid. Her muscles tensed, though she tried to stay relaxed, and her heart beat faster. The rush of the current drove them straight towards the hole. She strained against the oars. The raft continued towards the hole until right at the last moment, she forced the raft toward the channel on the left, right where she wanted to be. As quickly as they entered the rapids, they left it and resumed floating down the river, and before anyone in her raft was ready, before they'd dried off, Tess pulled ashore to make camp.

53

Day 8. Evening

West stood atop the baggage piled on his raft and looked up and down the sand. He planned the night's camp and directed where the rafts should dock and tie off, where they should set up the camp kitchen, and where they should locate the river toilet. He told everyone what to do.

"We could raft a little longer, it's early enough," Tess said, "but this is the best camp to get us to Havasu Canyon at the right time tomorrow morning. We'll spend most of the day there."

"I saw the most amazing photos of Havasu," Linny said.

Claire grabbed a beer and walked to the edge of the water. Before opening the beer, she pulled her next-to-the-last flask from her bag and took a long drink. Nothing happened that Linny didn't know about. She knew every rock formation they saw and remembered reading about every place they visited. Once again Claire faced up to the fact that Linny remembered everything that Claire had read and forgotten. Usually Claire appreciated Linny's ability to recall facts and details; she liked being impressed by her friend. Day eight of this trip, though, and she'd had enough.

She was nursing her second beer when the kayakers pulled to shore and asked if they could join the camp. Tim said private boaters had claimed the small site a mile or so up the river, and when he and Ellie stopped there, the man they spoke with told them to keep going. West and Orion shook their heads.

"Hope they never need anyone's help," Orion said.

"This area's notorious for having few camps," West said. "Of course you can camp here. And join us for dinner. That should reward you for floating the extra mile."

Ellie and Tim pushed their kayaks onto the sand at the lower stretch of beach and removed their life jackets, both close-fitting, bright red and yellow, in the same style as those the guides wore, nothing like the pumpkin-style jackets that the commercial passengers wore. The couple tossed their jackets across the kayak hulls to dry and immediately started pulling off their wet, outer clothing, jackets and pants. Even when they'd finished, they wore more than the warm, late-afternoon air required, but Ellie, so thin, without any fat, shivered.

"Kayaking must be hard work," Claire said to Tess.

"I remember how hungry I was after a day in a kayak," Tess said.

"You still kayak?" Claire said.

"No, not any more. Only when I was younger, before I became a guide," Tess said. "Do you know the Kern River in California? I grew up on the Kern."

Claire knew the Kern. It was in the mountains, outside of Bakersfield.

"She's a river rat," West said, approaching the women. "The Kern was her first love, and now she's devoted to the Colorado. Basically, that's all you need to know about Tess."

Tess smiled. "Sounds weird," she said, shrugging her shoulders, "but it's true."

About a half hour later, the science rafts pulled up and also asked to camp.

"Did you try to camp a mile up the river?" Tim asked.

"No, we thought we'd try here," one of the guides said. "We didn't think we'd have a good chance camping with a private trip.

And we didn't really want to. We hoped a private trip hadn't taken over this camp."

The researcher guides pulled their rafts up behind the kayaks and tied off. The scientists scattered across the sand and their guides headed to the kitchen area.

"Let's plan a feast," one of them called out.

West crouched in the sand, before a large aluminum box of pots and pans. He started to pull out what they needed for dinner, banging the pots and pans, creating his own kitchen symphony and drowning out the reggae booming from Orion's speakers. Tess found the canvas bag that held the water filter and pulled out the biggest pieces. She threaded pipes, attached the handle, and dug the base into the sand. She loosed a five-gallon bucket from a tall stack and walked into the river until it was deep and less murky, and she filled the bucket with water.

Remembering her high school science, Claire knew that five gallons of water weighed more than forty pounds. She watched to see if any of the men would run to help Tess. No one did, and Tess carried the bucket back up the beach without apparent strain. Claire didn't think she could do that. She didn't think Linny could either. She didn't know about Dirk.

Once the water was set up, Tess opened a tin of oysters and a box of crackers and announced the appetizers. Someone from the science trip added chips and salsa and pickled asparagus. Tim and Ellie arrived at the table before the food was completely arranged, as if they couldn't wait any longer.

"When I was fourteen and kayaking, I was either on the water or eating," Tess said. "There was nothing else."

Ellie ate a few chips and salsa, and then two unadorned crackers, no oysters. Claire didn't think that was the kind of hunger Tess was talking about. Claire herself ate much more.

Dinner was simple and elegant—steak, rice pilaf, and salad. It wasn't the best choice for vegetarians, but no one complained, and Claire wasn't sure if anyone on the trip ate vegi. On a small plate at the end of the buffet, a few vegi burgers waited for those eschewing the meat. When Claire filled her plate, the meat substitute had not yet been touched.

She sank into a chair at the edge of the surf and stared at the water where the angle of the sun created a seamless pattern that merged the river's reflections and the sparkle of the water. Across the river, the cliffs glowed in the setting sun. Along the beach, warm breezes wafted over the sand, whispering clues to the canyon's mysteries. She enjoyed the meal as much as any dinner she'd ever eaten. The meat was tender and cooked just right, the food of gods.

Cocooned in the lingering warmth that rose from the sandy beach, she slowly sipped a cold Coors. She sat next to a woman geologist about her own age. The woman introduced herself and told Claire she'd done lots of fieldwork around the world, but nothing compared to being in Grand Canyon. Nothing in the world was as important to her as Grand Canyon.

"That's what my husband said on the night he moved out," the woman said, "and I knew then, and I know now, that it's true."

She told Claire that she'd devoted much of her life to Grand Canyon, and that she cared deeply about its preservation. Time after time, over the years, with the narrow focus of which her husband had complained, she'd rafted down the river collecting data and then sat in her office processing the information.

"And you think your data, or anyone's data, will convince the dam operators to change dam operations so more sediment comes through?" West asked.

The geologist shrugged, and Claire looked at her. It was obvious the woman had more to say but was restraining herself.

"There's always the possibility of a sediment pipeline," she said, "or increased floods when conditions are right, bringing in sediment from side canyons."

She was thin, with very straight, light brown hair and symmetrical, even features. She looked rather unexceptional, and not that different from Claire, in a large-canvass kind of way. Yet, Claire thought, they were nothing alike. The geologist's plain appearance seemed to hide immense passion, about her work and about Grand Canyon, and Claire had never had that much passion about anything. She hadn't cared so much about the law, even on the first day of her first job. Now, almost twenty years later, she was practically passionless. She wondered if everyone knew that. She wondered if it were written across her face.

54

Day 8. Evening

Evening approached, and the first stars emerged in the darkening sky. Most days, Dirk went off by himself as soon as dinner was over, as if he'd had enough grown-up time and needed to escape. Or at least that's how Claire saw it. That's how she would feel if she were on this trip as a sixteen year old. She remembered counting the minutes until she could leave the dinner table when she was a teenager, and now she was surprised if Greg and Sarah lingered after eating. She reasoned they were still young, still children, even though Greg was twelve, and she'd certainly had enough of her mother by that age.

Dinner was winding down when Orion called Dirk over and introduced him to a young man sitting next to West, a couple seats away from Claire. Orion said Will had graduated from college the year before and now worked for the Grand Canyon Study Group. He was on his eighth trip down the river. He had a girlfriend in town and the attention of all the young female scientists and the young female guides on the river. Orion immediately had Dirk's attention. In fact, he had almost everyone's attention.

"I had no idea," Tess said. "So, you're saying he's a playboy? That's it for me – I thought I was his only love."

"But Tessy," West said, "you were number one whenever he saw you!"

"Hey people," Orion said, "I'm trying to give Dirk here some valuable information about how things work in the world. Time for the rest of you to clean up the kitchen."

Claire loved that Orion had taken Dirk under his wing. She wondered if that was because of who Orion was, or who Dirk was, or if the two of them just clicked.

Linny, on the other hand, didn't look pleased, but she hung back. Claire knew that took quite an effort on her friend's part. Linny liked to participate in everything, and she wouldn't like someone she didn't know and hadn't chosen, advising Dirk.

"What do you do?" Dirk asked Will. "What was your major in college?"

"I should have majored in geology," Will said, "but that's not what I did. I didn't know I could get a job like this. So, I majored in engineering, cause I knew I needed to work when I graduated, and engineers can get jobs."

"Is engineering needed here?" Dirk asked.

"Yeah, in a way," Will said. "I know how to work with code and with equipment, and both are integral to the work here. It's just that I would have liked majoring in geology, I think, and I didn't like engineering."

"Well, it worked for you," Linny said, "to major in something concrete, with job prospects."

Claire was one hundred percent certain that Linny had majored in Philosophy, a subject that was not particularly concrete, at least not then, and one that had no job prospects that Linny would have wanted. She didn't feel as if she could comment, though. She stood up and walked across the sand towards her tent.

She was looking down at the sand, watching the light from the camp lanterns dim, when she looked up and Brent was there, before her.

"The evening's still young," he said.

"I'll be right back, I just need to get something from my tent," she said, and she hurried away and didn't return, not knowing what to do.

55

Diary Day 8

Today we hiked to Deer Creek Falls and to Matkatamiba Canyon. I'm writing this as a reminder to myself, so I'll remember to tell you about these amazing hikes when I get home. I took lots of photos so you can see these places. Linny also took photos and will send me hers. If I can find a book with photos, I think I'll buy it.

Even after only a week, we all know each other quite well. You wouldn't think a week is a particularly long time, but it feels like it is. Or maybe, Greg and Sarah, you always feel like a week passes slowly, but I'd forgotten that childhood sense of time. In part, it feels like summer camp. It may be time to look for a sleepover camp for Greg and then later, for Sarah. The experience is unique.

We all get up at the same time, stand in line to use the port-a-potty, and have breakfast together. We line up along the river with our water bottles to wash our faces and brush our teeth, spitting our toothpaste out into the current. Then we divide into five rafts, almost always into the same raft with the same people. Except for breaks to hike, explore, or have lunch, we are in the rafts until we stop to make camp.

That's a lot of togetherness, and we get to know everyone's quirks and defects. As a glass-half-empty kind of person (I know that's how you all think of me), I'm more aware of everyone's flaws than I am of anyone's strengths, although I have noticed that a couple people are quite impressive, and I am doing my best to be a good sport. The guides are definitely the most pleasant, all the time. I guess that's part of the job. Maybe you don't become a guide unless you can both handle and enjoy this particular style of togetherness. I think of it as collective solitude.

Dirk has become almost as agreeable as the guides. I think perhaps he is modeling himself on them, since he arrived here rather sullen. Or maybe he's just more relaxed, away from his NYC life, just like the rest of us. I don't know. I definitely like having him on the trip, though he doesn't say much to me.

The scientists and the kayakers camped with us last night, and that changed the group – adding new people to our dinnertime conversation. I liked listening to the researchers talk about Grand Canyon, explaining the ecology of the river and giving opinions on how the river should be managed. It seemed I was hearing the inside scoop.

Also, it was inspiring to hear the scientists talk about their work. They're collecting data for an environmental impact study, and most of them have been working on this one project for years. When the report finally comes out, it will determine operations at Glen Canyon Dam for the next ten years, and thereby determine conditions downstream on the Colorado River through the Grand Canyon. The guides say there's much less sand on the beaches now and that it's difficult to find a good camping spot, and they all agree that Glen Canyon Dam is to blame.

Someone mentioned the possibility of taking out the dam, and years ago I read Edward Abby who wrote stories about such things. But our guide wants the dam to stay. She says the river would be too wild without any dam. I guess everyone agrees there's a problem, but disagrees on the solution. At least there's no skepticism about the validity or role of science, and that's refreshing. Everyone sitting there at the river believed more data and sophisticated scientific analysis could improve the situation. I loved getting a glimpse of the scientific world for an evening.

The following is for me, and probably not of interest to anyone else:

For the last day or two I've been thinking how extraordinary it is to be part of the rafting group. I both feel a sense of intimacy with the other members of the group, and at the same time I have an awareness of deep isolation from everyone else. It may be my unique psychology, but I feel the paradox of joining in intimate contact while remaining separated in isolation, and I'm filled with contradictory emotions.

56

Day 9. Morning

U p, up, up," West called out. "We want an early start today."
Claire had worked to adapt to the rafting routine, and she thought she'd done well. She'd learned to rise in the dim obscurity of morning, amidst murky shadows, when only a mere hint of light bathed the tops of the mesas. She dressed automatically in layers, knowing it would be cold in the morning and scorching by afternoon. She poured herself a cup of coffee as soon as she entered the make-shift kitchen, and she ate breakfast whether she was hungry or not, knowing the kitchen would be cleaned and packed in an hour when she was actually ready to eat. She trained herself to use the toilet when it was available.

On that ninth morning she lay in her tent, submerged in a heavy slumber, when West's alert woke her. Neither a glimmer of light nor an inkling of sunshine reached her. All her training vanished, and her pride in following the river's rules evaporated; she couldn't force herself to move.

West and Orion walked through the camp waking the rafters. Claire could hear them at the different tents, announcing the start of the day and urging everyone to get moving. She was listening for the next announcement, somewhere across the sand at another campsite, when the walls of her tent shook.

"O.K. sleeping beauty," West said. "It's time for you to rise."

"Or, better option—I could join you," he said, after a pause, in a much quieter voice.

Claire didn't say a word. She barely breathed.

"O.K.," he said, "I'll assume that means you're getting dressed. See you in a couple minutes."

Silence again settled across the camp, except for sounds of someone in the kitchen. Perhaps, Claire thought, she'd imagined West speaking to her and shaking her tent. She tried to convince herself he'd been speaking to Linny, until she realized she hadn't seen Linny and West together in several days. Whatever they had going those first days on the river, had faded. Claire had noticed and not noticed at the same time.

No longer groggy with sleep, she combed her fingers through her hair and buttoned and straightened her shirt. She climbed from the tent, pulled her sleeping pad and sleeping bag out, and left them and her tent to dry. She was the first rafter to arrive in the kitchen.

Tess and Orion stood at the stove, mugs in hand, and poured coffee for each other. West walked up, and Tess poured for him. Theresa arrived next, and West poured for her.

"Theresa's little routine," Tess said. "She likes this polite formality, pouring coffee for one another, to get everyone's day off to a good start."

"There's other ways to get the day off to a good start," West said.

Orion looked at West and at Claire. When he looked at Tess, she shrugged.

"I'm sure there are," he said.

Claire went back to packing her gear, and when she finished she walked over to where Linny was folding her tent.

"Here," she said, "I'll hold this part so you can pull it tight."

Linny looked up and nodded, and they both crouched down to get the tent into the stuff sack.

"What's happened with you and West?" Claire said.

"Nothing much," Linny said. "Why?"

"I just realized that you seemed immersed in a river romance, and now I'm not aware of anything going on."

"Well, believe it or not," Linny said, "West didn't feel comfortable about Dirk."

"Does he have teenage kids?"

"No, no kids," Linny said, "but he said his mom had lots of boyfriends when he was growing up, and he hated being forced to spend time with them. He didn't mind her having boyfriends, but he didn't like being involved."

"That makes sense," Claire said.

"Well, not to me," Linny said. "Whatever West and I had, it had nothing to do with Dirk. I'm pissed."

57

Day 9. Morning

It was still early morning and cool on the river when they pulled alongside the rocks below Havasu Creek. Rafters had already begun arriving, blocking the creek's mouth with rafts and kayaks. Claire couldn't imagine where they all came from and why she hadn't seen them as they floated down the river. More rafts had accumulated than she'd seen at any of the other stops except, perhaps, Phantom Ranch.

She forgot whatever it was she'd been thinking as soon as she glimpsed the turquoise water spilling from the side canyon into the Colorado. The tributary flowed into the larger river, its water seeping around the parked rafts and stopped abruptly at the water of the Colorado's main current. She'd never seen anything like it, though it reminded her of a photo she'd seen of the merging of the Rio Negro and the Amazon River, where currents of different colors flowed side-by-side. The Colorado seemed the same as a couple days earlier, not nearly as clear as when they started out, with a translucent brown hue, and the aquamarine color of Havasu Creek was more intense than the Little Colorado, which had been somewhat milky. She'd thought that earlier confluence spectacular, but it was just preparation for this one. At first glance the electric-blue water of the creek seemed unreal and unnatural, yet the longer she stared, the more perfect she found it.

"Isn't this wonderful?" Tess said. "My heart lifts as soon as I get here."

"Crazy," Dirk said.

They tied the rafts to the rocks and climbed to a trail. A surprisingly level, horizontal path clung to the side of the vertical rock wall and wound around into the narrow canyon. The rafters walked single-file, and Claire followed behind Linny who followed Dirk. At the entrance to Havasu Canyon the rafters stopped, astounded, needing time to make sense of the sensational view.

As soon as they turned the corner, the massive, solid gray cliffs of the Colorado River disappeared, replaced by crumbly, vibrant red layers of rock, stacked high into towering walls and blocking out much of the sky. Between those tall, craggy bluffs, Havasu Creek tumbled down a series of dramatic rock formations into pool after pool of vividly colored water, dotted with huge, rounded boulders.

It wasn't just that she'd never seen anything like Havasu Canyon; it was also that she'd never, until that moment, imagined such magnificent, intricate beauty. Part way up the creek, a rock ledge spread under the flowing water and across the canyon, and the creek flowed over it, and as it fell it divided into numerous, tiny cascades. The deep blue turquoise water turned white as it spilled down each of the falls and glowed as if lit by an inner light. In the pools below the waterfalls, the water shimmered.

Before she could fully register what she saw, Dirk slid down from the path into the water of the lower pool.

"Fantastic," he called up to them. "Super warm."

"The small rock falls are made of travertine, due to large amounts of calcium carbonate in the water," Orion said. "These river terraces and cascades continue up the canyon, and several miles farther up the stream, you reach magnificent, very large falls, near the top of the trail. It's a real bear of a hike."

Claire stepped into the Garden of Eden, and looked up the creek into paradise—a patriotic assemblage of red walls, white rocks, white foam, blue water, blue sky. She stood in water that must have been at least seventy degrees, maybe warmer, a lot warmer than the forty-six degree Colorado. She sank down into the large pool, and a feeling of heavenly bliss enveloped her.

The water swirled past in a gentle flow through the rock-lined basin. She pushed herself closer to the falls to feel the rush of energy, then backed off, content to float and soak. The water was soothing, not the least bit frightening. The rafters followed Orion up the ledges, climbing onto the rock patios and swimming across one pool after another.

After a half-hour of playing in the river, Orion collared Dirk and offered to take him up the trail to the larger waterfall. It would take them most of the day, but the other guides were willing to hang out, and he was certain none of the passengers would complain. Everyone would be happy. Claire had been splashing next to Dirk, close enough to hear the offer.

"Cool," Dirk said. "Yeah, I want to go."

He paused and looked at Orion.

"I guess I better ask my mom," he said.

"I can do it, if you want," Orion said.

Dirk nodded and watched Orion walk off towards Linny who was sitting at the edge of the creek, dangling her feet in the water. Claire also watched Orion, and she saw Linny jump up in excitement. That excitement seemed to turn to anger in the next moment as Orion shook his head.

"She wants to go," Dirk said to himself but loud enough so Claire could hear.

Yes, Claire was certain that Linny wanted to go. Just this once, though, she hoped Linny would back off. Maybe, she thought, Orion could say something to convince her that he and Dirk should go without her. She stood there next to Dirk, watching Linny and Orion across the river. When Orion shrugged his shoulders and turned around, she knew he'd given up.

"Fuck," Dirk said under his breath.

Claire wasn't surprised; it was impossible for her to fight Linny. Linny always won. What Claire hadn't known was whether that was her experience and her relationship with Linny, or if that was how everyone experienced Linny. Now she knew.

Linny and Dirk took the snacks that Tess offered and put them in their daypacks. Mother and son then followed Orion up the trail alongside Havasu Creek. Claire watched until the river curved and she could no longer see them.

58

Day 9. Afternoon

No one mentioned Linny and Dirk until the rafters assembled for lunch. They sat on one of the flat patios overlooking the river, and Claire leaned against a rock, eating a pasta salad the guides had prepared earlier that morning, or perhaps, the night before. As soon as everyone had a bowl of pasta, the missing pair became the topic of conversation about which everyone had an opinion. Claire hoped Dirk was having a good time, because she was certain he would have enjoyed the meal. He would have loved the change from the usual sandwich assortment of meats and cheeses. She did.

"That woman is something else," said a man with whom Claire had never even had a conversation. "Couldn't let her son have one afternoon without her."

She wondered if Linny had even talked to the man, and she couldn't imagine Linny telling the man about her divorce and Dirk's change of school. He couldn't know Dirk's or Linny's situation. He couldn't know, as Claire did, that Dirk really did need time away from Linny with someone like Orion.

"They call them helicopter parents," his wife said.

Except, Claire thought to herself, Linny is anything but a helicopter mother. She doesn't involve herself in Dirk's life at home. He's on his own for breakfast, lunch, and many dinners. He's on his own after school. He's on his own on weekends. Back in New York, a move towards helicopter parenting might make a real improvement in Dirk's life.

"All I know is that kid would benefit from an afternoon hiking with Orion," West said. "That's what he needs at his age."

What he left unsaid was that Linny didn't understand, but knowing that West had put Linny off, Claire had to silently agree with the spoken and unspoken sentiment. She had to give West a lot of credit, for what he seemed to know about Dirk and Linny. As far as Claire knew, no one had ever rejected Linny, even for something much less important and appealing than sex. The more she thought about West, the more exceptional he became.

If she were in West's position, having just met Linny and Dirk, and not knowing anything of their story, Claire would never have understood Dirk's needs. West was a lot more perceptive than she would have expected, and he'd made a quick, accurate judgment. She herself might end up accurate, but she was never quick. She needed to know someone for many months or a year before she could begin to understood that person and make a critical evaluation. Sometimes it became a sore point with Paul. He was quick to judge, and he couldn't tolerate her slowness. He never admitted that he misjudged, though, and he often did.

Another thing about West was that not many people, especially men, would care about Dirk above Linny. She was so engaging, and he was so adolescent. She was so exciting, and he was so needy. It was impossible for Claire to understand how West had chosen Dirk over Linny.

West came up next to her and draped his arm across her shoulders. She didn't mind, though she was relieved that Linny wasn't there to see.

"What do you think?" he asked her, quietly enough so the whole group wasn't included in the question.

"I think you understand the situation perfectly," she answered without hesitation, and as soon as she spoke she realized that she was treating West as an intellectual and emotional equal. She was treating West as she treated Linny.

With Paul it was different. She never told him what she honestly believed. Their life together worked only if she controlled and manipulated him. She always needed to direct him to do the right thing.

"I like your friend," West said, "but she's clueless about teenage boys."

"Their lives are in turmoil right now," Claire said. "That's why we're here."

"And your life is calm and tranquil?" he said.

"That's never been my life," she said.

"Mine neither," he said. "What's your living situation?"

"I've two kids, ten and twelve."

"And no husband?"

"I have a husband."

West left to offer a second helping of pasta to the rafters. Claire, shocked by her response to West, by what she had and hadn't said, was certain that West fully understood her situation. She'd been quick to forget about Paul, mentioning only her children, but she'd also been unwilling to lie about her marital status. That probably said everything that needed to be said about their relationship.

As soon as West had left, one of the women rafters sat down next to Claire. She and Claire often found themselves in the same raft, and they sometimes ate together. Melissa's husband seemed to be on a different schedule, or to have different interests. Claire hadn't paid him much attention.

"You didn't want to hike up to the falls?" Melissa asked.

"No one invited me," Claire said, "though I probably wouldn't have gone even if they had."

"Do you think anyone invited Linny?"

"Her son was going," Claire said, "that's different."

Claire had defended Linny since they were in high school. It didn't even take a conscious decision for her to take Linny's side. Somehow West had slipped around her defense of seeing things from her friend's point of view. Or maybe Dirk had revealed his point of view, and West had merely arrived before she'd regained her usual perspective. In either case, she was back where she was most comfortable.

She and Melissa finished lunch talking about the beauty surrounding them and the strange features of a river trip. Melissa said it had taken her several days to feel disconnected from her life at home and to feel like she was truly in the canyon, and Claire agreed. Melissa said it took her and her husband a couple days to alter their automatic style of interacting, but they had. Claire said she kept a journal for her family, but the nature of what she wrote was changing. It was no longer a simple travelogue, reporting the day's sights.

"People say a journey like this can change your life," Melissa said. "I wonder if that will happen to any of us here."

"I'd had thought that before I came," Claire said, "but now that I'm here, that prospect seems a little too simple. I think it will take more than two weeks on a river to change my life."

Melissa nodded in agreement, and Claire shrugged her shoulders. Claire understood that both of them would be happy for some major changes. They also knew that wishing wouldn't make it so.

"What do you do?" Claire asked.

"I'm an attorney," Melissa said.

"Me too," said Claire, and they both laughed.

59

Day 9. Afternoon

It was late afternoon when Linny, Dirk, and Orion returned from their hike. Most of the rafters had been ready to leave for at least an hour, and several had begun complaining. If Dirk and Orion had gone off by themselves, Claire thought, the others might have been more agreeable. If they were waiting only for a teenage boy, they'd make allowances and allow themselves to enjoy the stunning canyon. Knowing they were waiting for Linny, they reigned in any indulgent goodwill they might have felt.

The sun had started its western descent, but it was still high enough to drench the banks of Havasu Creek in a radiant glow. Claire would have been happy to sit there for several more hours. It would remain warm, she knew, for at least that long. As soon as the hikers returned, though, the rafters prepared to leave. When Claire stood to join the procession headed towards the rafts, Linny caught up with her and pulled her to a stop.

"You should have come," Linny said. "You can't imagine how incredible it was. It was way up the canyon, nearer to the Indian reservation. Several Indians were there. I'm not sure what they were doing. No one else was there. We had the place almost to ourselves."

Claire let herself get caught up in Linny's story. That's how it always was – Linny oblivious to everything except what she was doing, and Claire tagging along. As always, she enjoyed the fantasy of joining Linny's world and escaping her own.

"Did Dirk enjoy?" she asked, and Linny stared at her uncomprehending.

"Of course," she eventually answered, shrugging her shoulders. "It was awesome. We didn't make it to the biggest falls. I'm not sure what Orion planned, but the hike we did was really hard, and we only made it to Beaver Falls. He seemed to imply that he and Dirk could have made it farther, up to Mooney Falls, but I don't believe it. The trail was rugged."

She described Beaver Falls, depicting it like some of the lower cascades Claire had seen, where the creek spilled over limestone ledges. She made sure Claire understood that Beaver Falls was much grander and more impressive. Very few hikers made it there from the rim, and though Orion told her that boaters often hiked there, none did while they visited.

Linny shed her pack and slid into the water. Dirk and Orion had already jumped in, too hot to wait another moment. Dirk crouched under one of the cascades. Orion floated face down in the pool for such a long time that Claire started to worry he wasn't breathing. When she started counting out the seconds to herself, wondering when to intervene, he popped up.

"You could have come," he said as he pulled himself from the water. "You'd have had a good time."

Maybe if you'd invited me, Claire thought, but she said nothing.

"I'll tell you about the Havasu Indians," Linny said as they walked back to the rafts where everyone else now waited. "I read about them in the river guide, and Orion told us some things as we hiked."

Claire listened with one ear. She was too aware of the stares and comments of the other rafters and amazed, as always, that Linny paid no attention to anyone but herself. Although part of her was horrified by Linny's oblivious behavior, another part of her was envious. She wished that she too could ignore the world around her.

How would it be, she wondered, if she just ignored Paul when he started to drink or when he lashed out at her? Before she even finished the thought, she knew that couldn't be the answer. Linny needed a compliant audience, someone just like Claire, and Paul was nothing like Claire. Linny wouldn't spend five minutes in the situation Claire had tolerated for many years.

Claire climbed back into the raft and took her seat.

"Hey," Tess said. "What's wrong? You want some of this?"

She held out a pink flask with painted roses on it. Claire had never seen anything like it.

"I bought plain silver flasks for the trip," she said. "I didn't know they came in pink, with a floral pattern."

"I thought I should express my feminine side while I sipped my bourbon," Tess said.

"Really? Bourbon? Thanks."

She was cradling the flask and enjoying the change in booze when Dirk and Linny climbed aboard. Dirk's eyes widened; Linny's narrowed. They both stared at her until she grew uncomfortable and handed the small canteen back to Tess.

"Isn't that the cutest thing?" she said. "Imagine, a girly flask."

Day 9. Evening

It had been a long day, and no one talked as the rafts floated the current and headed down the river. The sun hung just above the western cliffs, and afternoon disappeared into evening. The cliff shadows already extended across the river and onto the eastern shore, leaving just the top of the eastern mesas in sunlight. The canyon itself was eerily quiet, only the splash of the oars hitting the water and echoing back and forth across the river.

Tess assured her passengers there were no rapids coming up and they'd be safely on shore before dark, but Claire still worried. She worried about getting wet and cold. She worried about looking for a tent site in the dark and finding a rattler. She worried that the other rafters would blame Dirk and Linny for the late schedule. She worried that they'd blame her because she was their friend.

When Linny first returned from the hike, Claire had felt annoyed with her friend's self-absorption. Now she herself was too self-absorbed to bother with Linny's obtuseness. She had her own unimportant problems. How would she find the right camp spot in the dimming light? How would she bathe once the sun set? Would the whole evening be on a rushed schedule? What about the hour of solitude that she savored at the end of each rafting day? Would she feel unsettled without time alone?

"Isn't it magical to be on the river as the sun goes down?" Tess said.

The simple question released Claire from her preoccupation and changed her perspective, and she nodded her head. Tess was right—it was magical, and Claire drifted in the canyon's spell.

Although the river grew increasingly less visible in the gray light, Claire no longer worried. She trusted Tess and ignored the lurking menace. She dismissed the drama of the day. As the dusk wrapped around her, she pulled her own discreet flask from her bag, and after she'd taken a drink, she turned and offered one to Tess. In front of her, Linny talked to dispel the descending darkness.

Tess said they wanted to continue down the river, closer to Lava Falls, so they could run the rapids early in the morning. That was the plan, but they didn't make it. Suddenly the dimming light went almost black, and West, in the lead raft, pulled to shore alongside a wall of rocky ledges at the mouth of a narrow canyon.

"Storm's coming in," he said, "and we need to set up camp, pronto."

"It's almost as dark as that time I was below Cardenas Creek, near river Mile 71," Tess said.

She told them how a huge thunderstorm had rolled in, triggering a landslide. She'd pulled to the bank upriver from the slide area, as rocks the size of autos flowed into the canyon, like bowling balls rolling down a lane. The massive landslide blocked the Colorado, and for almost an hour the current disappeared, until the river breached the jumbled dam and spilled across the rocks, and water again swept down the canyon.

"But don't worry," she said, "That won't happen here, today. Different topography."

West, Riz, and Theresa jumped to shore and tied the rafts around large boulders. The slow crawl down the river was over; things now happened quickly. Tess told them they would dispense with a full kitchen set up and would modify camp. The passengers dragged themselves from the rafts and climbed onto the stone ledges.

West lifted gear from his raft and handed pieces one at a time to Orion who handed the gear off, directing where it should go.

They dragged tables and boxes onto the rocky ledges; they moved food and cookware. Though they unloaded less than usual, the effort was exhausting and a testament to the benefits of camping on a flat sandy beach. Every muscle in Claire's body ached, though she merely passed the gear from the person standing before her, closer to the raft, to the person standing behind her, farther from the raft.

Without a moments rest, they moved from unloading gear to setting up the limited kitchen. Tess directed them to a shallow cave, to shelter the kitchen from the wind that had picked up and from the rain that would soon come. She said they would eat as early as they could, as soon as possible, so they could finish their clean up chores before the hard rain came, and while they still had enough light to see. They had dinner ready within record time, perhaps forty-five minutes, just as the first raindrops fell.

Claire hunched over her bowl and mechanically spooned beef chili into her mouth. In every bite she tasted the bland, unwanted crunch of sand and an added tincture of tasteless rainwater. It was the least appetizing meal they'd had, and she couldn't quite finish the portion she'd taken.

"How do you think the early Indians kept their teeth under such conditions?" Linny asked.

"It's one of the ways to identify Native American teeth," Tess said. "They're ground down."

Claire emptied the remaining chili from her bowl when she'd had enough, and then she washed her spoon and bowl, but she didn't offer to clean the pots and pans or tidy the kitchen as she often did. Instead, she clambered across the rocks, lugging her gear and looking for a spot to lay her sleeping bag. West pointed out a wide, accessible ridge, and he told her how to set up her tent on the hard surface, staking it with piles of rocks, rather than tent pegs.

"This is a good spot," he said. "Somewhat sheltered, mostly out of the wind and rain, and not too far away."

She followed West's instructions, and when the tent was up and sufficiently secure, she threw her pad and sleeping bag inside, and she crawled in. Usually she changed into a clean tee shirt for sleeping, and pulled off her shorts and slept in underpants, but the whole camping arrangement seemed so tentative that she remained fully clothed, ready to abandon her tent at a moment's notice. She smoothed the fabric of her sleeping bag and lay down with her eyes closed. To calm her mind as she waited for sleep, she started to list everything good that had happened that day, starting when she first woke up. That was how she fell asleep at home each night—listing the joys of her day, from morning to night, and deliberately ignoring the hardships. She made it through the whole day, naming everything good, and then she started over again. She was not at all sleepy.

Wide-awake, she felt each bone in her spine press into the bedrock, as if her pad and sleeping bag weren't even there and she lay directly on the slab of hard rock. She turned on her side, with her back to the river, and tried to ignore the stiffness in her knees and the ache in her pelvis. No luck—she was too old to sleep on hard surfaces. After a while, she sat up and looked out through the mesh screen door of the tent. Lightning flickered across the sky, and in that light she could see the rain pounding onto the riverbank. In the next moment, with the lightning gone, everything turned pitch-black, the river invisible. Claire imagined that for a hundred miles there was no sound, other than the canyon echoing the roar of the rapids, the fall of rain, and the crash of thunder. She felt far removed from her usual life, with little connection to home or family.

61

Day 9. Evening

As she looked out the door of her tent, the faint outline of a figure walked in front of her and stood a few feet away. Her eyes slowly adjusted, and she saw long, muscular legs in a pair of flip-flops. The legs faced her tent, straight on, and the person must have been looking right at her, but Claire couldn't see who it was. She held her breath, her body rigid and locked as she peeked outside. She thought she should call out, either in fear and warning or just curiosity, but she didn't. Instead, she watched as the person walked a foot closer to her tent and stooped into the vestibule at the tent door. With his face inches from hers, she recognized West.

"Can I come in?" he said.

She unzipped the fabric and scooted to the side. He didn't say anything more, but slipped off his rain gear, stashed it near the door, and climbed in to sit next to her. Neither of them said a word, and she wondered whether it was up to her to say something or do something. She was still thinking about it when West grabbed her hands, taking both her hands in one of his, and pulled her arms over her head and pushed her down onto her sleeping bag. Without saying a word, he slowly unbuttoned each button of her blouse, starting at the top, and when all were undone, he pushed the sleeves off one arm and then the other, so she felt the fabric smooth against her skin, sliding from her shoulder to her wrist, across the smooth, tender part of her upper arm, and across her curled fingers.

He reached behind her and unhooked her bra. He slid the straps down her arms and tossed the bra aside. Her breasts lay fully exposed, but he didn't touch her. He grabbed her swim shorts at the waistband and, in one quick movement, slid them down her legs. She lay there completely naked, and her skin tingled with the exposure, but still he didn't touch her.

She couldn't see much of anything in the almost pitch-black night, but she could feel him examine her, and could feel his eyes roam across her body. He started with her feet, and she felt his gaze climb up her legs. She didn't think he could see very much except when the lightning flashed, and even then, she imagined, she looked more theatrical than usual. It seemed an hour had passed while she lay still and he didn't move, until he was looking into her eyes, his face close enough for her to see. Then he moved back and pushed her down with the force of a linebacker, and his thigh pressed her between her legs, almost numbing her, and his free hand grabbed hold of her arm, and she couldn't have moved if she'd wanted.

He licked her ear and traced his finger across her chest, and she shivered down to her toes. He continued to stare at her. He ran his hand across her midriff, very gently, then more firmly, first in straight lines back and forth, then in a circular motion spiraling out from her navel. Though his hands had calluses, they were smooth enough, and Claire felt as if the caress were polishing her skin. As the spiral grew his hand found her breasts and ran down her thighs. He returned to her belly button, circling round and round, then pulled at her nipples. Her body relaxed and her skin throbbed, every nerve alert with pleasure.

When he rolled onto her, the weight of his body seemed to spread her across the floor of her tent until her solid frame disappeared. West appeared huge on the river. In her tent, he was even bigger. He didn't say a word, and he quickly entered her, and pumped hard against her.

62

Diary Day 9

I climbed into my tent early, right after dinner, and the storm raged around me—a dark, impenetrable sky, loud cracks of thunder shaking the canyon, peels of lightning exposing the gloom. But it was too stormy and the weather too wild to write. I am writing this the next morning. Listening to the morning chatter of swallows and the rush of the racing river, it's possible to forget the previous night's bleak spectacle. For all the evidence of the morning, last night might not have happened. In the soft light and peaceful quiet of sunrise, the black, shadowy river courses through the canyon and again appears normal. A light breeze whooshes overhead, as cool air rises from the water and mixes with warm air radiating from the cliff. At this moment, it could be any day on the Colorado.

That is part of the magic of Grand Canyon. Every day here is both unique and no different from any other day. Each day on the river we drift through new rocks and run extraordinary rapids, yet the days flow one into another without clear distinction. The minutes and hours seem interchangeable, until we encounter a storm or a challenge.

Yesterday was a particularly tumultuous day. Linny and Dirk hiked up Havasu Canyon with one of the guides while the rest of us played in the warm pools of the smaller river. It was heavenly, and I'm not sure why that upset the delicate balance of the group, but it did, and everyone reacted. Perhaps it's something that Greg and Sarah will understand better than I do, since it felt like a situation that came straight from the schoolyard. For hours after the hike, no one was quite himself.

63

Day 10. Morning

Claire woke with a start, expecting to see West lying next to her, and not sure what to do about that. She could make light of the situation, or she could take it seriously; she could start the day with a continuation of their night-time camaraderie, or she could behave more aloof. Her moment of indecision passed. West wasn't there—she was the only one in her tent. She looked outside. His raincoat and flip-flops were gone. Except that every nerve in her body told her last night had happened, she might have dreamed it all, and for a moment she felt cheated by his early exit. She would have liked to have him to herself for a few minutes of daylight. She would have liked to see her changed status reflected in his eyes.

The rational part of her brain kicked in, and she silently thanked him for leaving. Seeing her image in his eyes was one thing, and seeing her reflection in everyone else's eyes, something very different. By leaving early, he had spared her. Whatever she might feel in that early, morning glow, she didn't want anyone else to know, and she didn't want a showdown with Linny. She didn't want a misunderstanding with Dirk. She didn't want the possibility of a later confrontation with Paul. She supposed what she wanted was to protect herself. She was, she knew, always so damn rational.

The day was already warm, sunny and dry by the time the rafters had a first cup of coffee. Perhaps to make amends for the compromised dinner of the night before, the guides prepared a feast for breakfast. Bowls of freshly cut oranges stood at either end of the buffet table, and in between—stacked plates of blueberry pancakes, scrambled eggs with chives, and crispy bacon.

"And there's gingerbread cake for dessert," Riz said. "We're cooking it in the dutch-oven, on the rocks behind the large boulder—should be done in about five minutes."

Claire piled up as much food as she thought she could eat, and she walked over to see the dutch-oven which sat atop a layer of glowing charcoal-briquettes. West was lifting the top off the cast iron pot with a pair of pliers. It was covered with similarly glowing briquettes.

"Want the first piece?" he asked Claire.

She shook her head. "I just came to see," she said as she looked in at the golden brown cake right before he set the top back down.

"A couple more minutes," he said.

"Looks perfect to me," she said.

"Timing's everything," he said. "If you make a move too early, it's all ruined."

"Can I have the first piece?" Dirk asked, coming up behind Claire.

"Absolutely," West said. "Has your name on it."

"We have to get fortified before Lava," Dirk said.

"Is that what this is all about?" Claire asked.

West and Dirk took turns explaining the seriousness of the upcoming rapids—a thirty-seven foot drop, a class ten run, the most dangerous rapids of the river. She didn't know which of them was more impressed with the upcoming peril. They were both as excited as she'd seen either of them.

"Can I walk around the rapids?" Claire asked.

"No need," West said. "We've got large, sturdy rafts, the best guides around, and lots of experience. Only problem is the river—

it's way higher than usual, and that can change the rapids. But, we'll handle it."

"I'm ready!" Dirk said, and West and Claire laughed.

Why had she asked to walk? The guys were probably just having a macho moment, she thought, describing the rapids in the most dangerous light possible, to egg each other on, and then she responded as if each word were the factual truth. Sometimes, she thought to herself, she was so impossibly literal.

"Lucky for me" she thought, "that West and I didn't say anything to each other last night. I'd have answered a question he hadn't asked, and I'd have asked about the remaining four nights of the trip. That would have been a mistake. I'd have wanted to know what the plan was, when the only real plan had to do with last night, that very moment."

She wasn't often an in-the-moment person, but she'd been one the previous night. She didn't regret anything.

They were cleaning up when the kayakers floated by. Tess called to them and tried to wave them over, but either they didn't hear or they ignored her. The rafters watched the kayaks skim in large meanders across the water, marking long, gentle ripples across the current.

"What do you think?" Tess asked West.

"We'll catch up when we stop to scout," he said. "You know how long it takes kayakers to scout Lava. This river's too high, they shouldn't kayak. Especially Ellie. Something unusual's going on here."

Claire and Linny stood together watching the kayaks disappear around a bend of the river when Orion announced that the rafts would be emptied and reloaded, and everyone needed to help. Claire walked over to Tess' raft, assuming Linny was right behind her. When she turned around, she saw that Linny stood at the stern of West's raft, talking to West. Dirk was already on Tess' raft, untying and unloading.

"Why are we doing this?" Claire asked Tess.

"We need to be as tightly packed as possible," she said. "Don't want the gear to interfere in any way, and we've gotten a little sloppy the last couple of days. It always happens."

"Talking to Dirk and West got me a little nervous," Claire said to Tess before they took off. "Where do you think I should sit?"

"You're fine where you've been," she said. "Just be sure to hold on. Try to stay inside the raft."

64

Day 10. Morning

The sun had begun its overhead somersault, transitioning from morning to afternoon, when they pulled around a bend in the river, and the water suddenly turned choppy. At that same moment the current grew faster, and they heard the deep, menacing roar of Lava Falls.

"Aren't we going to scout?" Claire turned around and asked Tess.

"Don't worry, we're not there yet," Tess said. "We still have about a half-mile to go."

They pulled to shore before the rapids, right behind the yellow and red kayaks. The guides secured their rafts, and everyone, guides and passengers, climbed out. With Theresa leading the way, they walked single-file up a path to the top of the bluff overlooking the river. The trail was steep and rocky, and the climb exhausting in the hot sun. Claire wished she could remove the lifejacket that she wore, but the guides insisted everyone wear a jacket. Orion told a story of a passenger who fell into the rapids while scouting. Claire wasn't sure if the story was true, but she understood the moral.

They hiked to the top of the cliff for a clear look at the rapids. Tess explained that the bird's eye view would show where the current was fastest and slowest, what route to take, and what dangers to avoid. She said the rapids' features changed all the time, that all rapids changed as river conditions changed.

With no experience scouting rapids, Claire had no frame of reference for her view of the river. She knew the river dropped down a falls, but she couldn't really see it. There was too much whitewater and too much confusion. All she saw was a long stream of foaming water that didn't look navigable. The waves were too big, the roar was too loud, and the run was too long. She didn't imagine anyone could learn anything from scouting. Perhaps the exercise was to increase the tension, the point to scare the customers. She would have been happy to wait in the raft, but that hadn't been offered as an option.

"Frightening, huh?" Orion asked.

"What do you do about it?" Claire asked.

"We find a way to run it," he said. "See, there's a possible channel on the left, but if you go there, you have to worry about the big hole on the left, and that hole is just about the scariest thing on the river. Or you can run down the middle, but then you face down the waves. At all cost, you have to avoid the falls."

Claire looked, but she couldn't see what Orion described. The rapids appeared scary and undecipherable. As they stood watching, four paddle rafts pulled away from the shoreline and lined up for the descent. The first raft headed straight down the center then pulled to the left, where Orion had pointed out a channel. Claire narrowed her focus and stared intently, but she couldn't see a channel. All she saw was a large raft, it's occupants paddling furiously, thrashing through big water and bouncing back and forth among the waves. As the raft neared the end of the whitewater and floated into calm waters, everyone watching from the bank cheered the raft's success. Claire turned back to watch the next raft.

The second raft was already in the run, but it wasn't pulling left as the first raft had done. The second raft continued straight down the middle of the river. Claire realized how big the waves in the center were only by seeing them crash over the raft. They could have been double the size of the waves encountered by the first raft. About half way through the rapids, the front end of the second raft rose up on a huge wave, and the whole raft tilted onto its right side. Claire held her breath, afraid that the raft would flip, trapping the rafters underneath. In seeming slow-motion, the raft remained on its side, sinking deeper into the water, until almost a quarter of the raft had disappeared, and two paddlers from that bottom side slid from the raft into the river. A collective gasp sprung from those watching on the high bank.

"Over there!" someone yelled, pointing to one of the swimmers and then the other.

The raft righted itself, and to Claire, standing on the top of the bluff, it looked like someone could easily grab the swimmers and pull them back. They didn't appear to be that far away. She watched and waited, but no one grabbed them. The swimmers rushed down the river, getting farther from their raft, until paddlers in the raft waiting below picked them up.

"Why didn't their fellow paddlers pull them back in right away?" Linny asked.

"It's not as easy as it looks from here," Orion said. "You think you could do it when you're watching, but on the water it's a whole other thing. They all did a really good job."

Claire looked back to the river. All four rafts had run the rapids and were pulled ashore below the whitewater.

"No one wants swimmers in Lava Falls," West said, "but if someone swims, that's as good as it gets, especially in this water."

Claire looked around the throng of spectators to find Tess. She stood back from the others, talking to the kayakers. Ellie, the young woman, shook her head back and forth as Tess spoke. Claire had no idea what anyone was saying, but it was clear that Ellie disagreed with Tess. Occasionally, the young man, Tim, shrugged his shoulders. West walked over and started arguing with Tim and Ellie. Claire couldn't make out his words, but his tone was angry. After a few minutes he walked away.

"O.K. back to the rafts!" he bellowed.

Claire saw him catch Tess' eye and wave her down the trail. She nodded and put her arms around the kayakers, and the three of them started walking back to the river, behind the rafters.

65

Day 10. Morning

With the rafters back in their boats, the guides lectured. Tess told her group the plan. Theresa would go first, followed by Mark and Riz. Then the kayakers would take the run. They'd be followed by Orion, Tess, and West. At that moment, no trips were queued ahead of them, and they would be the next rafts to run Lava. The rafts and kayaks queued up in the designated order to wait their turns. Claire peered downstream, to see how the rapids looked from river level, but the river completely disappeared from view ahead of Theresa's raft. As that raft moved into the current and floated down the river, it quickly vanished from sight.

When Tess explained the order of descent, Claire had been relieved her raft was second to last. She figured she'd watch the runs of the first rafts with the security of knowing West followed. She quickly changed her mind. She watched without seeing. Ahead of them, one after another, the rafts and kayaks moved into place and dropped from sight.

Claire turned to look back at Tess. Tess' face, usually calm and relaxed, strained at every muscle and nerve and looked nothing like the face of the woman who had ferried them down the river the past ten days. A twitch that Claire hadn't noticed before flickered across Tess' left cheek. Tess' lips were pulled so tight they almost disappeared.

Claire turned back around and looked ahead. Her stomach cramped.

"They deliberately build up the tension," Linny said. "For people who like excitement."

"That makes sense," Claire said. "But the guides said the water's higher than usual. I guess that means the river's flooding, though they didn't use those words."

"Maybe that's a problem for the kayakers," Linny said.

After Mark and Riz took off, Tess moved downriver, to wait her turn. Hoping for a sense of stability or at least a feeling of security, Claire moved her legs against the tube and forced her feet underneath. She found a strap tied to the rowing frame and wound it around her right hand. She found a strap tied off behind her and wound it around her left hand.

Eventually everyone ahead of them had entered the rapids, and Tess' raft moved to the front of the line. Claire stared straight ahead, waiting and seeing nothing, and then Tess started rowing. The raft sped past narrow beaches and towering cliffs and entered the rapids, and all at once nothing but river water was visible. The sky, the shoreline, the tall cliffs disappeared. In front of them waves rose up and curled over the bow. They broke and pounded the raft, and water surged across the outer tubes, doused the rafters, and gushed onto the floor of the raft. The water was icy cold, and Claire shivered when it washed over her.

Tess followed Orion, but Claire couldn't tell where in the river they were, whether they'd headed for the left run, or taken the center. For all she knew, they'd gone right. Occasionally she saw Orion's raft and then, ahead of Orion, Claire could see the red kayak, racing ever farther downstream, bobbing in the river spume. The kayak shot up and down the waves and veered left and right. As Claire watched, it tipped onto its side, thrashing in the waves, water spilling across its length. It was quite a distance away and difficult to see, hidden at times by the waves and the water. Claire couldn't be certain, but she thought she saw Ellie inside, floating on the water, jounced by the waves. She thought she saw Ellie flaying a paddle against the current, struggling to straighten, being dragged down the river.

The water was higher, swifter, and more turbulent than anything they'd yet experienced. Instead of skimming along the current, the raft bounced back and forth between waves. Everything accelerated. Claire wondered if Tess were having trouble controlling the raft. In every direction, rock and water closed in on them, leaving room for nothing else. The water flowed past them frothy, churned, impenetrable, and racing to an unseen finish line. From the crest of a wave Claire saw the river currents pound against the colossal cliffs, like ocean waves against a sea wall.

Ahead of them, Orion pulled his raft alongside the kayak and leaned out of his raft, over the water. The kayak sped out of reach as Orion made a grab for it. A wave washed over Tess' raft, Claire blinked, and when she looked again, Orion's raft was again besides the kayak, and Orion jammed his oars inside his raft, stood tall, leaned across the outer tube and yanked Ellie from the kayak into his raft.

Orion immediately dropped Ellie and grabbed the raft's oars, but he couldn't prevent the raft from spinning, and he headed down the river backwards. The empty red kayak sped down the river ahead of him.

Claire hunched over her legs, and the shoulders of her bulky, orange pumpkin vest pushed against her ears. She squeezed her eyes shut against the drama engulfing her. Waves splashed across the raft almost continuously, keeping her soaked and chilled. They came up to the yellow kayak bouncing in the current. Tim sat straight, staring ahead, holding his paddle out of the water. The kayak made no progress, trapped on the outskirts of danger, but Tim seemed not to notice.

"Kayaker," Tess yelled. "Paddle!"

"Paddle now!" she yelled again when he didn't respond.

He looked at Tess and started to paddle, skimming across the water and quickly moving ahead of the bulky raft. The raft, running the main current, powered into the next wave. Claire wasn't prepared: she hadn't re-secured her handholds; she hadn't refocused her mind on the rapids; she was twisted and facing the side of the raft where Tim had been the previous moment. In an instant she was airborne, without a tether to the raft. Certain she would land in the water, she already felt she was drowning. Floating through air, she felt suffocated by water, and in that moment, time stood still. Her life didn't flash before her eyes, nor did she find meaning in her existence. Instead, she felt gripped with terror, knowing she was about to drown and was unable to help herself.

West had drilled them with rules that first night on the river, including what to do if you were washed overboard, and in a flash she knew she'd forgotten everything he had told them. Instead of being prepared, which she always was, even for the least important matter that no one else took seriously, she was running the largest rapids on the river unable to remember anything she'd been told. All she knew was that the waves of Lava Falls were too big, the run was too long, and the volume of water was too great. She was sinking, unable to see or hear anything but the river, crushed by her understanding of what it meant to swim the rapids, when a hand grabbed the collar of her life jacket and flipped her back into the raft.

Sitting in a heap on the rubber floor, soaked and shaken, Claire looked up to see Dirk beside her. He crouched with his hand hovering next to her, at the ready to grab her again, and he focused every bit of his attention on her. He looked thirty, rather than sixteen. She couldn't speak, but she grabbed his hand and squeezed it. He didn't say anything, but Claire thought the muscles in his face relaxed. Linny sat in front of them, looking ahead, seemingly unaware of the scene unfolding behind her.

The enormity of the danger she'd faced and the shock of her rescue flooded through her, and she squeezed Dirk's hand tighter as tears filled her eyes. A moment later, her whole body started to shake, convulsing from the inside out, and her stomach heaved, her lungs collapsed, her heart pounded. She couldn't hold any part of her body still; nor could she breathe. She slipped her hand from Dirk's, grabbed a strap dangling near her seat, and stretched out on the floor of the raft. One wave after another washed over her, and each wave of frigid, dirty water submerged the raft. The water ran under her lifejacket and under her clothes and down her skin. When she couldn't hold her head up any longer, it lay in a puddle. Whatever sediment survived in the river found its way to her, covering her in a fine silt. She felt dizzy, nauseous and light-headed, and more than anything, she felt scared. She felt great compassion for Tim seeing his wife pulled limp from her kayak, and she feared for Ellie.

"What if you hadn't grabbed me?" she whispered to Dirk.

"You'd have been O.K.," he said. "You know the rule West told us in case we got washed overboard—sit up with your legs in front of you, facing downriver."

66

Day 10. Afternoon

In the calmer waters below the rapids, the rafts gathered around Tim's yellow kayak. Ellie's body appeared lifeless and lay unmoving across the rear tube of Orion's raft. As far as Claire could tell, the kayaker hadn't moved a muscle since the guide dumped her there, yet it seemed impossible to imagine that she hadn't responded to Orion grabbing her and throwing her to safety.

Claire peered at Ellie but the young woman didn't move, and Claire was too far away to read the expression on her face. Without realizing what she was doing, she made a decision that she couldn't help the situation, and she looked away, only later realizing that in that moment, she abandoned the young woman. In that same moment, Linny jumped up and climbed onto Orion's raft. Tess followed. Orion scrambled over to the kayaker and pulled off her helmet. He tossed it aside, and it rolled onto the floor of his raft. As soon as he could pull himself from the skirt of his kayak, Tim sprang onto the boat.

With the guides, Linny, and Tim now gathered around Ellie, Claire looked back at the kayaker. She could no longer see her, only those surrounding her, but with the others taking charge, she assumed everything would be all right. The sense of urgency that had gripped her while they ran the rapids slowly abated.

West pushed Linny aside and lay his hands on Ellie's chest. Linny protested.

"No, I'll do this," West said. "Tess, you tell me everything we need to do. Say it all out loud."

"Get the satellite phone. Call for help," Tim said.

"We can do that, but we can't wait for help," West said. "Riz, call for help."

"Tess, breathe her," West said as he continued to compress Ellie's chest.

Tess stood next to West. On the other side of Ellie, straight across from them, Tim sat and held Ellie's hand and whispered into her ear. He looked straight into Ellie's face.

Tess leaned over Ellie and yelled "Now." West stopped pushing.

Tess called out, "Tilt her head, lift her chin, pinch her nostrils," as she did each of those things, and then no one talked, and she took a deep breath and placed her mouth over Ellie's. She breathed into Ellie until it seemed her own lungs must be empty. She raised her head, drew another deep breath and again breathed into Ellie. When she finished, she pulled back up and released Ellie.

"Over," she said.

West again started to compress Ellie's chest, counting out loud. Tim sat, holding Ellie's tiny hand in his large, left hand and staring into her face. He may not have noticed that Tess had blocked his view for two minutes while she placed her mouth over Ellie's to stimulate her breathing. With the tips of the fingers of his right hand, he gently brushed Ellie's hair back from her forehead; his own face distorted in misery.

Tess grabbed the hand of Orion who stood behind her, and she held tight until she again stepped forward, calling out her actions and breathing into Ellie. For many long minutes West pumped Ellie's chest and Tess gave resuscitating breaths.

Claire wondered how they could keep it up after rowing. She supposed the adrenaline rushing through their bodies was that much greater than what she felt. She felt depleted. She wanted to fall back to the floor of the raft. She wanted to leave the nightmare. The guides worked like robotic machines. At some moment, which seemed to Claire no different than the moment before, West and Tess stopped.

"That's it," West said.

"That's it," Tess mechanically answered.

Claire stared across the rafts in disbelief. West walked around Ellie and sat down on one side of Tim; Tess sat on the other. Tess held Tim's free hand, the one that wasn't holding onto Ellie.

Tim whispered into Ellie's ear. He let go of her hand and smoothed her hair. He passed his right hand across her eyes, shutting the lids. Everyone on Orion's raft looked away. Tears streamed down Claire's face. She heard several rafters sobbing. Someone wailed.

67

Day 10. Afternoon

N o one talked much after Lava Falls. They continued down the river, swollen and turbulent, and Claire sat in her usual seat in Tess' raft, surrounded by the other rafters, but feeling painfully isolated. She watched everyone and paid attention to everything that happened, but little registered, and nothing mattered. When they reached a large beach, they pulled to shore and secured the rafts. It seemed like most of a day had passed, and it could have been midnight, but instead the sun shone directly overhead and beat down on them. Afternoon breezes had not yet picked up; the air was still, and the sun scorching hot.

Orion pulled an orange tarp from beneath his seat and spread the stiff plastic across the middle of his boat. Standing on opposite sides of the tarp, West lifted Ellie's head and Orion lifted her feet, and they lay the body across one end of the plastic. Ellie weighed very little, and the two men were exceptionally strong, but it looked like they could barely manage to move her. Tess stood and watched, tears filling her eyes and spilling down her cheeks. Occasionally someone's cries echoed across the river. Claire moved across the sand until she stood alone, away from the others.

West and Orion pulled the end of the tarp across Ellie's body and then rolled her. At the other end, they pulled straps under and over and tied them. They carefully lifted the long, thin, orange package onto the back of West's raft and secured it out of the way and partially hidden. Tim started out watching, but as soon as Ellie's body was covered by the tarp, he turned away. At that point, the orange package looked nothing like Ellie. It didn't even look like a body. Wrapped in the stiff tarp it now seemed larger and less flexible. There was no indication of a head, torso, or feet. Tim walked off across the sand, past Claire, and sat by himself at the farthest edge of the beach, where the sand disappeared into the river, and a cliff wall rose to the sky.

Someone prepared food, and they ate a very late lunch. Tim didn't join them. As they sat on the beach, joylessly eating, Tess talked. It seemed she couldn't stop talking, and she told a story that she said the other guides knew.

"That didn't look like Ellie," she said. "Nothing like Ellie. And when my father lay in his coffin, after he drowned, he looked nothing like my father. I didn't see him when he was pulled from the river, but I'm sure he didn't look like my father then, either. Of course, seeing him in the coffin, I knew it was my father, just like we know this is Ellie. I was there when he drowned in the Kern River. But I didn't save him, just like we didn't save Ellie."

"You probably don't know the story," Tess continued, looking at the rafters sitting in a loose circle around her, "so I'll tell you. My father was teaching me to kayak. Over and over I had to get in the kayak and paddle out to a pool in the river, then roll the kayak, straighten out, and paddle back to shore. The river level rose, but we kept going. One time, after I'd been doing it for hours, I couldn't complete the roll. I think the current had changed and the water was not only higher, but also rougher. Strong currents had formed, maybe even a bit of a whirlpool. I was under water too long, and I couldn't breathe.

"My father pulled me out and pushed me to shore. I lay on the bank, catching my breath, gulping at the air, unable to get enough into my lungs, but realizing I was alive. I remember that feeling of knowing I was alive. Slowly I let go of the certainty I'd felt that I would die. I said something to my father, but he didn't answer, and I thought he must be more exhausted than I. The significance of his silence didn't register. Only later, much later, did I prop herself on my elbow and turn to look at him, and see he wasn't there. I was alone on the sand. My kayak was caught in the brush across the river. My father's kayak was pushed onto the rocks just below the sand where I lay. I knew immediately that he'd rescued me, but not himself."

And yet, Claire wanted to say, you chose to become a rafting guide. That was her first reaction, wondering how Tess could do that. It was not something Claire would do, not how she'd respond. She was pretty sure she'd never go near a river again if that had happened to her, even considering her ambiguous feelings about her father. Yet Ellie had almost drowned, and she continued kayaking the river until she did drown. It was impossible to understand what motivated some people.

No one said anything for a while. Eventually someone asked what would happen next, and Riz answered that when he called emergency, they said a Park Service boat was at Phantom and would catch up with them to take Ellie's body.

Within an hour, a sport boat came racing down the river and pulled to shore alongside their rafts. The Park Service Ranger cut his motor and waved West over.

"A kayaker drowned," they heard the ranger say. "I'm looking for the body. Dam breached; river's running high. They don't think the dam will fail."

Riz walked down the beach to get Tim who was still sitting by himself at the edge of the river. West took the ranger over to his raft. Everyone else remained sitting where they were, barely breathing, watching the ranger now, instead of Tess. Claire wished she could force herself to get up and walk farther away, to where she couldn't see or hear anything, but she couldn't move. She wanted to distance herself and do something other than watch the transfer of the body and hear what the ranger and Tim and the guides said. Still, she didn't move. She sat where she'd been since they'd arrived at the beach, and, along with the other rafters, she stared at the orange tarp.

Tess turned to the rafters and explained who the ranger was and what would happen. Abruptly, she stopped talking. Claire thought she might have stopped in the middle of a sentence, though she wasn't quite sure, since she'd been trying not to listen. The rafters turned from Tess and again looked at the ranger and the body wrapped in the tarp.

Claire thought that Linny should take Dirk away, somewhere across the beach, somewhere where he couldn't watch. If Greg were there, she would force herself to walk away to protect him. If Dirk were her child, that's what she would do.

Linny dragged her chair next to Dirk's. She hunched over her knees while she stared at West and watched him lift the package that was Ellie. She focused all her attention on Ellie and in so doing, she drew Dirk, and everyone near her, deeper into the drama. Claire felt herself pulled by Linny into the center of the action, though she'd just tried to turn away. Linny had that kind of power.

"Do you think this is right? Linny said. "I'm not sure West is treating Ellie with sufficient respect."

"She's gone mom," Dirk said. "If Tim's O.K. with it, it's O.K."

"It matters to me, not just to Tim," Linny said.

"But you didn't even know her," Dirk said.

It almost looked like Linny was going to slap Dirk across the face. Her face had that concentration, and her hand moved slightly. Yet that was impossible. Why would they fight over Ellie? Dirk was right—Linny didn't even know her.

"Can you give me a hand?" Tess stood next to Linny and held her hand out to give Linny a lift from her chair.

Linny stood and walked away with Tess, and as soon as she left, Claire was able to free herself from the scene at the rafts. She walked away, filled with doubts as she did so. She left Dirk sitting alone, Dirk who had saved her from washing out of the boat. Did karma require her to rescue him from the tragedy on this beach? Yet Dirk wasn't her child. Linny approved his sitting there, watching.

Claire examined the rocks at the far edge of the sand. She found a small trail but didn't follow it. She stayed where the others could see her, but where she wasn't forced to see them. She was too far away to hear anything being said at the water. When she glanced back at the guides, to stay in touch with what was happening, the ranger and his sport boat had left, Tim and his kayak had gone, and Ellie's wrapped body had disappeared.

The rafters were rearranging the chairs in a semi-circle at the shoreline. Claire walked back and joined them. For a while, the beach was eerily quiet, and no one talked. Tess broke the spell.

"How could this happen?" she said to no one in particular. "How can this be? Witnessing one drowning in a lifetime is enough for one person."

Claire was certain Tess was right. This was Claire's first drowning, and she never wanted to see another. This was her third death, and she knew she'd experience many more.

She clearly remembered her uncle dying from a stroke when she was twelve. She took the phone call from her aunt's good friend who told her that her mother's brother had died, and she passed the news on to her mother as soon as she got home. They packed that evening, and she remembers her mother picking out appropriate clothes for each of them to wear. Her mother's friend Ellen came over to keep her mother company. Early the following morning her family drove to her aunt and uncle's home outside Boston and stayed for most of a week.

What Claire remembered most distinctly was that on the days following the funeral, which took place the day they arrived, her aunt took the T downtown everyday in the early afternoon. The extended family, Claire's aunts and uncles and cousins, gathered together in her aunt's house, and after eating lunch around the large dining room table, someone put up another pot of coffee, someone cleaned up from the meal, others sat on the sofa looking through photo albums, and her aunt left for her office for a couple hours. Saying she had important work to do, she grabbed her briefcase and a jacket and walked out the door.

Claire had thought it rude, and she had expected someone in her family, which was usually very vocal in its complaints, to object, but no one said a word. At the time, she had no idea what her relatives thought about her aunt's behavior. Now, she also had no idea what she thought about it.

Years later, when she was in college, she attended her second funeral in a gritty village outside Mexico City. Pick-up trucks, piled high with garden produce and weighted down with laborers, scraped along rutted dirt roads. Large families squeezed into runty rooms, with too little space for too many people. She was traveling over spring break with her roommate Angela who called a cousin of her grandmother's in Mexico City and learned that a distant relative had died in an auto accident on the road outside the village. No one asked what she and Angela wanted to do; they just made arrangements for the Americans to join the family in the village.

The girls arrived to find the few dismal shops boarded, the transport office locked shut, and the crumbling city hall closed tight. The town mourned. Men and women cried, wiped tears, and cried again. For that man she hadn't known, Claire spent several days in mourning, and no one went to work. She remembered wanting to tell Linny about the funeral, but Linny had spent her vacation on a service trip to Guatemala, and she had many stories to tell and no time to listen to Claire when she returned.

Until now, Claire hadn't known anyone her age who'd died. Certainly no one younger, like Ellie. And no one who'd died by drowning. Tim had looked devastated. Her aunt (much older) appeared more dazed than devastated. The whole Mexican village completely shut down, and Claire never even understood who was related to the deceased man. Which was the normal response to death, she wondered? She remembered reading a shocking essay by Ralph Waldo Emerson about the death of his son and how shallow his grief, how it left no scar.

Who would mourn if she died? Would Paul be as distraught as Tim? Would she be if Paul died? Perhaps they would each behave like her aunt did and continue with their work. She couldn't look back at her aunt and uncle's marriage and understand anything. She was only a child at the time. Had their passion dulled, or was something else going on? She didn't remember ever feeling passionate about Paul, but that must be wrong. She wouldn't have married him if she felt then like she did now. Maybe she just couldn't remember back so many years. She was a different person then. He was a different person. She no longer remembered who either of them were or what either of them had felt.

She shut her eyes to stop herself from thinking. It was ridiculous to worry about her funeral. If anything, being in the canyon had underscored her basic insignificance. She understood that she wasn't a person with a large impact on the world. Perhaps the Mexican man had truly left the whole village crying. What determined the impact one had in the world?

"I understand why I became a river guide," Tess said to anyone who would listen. "My father loved the river. I honored him by coming here. Besides, a person needs to face her fears. If you turn from them, you'll spend your life running away. If you fall off the horse, you need to get right back on."

Conventional wisdom, Claire thought, but I've never faced my fears like that. I haven't even identified them, and I gave up riding horses years ago. She tried to think of a fear to face, but her mind went blank. Perhaps, she thought, she had too many fears to make identification of a single one meaningful or significant.

"Ranger said a rafter also drowned in Crystal. The dam breached for some hours, and the flow got high and erratic," West said. "Some problem with the spillways being compromised by erosion, making them unusable, and sending the water over the dam, but they're expecting the flow to normalize, and hoping the dam doesn't fail. This is the first time it breached, so they don't know how it will hold up. First time they used the spillways and found they were eroded. Maybe we should have waited before running Lava."

"Unless it all gets worse," someone said.

No one said anything else for a long time.

"What happens if the dam fails?" someone asked.

West shrugged and shook his head. "Don't know."

Storm clouds blew in and settled into the canyon. Not as frightening as the previous night, but substantial enough that they couldn't be ignored. An intermittent, light rain started to fall. Claire felt a soft mist, and then individual drops splatter onto her exposed arms and legs. She quickly set up her tent and climbed inside. Later, when she heard the call for dinner, she pulled on her raincoat and walked down to the kitchen. The guides had strung a small tarp over the kitchen and a larger one nearby and had moved the chairs underneath the larger one.

The rain fell harder, and raindrops pitted the river's surface. Claire stared at the spectacle. The river transformed into a Seurat canvas, as mesmerizing as the paintings. The rain grew heavier, and a curtain of water dropped off the tarp. The shoreline faded, like chalk lines erased from a blackboard, and the Seurat vanished.

The sky turned black, an impenetrable screen having fallen across its features. A clash of thunder and a streak of lightning punctuated almost every movement on shore. The rafts bobbed in the water, slammed by the waves and a seeming target for the lightning, the canyon transformed into an enormous, sporadically illuminated, pinball game. Over the course of dinner, the rain fell with enough force to halt all conversation, and then, a moment later, it merely misted the already dry desert air. In the quiet, someone talked to fill the silence.

Claire walked upriver, stopping only when she'd disappeared into the shadows amidst the rain and thunder. Standing exposed in the storm, the rest of the world disappeared, and she stood unmoored in time or place, almost a figment of her own imagination. When she returned to the other rafters, she stood in the dark at the edge of the river just beyond the circle of chairs. When she left to walk to her tent, West followed. At the vestibule to her tent, her told her he needed to work on his raft for a few minutes.

"I'll be back in a half hour," he said.

68

Diary Day 10

Even though it seems awkward, I'll try to tell you everything about today. You'll understand at the end.

The day started with a focus on running Lava Falls. It is huge—the biggest and scariest rapids on the Colorado River. In some ways, all of our time on the trip was leading up to this one event. The guides prepared a special breakfast with more food than anyone but Dirk could possibly eat. We even had breakfast dessert—a gingerbread cake baked in a Dutch oven. Baking a dessert in the desert is quite a feat, and the cake was delicious.

We floated down river and pulled to shore at a rocky beach. At that point we'd been hearing the roar of the rapids for quite a while, and I'd been expecting us to pull over for at least a mile or two, which just increased the tension.

The guides tied the rafts to large boulders along the shoreline and told us to keep our life vests on. We formed a procession and hiked along a rocky, narrow trail that climbed up the cliff to overlook the river. From the top we could see the rapids spread out below us, and we watched four large rafts coast down the river and head into the waves. The first waves curled over the rafts as if they were toys, and the water washed across the boats and the rafters, obscuring them from view. One of the large waves raised the second raft and tilted it on its side; two passengers slid out into the river current.

We watched it happen, and it was far enough away that it looked as if it were progressing in slow motion. We had no ability to help. The rafters swept through the current into the calm water below the rapids. No one pulled them back into the rafts until they were through the turbulence. It looked like someone could have grabbed them earlier, but our guide said it was much more difficult than it appeared.

Then it was our turn. We climbed back into the rafts and the guides lined up in a predetermined order. My raft was second from last. The drop into the rapids was so steep that it was impossible to see anything as we waited upstream. It looked like the end of the earth—as if the earth actually was flat, rather than curved, and we were perched at the edge. Each raft floated to the edge and disappeared. Then it was our turn, and we descended. Once the waves hit, I lost all sense of direction. From the cliff I'd been told what rocks we wanted to avoid, and what channel we wanted to run, but once we entered the rapids, it felt as if the raft were being battered and pushed, and all I could do was hope the guide retained some control. I certainly had no force at all. It felt as if the raft were running itself.

And then a wave hit, and I was knocked out of the raft into the air. I had no way to reconnect with the boat. It flashed through my head that if I landed in the water, I would remain in the water, and I wasn't sure I could survive. All of a sudden, a hand grabbed my life vest and jerked me back into the raft. Dirk had rescued me, and he held onto me until I was securely back in the raft.

When we gathered in the calm waters below the rapids, we found that a young woman kayaker, one who'd spent time with us on the river, had drowned. Our guides and her husband tried to save her, but they couldn't. The river had flipped her kayak onto its side, and the water had overpowered her, and by the time anyone could reach her, it was too late. She was very young and beautiful, and it was incredibly distressing to everyone to witness the tragedy. In many ways, it seemed hard to believe, and I kept waiting for Ellie to come back to life.

The river level is exceptionally high, apparently from a temporary breach of Glen Canyon Dam. No one is sure if the dam will fail and the river flood catastrophically higher. Everyone keeps wondering if we had done things differently, whether Ellie would be alive.

This night another storm developed, and this time it seemed particularly appropriate. I have never been through anything as difficult as this day. I almost wish I were home, except there is magic here, and I need to see what comes next.

69

Day 11. Morning

When Claire woke, there was again no trace of West, his raincoat or flip-flops. He'd slipped from the tent without her noticing, just as he had the previous morning. Claire felt only unambiguous relief and gratitude for his timely disappearance, and she silently thanked West. He was one amazing man. She'd enjoyed the second night even more than the first.

Did he know exactly what she wanted, she wondered, or was this also what he wanted from her? It had been so long since she and Paul wanted or needed the same thing, that it was hard for her to imagine such a situation. Perhaps being in Grand Canyon attuned West to what others needed. Perhaps that's just how it was, with no rhyme or reason. Claire rarely had a definitive explanation for why anything happened, ever. As Paul used to say years ago, it is what it is.

On October 18, she'd turned forty-five years old. She couldn't think of herself as the object of someone else's desires. Even when she was younger she never thought of herself in that way, though she sometimes now thought that she should have. Now, when she saw photos of herself in her twenties and early thirties, she looked in amazement at how beautiful she'd been, in that way that many young women are beautiful, and she remembered Paul's mother telling her that if she waited twenty years she'd love the photos of herself that she then found so unflattering. It hadn't taken twenty years. Unfortunately, though, she only became conscious of a young woman's power when she was no longer a young woman.

She had no explanation for why West had spent two nights with her, and the more she thought about him, the less she understood him. Things worked so easily with him, yet they hardly knew each other. Things hadn't gone so smoothly for Linny and West.

Breakfast was plentiful, but nothing like the spread prepared the previous day before the run of Lava Falls. Though delicious, the food seemed less appetizing to Claire, and everything about the day felt diminished. The sun didn't shine as bright, as if viewed through an invisible translucent shade. The river flowed high, more terrifying than exciting. The cliffs bolted black and shiny straight from the river without the interesting sandstone layers evident upstream. The guides dawdled and spoke with less enthusiasm. The rafters had lost the confidence they'd slowly gained.

"We're going to look at the geology today," Theresa said. "We'll examine the ancient lava flows along the river."

Claire wondered if that were always planned, or if the guides sought a way to transition from the drama of the previous day. Not that it mattered. Whether it was prearranged or spontaneous, it seemed a good plan, and she'd be happy to spend the day looking at lava. She'd be happy to do anything that didn't involve a risky descent down dangerous rapids in a flooding river.

Linny and Dirk sat together upstream, away from the rest of the rafters. With their backs turned toward the circle of chairs on the beach, it was impossible for Claire to see their faces. From their postures she was certain they were arguing, and she thought they could be arguing about anything. There was so much for them to disagree about.

Suddenly Linny got up and turned around, as if she knew Claire were watching her and wanted to catch her in the act. She walked over to Claire and glared at her.

"Well, now he knows you aren't so perfect," she said. "I saw West leave your tent early this morning, and I told Dirk."

Linny was gone before Claire could answer, and in fact, Claire had nothing to say. Linny had gotten it all wrong. Linny, not Claire, had been the perfect one. Claire had always tagged along behind Linny, trying to catch up and had always taken Linny's discards. Claire had always tried her best to be someone Linny would like, someone Linny could accept. Linny had no basis for accusing her of not being perfect—that had never been a possibility.

Claire understood Linny's anger about West, though. Linny hadn't discarded him—he'd discarded her, and that should have sidelined him for the rest of the trip. Claire shouldn't have given him the time of day. She should have taken sides and supported her friend.

She caught up with Linny as she started to take down her tent. Claire took the role of assistant, folding the tent poles and smoothing the tent fabric. When it seemed that Linny had calmed enough to hear her, Claire apologized.

"I can't explain what happened," she said. "I have no excuse. Everything about it was wrong. Nothing is more important to me than your friendship, and I mean that. Forgive me."

When Linny looked up, Claire could see tears leaking from the corners of her eyes. Her own eyes welled up in response.

"Maybe it was the horror of the day," Linny said. "Ellie drowning and all."

Claire nodded. She knew that didn't explain her first night with West, and she knew Linny would never forgive her if she later found out about the earlier indiscretion, but she accepted Linny's excuse on her own behalf. She didn't know what else to do. She couldn't bear Linny's anger. She hadn't come on this trip to destroy their friendship, and she wanted everything to be as it had been.

"Anyway, West and I weren't a good fit," Linny said. "No reason you shouldn't give him a try."

"No," Claire said. "That's wrong. There was every reason not to."

"I didn't really say anything to Dirk," Linny said. "I just said that to you because I was angry. Dirk and I were arguing about school. Nothing important."

"That's important," Claire said. "Certainly more important than whatever West and I do."

"West didn't like anything about me," Linny said.

"He didn't know you."

"Steve certainly knows me," Linny said, "and he doesn't love me. Dirk knows me, and he's always angry at me. You have no idea how simple and sweet your life is."

70

Day 11. Morning

Dirk fumed as they boarded the rafts for the morning's short excursion. Claire wanted to talk with him, to try to calm him down, but she wouldn't interfere with Linny's handling of the situation. She couldn't risk Dirk turning against her or risk angering Linny again. It seemed so long ago that she'd arrived at Lees Ferry to tell Linny about Paul's drinking and her own unhappiness. The immediacy of her problems had disappeared, and she'd gotten tangled up in Linny's troubles and the river's own crises.

They'd come to the Colorado River for an adventure, but they'd ended up in a tragedy. For a fleeting second, Claire thought that Linny had no more luck or hold on life than she did. Immediately, though, she knew that wasn't true. She hadn't paid sufficient attention to Ellie and hadn't known she was in trouble, but Linny knew. Linny paid attention to everything—to Ellie and the others—while Claire disengaged from those around her, like she always did.

Once they were on the water, floating the current, Dirk seemed to let his anger go. As they took the safest route, avoiding eddies and large waves, Claire too lost her own train of thought. The river, wild but for the moment not terrifying, tumbled into the deepest section of the canyon, into an earlier time, and Tess told them they had dropped into the Precambrian period of history. Schist, a dark metamorphic rock, created a deep inner gorge that jutted straight from the river towards a clear blue sky.

"These rocks are about 1.7 billion years old," Tess said. "And see the veins of pink and red Zoroaster granite? That was magma that shot through this tectonic mountain range and then cooled."

She pointed out much younger rivers of cooled lava cascading down the steep side canyons. At one lava flow, the dark rock seemed to descend straight from the sky. A little further down river, the rock reared up directly from the water. They pulled to shore, and the guides pointed out the remnants of a lava dam. A few miles later they passed a layer of basalt columns wedged into the cliff.

"This is so incongruous," Linny said. "Everything else in the canyon is flowing and weathered and eroded, and here, in the oldest section, vertical, sharp columns tower above the water."

"Don't you just love that?" Tess said. "The canyon always surprises."

"But how did it happen?"

"The columns formed as the lava slowly cooled. So, the lava flows are fast cooling and the basalt columns are slow cooling," Tess said.

The rafts floated the current, and for a while, no one said anything. It was hard for Claire to envision the canyon with lava flowing down from volcanoes on the rim, and some of that lava cooling quickly, and some taking a long time to cool. She'd followed the discussion of geology when it involved the deposition of sedimentary layers by receding waters, but the chaos of volcanic eruptions and molten flows and fast and slow cooling lava seemed more than she could comprehend.

The rafts pulled up at a long, narrow beach.

"If it's O.K. with everyone," West said, "we'll look for the medicine pouch before lunch."

Not all the rafters knew about the old man leaving his pouch on the beach and asking Tess to find it. West explained. No one said anything.

"The old Indian told me to look for his medicine pouch on this beach," Tess said. "So, we'll start looking here, fanning out across the sand."

She said it matter-of-factly, as if it were all set—they'd spend ten minutes walking across the sand, and they'd find the medicine pouch. The beach spread as far as they could see in both river directions.

"Are you serious?" Linny said. "This beach is practically endless."

Tess shrugged. "The elder said we'd find it, and I don't know why he'd say that if it weren't true."

She started pacing across the sand, heading upstream. She didn't have any better plan than walking up and down across the sand looking for the medicine pouch. She walked several yards, her head turning from side to side as she scanned the sand. She tried to imagine where a ceremony would be held, but one place seemed as likely as the next. A crow flew overhead, it's wings barely moving, its flight in no way disturbing the tranquility of the moment. Minutes later it began to caw and circle above them.

The cawing grew louder and more insistent, until no none could ignore it. Tess stopped walking and watched the crow circle the beach, fly back to the raft, and circle the raft. With an ear-piercing scream, it swooped down into her raft and tangled the strap of one of her flip-flops around its right foot.

"No," she yelled, running across the sand back to her raft. "That's my favorite pair!"

The crow flew up before she could reach it. Cawing loudly, it circled above them; the guides and rafters watched. Suddenly it swooped down and flew west, away from where they stood.

"No," Tess yelled after it.

As they watched, it dropped the sandal onto the crest of a small dune. Tess ran to retrieve the flip-flop. She stopped a yard or two short and stooped down. When she stood up and turned to the rafters watching her, she held up the medicine pouch. The crow flew above the cliffs and disappeared.

"O.K." West called, "Time for lunch!"

71

Day 11. Afternoon

It was as quiet a lunch as they'd had the day before. No one said much of anything. No one mentioned Ellie or asked about Tim. No one commented on the morning's geology, the huge columns resembling majestic porticoes springing from the cliff walls, angular tubes slumping down a rocky cascade. No one asked about the medicine pouch.

Claire took refuge in the silence. That wasn't particularly unusual for her, but she thought it unusual for Linny.

The river flow continued high—as if that were the new normal—but no one mentioned it.

Claire looked for Linny but didn't see her. Dirk sat alone, slightly apart from the others, watching the current. He clutched a sandwich in each hand, almost like a toddler, a very big, almost grown-up toddler, holding a cookie in each hand.

"Where's your mom?" Claire asked.

Dirk turned his head and looked downstream, and Claire followed his gaze. Where the river turned to the right and the sand narrowed and the beach almost disappeared, Linny sat with her back against a rock and her legs stretched out towards the water, staring at the river.

"I wouldn't bother her," Dirk said. "She's really grouchy."

"I'm tough," Claire said, "even if I don't look it. I can handle her."

"No, you look tough," he said as Claire headed across the sand.

She hesitated for a moment, surprised by his comment, but she didn't turn around. She walked to where Linny sat and dropped down beside her.

"What's going on here?" Linny asked. "What?"

Claire shook her head.

"Scientists here are researching the river, and I think we're in the twenty-first century," Linny said. "Then a Medicine Man manipulates a crow to lead us on a hunt, and I don't know where we are. Whatever happened on the beach certainly wasn't science. And it didn't feel like the twenty-first century."

"Maybe," Claire said, "the canyon distorts things, or at least changes our perception of what's going on."

"What the hell does that mean?" Linny said.

Claire shrugged her shoulders and shook her head, unable to answer. She didn't understand what had happened, only that it had been real.

"I've got real-world problems and a real-world life," Linny said. "Ellie's death is as real-world as it gets. Who has time for this shit?"

Claire didn't answer. Here they were, surrounded by ancient rocks and magnificent beauty, at the mercy of natural forces, with no obligations other than the basic requirements of camping and living—surviving. Grand Canyon was certainly the place to ponder the nature of reality. She felt she needed more information, and she wanted to know how others interpreted the morning's events. She had no thoughts beyond that. Linny stared at her for a while, then she turned away and scanned the sand at her feet. Claire followed her gaze. Several odd little creatures marched nearby.

"They're so adorable," Claire said. "So soft and fuzzy – with bright red fur!"

"They're called velvet ants," Linny said, "but they're really wasps. They sting, but nothing as bad as red ants, which have one of the worst stings in the canyon. If they get you, you'll want to cut off your foot, or your hand, or wherever they've stung you."

"These creatures don't have wings," Claire said.

"I know, but they're still wasps. Appearances can be deceiving. Maybe the canyon has distorted our perception, as you said."

"We're going to check out some pictographs on the cliffs!" Riz yelled across the beach. "Leaving in five minutes!"

72

Day 11. Afternoon

Claire pulled her camera from the small ammo box holding her personal gear and unclipped her daypack and water bottle from the red strap looped around the raft frame. She was ready, even anxious, to go. She needed something to do and something to think about, and Indian art fit the bill.

Linny continued to sit at the far edge of the beach; she hadn't moved. Claire hoped Linny wasn't obsessing about Claire's night with West, or why West had rejected her. Knowing Linny, she'd probably moved on to something new. Probably only Claire worried about West.

Claire filled her water bottle and looked back down the beach at Linny. After a moment's hesitation she walked along the river until she reached her friend. Linny still watched the velvet ants scurry across the sand, but she looked up at Claire.

"Nothing's working out for me," she said.

"At the moment," Claire said, "nothing's working for anyone. We just need to act normal, until we are normal. That means getting your pack and water bottle and joining the hike."

She held her hand out to Linny to pull her up. Linny hesitated, then grabbed Claire's hand. They joined the rear of the hiking group. Dirk was at the front of the line with Orion.

"It's about a mile hike to the pictographs," Orion said to the hikers as they headed for the tall cliffs. "Pictographs are drawings on the rocks, and petroglyphs are carvings in the rocks. On the jumbled blocks of sandstone back there, at the base of the cliff, we'll find pictographs, drawings."

They trudged over the sand and through the brush, a mix of willow, tamarisk, and mesquite, on a narrow, well used trail. With each step away from the river, the temperature rose. Claire couldn't remember if there'd been clouds in the sky earlier in the day, but if there had been any, they weren't there now. The sun was overhead, strong, and fully exposed. Under other circumstances, Claire might have turned back, any interest in Indian pictographs having evaporated after five minutes in the desert heat. Time and again she stopped to have a drink of water, prepared to fall behind the other hikers, but they also slowed. The mile walk felt like a ten-mile march.

As they neared the cliffs, Claire saw that the ocotillo at the base had started to bloom, and barrel cacti and creosote bushes grew from cracks in the rocks. A series of drawings danced across the bluff in a horizontal band—stick figures, animal figures, celestial representations in red and faded pink paint. Even as she resisted, too hot and tired to care, the pictographs transported her to another world.

"The experts tell us these are part of a Ghost Dance site from the late 19th century," Orion said. "It was a practice of the Paiute Indians to reunite the spirits of the dead with those of the living. The Navajo never joined the Ghost Dance Movement. They were afraid of ghosts."

Claire looked around her—no condescending smiles, no patronizing shakes of the head. All of them had witnessed the death of Ellie, and they'd watched a crow, purportedly guided by an Indian elder, direct a search party. Claire didn't know if she believed in spirits and ghosts, but she understood the Paiutes' interest, and she couldn't fault the Navajo for being frightened.

"I'm headed back," Linny said, and she started down the trail to the river.

"I'll walk with you," Claire said as she jogged to catch up.

"I can't handle this spiritual woo-woo," Linny said. "I've got to get Dirk to a boarding school for September. Yes that's a rarefied problem, and it means I have a lot of money, but it's a real, actual problem that requires a real-world solution. And either Steve or I, or maybe both of us, need to find a new place to live in a city with few vacancies. Reality. Life. I can't wait for an Indian psychic to guide me. New York living is hard. Not like here. Not like California.

"Maybe in California you let psychics guide you—I don't know. Somehow everyone manages, the kids go to school, you and Paul get along, you clean or don't clean your house. You don't worry about someone reporting you to the co-op board if your housecleaner goes back to Haiti and you can't find a replacement.

"And life here in Grand Canyon – even simpler."

Claire walked behind Linny and didn't say anything. She'd never had a housekeeper, and she'd never met anyone from Haiti. She and Linny had had similar conversations before, with Linny insisting that the rules in California were so much looser, that life for Claire was so much easier. Linny saw herself caught up in a whirlwind, without any options. She never recognized the choices that having money provided, and she never looked closely enough at Claire's life to make out the details. She was unable to see that she always had the choice to step out of the rat-race.

In the past, Claire had answered Linny by insisting that Linny chose how she wanted to live, that she was educated and wealthy and had more opportunities than almost anyone in the world. This time, though, Claire didn't say that. It was the eleventh morning of a Grand Canyon trip, tall cliffs rose around them, and the Colorado River raced before them. This time, Linny's complaints resonated differently with Claire. She felt sorry that Linny couldn't clearly see her situation, and she thought she'd arrived at a better understanding of her own life.

Perhaps the canyon had changed her, like the trip brochures said it would. Though the guides drank throughout the day, and Tess in particular started early and finished late, Claire hadn't finished her last flask. For the first time in a very long time, she wasn't' waiting for her next drink. Watching the sun rise over the eastern cliffs and set in the west rejuvenated her. Tracking the sun across the open sky, from rim to rim, filled her day. She'd spent joyful hours scanning the river bank and cliffs, trying to spot a beaver or a mountain goat. Now she watched the water level, worried the river would flood. She understood and accepted her dependence on the guides to protect her. She was beginning to accept her fundamental lack of control.

Life back in California, in Santa Cruz, seemed far away and very remote, and she hoped to return home to live a decent life. She couldn't see why that wasn't possible, and if that were true for her, it was also true for Linny. They both had options.

No matter what Linny said, life in Grand Canyon was not simple. In all important ways, life was harder in Grand Canyon than in California or New York. Life in Grand Canyon was reduced to the basics. There was sufficient time and energy only for essentials, and if anyone in the canyon got distracted, even for a moment, the consequences were dire. They had all seen that.

Keeping one's eye on the ball seemed a good way to live, and Claire thought she could return to California with that perspective. She didn't know exactly what that meant for her life, and she didn't know what it might mean for Linny's life. It sounded right though.

73

Day 11. Afternoon

P enny for your thoughts," West said as he sat down next to Claire.

"I'm thinking that my husband drinks too much and he's mean to me and the kids, and my mother was mean when I was growing up," Claire said. "I went from one mean person to another, instead of looking for someone nice. Why did I repeat the pattern? Why didn't I find someone nice?"

As soon as she finished speaking, Claire regretted what she'd said. She had no idea why she'd done it.

West shrugged. "I don't know much of anything."

"Right," Claire chuckled, relieved that West let her confession pass without comment. "Why is it I wouldn't be surprised if you had a PhD?"

"Post hole digger, I've got one."

"You have a ranch?" Claire asked.

"Some land, out near Kanab, Utah."

"Are you there in the winter, when you're not guiding on the river?"

"Sometimes I travel a little, if I have the money, or I hire myself out as a ranch hand if I don't. Mostly I like to spend time at home."

"I think I've got too much time at home."

"Can you guys help with dinner prep?" Tess asked as she walked over.

"You're unrelenting," West said, and he walked towards the kitchen.

"I'll come in a minute," Claire said. "I need to set up camp and wash up. I was too wiped out when we got here."

"Yeah," Tess said, "it was a long day. But we're back on schedule."

Claire looked around her. They had pulled onto a long beach at the mouth of a big, wide canyon. As they pulled the rafts on shore Tess had announced that they would hike up the canyon in the morning.

"Meaning," she said, "that we've arrived at camp unusually late, and we need everyone to help and no one to wander off exploring."

Claire had pulled her bags from the raft and dropped herself onto the sand. When she turned to look for Linny, she saw her friend setting up her tent. When she looked again, she saw Linny heading up Parshant Wash, the large canyon Tess had placed off limits. Claire had looked because she'd known Linny would go. It wasn't exactly that Linny didn't think the rules applied to her. It was more that she had to do whatever was interesting and exciting at the moment, and Claire both admired and censured that trait in her friend.

By the time she made it to the sandy kitchen, the prep work was all completed and the cooking had started. West, who assisted with prep, was no longer there, but Tess, who was cooking, welcomed all assistance.

"This will get you in the mood," she said. "The menu is: chili relleno casseroles, cooked in dutch-ovens with charcoal, a napa cabbage coleslaw, and refried beans. Cookies for dessert. If we have time, I'll make some pitchers of margaritas – we've got tequila and limes and everything else we need. Even have some ice available. It's so beautiful here, we have to make a special dinner."

That's it, Claire thought. In the canyon, someone, perhaps everyone, was paying attention to the beauty of each moment, and time rarely slipped away unacknowledged. Now that she thought about it, every day probably deserved a special dinner, for one reason or another, but she'd never thought about it like that. She might never have cooked a special dinner except for a birthday or anniversary celebration, and over a year's time, there were only a handful of such special days.

74

Day 11. Evening

Though she was drinking less, Claire noticed that everyone else drank more. Perhaps the increased alcohol consumption related to their nearing the end of the trip and feeling sufficiently comfortable and relaxed to let go, or no longer needing to ration. Or it could be the tragedy of Ellie's death. Or the uncertainty of the river flow. For her, it was different. She drank in the beginning from habit, tension, and insecurity. That's also why she drank at home. She hoped she'd figured out how to manage her anxiety without alcohol. She wouldn't know until she was back home.

Even before dinner officially started, the guides and passengers finished off the beers they had cooled in the river. That forced the guides to scour the rafts for replacements, and with only three days left on the river, supplies were, apparently, getting low. Orion, Riz, and West collected what beer they could find and dumped the cans into the drag bags suspended in the current. Before those replacements had sufficiently cooled, someone found the tequila and started pouring shots. Tess never made margaritas, but the rafters quickly drained two bottles of the cheap booze.

Dinner, though delicious, was almost an afterthought, and even Tess, who'd done the cooking, didn't appear to mind. As soon as they finished eating, the guides cleared the dinner dishes and brought a couple bottles of whisky onto the beach. Several passengers scampered back to their tents and returned with additional bottles. Clearly, this was the night to share.

"You going to share what you brought?" Dirk said, and Claire turned to look at him, amazed at what he knew about her.

He sat next to Claire, and she glanced at him and turned away. This wasn't a conversation she wanted to have, even though it was an extraordinary thing for him to say, considering they'd hardly had a conversation. It reminded her how her kids always knew the situation with their father, though she worked hard to keep them uninformed. What was that process, she wondered, by which children knew the score on the adults in their lives? They looked so young and innocent, but they often knew everything the adults around them were trying to hide.

Claire nursed a beer. She drank neither the tequila nor the whisky. Linny drank both. Conversation swirled around them with inexplicable stops and starts, and Claire gave up trying to follow what anyone said. Linny argued with someone, then Tess expounded her theory of survival. From the corner of her eye, Claire saw Dirk pour himself several shots of whiskey. It seemed that everyone in the group made a point of not noticing, except Linny, who seemed genuinely unaware.

What Claire wanted, more than anything, was to talk about everything that had happened in the past couple of days. She supposed it was the lawyer in her, but now that she'd had a little time to process the information, she wanted to understand exactly why Ellie had died and what they could have done to prevent it. She didn't want to assign blame; she just wanted a better grasp on what had happened. Should they have paid more attention to Ellie? Had the others? The young woman had caught Linny's eye, and Claire wondered why. Had Ellie wanted their attention? What about Tim? Why didn't he and Ellie protect themselves after Ellie almost died in Hermit Rapids? Did the high water make the tragedy inevitable?

Claire also wondered whether this was a common occurrence on the river—whether rafters or kayakers often drowned, even when the water flow was normal. Should the guides have known there was a problem? Did they know, but find themselves helpless to do anything about it? What could they have done? Were the river-permit rules too lax?

Claire was certain that kayaking down the Colorado was a known, risky adventure, and she wasn't looking to pin liability on anyone. She just wanted to understand the tragedy in human terms and know how it could have been prevented. Clearly there were warning signs.

What about the river? The ranger told them the dam had breached; they'd known the water was high. Should they have continued down the river? And now what? Would the dam stay breached and the water high? Would the dam fail and the river flood? Were they prepared?

Question after question ran through Claire's head, over and over, as if on a reel. She realized, with a start, that she'd had over a week's relief from that particular brain torture, her normal way of being. Always, after she'd run through questions that bothered her, she couldn't get their repeated repetition out of her head.

Claire tried not to listen to the conversation that swirled around her—it wasn't what she wanted to talk about. At one point, she heard Linny talking about her. Her immediate reaction was to pay attention, but then she very deliberately forced herself to turn away and retreat into herself without listening. In the past, she would have needed to know what Linny was saying about her, what Linny thought of her. Now she realized how little Linny knew her, and how little Linny's opinion ultimately mattered. If Linny didn't understand Claire's life, which she didn't, it couldn't matter what Linny said about her. Whatever story or anecdote Linny was telling about Claire, it had more to do with Linny than with Claire. Years ago she'd realized that about her mother, but she hadn't, until this evening, understood that about Linny. It now seemed that Dirk, Linny's sixteen year-old, knew Claire better than anyone did.

"You're still nursing the same beer you took before dinner," West said. "That's a change. What's the matter?"

Claire looked over at the rugged guide who'd squeezed in next to her, placing himself between Claire and Linny and most of the rafters. She didn't answer.

"I'm not judging or criticizing, just wondering," he said. "Every guide on the river has or had a drinking problem, so we know."

"O.K.," Claire thought to herself. "She'd slept with West—twice, to be exact. But she didn't know anything about him, and he didn't know anything about her. He was just another person who thought he knew her, but didn't know a thing. At one time Paul knew her, but now he didn't bother giving her a thought. She was perhaps the last thing on his mind."

Claire pushed her bottle into the sand and stood up.

"Goodnight," she said to West and walked away from the camp circle to her tent.

As she walked, she thought about what had happened with West. But what did happen? She'd been married fifteen years, and she'd always been faithful and never even seriously tempted to cheat. So, what had changed? Was it West, or the Grand Canyon, or the situation at home?

West was certainly different from any man she knew. Tall, six feet three or four, with the dark leathery skin of a fifty year-old boatman and the muscles of someone who had spent a lifetime working on the river, he could be Grand Canyon's real-life action figure, and she found everything about him sexy. Still, that explained nothing. She'd known other sexy men, and she hadn't jumped into bed with them. She wasn't a teenager. Power and intellect also impressed her, and she'd known many men sexy with those traits, but she'd never been seriously tempted.

Grand Canyon was different from any place she'd been. The wilderness was remote, the scenery spectacular, and the days filled with adventure. Claire felt immense gratitude for the opportunity to raft the canyon. She knew that sounded a little corny, but it was how she felt. Her sense of gratefulness was palpable. She thought it must be how all the trip participants felt, and that explained some things, but it didn't explain how she and West ended up together. She hadn't come to Grand Canyon to find a lover.

75

Diary Day 11

We started the day examining the rocks and learning about the canyon's geology. The river plunged into the deepest part of Grand Canyon, and we coursed down through prehistoric rock. Our rafts swept between immense towering cliffs, and the canyon expanded and narrowed around us as we went ever deeper. In an area of black metamorphic rocks formed more than a billion and a half years ago, neon pink veins shot through the shiny dark rock—the remnants of hot magma that solidified after the lava rocks cooled. A short time later, we floated past a section of basalt rising into enormous columns, as if carved straight from the cliff. It all seemed magical, and I wished I knew more science, to understand it better.

The real magic, though, began later in the morning. Back at Phantom Ranch, an old Indian medicine man had introduced himself to our river guide, and he asked her to retrieve the medicine pouch he'd left behind on his recent trip down the river. I'd forgotten, or maybe I thought we would just ignore the Indian's request, but our guides remembered. Before lunch we pulled up to the beach where he said he'd left the pouch, a narrow strip of sand almost two miles long.

The beach was sand and more sand—not much else. Wind had formed several rows of small dunes at the far back, near the cliffs, but other than these rises, the beach was an indistinguishable expanse, except in the few places beyond the dunes, where the cliffs had fractured and large rocks had slumped down into piles of debris. In all directions, from the cliffs to the shoreline, for a two-mile stretch along the river, the beach was unremarkable.

The guides told us to spread out and look for the medicine pouch. Spread out over two miles! I joined the others, kicking across the sand, not having any idea where to go. Everything else on the trip had been so well planned; this seemed quite the anomaly. As far as I could tell, no one knew what to do. I certainly didn't know what I was doing.

I can't remember what I thought next, so I'll just tell you what happened. A crow started circling overhead and cawing, and it got louder and louder, and everyone stopped walking and looked up into the sky. While we watched, the crow flew over Tess' raft (my raft) and dove down into the back where Tess kept her things, and it grabbed Tess' sandal in its right claw. Then it flew back overhead, circling over all of us. Tess waived her arms and screamed at the crow, but it flew in circles high above the sand. Then it took off flying across the beach towards the cliffs. Tess ran after it, yelling and trying to attract its attention so it would drop her sandal.

As we watched, the crow did drop the sandal, and it fell to the sand. Tess ran over to retrieve it and there, next to the sandal, she found the medicine pouch.

76

Day 12. Morning

Claire woke early, remembering the plan to hike up Parashant Wash even while her eyes were shut tight. When she opened her eyes, a very faint light filtered through the darkness, the dim start of morning in the canyon, and she sat up and started to dress. She liked the plan to spend the early morning off the water, exploring the canyon. In the afternoon it would be too hot to enjoy a hike through the rocks and across the desert sand; in the afternoon, they'd all want to be back on the river.

She dressed as quickly as she could, took down her tent, and stuffed her bags. She walked to the camp kitchen, thinking she'd be one of the first to arrive for coffee, but most of the rafters already stood facing the river, staring at the water, coffee cup in hand. As she stood looking at everyone, trying to understand why they were all up so early, she caught Tess' eye, and the young guide shrugged her shoulders and smiled. Apparently they were all anxious to go hiking and postpone progress down the river. Everyone knew the trip was coming to an end.

Claire drank her coffee and ate her breakfast, paying attention to neither her food nor her surroundings, more distracted than she'd been any morning in the canyon. Her thoughts were elsewhere—about taking off the river in two days, about being back home the following day. For a moment there, she'd thought things had changed, but now she thought that nothing had changed. She was the same person, and she'd go home to the same children, the same husband, and the same life. If she hadn't been changed by her adventure, her family wouldn't be changed by her absence. Maybe she'd set clearer boundaries with Paul, but she had no illusions that would significantly change her life.

West offered to clean up the breakfast mess and box the kitchen gear while everyone hiked up the wash. Orion and Tess led the way, accompanied by Dirk. Claire walked with Linny, studying the crunchy pebbles of the dry streambed that filled the gully between the golden cliffs.

"What amazing light," Linny said, and Claire looked up.

Ahead of them, bright sunlight streamed down between the majestic, massive walls, highlighting a small section of the canyon and lifting it from the deep shade that held the rest of the narrow gorge. The lighted rocks looked regal—their colors richer and deeper than those of the surrounding panorama. The sunlit air disappeared—clearer and sharper. No one had provided a description of this hike, and Claire had expected it to be unexceptional—nothing like Deer Creek or Havasu. She'd thought the guides had improvised a needed break from the river. The landscape, in its own way, was as spectacular as anything they'd seen on the trip.

They marched single-file through broken cliffs resembling columns, until Orion announced they'd reached the Book of Worms. They stood before a huge slab of rock covered with fossilized worm tracks, a rock section looking like a book opened on the ground, its pages upright and covered with innumerable worm tracks. Tess said the wormholes were 550 million years old.

Riz pulled out a sheet of paper and read a quote from John Muir's, Grand Canyon of the Colorado.

"The whole canyon is a mine of fossils in which five thousand feet of horizontal strata are exposed in regular succession... forming a grand geological library—a collection of stone books covering thousands of miles of shelving tier on tier conveniently arranged for the student. And with what wonderful scriptures are their pages filled—myriad forms of successive floras and faunas, lavishly illustrated with colored drawings, carrying us back into the midst of the life of a past infinitely remote. And as we go on and on, studying this old, old life in the light of the life beating warmly about us, we enrich and lengthen our own."

77

Day 12. Morning

They returned to the beach to find that West had cleaned the kitchen, packed the gear, and loaded the rafts. He'd struck down the campsite and returned the beach to its natural state, clear and unblemished except for numerous small bushes scattered across the sand. Claire stood for a moment admiring the casual, understated beauty of the beach, so different from many of the majestic canyon tableaus. Where much in the canyon mirrored the immensity of the universe, leaving Claire feeling small and inconsequential, this beach didn't minimize her but merely impressed her with its simple charm.

They climbed aboard the rafts and headed down the still swollen river. The landscape changed again. The massive cliffs disappeared, replaced by huge canyon walls that sloped away from the river and allowed a more expansive view of the desert. In all directions the canyon opened and widened, the dry, rocky terrain extending to the horizon. It was no less imposing than the inner canyon.

For several miles the river ran mostly south and southwest, and the water moved quickly, and they made good time. When they stopped for lunch, it was not yet noon, and the sun was not quite overhead. Across the river from where they pulled the rafts ashore, the canyon sprouted showy crimson ocotillo. The plants seemed to grow in arrangements, numerous large, spiny stems jutting from small sandy crevices in the cliffs or along the narrow borders of flatter rocks.

"Ocotillo like the sunnier, open areas of the lower canyon," Tess announced. "That's why they're now so abundant. We'll see them all day today."

Behind the beach where they'd hopped ashore, Riz led them on a short hike through the weeds. He pointed out a plant he called Desert Tobacco—small, with purple flowers of five petals. He also pointed out numerous archeology features—the ruins of a pueblo and the remains of a roasting pit from an early occupation of the canyon by ancient Indians. The Indians returned to these sites every year on their migrations, seeking out favorite places and reusing the same buildings and fire pits. Riz said that modern Indians insisted that the agave found here, closer to the water, was sweeter tasting than the agave up on the plateau.

With the big rapids behind them and canyon views opening to the larger desert, the trip changed. Claire felt an urgency to organize her thoughts and make sense of all that had happened. She needed to make plans for her return home.

Thinking about her family made her sadder than she wanted to admit. A depression pulled at her; her thoughts burdened her. Her kids were basically good, but she found little joy in rearing them. She blamed Paul. She blamed herself. Nothing was going to change. She didn't have the courage, if that's what it took. She'd had almost two weeks of adventure, yet nothing had been resolved.

She looked at the ancient ruins Riz pointed out, with no sense of awe. She was unimpressed—perhaps running out of enthusiasm. Could be that's what happened at home—too much going on, with too much repetition, and she couldn't sustain her interest. Day after day, family issues and family patterns stayed the same, repeating problems that had surfaced the day before, and the week before that. Of course she was bored and unhappy. How could she not be? Who wouldn't be?

Linny pointed out the large number of beautiful velvet ants scurrying back and forth across the brown dirt. If she hadn't already told Claire and everyone else that the ant was a wasp with a particularly painful sting, Claire, or one of the other rafters, would have picked one up and petted it. They were that cute, almost irresistible. If Sarah were there, Claire couldn't have stopped her from petting the wasp and getting stung. Seeing the puff of soft, red hair, Sarah would never have listened to her mother's warning. Maybe she'd have listened to Linny or to Tess.

They climbed back into the rafts, and Claire took the seat she'd occupied most of the trip—on Tess' raft, behind Linny and across from Dirk. Somehow, she was neither bored nor burdened by that configuration. If anything, she found comfort in floating the canyon with Tess rowing, and her friend sitting in front of her. In any case, the day was heating up, and it felt good to be back on the water.

78

Day 12. Afternoon

Two rapids this afternoon," Tess said. "One at Mile 205, sometimes called Kolb Rapids, and one at Mile 209. Nothing like the big rapids we've run. Neither is particularly difficult, usually just referenced by their mile locations, but they both have a wave and a hole that require attention. The problem today is that the water is high and fast, and we aren't really sure what's happening."

Claire had noticed that the river level was extraordinarily high and the waters rough. Although she'd accustomed herself to Tess and learned to appreciate the young guide, the high water made her nervous. Her mind wandered back and forth across the canyon, over the guides and trip participants, and settled again and again on West. She turned in her seat and searched for his face.

The current was swift and scary, but still the heat was brutal. Tess rowed, keeping the raft steady in the current, and they moved swiftly down the river. She was relieved by the absence of wind, yet wished for a slight breeze. Beads of sweat ran down the edge of her face, and her sunglasses slid down her nose on the sweat that dripped from her forehead. She leaned over the water and splashed some of the cold river water onto her arms and legs.

Claire was turned around looking for West when she saw Tess splashing.

"That looks good," she said.

"Don't worry," Tess said, "You'll get wet in the rapids."

"Hey," she yelled above the noise of the river. "Looks like we're pulling over to visit the science trip."

One after another their rafts pulled off the river onto a sandy beach and eased in among the rafts and motorboats tied-up along the shoreline. A couple of umbrellas had been set up on the beach, and the guides were huddled there in the shade.

The scientists could be seen on a rise above the beach, and as soon as the raft passengers disembarked, Orion led them across the sand up a short weedy trail to an over-heated archeological site where the scientists had assembled. Claire didn't see Brent. A young woman came over to discuss their work.

"Seems like explaining things to all the raft trips would be a real hassle. Why do you do it?" Claire asked.

"Not everyone stops," the woman answered, "and Park Service rules. It's the price of working in the Canyon."

Claire wondered how Linny felt about being a cost. She herself had no reaction.

The woman, who introduced herself as Cheryl, was the archeologist in charge of the investigation.

"This is a totally cool spot," she said. "There are still artifacts here—they haven't disappeared—and the site has an interesting history. Years earlier the Park Service tried to protect this archeological feature by advising rafters to leave it undisturbed. That didn't work, so to protect the archeology, the Park Service instead closed the beach to commercial and private trips. Unless a Park Service archeologist is present, no one is allowed to stop here. You are seeing something very special."

Looking around, her eyes focused by the introduction, Claire could see that the site was different from others they'd visited. The main part of the ruin rose from sand near the base of the cliff. Partial walls formed rooms, and what must have been doors connected rooms to each other. It looked like the ruins of an ancient village buried beneath the sand. Walking closer to the site, she saw potsherds scattered on the sands. The archeologist picked up one after another and identified them as Tsegi Orange Ware, Red Mesa Black-on-White, and Black-on-Red Ware. She dropped them back to the sand. She pointed out a plain, large, curved neckband from a water vessel. They skirted the perimeter of the ruin, and it was like walking through an open-air, desert museum.

After a while, to escape from the heat, Claire found a small sliver of shade under a large creosote bush. She sat for a few minutes with her eyes lowered to the baked dirt, and she listened for desert sounds. The sun burned everything in sight, and every living thing seemed at rest: scorpions, velvet ants, even beetles had disappeared. Claire sat cross-legged and stared into the shimmering, hazy atmosphere, aware of her place in the barren desert.

"The jurisdiction over this site is in dispute," Cheryl said. "The United States government claims that the site, below the high water line of the river, is under its control. The U.S. set the boundary between Grand Canyon National Park and tribal lands at the Colorado's high-water-line. The tribes adjacent to the park, however, assert a boundary in the middle of the river, and they claim that tribal lands extend from the high, wind-blown plateaus into the main current of the Colorado. Neither the government nor the tribes talk of compromise. Instead, with both deeming judicial adjudication of the dispute too risky, and with both fearful of potential loss, the U.S. and the tribes agree to disagree. All parties accept a status quo of ambiguity and leave the boundaries unresolved. As a result, the U.S. regulates use of the area, but the Indians come and go as they want, crossing into protected areas and visiting closed sites."

As she talked, she picked up a thin plastic produce bag, torn in several places, its forest green lettering faded. It appeared to be filled with a thick white powder.

"What's this?" she said.

"Some kind of hallucinogenic drug?" Dirk said.

Everyone looked at him. "That's what happens when you go to high school," Claire thought. "It's going to happen to Sarah and Greg. I'm not ready."

The researcher tore the bag open. The contents, looking like ground shells, spilled from the plastic. Numerous solid white chunks, the size of small tootsie rolls, as bleached as the candy was dark, settled into the palm of her hand. She dropped the sack and knelt to examine its contents.

"Crudely cremated bones," she said. "Human."

"Cool," Dirk said, and again everyone looked at him.

Cheryl pulled a very small trowel from her pack and used the tip to poke the largest pieces. Sliding the smooth blade into the powder, she scooped up as much as she could and sifted back and forth until only one large piece was left.

"A human tooth," she said. "Standard fare of Southwest archeology. It's flat, worn, and easily identified as Native American."

She held the tooth between her fingers and pointed out a small nail protruding from one side.

"Never saw this in the field before," she said.

She described the nail as a distinct model used years earlier in museum exhibits, and she said it provided definite confirmation that the tooth was human. She took a cotton sampling-bag from her pack and scooped the plastic bag, the partially cremated bones, the ash and powder, and a small amount of sandy dirt, into the sack.

"Probably a cremated human skull," she said, "stolen from a museum, unprofessionally cremated, and brought here for burial in the canyon."

"I know about this," Linny said, and everyone turned to look at her. She told them she'd read an article in *The Coloradoan* when she'd searched on Google for information about Indian country, the southwest, and Grand Canyon.

A Colorado skinhead had been arrested for breaking into museums and stealing American Indian skulls and skeletons. He smashed them and sent the smashed bits to Indian tribes, mostly in Arizona, to rid Colorado museums of an Indian influence. The article quoted an elder of some tribe who said sacred remains should never be put in museums.

Claire didn't hear the rest of the discussion. She thought how much she loved museums, how she'd always appreciated examining the artifacts kept there. Only Linny would know about skinheads and elders who didn't want those museum displays.

79

Day 12. Afternoon

The rafts pulled off the beach and headed down the river. Tess found her small flask, took a long drink, and stuffed it in her pocket. This looked to be the kind of afternoon that needed drinking. The rapids would be small enough, but the current was crazy, and she wasn't sure what was going on.

The sun flashed on the river, but the water didn't shine. The river looked swollen and dirty. Although Tess knew it improbable, the river seemed more threatening than it had just a short while ago. It seemed to have risen noticeably in just the past hour. Choppy waves splashed against the rafts' tubes, and the water looked increasingly opaque. Occasionally, branches and logs and small bushes swept down the currents. She'd never before seen that.

They hit the Rapids at Mile 205. She slid the raft into the rapids at the edge of the hole, but couldn't control the raft. Instead of skimming the hole, the raft bounced back and forth across the river. The current was too powerful. She could only go where the water pushed her, and it pushed her down into the hole. Water splashed across the bow; she entered the rapids and braced herself. Tension gripped her shoulders and spread down her back. She strained at the oars, her hands so tightly gripped on the rubber handles it looked like they were molded in plastic. Her knuckles turned white. She no longer sat back in her seat; instead she leaned forward. The water was so crazy it pulled the raft forward into the tail of a wave. The usual spray of water was lost in the general tumult. Tess had never seen the rapids like that.

She stood up on her seat and looked downstream. She didn't recognize the river.

They continued down the river, and the raft raced left and right, and down the middle. Tess did her best to control it. Tree limbs and branches, looking too heavy to float, now surfed the waves. Slabs of driftwood converged into numerous small dams, while other free-floating logs and debris rushed downriver. With each wave crest, water gushed across her front tube. The Colorado no longer looked like a river. It looked more like the mouth of a bay or an open ocean. It looked like the scene of a flood.

Tess heard the distinctive whir of a helicopter, the sound low, coming down the river. The helicopter flew into view. Plastered to the body, below the rotors, was a large sign

"Danger. Immediate flooding. Dam emergency. Seek high ground."

Almost immediately the bottom of the raft scraped across a rock and pitched into a drop. The right side of the boat slammed into a boulder. The rocks usually exposed in the river vanished under the high water, and the raft tumbled down the river over out-sized boulders. Debris floating on the water battered the small inflatable. Tess pulled at her oars to keep the raft afloat. It smashed into the small trees and large branches that suddenly surrounded it, and it bounced off the rocks submerged in the churning current. The water was like nothing she'd ever seen on the Colorado, nothing she'd ever experienced, maybe like the river before the dam.

"Shit! Hold on!" she yelled.

The river rained from above and drenched the raft below. The current forced them further downstream. Tess tried to catch her breath but had no time to breathe. She pulled hard on her oars, trying to steady the raft. They tumbled down a drop that she didn't remember being there. Water poured into the raft from the huge waves. Ahead of her Tess saw her passengers clinging to straps.

She couldn't possibly find a place to pull to shore, certainly couldn't find a spot where they could climb to higher ground. She had no choice but to row the raft as best she could.

A logjam blocked the farthest right channel of the river, and for the first time in many years, Tess prayed she wouldn't flip. The water was so violent merely running the current had become treacherous. Logs, branches, even clumps of mud hit the raft. The rafting was out of Tess' control; flipping was a real possibility.

Sooner than expected, Tess heard the roar that announced the approach of the next rapids. Claire heard it too, but before she could reposition herself and tighten her handhold, the raft bumped at the edge of a large hole at the center of the rapids and dropped down, and a wave erupted directly underneath the raft and bounced it into the air. The following seconds unfolded in slow motion, for what seemed like an eternity. A foam rose from opaque depths, and Claire hovered in the rapids' mist, without a handhold, suspended high above the raft. Without seeing anything or feeling anything, she understood that the raft had pitched down into frothy water and was itself submerged. Icy water from a wave gushed down her life jacket and further drenched her already soaked shirt. The wave engulfed her, blocking her vision and surrounding her with the deafening roar of the water. She was unable to think, and barely able to breathe.

The paralysis that gripped her broke, and Claire screamed out in fear. She could barely hear herself, and she knew no one else could hear her. Just then another wave hit. Consumed by cold and terror, she squeezed her eyes shut, unable to do more. She couldn't see anything or hear anything. She felt like she was having a heart attack. She had no idea which way was up. Her shallow breathing stuck in her nose and throat, caught in the upper reaches of her chest and around her collarbone. Instead of her body filling with breath, it filled with heartbeats and pulses and surges, and she could feel each beat of her heart, as if it were ready to explode.

The water drained away, and the raft emerged below Claire, off to the left. She was neither in the raft, nor above it; she wasn't anywhere she should be. She knew without thinking that in a moment, she would be under water, submerged in the swollen river. She understood in the blink of an eye everything that had happened and everything that would happen. Panic consumed her, but before she fully understood the enormity of swimming down a flooding river, Dirk grabbed the strap of her life jacket and flipped her back into the raft.

His fingers encircled the strap of her life jacket and pulled her back to her place on the raft. He yanked her closer, and she tumbled into the boat, landing on the floor; she curled into a fetal position. Water pounded down on her, then drained away. She lay still, unable to move. One wave after another washed over her. The frigid water ran under her lifejacket and under her clothes and down her skin. She raised her head and finally caught her breath. Dirk stared at her.

"How many times can you save me?" she asked him, but he didn't hear her. Eventually he released his grip.

Claire was too shaken to do more than lay in a ball. She shut her eyes and felt the pounding river below the raft's rubber floor. If Dirk hadn't grabbed her, she'd be in that water, and Linny would be frantically searching for her. Life can change dramatically in a second. She pulled herself up onto the raft tube and took her seat.

She thought she might throw up. She pulled the straps on her jacket as tight as she could, compressing her chest even more and hoping for some stability or at least a sense of security. She moved toward the center of the raft and pushed her feet into the space beneath a tube. She found one strap that was long enough to wind around her hand and got a good grip. Though she searched, she couldn't find a second handhold. She cinched her hat tighter and moved her legs from underneath her to out in front, knees bent, feet braced as best she could. Even sitting in the middle of the raft, she didn't feel safe, but she had nowhere else to go. The raft sped past towering cliffs. The canyon narrowed and the river's turbulence grew fiercer.

Waves splashed across the raft almost continuously, keeping everyone soaked and chilled. The enormity of the danger and the shock of her rescue hit Claire, and she began to shake. Convulsing from the inside out, her stomach heaved, her lungs emptied, her heart pounded. She couldn't hold any part of her body still; nor could she breath.

80

Day 12. Afternoon

Tess was too focused to remember if any beaches had existed in this stretch of the river. If they had, they were gone, under water. Instead, there were only the waves of brown, flooding water, and the awful debris. The Colorado now surged through a canyon of rock and water, and rock and water closed in on the rafts, leaving room for nothing else. The only vegetation in the canyon now floated down the currents, racing to an unseen finish line.

The helicopter returned, first appearing in the distance like a small bird, down river against the horizon, and heading up the canyon. As it approached, it grew larger, no longer a bird, and it developed a main rotor and a tail rotor, a cockpit, and landing skids. Its weak puttering sound grew louder, until its incessant noise filled the canyon. It continued past the rafters, heading back up the canyon, announcing its warning.

Tess strained at the oars. The water rose higher and moved faster than she had imagined possible, obliterating everything in its path. Only the rocky cliffs and the rising river remained. Rowing was almost impossible. Even with all her concentration, she was barely able to keep the raft right-side-up, headed down the river. When she was drowning in the Kern, she'd thought she could make it. Now she worried they were doomed. She didn't have enough power to force the raft across the river and out of the current. She didn't know how they'd get off the water, even if she could find a place to pull out.

Only the adrenalin surging through her veins kept her oars in the oarlocks and her raft skimming the river. The effort needed to succeed at that point was beyond human. It wasn't something she could will herself to do. The water flowed high and fast, and any rapids disappeared in the swell, though that made them no less dangerous. The rocks that once hovered in the mist above the river, now hid below the water, an unseen threat, looming even larger. With more water, some of the whirlpools and holes disappeared, but others grew infinitely stronger, and she didn't know what to expect from one minute to the next. The river transformed itself into something unrecognizable, and it grew more frightening than she ever imagined possible.

She rowed on autopilot, doing everything she could do that required no thought, everything she'd been trained to do, everything her father had taught her. She abandoned her thinking mind and acted totally on instinct.

She worked her oars, trying to pull the raft to the left, to follow the raft before her. She searched the shoreline for an eddy. All they needed was the slightest indication of an eddy. A mere hint would do. They could escape the current and slow their rafts, if an opportunity arose. She prepared for success, as she'd been trained to do, but the swollen current pushed her downstream without regard to where she aimed the raft or tried to row. Waves broke against the raft and washed over her, bouncing her from her seat with every surge. Each wave of frigid, brown water submerged the raft.

Water sloshed across the outer tubes of the raft, and the river, filling with debris, threatened to trap them in a tangle of garbage. Small trees rolled in the water and knocked into the raft, and their roots, still filled with clumps of sand and soil, hovered above the river. The monumental force of the water pushed the raft out from the jumble and farther along. Tess felt dizzy from her exertion, nauseous and light-headed, and scared from the increasingly probable likelihood that they wouldn't make it. A wave splashed across the raft and for that moment she couldn't see. Her body stiffened against the force of the water. Her elbows locked as she struggled to keep her grip on the paddles, and her knees straightened as she braced her feet against the rowing frame. The wave washed away.

Tess let up on her left oar. She maintained her tight grasp on the handle, but relaxed the power of her pull mid-stroke. At the same time, she pushed harder on the right oar and forced it to remain in the water for one extra moment and then another. She braced herself against the rowing frame and leveraged all the strength she had into the right oar. She stared toward the left riverbank, willing the raft to move there, knowing that she had to get there. She didn't budge from the center of the current, and she continued to surge down the river with little control over the raft. Nothing she did had any effect.

She held her breath and squeezed every ounce of her effort into pulling on her oars, but still the raft didn't budge from the main current, and she raced downstream. She breathed quickly to pump oxygen into her blood and fuel her muscles, but her muscles grew no stronger, and she gasped for air. The raft remained in the center of the river. Tess couldn't breathe her way to being more powerful. She couldn't will the raft to move. Whatever she did, the raft stayed mid-current, rushing downriver.

With every pull on her oars, there seemed less and less room for the small raft. The river filled with debris. Tess pushed her oars against the rubble and struggled to keep the raft steady. Still, it tossed from side to side. She braced her feet against the rowing frame so she wouldn't be thrown out. She had no time or energy to think about her passengers. They were all in the raft; she hoped they were all right.

A bump from behind punched the raft forward, jamming the paddle of Tess's right oar down under several huge logs. The grip jerked from her hand and the oar, caught beneath the logs, snapped to attention. The oar popped from the oarlock, and only a small, nylon cord tethered the oar to the raft. Tess knew her odds. She had little chance of survival with two oars; she had no chance with only one oar. She clutched at the left oar to anchor herself in the raft, and she leaned out, as far as she could, over the right side tube to retrieve the right oar. She leaned farther, extending out over the river, and her feet slipped from the cross bar and she lost her footing. The left oar suspended her above the floor of the raft, and for a moment her only anchor was one oar thrashing in the water. She scraped her feet along the outer tube and reached the handle of the right oar. The fingers of her right hand wrapped around the foam oar-grip and pulled the oar free.

"Fucking impossible!" she yelled to no one.

"Hang in there!" roared a voice coming from behind her.

Another bump jolted the raft and again knocked it ahead, and Tess squeezed the oar grips and struggled to maintain control. She couldn't turn around to see who was there. She thought she might have imagined the voice of a savior. Most likely she was alone. Another bump jolted her raft, and this time she knew someone was pushing her from the current. She pulled on her oars with the little strength she had. Knowing she wasn't alone on the river reassured her and she found reserved strength. Her hands clamped the grips so tightly they compressed the non-compressible foam. Her oars cut through the water with renewed potential. She wasn't assured of a good ending, but she'd fight til the end.

She angled her raft to the left and pulled on her oars. Behind her, her savior pushed. The raft moved from the center to the edge of the main current. It headed toward a narrow side canyon. She saw a small eddy and aimed her raft there. She still wasn't sure she could make it.

81

Day 12. Evening

The science boats had pushed each of the oar rafts into the eddy. No one seemed to know how it happened, and everyone was too exhausted to talk about it. They were all safe, and for the moment, that was enough.

"We need to get the fuck out of here," West said. "Off this fucking river. Out of the fucking canyon."

Everyone nodded. This was the first they had seen of West's anger, and it scared them. The brown, muddy water of the river looked ever more wild. That scared them too. Only Tess seemed to take it all in stride.

The campsite was less than ideal—a narrow dash of sand at the mouth of a small side canyon—and much too small for a group their size. Where they usually spread out, tucking their tents into the dunes, disbursed among the bushes or scattered in the weeds, the cramped beach forced them to line up, one tent next to another, with no illusion of privacy. Even the groover, the river toilet erected at the far down-river edge of the sand, lacked any real sense of isolation. They set up a partial kitchen at the opposite end of the little camp, close to the river, and hoped the water didn't rise too much overnight. No one complained.

Claire dug through her dry bag, searching for her sleeping bag. She worked to set up her tent. She felt completely drained. She heard Tess saying how thankful she was that the scientists were right behind them, how lucky everyone was, but she didn't feel lucky. She saw it all differently. Maybe her family's complaint that she was a glass-half-empty person was true, she thought. Or, maybe she just knew how close she'd come to drowning.

She looked around to see what Linny was up to. Linny's tent was already up, and Linny stood at the river's edge to help Tess with the water buckets. It seemed that just as Claire had become worn out and tired from the trip, unable to help, Linny helped more.

Claire wanted to rest in her tent, alone, but she forced herself to walk back across the beach to join Linny and Tess in the kitchen preparing dinner. Everyone acted as if it were a normal evening. Claire wanted to feel like that too.

Tess was in the middle of telling Linny how she had decided to become a rafting guide after the death her father.

"For several months my mother and I lived in shock. Neither of us knew what to do without my father in the house. My mother went to work, and when she got home, she cleaned and cooked, as she had before. We had lost our appetites and ate very little, and every meal my mother prepared also included enough food for my father, and soon the refrigerator and freezer filled with leftovers.

"Everything about our lives was wrong. I finished high school and left home on June 23rd, three days after graduation. I came straight to Grand Canyon and rowed the Colorado the day after my eighteenth birthday. Everything about my life has been right since then. My interest in Grand Canyon far exceeds my interest in anyone or anything else."

"I get it," Linny said, nodding, and Claire wondered what, exactly, she got.

"This trip has been an amazing experience for me," Linny said. "As Claire knows, I've never spent much time in the outdoors. This is my first time camping, first time rafting. It's all new and exciting, especially coming from New York City, where running in Central Park is spending time in the wilderness. And the danger is real and immediate, and requires your full attention. I've never experienced anything like that.

"There have been big changes in my life recently. I no longer need to stay in New York, and I'm open to new adventures. I want to guide on the Colorado. How do I learn to row and become a guide?"

"You start by volunteering as a swamper," Tess said.

"O.K., that's what I'll do. I'm going to tell Dirk right now."

By the time Claire had processed what Linny was saying, her friend had jogged across the sand and stood before Dirk. Claire ran to catch up, but Linny had already said whatever it was she planned to say.

"What?" The word burst from Dirk in an explosion of sound.

"So, this is your way of telling me that you and dad are getting divorced, I'm going to boarding school, and you are moving away," Dirk said.

"Don't be so dramatic. You knew before we got here that dad and I were separating. And then I told you about boarding school. It won't matter to you where I am, you'll be at school. And your dad has enough money to pay for school; you don't need my income.

"I really don't know why you're so upset," she said. "Where I am or what I'm doing, won't change your life a bit. We're talking about my life, not yours. Don't be so self-centered and juvenile. Your life has already been decided, as we discussed. Now it's time for me to figure out my life."

"We didn't discuss anything about me or my life," Dirk said. "You told me."

"Well, same thing," Linny said. "What could we talk about? You need to go to school, and I found a school that would take you at the last minute, at this late stage in your education. There aren't a lot of choices."

"I could stay where I am."

"That's not an option."

"Of course it is. There's divorced kids at school. Lots of them. You just don't want any responsibility and you think I'm a burden," Dirk said. "And what do you care?" He turned to look at Claire, challenging her.

"Do you want to come and live with us and go to school in California?" Claire said. "Public school."

82

Day 12. Evening

Even at age forty-four, Claire didn't yet understand herself—why she did things, why she said what she did, why her life was as it was. After she asked her question, it was quiet and still enough to hear the passage of time itself, as minutes rolled in up the canyon and blew out across the mesas. The contrast from just a short while earlier, when she was poised to sink into the river and the raft was on the verge of flipping, struck Claire as extraordinary. She was certain the two times were related, but not sure that it mattered, now that she'd made her offer.

"What?" Linny and Dirk both shouted.

"What are you talking about?" Linny asked.

Claire shrugged her shoulders. She hadn't known she was going to say anything until she'd already spoken. She certainly hadn't planned to invite Dirk to live with her. She'd spent almost two weeks with Dirk and said few words to him. He'd saved her twice, but that didn't obligate her to take him in. As far as she could tell, she'd spoken without thinking, and she herself wondered what she was talking about.

"You have no idea what it's like having Dirk live with you," Linny said. "It's really hard and not a lot of fun."

Claire still had nothing to say. She lived with two children and Paul. She knew a lot about what it was like to live with someone, whether Linny thought she did or not. But how could Linny say these things in front of Dirk?

"I'd like Dirk to come live with us," Claire said, and this time she meant it.

The danger of the river faded, replaced by the possibility of California. Dirk immediately began asking questions. He wanted to know the name of the school he'd go to, the size of the school, how he'd get to school. He asked her how old, exactly, her kids were; what they did after school and on weekends. Would they like him living with them?

Claire answered the questions as best she could, except for the last one. She didn't think Sarah and Greg would like Dirk, at least not at first, but she didn't say that. She said she didn't know. She said they were easy-going kids and she wouldn't have invited him if she hadn't thought it would work out for everyone. Even as she said it, she knew it was partly a lie. She hadn't thought about anyone or anything when she'd blurted out the invitation. She was only starting to think now. Dirk didn't ask anything about Paul. Claire figured that in his day-to-day life, parents weren't that important.

Linny stood quietly saying nothing while Dirk asked his questions. Claire knew Linny wasn't accustomed to being on the sidelines, and if she'd seen a way to insert herself into the middle of the discussion, she would have. At the moment, she had no choice except to listen. When there was a pause in the conversation, she added that she thought it could work. Dirk turned to look at her, then turned back to Claire. That apparent transfer of power from Linny to Dirk or to Claire, it wasn't clear, made Claire uncomfortable.

"This only works if your mom and dad think it's a good idea," Claire said. "We all need to think about it and talk about it. And together we need to work out the logistical details."

"You mean like how much allowance I get?" Dirk asked.

"No," Claire said, "That's not what I was thinking about."

"But what would I get?" he asked.

Claire shrugged. When she caught Linny's eye, Linny smiled and nodded, once again the expert who knew how this played out.

"It's important," Dirk said.

"Agreed. I understand," Claire said. "I just don't have an answer."

Even as she answered Dirk, she noted how she felt no irritation with him, and how unemotional she remained responding to him. She would have answered Greg differently. She would have commented on his selfishness, and her body would have stiffened with the anger she felt towards him. Her heart would have raced. Of course, she said to herself—that's why this can work. He's not my kid.

Linny took over the conversation. She knew about California schools, with their limited funding and poor ratings. She said it was unlikely that a school in the Santa Cruz Mountains was any good. No one would help Dirk get into a good college, and with his less than stellar grades, he might have to stay in California for college.

Everything Linny said was probably true, though Claire didn't really know since her kids were young, and they were not yet thinking about college. Claire did know that she hadn't thought about any of it. Nor had she thought about any of the issues Linny and Dirk discussed for the next twenty minutes. All she could think about was how Linny planned to stay in Arizona and become a river guide.

Linny had gone to the better college. She'd married the better man. In almost every way that mattered, she'd been more successful. If either of them were to chuck it all to run rivers, it should be Claire, especially considering Claire was the only one of them with any outdoor experience.

Yet Claire never considered staying in Grand Canyon. She'd spent those incomprehensible, unfathomable nights with West, but never imagined disappearing into the wilderness. Even her most secret fantasies, the ones she'd never acknowledged to herself, kept her in Santa Cruz, making sure no one truly failed.

"Will I have my own bedroom?" Dirk asked, breaking through Claire's reverie.

"Yes," Claire said. "We have a guest room that can be yours. You will need to share a bathroom with Greg and Sarah, though."

"Definitely not yet a problem," Linny said, rolling her eyes, "Dirk's happy peeing and washing in the river."

83

Day 12. Evening

Word spread quickly down the beach, and everyone had something to say to Claire. Most of the comments were critical of Linny and supportive of her, but since no one really knew her or Linny, Claire knew the comments were, on the whole, irrelevant.

West sat next to her and put his arm around her.

"I wish I could know you better," he said. "I like everything about you."

Claire would have normally responded with a joke, something to take the focus away from her, but she didn't have the energy. She looked at West and shrugged her shoulders. She couldn't imagine a life where she would know him better, and he wouldn't like her if he knew her better. He had confused her with Linny. Linny watched them from the other side of the group.

One of the guides called West to help with securing the rafts for the night. As soon as he stood and walked away, Brent sat down next to Claire. He didn't put his arm around her, but he sat closer than she expected. Before he'd said a word, Claire saw Tess watching them and scowling.

"You're more special than I even realized," he said. "Maybe I could visit you sometime. I travel to Palo Alto and Santa Cruz on business."

"I'm married with two children," she said.

"No wedding ring," he said.

"I read it was safer to raft without."

Brent nodded. After a couple minutes, he stood and walked away.

Later that night, when she'd decided to go to bed, Tess walked over.

"That's the right thing for Dirk," she said. "Not sure if it's the right thing for you."

84

Diary Day 12

So much has happened it's nearly impossible to remember the morning's activities, but if I don't record it now, I will certainly forget. The day got off to a perfect start, with the group hiking up a side canyon between massive cliffs. Our destination—The Book of Worms. It looked like the prop for an Indiana Jones movie, without the booby traps and gruesome deaths. I took photos, so I can show you.

Everyone enjoyed the time off the river, walking in the canyon. It all seemed more manageable, on a more human scale, even though everything remained super-sized. Perhaps I'm used to being here. Anyway, when we returned to the rafts, I was again ready to float.

Since the big rapids were behind us, the tension we'd felt on the rafts had vanished. Large red ocotillo, in full bloom, studded the cliffs, making the canyon feel softer, more like a painting. We were all MUCH more relaxed. Too relaxed. The water was rough and wild, and the river was higher than we'd seen it.

We stopped a short time later, when we saw the science rafts pulled onto a beach. The archeologists in the group were investigating an ancient village, and they let us walk among the ruins. Even though we'd already seen lots of archeology sites, this place was spectacular. The ruins were so extensive, I easily imagined living there, overlooking the river. It seemed quite a comfortable life. Again, I have photos.

Back on the river, the water looked crazy. It was muddy and choppy and nothing like the river we'd been running. Tess said the rapids coming up were small, and the only problem was the river was fast and high. As soon as we hit the first rapids, I knew something dramatic had happened. The raft veered down the river, seemingly out of control. Then, right before the second rapids, a helicopter flew overhead trailing a banner warning everyone to get off the river. The dam upstream had problems, and the river was flooding. Unfortunately, there wasn't anywhere for us to go, and we zoomed down the current.

When we hit the second rapids, things happened too fast for me to follow. Before I understood what had happened, I was in the air, and the raft was no longer underneath me. It was scary and frightening. Dirk grabbed my life jacket and kept me in the raft. The experience was quick and intense. I guess Dirk keeps his cool in extreme situations.

We continued down the river until one of the science motor rafts came up behind us and pushed us to a narrow beach. All of the rafts and science boats made it to safety, and we camped together for the night. No one talked about the plan for tomorrow. I have no idea what we'll do.

85

Day 13. Morning

As soon as the sun found a notch in the cliffs, sunlight streamed through the mesh door of Claire's tent, directly into her eyes, and woke her. She unzipped the door and sought out the warmth of the light. It was still early enough to feel the coolness of the night lingering in the morning air.

She dressed quickly and walked to the river. Many of the rafters, guides, and scientists were already there. The water was as muddy and debris-filled as the day before, but it was calmer—nothing like the day before. She sought out one of the scientists to ask what it meant.

"Not sure yet," he said. "A serious breach caused yesterday's flooding, and we think we avoided total failure and a more serious catastrophe. We think the reservoir filled, and it got out of control, and breached the dam. We don't know the details, and we don't know yet if anyone drowned yesterday."

"So we'll get back on the river this morning?" Claire asked.

"It looks O.K."

Claire turned away and saw Linny packing up her tent. Anxious to know what Linny and Dirk had decided overnight and not knowing what she herself thought, Claire hesitated. She went back to her tent and packed up. She stayed away from Linny as along as she could.

She watched the canyon change. Morning shadows retreated down the gray cliffs behind her. Pink and purple bluffs emerged from the early morning murk, like the colored lips and tinted eyelids revealed beneath a burka slipped back from a shrouded face. Claire wanted to understand how it could be that Linny, not she, would wake each morning to this beauty.

The guides grouped everyone in a circle for breakfast, disrupting the usual routine of morning autonomy. Once everyone was seated, West said he and Brent wanted to talk Grand Canyon politics. A couple rafters groaned, but West looked at them, shrugged his shoulders and continued.

"Don't know what the researchers will say, but I know that yesterday's crisis was all about politics. Now that you've hiked the canyon, run the river, and camped in the desert, you know a little of what's at stake out here," he said. "You'll read in the news about Grand Canyon, and now you'll know what they're talking about."

"What you need to remember," Brent said, "is that things here are often not as they seem. It looks like there's plenty of water, but there isn't enough, and the flood yesterday was certainly linked to that discrepancy."

Linny started asking questions before either man had said much of anything. She summarized that due to a prolonged drought, water from the river was no longer sufficient to supply all the communities that depended on it. She mentioned the problems with the dam and how it limited the amount of downstream sediment. She explained how the archeological sites were at risk of being destroyed.

Some of this Claire knew, but not all of it. No one else had a word to say, and West began responding to the issues Linny raised.

Claire watched West. Maybe, she thought, he would have been more interested in Linny if she'd spoken up earlier and he'd realized how smart she was. She watched them both a little longer and realized that Linny impressed Claire more than she impressed West or the others. No one else seemed to revere her as Claire did. Claire looked over at Dirk. He paid no attention to his mother.

Perhaps it was her role, Claire thought, to think Linny was amazing.

"Linny has nailed some of the hot topics," Brent said, when West stepped back and nodded for Brent to take over. "First is the allocation of water. The Colorado River, from its headwaters to the Gulf of Mexico, is 1450 miles long. Agriculture demands about three quarters of the water in the river, and in exchange, it produces about fifteen percent of the nation's food. Forty million people also depend on the river for their water. By law, the states bordering the upper river, Colorado, New Mexico, Utah, and Wyoming, can use a certain amount of the water. California and Nevada, bordering the lower river, get a certain amount. Arizona gets a special allocation, and Mexico gets a certain amount of the water. Unfortunately, those allocation amounts were determined based on data in wet years. Now we're in a long drought and there isn't enough water to meet all the allocations. But everyone still needs the water, so reservoirs are being depleted. And the reservoir itself increases evaporation and decreases water supply. No one knows what will happen.

"Second, you've heard us say that Glen Canyon Dam is reducing the sediment in the river. It's restrained by the dam, filling up Lake Powell. As a result of the dam and the diminished sediment, the Colorado's become a clear, cold river. It used to be a warm, muddy one. That changes the fish that thrive here, and it changes the plants along the river's edge. One of the questions is what remedial action is required to protect endangered species. You could take down Glen Canyon Dam and return the river to a more natural state. You could build a slurry pipeline and take sediment from above the dam to the river below the dam.

"To protect the archeological sites, the river and beaches need a lot more sand and floods that bring the sand up the beaches to the sites farther from the river. If you get sediment downstream without removing the dam, the next problem is arranging floods to move the sediment onto the beaches.

"To put it simply, one way or another, dam operations need to change if this river is to remain healthy. If the dam stays, most of the scientists believe the river flow needs greater fluctuations than dam operators now allow. That means controlled floods, timed to coincide with storms, so runoff from the tributaries can increase the sediment load of the river. Sediment on shore can build sandy beaches, and sediment in the river can create a backwater habitat of ponds for native, juvenile fish. Sediment is needed in the river to create a turbid environment for those native chub to thrive. It's pretty straightforward in theory, but rather complicated in practice."

Claire waited for Linny to interrupt and say something, and it didn't take long. The scientists had told Linny that a lot of ambiguity about how to keep the river healthy still remained, and they blamed that ambiguity on a lack of information and a need for additional facts. Linny posited whether science was sufficiently developed to provide a definitive resolution of all these issues. West answered that Linny was needlessly confusing the situation.

"There's ambiguity about how to manage the canyon as a whole," he said. "There's no dispute about the need for more water and more sediment and more floods."

Brent said Linny raised an interesting point. He didn't yet know exactly what caused yesterday's flood, but he was pretty sure it had to do with the data collection of the science group. He believed the data would provide answers, maybe answers some wouldn't like.

Tess said that she had thought that in river rafting a person needed myopic focus to survive the waves of the next big rapids— that nothing mattered on the river except the next few hundred feet downstream. On the other hand, for an environmentally sustainable Grand Canyon, the river was merely one feature of a vast landscape.

One of the scientists walked over and said she'd gotten through on the sat phone.

"Apparently, the dam is O.K. and the flow is being regulated again. No further flooding is expected. No official word on what happened or why."

With that, the researchers were ready to go. They loaded their gear and took off.

"And that brings us back to my original point," West said. "There's a lot at stake, and many things threaten Grand Canyon. When you go home, please pay attention to the news about this place."

"There's also magic in the canyon," Tess said, "and the magic keeps this place together. Environmentalists see danger and destruction everywhere, and it's probably true. But with all those problems, here we are, in heaven. It's a complicated world."

Claire didn't, for a moment, doubt the complexity of Grand Canyon. She did doubt the existence of magic. She was still trying to understand the implications of what everyone said, when Linny again started to speak. Now, though, she no longer spouted off what she'd heard or what she'd read; now she was problem solving and making a plan of action. Linny thought the water allocation laws should be changed to reflect changed climate conditions. She wanted to know how much water was used to raise alfalfa and other cattle feed. She wanted to know whether the Indian tribes had a water allocation. She wanted to know whether removing Glen Canyon Dam was a serious, viable consideration. She proposed a letter-writing campaign and a lobbying effort.

Claire looked around the circle of rafters, and everyone seemed caught up in Linny's plans. She stared at Dirk. He alone appeared unmoved. He ate his breakfast and a second helping. He didn't seem to be listening to his mother or the discussion that gripped the rafters.

"Are we going on any hikes today?" he asked.

"We've got a lot of river to cover," Tess said, "but we'll stop at Pumpkin Springs. You'll like that."

"O.K." he said, and he walked into the kitchen and began washing the breakfast dishes.

It was the only time Claire remembered him helping without being asked. Neither he nor Linny had said anything to Claire about where Dirk would live next year. Claire thought perhaps his new helpfulness offered a clue to their decision, but if it did, she couldn't decipher it.

86

Day 13. Morning

They broke camp and began loading the rafts before either Linny or Dirk mentioned Dirk's situation. Claire felt the tension spread through her body, and she imagined Linny and Dirk conspiring to obtain the most advantage from her offer. She was on the verge of telling them to forget it, angry that something with such a major effect on her life was being analyzed and evaluated without her, when Linny took her aside. The touch of Linny's hand on her arm immediately calmed her.

"Do you know what you're doing?" Linny asked.

"No, not really," Claire said, unable to pretend that she knew more than she did.

"I haven't talked with Dirk," Linny said, "but I'm sure he'd like to live in California. Who wouldn't? It's everyone's dream. But I don't want to burden you, and I certainly don't want to jeopardize our friendship. I feel conflicted about what might be best for Dirk and what's best for you."

Claire instantly remembered why she and Linny had remained friends all these years. It wasn't just that Linny was so impressive, though that certainly was part of it. Claire understood that Linny didn't worry about many people, but Linny did care for her, in a way that no one else did. No one else in her life hesitated to be a burden to her. Not her mother, or her brother or sister, not her husband or children. She couldn't begrudge Linny her new adventure. It wasn't as if only one of them could take the adventure and Linny claimed it first, knocking Claire out of the running. The truth, as she well knew, was that she was never going to choose such a life.

As soon as he saw them talking, Dirk hurried over.

"I want to go," he said.

"I thought you would," Linny said. "There's lots to figure out."

"You're real smart," he said. "You can do it."

"Claire's an attorney," Linny said. "You won't be able to manipulate or fool her either, you know."

Dirk looked from his mother to her friend and shrugged his shoulders. He left them and walked across the sand to the water, walking into the river until it rose up his calves. He punched both fists into the air in celebration.

"You're ready for a teenager?" Linny asked.

Claire shrugged, in a very good imitation of Dirk, and they both laughed.

87

Day 13. Morning

The water moved swiftly and the raft tumbled down the river, bumped logs and other debris, but after the scare of the previous day, nothing bothered Tess. She was happy to be guiding, ready to show her passengers the next sight. The sun wasn't yet overhead, and it wasn't yet time for lunch, when a huge, enormous rock formation, perched above the river in the shape and colors of a pumpkin, jutted out from the canyon wall. Water dripped into the bowl of the formation and spilled over the edges down to the river. Tess saw it all, as she did every trip, as if it were her first time.

"Pumpkin Springs, formed from travertine limestone," she said. "The water's nice and hot, but there are very high levels of arsenic and metals like copper, lead, and zinc, so no bathing, no drinking. We'll pull off for photos and an up-close inspection."

Before either Claire or Linny moved from the raft, Dirk had climbed over the rocks and was leaning into the pumpkin, his hands swirling in the hot water. He leaned so far over the edge that it looked like he would lose his balance and tumble into the water. Orion grabbed his life jacket and pulled him back.

"Very nasty stuff," the guide said, and Dirk nodded and stepped down.

"Clear back," Tess said. "First we do photos, then you can get closer for a personal look."

Dirk and the few rafters leaning over the rim now backed off. Claire pulled out her camera, looked through the finder, and understood why special arrangements were being made for taking pictures. The sight was impossibly photogenic, and this ten-minute stop would end up the highlight of everyone's slide show. Claire took several photos, with different cropping and from different angles. She tried to remember what Tess had said as they pulled to shore. Certainly everyone would ask her about this place as soon as she showed the photo.

"This is great," Linny said. "Tess, are there rivers with bathable hot springs? That would really be fun."

Claire didn't hear Tess' answer. She had walked away from Linny, closer to the pumpkin. Already their worlds were diverging. Linny thought about rafting down a river with hot springs. Claire worried about supervising a teenager. She didn't worry about Dirk fitting into her family. She'd do what was needed. Dirk would thrive, and her family would ultimately accept him.

"Back to the rafts!" West called, and in five minutes they were back on the river floating down the current.

"Settle in Dirk," Tess said. "We've got a lot of miles to cover. It's a day to rest, after the exertion of yesterday."

"No problem here," Dirk said. "I'd sleep if I knew I didn't need to rescue Claire."

"You're off duty, sleep."

Claire listened, amazed. She thought she was helping Dirk out. Could he, instead, be saving her? Should she tell Linny about the hornet's nest she'd invited Dirk into? She tried to recall the intensity of feeling that consumed her at home, how she'd left bursting with anger, ready to leave, and too agitated to care how it all worked out. She no longer remembered what had pushed her over the edge. Perhaps it was just the alcohol.

She imagined Tess saying the canyon had worked its magic, but she knew this was neither Grand Canyon nor Indian magic. This was spending time in nature, which laid bare the truth below the surface, allowing artifice to fade away. Perhaps the canyon disclosed emotional truth in addition to exposing geologic history. The truth was that she could handle her life. She was capable of taking care of herself and her children, and also helping Dirk. Paul could get this shit together, or he could leave. She was staying.

88

Day 13. Afternoon

E arlier that morning, while the other guides cleaned up from breakfast, West had prepared a cold quinoa salad and a cold tomato soup and packed it all into several containers placed in the lunch cooler. It was served for lunch.

"Our last lunch on the river," Tess announced. "Tomorrow we'll eat lunch at the takeout, as we de-rig the rafts. The guides who drive down the trailers and trucks will bring coolers of lunch food. We're pretty empty at this point. Down to dried and canned staples."

Everyone turned to stare at Tess, and traces of shock spread across the faces of the rafters. Tess looked from one face to another, nodding. They all knew the trip ended the following day, but no one had really thought about what that meant. Tess had been through it all before. She knew to give a gentle reminder. When she looked at Claire, she added a slight smile, as if she knew Claire had already been preparing.

Tess had asked West earlier that day if they would do the usual end-of trip. Considering all that had happened, it didn't seem quite right, but he was emphatic that they would. Tess thought they should talk about Ellie and the flood. West said they would roast the guides and passengers like they always did.

"So it's time to wrap up the trip and review what's happened," Tess said. "We'll do some fun things tonight, but if you have any questions, or if you want to discuss something, you might bring it up now or sometime this afternoon."

Linny turned to Claire. "What happened on this trip," she said. "I dragged Dirk here not knowing what else to do with him as I tried to hold my life together. I spent the trip trying to salvage what I could from the wreckage of my life. Turned out great for Dirk, though."

Linny turned away before Claire could answer, which was good, since Claire had no answer. She'd stopped listening with the word salvage. In Claire's mind, no matter what happened, Linny didn't salvage. She made bold choices, and she invariably succeeded. Claire, on the other hand, treaded water, desperate to survive. How did Linny not understand that? Claire considered herself a person with no firm beliefs, whose defining characteristic was her ability to accommodate. Perhaps that disguised her and hid her from Linny.

As Claire watched Linny climb into the raft, Tess walked over. "The more I think about you taking Dirk, the better I think it is."

"I asked him without any real thought," Claire said. "Maybe it's not the right thing to do."

"Are you kidding?" Tess said. "It's perfect. Dirk needs to live somewhere without too much direction, where he can slow down and grow up. That's not living with Linny. Linny will love the river, though. River guides are people of action. We don't wait for other people to make choices. We couldn't sit still if our lives depended on it. Luckily our lives depend on making split-second decisions without any time for thought—perfect for Linny. Dirk will love being with you."

Claire climbed into the raft wondering whether Tess, with her lack of education but years surviving in the wilderness, really knew that Claire could help Dirk. How could Tess understand what Claire needed, when Claire didn't know herself what she wanted?

Just as Claire started to doze off, Tess declared their entrance into Lower Granite Gorge, and that started Linny explaining what she knew about the canyon's geology.

"I want to impart a little knowledge to you, Dirk, before you leave me," Linny said. "So, listen up. At the launch, if we knew what to look for, we would have seen the Echo Cliffs, and if we looked west, we would have seen the Chocolate Cliffs and the Vermillion Cliffs. Now we're surrounded by the oldest rocks in the canyon—granite and schist. This is the deepest we'll go into the geologic record."

Linny had so much to say. The only time Claire spoke with authority was in a courtroom. When she was home, or floating down a river, her mind seemed empty. She couldn't remember ever imparting knowledge.

"You listening, Dirk?" Linny asked.

"Yes mom," he said. "Thank you."

"I'm listening too," Claire said. "Thank you."

Linny laughed, the other rafters and Tess laughed. Dirk smiled a rare smile. Tess took over the discussion. She had lots more to say about the canyon's geology. She explained how the limestone, sandstone, and shale in the upper reaches of the canyon formed from particulate deposits by wind or water in the Paleozoic era, roughly 570 to 245 million years ago. The dikes of granite in the lower gorge were igneous rock, cooled into solid form from a molten state. This granite was found in larger expanses of schist, a metamorphic rock that formed when older sedimentary and igneous rocks changed under pressure, temperature, or chemical activity during the Proterozoic era, 1700 to 825 million years ago.

For a while, no one said anything. Claire contemplated the huge numbers rattled off by Tess and decided she had no idea of what they meant. Instead, she tried to remember the rock formation types.

"There are a lot of missing years there," Linny said, turning to look at Tess.

Claire had no idea what she was talking about.

"The Great Unconformity," Tess said. "We're missing the geologic record for 255 million years. And if you want to be precise, there's an Earlier Unconformity for the period 1700 to 1250 million years ago. I just ignored it when giving you the rock formation dates."

Claire was certain Linny was genuinely interested in the geologic record; that's how she was. Claire, though, couldn't keep it straight. She stared at the cliffs as they floated by, and she looked into the still muddy water as they sped down the river. She worked hard to see anything specific and felt proud when she identified veins of Zoroaster Granite in the Vishnu Schist. She envisioned the rocks bolting straight from the river as emissaries from the earth's buried past, and with the wonders of nature on full display, she relaxed and floated through a unified, harmonious world, the environmental problems of the canyon forgotten.

89

Day 13. Afternoon

N o one talked for an hour or more until Tess resumed the discussion as if only a few minutes had passed.

"To continue this morning's conversation," she said, "Glen Canyon Dam is changing the river, as every dam changes every river.

Years ago, the river had significant amounts of suspended sediment. The water looked cloudy, sometimes even murky, and occasionally as muddy as it is now."

Except for the past few days, she said, the river mostly flowed as clear as tap water. She said she'd worked one summer on the upper Salt River where the water also ran clear by the end of the summer.

"But then it flooded in the winter and carried huge amounts of sediment, more than enough to make up for a clear summer. That's how western rivers are supposed to be."

She looked down at the water. The Colorado moved swiftest in the middle of the river. Near the left bank, the current tumbled over rocks piled up at the river's edge. Below the rocks, the water moved too quickly to spread along the bank, and it bumped into the shore, piled up, and bulged until there was so much water in one spot that it flowed in two directions, both upstream, curving back on itself in an eddy and creating a small pool, and downstream, gurgling as it spread onto the sand. For a moment, the river flowed with visible currents, like a stereoscopic image brought into relief, and it hypnotized her. When she blinked and lost her focus, the river again flowed an undifferentiated rush of water.

In the late afternoon, the winds picked up and made it difficult to row. Tess pulled her baseball cap down lower onto her head, and she turned the raft around and rowed backwards.

At first Claire sat hunched in her seat, facing upstream, with her back to the wind and her head tucked down onto her knees. Occasional gusts blasted up the canyon, pushing the raft upstream, and Tess strained at the oars and forced the raft downriver. Tess rowed with her head tucked down, each pull on the oars long and slow, and at times they barely made headway. Claire turned around and watched Tess closely—there was no evidence that she was tired after two weeks of rowing.

The wind slowed them down, and it was a long day on the water, as Tess had told them it would be. When they started out, Claire had thought only about setting up camp in the evening and having a late dinner. She hadn't thought about the guides having to row in the dimming light. She tried to picture Linny as a guide, rowing into the wind at the end of a hard day. It was beyond her imagination.

As dusk approached, the winds calmed. Tess turned the raft around to face back downstream. The sun dipped behind the cliffs, and they continued down the canyon. Shadows spread from the beach onto the river, turning the water an opaque black. When it seemed they might never reach camp, the rafts pulled to shore on the eastern bank.

90

Day 13. Evening

They made camp, and the guides headed for the kitchen. West made an official announcement, before anyone started to prepare dinner, that it was to be a special, farewell meal, and they didn't want any help. Linny commented to Claire that she was too tired and hungry to offer help anyway, and Claire agreed. She hoped she wasn't too exhausted to enjoy the meal.

She needn't have worried. These guides knew how to throw a party, even at the tail end of a strenuous trip, without the benefit of a refrigerated cooler. They cooked huge pots of pasta, toasted garlic bread, made a salad of cabbage and shredded carrots, and brought out boxes of Clair's favorite cookie – the chocolate covered Le Petite Ecolier – which she hadn't had for years. Claire stuffed herself, enjoying her last dinner under the desert sky. After everyone finished eating, the guides smoothed out an area along the water's edge and lined up all the liquor that remained. There was still quite a lot of booze.

Claire thought for a moment about cutting loose and drinking till she passed out, with a vow to stay sober at home. Instead, she took a gin and tonic, heavy on the tonic, and promised herself she would nurse the drink for the rest of the night. Linny poured brandy into a cup. Dirk took a beer.

For the next hour the guides re-enacted events from the trip. It started with Tess taking on the role of Linny, arriving late with her cell phone and wanting to make arrangements for cell coverage in the canyon. Riz pretended to be Dave, from Massachusetts, who had trouble setting up his tent the first few nights. Claire waited for someone to pull a flask from a bag, looking around to make sure no one had seen, but no one impersonated her or satirized her, or perhaps she just didn't recognize herself in any of the skits.

Her attention drifted. She'd hated camp skits since she'd been an eleven year old at camp. She didn't care for the humor, and she hated the attention it focused on the subjects. When she looked around, everyone seemed to be having a good time.

Later in the evening, after many of the rafters and guides had had too much to drink, Linny stood up and recited a poem she'd written for the occasion. It was titled *Refuge on the River* and began with the line: "With the future blocked and the present exploding, I took refuge in a distant canyon."

The poem, juvenile and unsophisticated, was structured with alliteration and a simple rhythm, but everyone enjoyed it. It was unpolished and naïve, not something Claire would acknowledge writing. Nor would she ever read it aloud to a group. It was a great thing for Linny to do, though, and Claire knew that no one would remember anything about the poem, only that Linny had put on a show that everyone had enjoyed. In the midst of everything going on, Linny had entertained them.

91

Diary Day 13

Just in case things change and what's on my mind tonight isn't what I remember when I get home, I want to record a brief outline of my thoughts. At the very least, it will give us a framework for some serious conversation.

I've invited Dirk to come live with us. His situation at home is problematic since Linny and Steve are separating, and there's nowhere for him to live. His parents were planning to send him to boarding school. He doesn't want to go. I like him, and I sympathize with him. He can take over our guest room and go SLV High.

Having Dirk live with us will change things a lot, but I think it will be good for all of us. He doesn't know how to drive, since he's grown up in New York City, but he can learn, get a driver's license, and help with the car shuttle. He knows nothing about living in the country, but everything about living in the city. He's been in one of the best schools in the US, and he can tell Greg and Sarah some of the things he's learned.

Dirk's excited to come to California, and having a new pair of eyes in the mountains will help us see the beauty that we're taking for granted. We all live very sheltered lives, and there's so much we don't know and so much to learn. Having Dirk live with us will introduce all of us to a different way of living – not better or worse, just different and, hopefully, interesting. It will expand our points of view.

Having someone else in the house may put us all on our best behavior, and that has to be a good thing.

I realize a change like this is something we should talk about before making such a commitment, but I was here by myself, and it really seemed like the right thing to do. I feel like I've been too passive for too long—though I know each of you will disagree and say I'm too aggressive. Anyway, I needed to do this.

Dirk's a really nice kid. Linny's been my best friend since I was a girl.

All day we've talked about Grand Canyon and how special it is. The big question is—what makes it so special? Why did John Wesley Powell make one trip and then another? Why did Robert Stanton make one aborted, failed trip and then another? Why has one guide after another arrived as a teenager for a summer job and stayed for a lifetime? Why has my friend Linny decided to leave New York to become a rafting guide?

92

Day 14. Morning

Claire slept soundly and woke while it was still dark. Shortly after she opened her eyes, Riz walked through camp calling everyone to breakfast. In the cold dewy air, well before daybreak, they climbed from their tents to get a very early start and assembled on the beach for their first cups of coffee under the still pitch-black sky. Bt the time they finished eating, the black sky had dissolved to gray. In that first light, they broke camp and dragged their bags, sleeping pads, and chairs across the sand. The guides loaded the equipment back into the rafts and tossed the bags on top. For the first time in two weeks, no one tied the gear down.

Claire stood at the edge of the beach and looked out across the river to a narrow strip of sand that hugged the rocks of a small riffle. Too small to accommodate camping and tucked away from easy raft access, this white-sand beach lay unspoiled, with no footprints. It was utterly exquisite, an utterly spectacular sight. She hadn't noticed it the evening before when they rafted by. She supposed it had been too dark, or she was just too tired. She was certain there had been much in Grand Canyon that she hadn't noticed.

Linny and Dirk stood apart from the group, away from the river. Both had long, serious faces. At first Claire felt that she should be included in this conversation, since Dirk would soon be living with her, but she quickly understood that Linny and Dirk had a lot to talk about that didn't include her. For the first time in Dirk's life, they would live apart. She started to think about all the things she needed to discuss with Paul, but shook her head to stop herself. There'd be time to think about practicalities on the airplane ride home. She wouldn't waste her last hours in the canyon worrying. She'd made the decision to invite Dirk. That was the only thing that mattered.

She felt in control, in a way that she hadn't felt for years, if ever. She could choose what to think about. She could choose what to do and how to behave. She was more relaxed than she'd been during the whole trip. Perhaps it was the knowledge that they'd arrive at the take-out by lunch, and they were, in effect, out of the wilderness. Perhaps it was that the river was calm enough to forego strapping the bags down. Perhaps it was the evening fun, or perhaps it was that Dirk was coming to California and her life would change. She thought it might just be that she'd been decisive. Whatever it was, she felt at home in Grand Canyon and awakened to the beauty around her.

Tess rowed down the still-sleeping river, past a single duck and a few solitary birds. In the early morning haze, Tess heard the song of the river. She caught snatches, then whole tunes, of an aria, sometimes a chant. The pure joy of living echoed against the cliffs in moments of silence, until the canyon again filled with music as the river ran through the geologic layers, scouring newer and older rocks, making a path through the earth's history.

The sun rose above the cliffs and heated the rocks, and Tess could feel the heat radiating from them. On a long flat stone on shore, a tiny lizard did push-ups. At some point, the quiet and stillness of the river disappeared, and the sound of engines and voices carried up the canyon.

"We're getting close," she said. "Prepare yourself. It's not pretty."

93

Day 14. Morning

Big trucks lined one side of the beach, like visitors from a foreign universe. One stereo blared hip-hop, another the music of Phish. Piles of equipment littered the sand. Garbage cans overflowed.

"Not pretty?" Linny said. "This is obscene."

Claire turned around to see Tess shrug. Tess lifted her sunglasses onto her head, and her eyes darted back and forth, scanning the beach. She seemed to find what she was looking for and broke into a grin. In a small group on the sand stood several people waving and holding up bottles of beer.

The rafts pulled to shore right next to each other, one after the other. As soon as the passengers disembarked, the guides issued instructions on where to line up and what to do, and they quickly and efficiently began to unload the rafts and load the large trucks. In little more than an hour, the soft bags were piled into the back of a pickup truck, the metal cases and kitchen equipment were loaded into a large cargo truck, and the empty rafts were lifted by cable onto two flatbeds, one raft on top of another.

All the certainty and calm that Claire had felt so plainly and strongly earlier that morning vanished. Only the guides looked comfortable—everyone else appeared miserable. Claire looked for Tess and found her crouched in the shade of one of the trucks, digging through a cooler. When she turned back to find her a few minutes later, Tess had set up a folding table and was laying out a lunch spread. Clearly the trip wasn't yet over for the guides.

Linny and Dirk lined up for lunch before Tess had finished. It seemed out of character for Linny to be so hungry, and for a fleeting moment, Claire thought she and Dirk might be avoiding her. She immediately dismissed the thought, telling herself it was her usual feeling of insecurity with regards to Linny. She got into line behind fellow rafters, and when she reached the buffet table, she made herself a sandwich.

At least two other raft trips had pulled onto the Diamond Creek Beach since they'd arrived. Newly arrived trucks traded places at the water with the earlier trucks. Newly arrived rafts took the place of the rafts already loaded onto trucks. Life jackets piled up on the sand. West bellowed for their group to assemble at the downstream side of the beach, at the water's edge.

As Claire walked to the designated meeting area, Linny grabbed her arm.

"We need to talk for a minute," she said. "Dirk and I talked this over, and we've agreed to slow things down. I'm not going to leave New York right away, and we're not going to send him away. Steve and I will work out the logistics of keeping him at his school. It's the only thing that makes sense.

"Dirk's concerned that you'll be angry, but I told him not to worry. Who'd be angry to return to family life without a teenager?"

Linny smiled, and Claire returned the smile. They both laughed, as if they understood each other. Claire knew that Linny didn't understand her at all. Linny thought she and Paul were happy, her kids were well adjusted, well behaved, and well cared for. Linny had no idea about Claire's life. She was correct, however, in knowing that Claire would be fine without the addition of Dirk. All of the sudden, everything seemed simpler to Claire. Once again she only had Sarah, Greg, Paul, and herself to worry about. That was something she should be able to handle.

She wondered if she understood Linny.

Day 14. Afternoon

Each of the guides thanked the passengers for making the trip so special. Many of the passengers thanked the guides and handed West, as the head guide, the tip they'd come prepared to give. Almost everyone exchanged names and e-mails.

With a last look at the river and canyon, Claire climbed into the van that would transport them back to Flagstaff. She took a seat at a window, near the front. As soon as everyone was on board and the van had started up the dirt road toward Peach Springs, she pulled her notebook out from her small daypack. Leafing through the pages she quickly found the last entry in her diary and ripped out the page.

About the Author

Michelle Rubin has rafted the Colorado River through the Grand Canyon on numerous geology and archeology research trips. Her husband has worked in Grand Canyon for many years, and she spent those years observing the canyon and filling her notebook with imagined stories. She has traveled extensively in the Americas, Europe, Asia, Africa, Australia, and the South Pacific Islands.

Before writing, Michelle received a BA in English from the University of Rochester and a JD from Albany Law School. She practiced law in California.

Made in the USA
San Bernardino, CA
09 July 2017